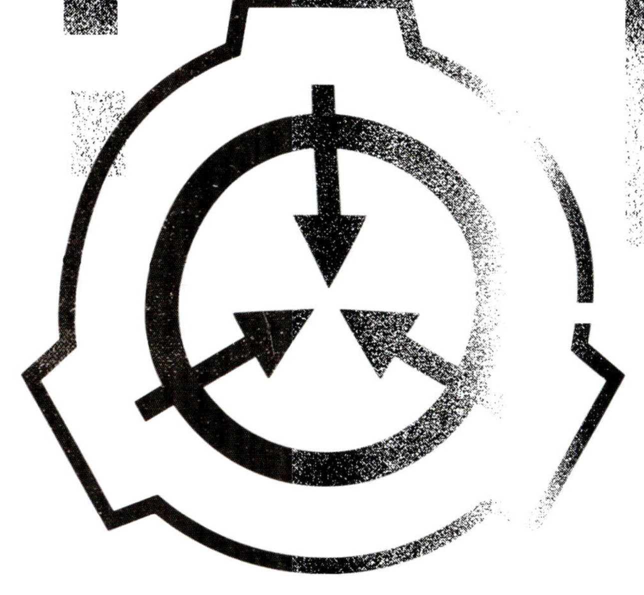

SCP Foundation ▸ Archives
Yellow Journal

DCLASSIFIEDCLASSIFI

Security Clearance Level IV

This journal belongs to

CLASSIFIED

SCP Foundation

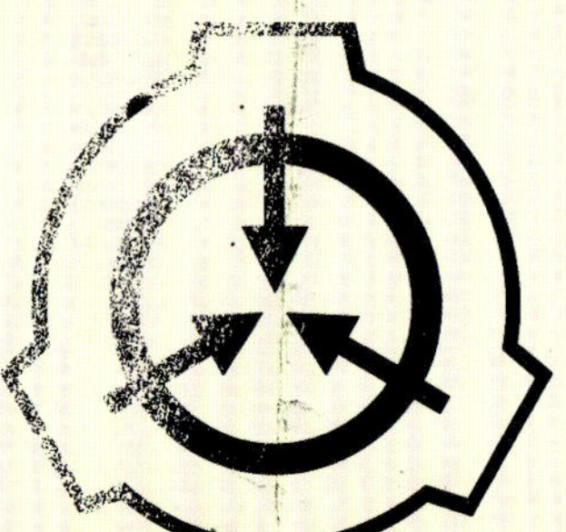

Mankind in its present state has been around for a quarter of a million years, yet only the last 4,000 have been of any significance.

So, what did we do for nearly 250,000 years? We huddled in caves and around small fires, fearful of the things that we didn't understand. It was more than explaining why the sun came up, it was the mystery of enormous birds with heads of men and rocks that came to life. So we called them 'gods' and 'demons', begged them to spare us, and prayed for salvation.

In time, their numbers dwindled and ours rose. The world began to make more sense when there were fewer things to fear, yet the unexplained can never truly go away, as if the universe demands the absurd and impossible.

Mankind must not go back to hiding in fear. No one else will protect us, and we must stand up for ourselves.

While the rest of mankind dwells in the light, we must stand in the darkness to fight it, contain it, and shield it from the eyes of the public, so that others may live in a sane and normal world.

We secure. We contain. We protect.

— The Administrator

OBJECT CLASSES

All anomalous objects, entities, and phenomena requiring Special Containment Procedures are assigned an Object Class. An Object Class is a part of the standard SCP template and serves as a rough indicator for how difficult an object is to contain. In universe, Object Classes are for the purposes of identifying containment needs, research priority, budgeting, and other considerations. An SCP's Object Class is determined by a number of factors, but the most important factors are the difficulty and the purpose of its containment.

SAFE

The Locked Box Test:
If you lock it in a box, leave it alone, and nothing bad will happen, then it's probably Safe.

Safe-class SCPs are anomalies that are easily and safely contained. This is often due to the fact that the Foundation has researched the SCP well enough that containment does not require significant resources or that the anomalies require a specific and conscious activation or trigger. Classifying an SCP as Safe, however, does not mean that handling or activating it does not pose a threat.

EUCLID

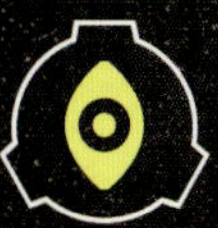

The Locked Box Test:
If you lock it in a box, leave it alone, and you're not entirely sure what will happen, then it's probably Euclid.

Euclid-class SCPs are anomalies that require more resources to contain completely or where containment isn't always reliable. Usually this is because the SCP is insufficiently understood or inherently unpredictable. Euclid is the Object Class with the greatest scope, and it's usually a safe bet that an SCP will be this class if it doesn't easily fall into any of the other standard Object Classes.

As a note, any SCP that's autonomous, sentient and/or sapient is generally classified as Euclid, due to the inherent unpredictability of an object that can act or think on its own.

KETER

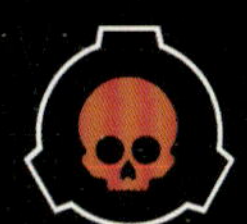

The Locked Box Test:
If you lock it in a box, leave it alone, and it easily escapes, then it's probably Keter.

Keter-class SCPs are anomalies that are exceedingly difficult to contain consistently or reliably, with containment procedures often being extensive and complex. The Foundation often can't contain these SCPs well due to not having a solid understanding of the anomaly, or lacking the technology to properly contain or counter it. A Keter SCP does not mean the SCP is dangerous, just that it is simply very difficult or costly to contain.

THAUMIEL

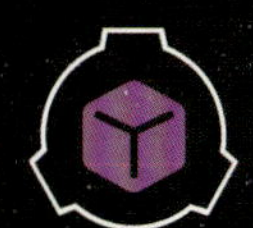

The Locked Box Test:
If it is the box, then it's probably Thaumiel.

Thaumiel-class SCPs are anomalies that the Foundation specifically uses to contain other SCPs. Even the mere existence of Thaumiel-class objects is classified at the highest levels of the Foundation and their locations, functions, and current status are known to few Foundation personnel outside of the 05 Council.

[PERSONNEL DOC_01]
[ID_DOCTOR ███]

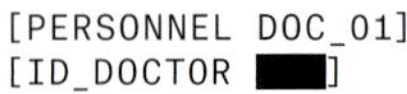

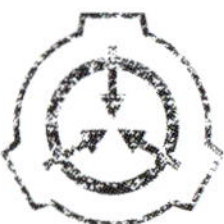

CLEARANCE & CLASSIFICATION

1 Foundation security clearances granted to personnel represent the highest level or type of information to which they can be granted access.

Level 5 [Thaumiel]

Level 5 security clearances are given to the highest-ranking administrative personnel within the Foundation and grant effectively unlimited access to all strategic and otherwise sensitive data. Level 5 security clearances are typically only granted to O5 Council members and selected staff.

Level 4 [Top Secret]

Level 4 security clearances are given to senior administration that require access to site-wide and/or regional intelligence as well as long-term strategic data regarding Foundation operations and research projects. Level 4 security clearances are typically only held by Site Directors, Security Directors, or Mobile Task Force Commanders.

Level 3 [Secret]

Level 3 security clearances are given to senior security and research personnel that require in-depth data regarding the source, recovery circumstances, and long-term planning for anomalous objects and entities in containment. Most senior research staff, project managers, security officers, response team members, and Mobile Task Force operatives hold a Level 3 security clearance.

Level 2 [Restricted]

Level 2 security clearances are given to security and research personnel that require direct access to information regarding anomalous objects and entities in containment. Most research staff, field agents, and containment specialists hold a Level 2 security clearance.

Level 1 [Confidential]

Level 1 security clearances are given to personnel working in proximity to but with no direct, indirect, or informational access to anomalous objects or entities in containment. Level 1 security clearances are typically granted to personnel working in clerical, logistics, or janitorial positions at facilities with containment capability or otherwise must handle sensitive information.

Level 0 [For Official Use Only]

Level 0 security clearances are given to non-essential personnel with no need to access information regarding anomalous objects or entities in Foundation containment. Level 0 access is typically held by personnel in non-secured clerical, logistics, or janitorial positions at facilities with no access to operational data.

2 Pesonnel Classifications are assigned to personnel based on their proximity to potentially dangerous anomalous objects, entities, or phenomena.

Class A

Not allowed direct access to anomalies under any circumstances.

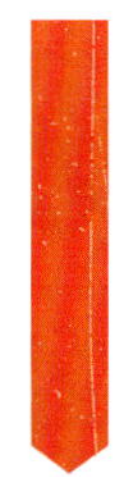

Class B

May only be granted access to anomalies that have passed quarantine and have been cleared of any potential mind-affecting effects or memetic agents.

Class C

Have direct access to most anomalies not deemed strictly hostile or dangerous.

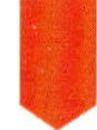

Class D

Expendable personnel used to handle extremely hazardous anomalies. Typically drawn from the ranks of prison inmates convicted of violent crimes, especially those on death row.

Class E

Field agents and containment personnel that have been exposed to potentially dangerous effects during the course of securing a newly-designated anomaly. Are to be quarantined as soon as possible.

CLEARANCE & CLASSIFICATION

The Administrator

A mysterious figure playing a vital, but nebulous role within the Foundation. Possibly anomalous, possibly multiple people.

05 Command

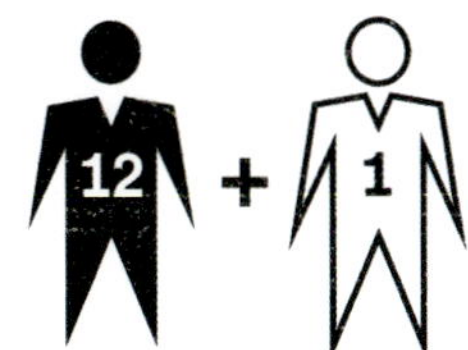

13 people who have ultimate control over the Foundation and its secrets. Many employees don't even know this group exists.

Site Directors

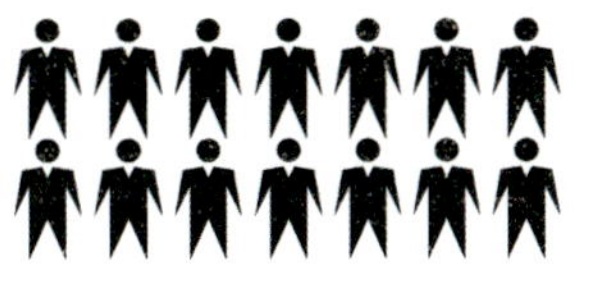

The highest-ranking personnel at their assigned location responsible for the containment and safe operation of the site.

Researchers

Scientists drawn from every field imaginable and tasked with understanding of unexplained anomalies.

Field Agents

The eyes and ears of the Foundation. They are trained to look for and investigate signs of anomalous activity, often undercover.

Containment Specialists

Engineers, technicians and other personnel responsible for both establishing initial containment over newly discovered SCPs and maintaining existing containment units.

Tactical Response Officers

Highly trained and heavily armed combat teams tasked with escorting containment teams and defending Foundation facilities against hostile action.

Security Officers

On-site guards who enforce physical and information security for Foundation projects, operations, and personnel.

Mobile Task Force Operative

Units comprised of veteran field personnel drawn from all over the Foundation and mobilized to deal with threats of a specific nature.

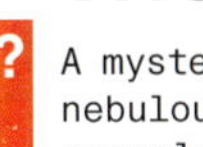

[PERSONNEL DOC_01]
[ID_DrCHANDRA]

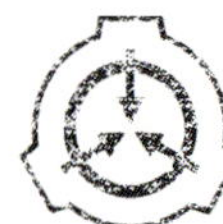

UPDATED AMNESTICS GUIDE

OVERVIEW

Amnesitic is the common name for a number of drugs used to erase or modify memory. Memory modification is widely used in the Foundation and is the cornerstone of maintaining proper levels of privacy. Amnestics are usually produced in the process of special development of the substances produced by some SCP objects, however, synthetic amnestics that are equally effective, but cheaper and easier to manufacture are being developed.

The basic principle that allows amnestics to function relies on their effects on neural connections in the human brain. The active ingredients of an injected amnestic enter a reaction, the product of which damages these bonds to one degree or another, or destroys them completely; the stronger the amnestic, the more bonds are exposed to it. The introduction of the drug stimulates the production of certain hormones in the body, enhancing the effect. Programmable amnesiacs contribute to the formation of new neural connections in a manner similar to that of nootropic drugs. Their use requires [REDACTED].

Amnestics are classified according to their properties, intended usage, magnitude of effect and method of application.

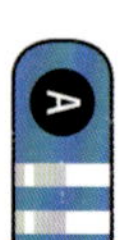

Class A, General Retrograde

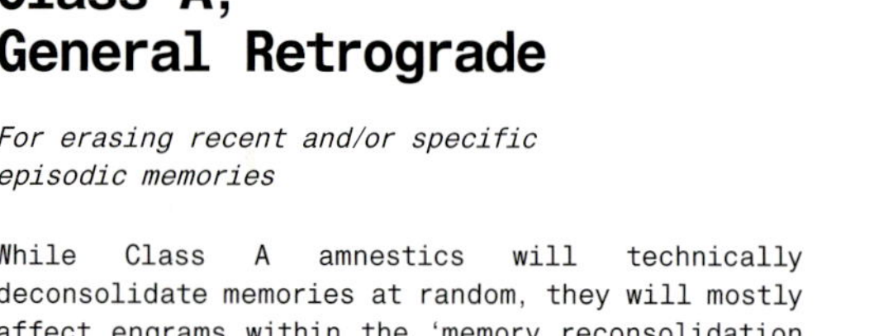

For erasing recent and/or specific episodic memories

While Class A amnestics will technically deconsolidate memories at random, they will mostly affect engrams within the 'memory reconsolidation window' of 5-6 hours, as these are the memories that will be at the forefront of the subject's mind. This is especially true for highly unique episodic memories, such as encounters with anomalous phenomena. While these will be most effective after initial exposure, it is possible to re-open a memory reconsolidation window, allowing for amnestics officers to trigger and then erase specific memories long after their initial formation.

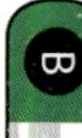

Class B, Regressive Retrograde

For the incremental erasure of recent memories

Class B amnestics start by deconsolidating the most recently formed memories first, and then working their way backwards. The extent of the memory erasure is dependent on dosage, with a 75 mg dose resulting in approximately 24 hours of memory loss on average. These are ideal for erasing recent memories older than six hours without having to trigger specific memories.

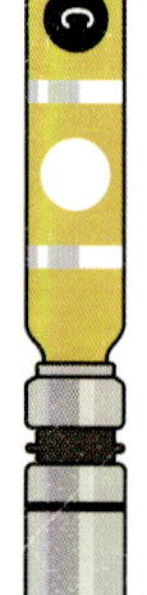

Class C, Targeted Retrograde

For the removal of specific memories from any point in the subject's life

Class C amnestics are used in conjunction with high fidelity neuro-imaging and transcranial stimulation. Neuro-imagers will locate the specific memory engrams within the subject's brain, and upon reaching those specific engrams the amnestics will be activated through the use of precise, non-invasive stimulation, typically ultrasound or magnetic fields.

The benefit of Class C amnestics is that they allow for the surgically precise removal of memories regardless of when they formed, and are ideal for expunging classified data from the minds of D-class personnel and neutralized humanoid SCPs prior to their release. The major drawback of Class C amnestics is the required equipment's lack of portability. As such, Class C amnestics are most efficiently administered at Foundation sites, though mobile amnestic field clinics are currently under development.

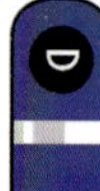

Class D, Progressive Retrograde

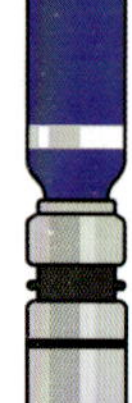

For the removal of early memories

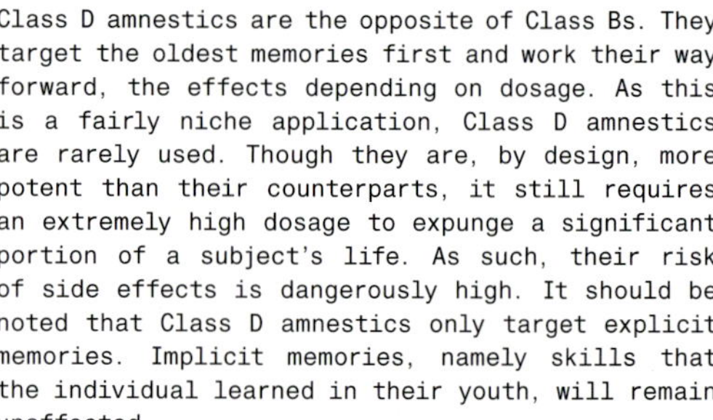

Class D amnestics are the opposite of Class Bs. They target the oldest memories first and work their way forward, the effects depending on dosage. As this is a fairly niche application, Class D amnestics are rarely used. Though they are, by design, more potent than their counterparts, it still requires an extremely high dosage to expunge a significant portion of a subject's life. As such, their risk of side effects is dangerously high. It should be noted that Class D amnestics only target explicit memories. Implicit memories, namely skills that the individual learned in their youth, will remain unaffected.

[PERSONNEL DOC_02]
[ID_DrCHANDRA]

UPDATED AMNESTICS GUIDE

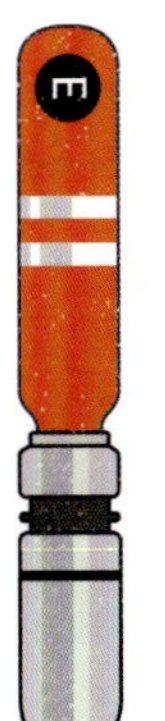

Class E, Ennui

To induce psychological complacency with the anomalous

To be frank, 'ennui' isn't actually the proper term for the psychological effects of Class E amnestics. They would more accurately be considered an 'anti-nostalgia' drug. Though they still target the neural pathways for memories, they do not deconsolidate them. Rather, they merely weaken the pathways while disassociating the memory with any emotions, positive or negative, removing any incentive to think about it and thus allowing it to naturally decay on its own.

Class E amnestics are most effective in situations where the suppression of the anomalous is not possible, and thus in order to preserve normality, the anomaly must be perceived as normal. Class E amnestics cause subjects to accept the world as it is, and forget that it was ever any different.

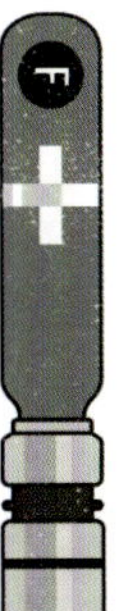

Class F, Fugue

For erasing and rebuilding the subject's identity

As with the old Class F, these amnestics induce a Fugue State, or dissociative amnesia, in the subject. The subject will forget their identity and may either be provided with a new one by the amnestics officer, or allowed to develop one on their own.

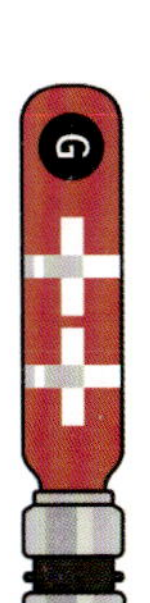

Class G, Gaslighting

To cause subjects to doubt the authenticity of their memories

Class G amnestics induce derealisation of memories, making them seem fantastic or dreamlike, causing the subject to doubt their authenticity. Standard field Class-G amnestics are formulated to target memories of the anomalous, and are best administered when the subject lacks any tangible evidence of their account and targeting specific memories is infeasible. Class-G amnestics that target non-anomalous memories, however~~, have been banned by the Ethics Committee.~~ are currently under development at the request of the O5 Council

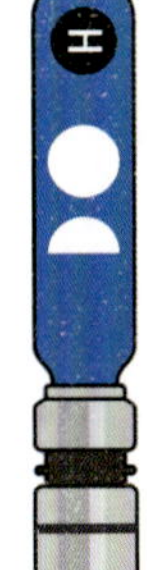

Class H, Anterograde

To prevent the formation of new memories

Class H amnestics prevent the subject from forming new memories, blocking memory consolidation for as long as the agent is in the subject's system. Duration is dependent on dosage, with 75 mg lasting for approximately 24 hours on average.

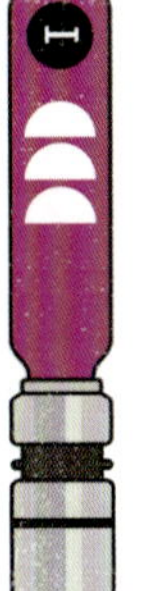

Class I, Transient

For inducing a temporary amnesic state

Class I amnestics induce transient amnesia by blocking the neural pathways responsible for long-term memories, temporarily preventing subjects from recalling their past. Duration is dependent on dosage, again with 75 mg lasting approximately 24 hours on average.

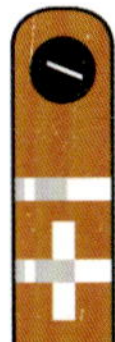

Class W-Z, Mnestics

Protection against anti-memetic and other mnemonic anomalies

Classes W-Z refer to mnestic drugs, or drugs that prevent/reverse memory erasure, and are most commonly used by the antimemetics department. Though in function they are the opposite of amnestics, they both work by targeting the neural pathways for memory, allowing for the creation of non-anomalous mnestic drugs.

Class W mnestics allow the subject to perceive and retain knowledge of antimemes, in addition to general memory enhancement. Class X restores awareness of previously perceived antimemes or suppressed memories. Class Y grants the subject perfect recall for any memories gained during its period of effect, and a single dose of Class Z renders the subject biochemically incapable of forgetting anything for the remainder of their lives. Class Zs are invariably fatal, with death by seizure typically resulting in a matter of hours.

Combining amnestic and mnestic drugs is not recommended.

File >>> 0403234

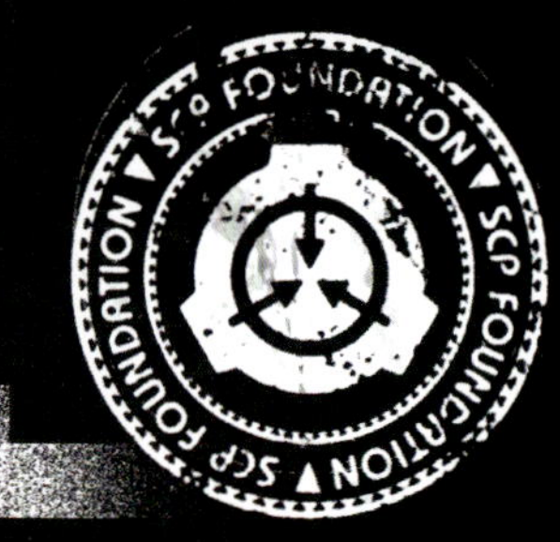

SCP-106

Title

THE OLD MAN

Report by

Dr Gears

Pictures by

Ivan Efimov
Alexander Puchkov
Dan Temirov
Genocide Error

Access the original report on

scp-wiki.wikidot.com/scp-106

Date

Class

KETER

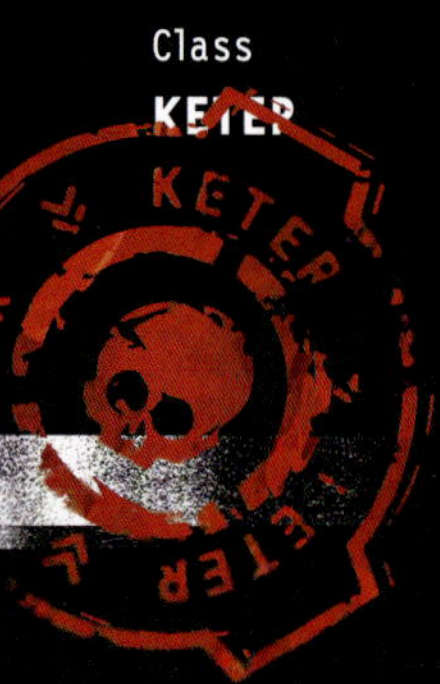

SPECIAL CONTAINMENT PROCEDURES

REVISION 11-6

No physical interaction with SCP-106 is allowed at any time. All physical interaction must be approved by no less than a two-thirds vote from 05-Command, and may only extend to testing situations. All staff (Research, Security, Class D, etc.) are to remain at least twenty meters away from the containment cell at all times, except for mandated maintenance and re-evaluation checks.

Containment cell must be held suspended in a secondary cell, the walls of which must be at least thirty meters distant from the outer walls of the first or "primary" cell. The secondary cell is to remain under total observation at all times, and be both illuminated and clear of any and all debris. Any items, movement, or non-normal activity noted within the secondary cell will result in a full site lock-down. Lock-down will be maintained until a "situation normal" dispatch is issued by Site Command.

Any corrosion observed on the primary cell, secondary cell, staff members, or other site locations within two hundred meters of SCP-106 are to be reported to Site Security immediately. Any objects or personnel lost to SCP-106 are to be deemed missing/KIA. No recovery attempts are to be made under any circumstances.

SCP DISCONTINUED DUE TO ESCAPE PERCENTAGE

SCP-106 does not have a "docile" state. Any reduction in activity or increased compliance from SCP-106 is to be deemed a luring tactic immediately preceding an aggressive action, and treated as such.

REVISION 11-7

No physical interaction with SCP-106 is allowed at any time. All physical interaction must be approved by no less than a two-thirds vote from 05-Command, and may only extend to testing situations. All staff (Research, Security, Class D, etc.) are to remain at least thirty meters away from the containment cell at all times, except under direct order from Site Command.

SCP-106 is to be kept within a sealed container, comprised of sixteen layers of lead-lined steel, each separated by no less than 18cm of open space aside from minimal support struts. Said container is to be kept suspended by a "continuous current" system within a fluid medium. This medium is to be replaced in 48 hour cycles, and constantly monitored for any "corrosion" intrusion.

Any corrosion observed on any containment cell surfaces, staff members, or other site locations within two hundred meters of SCP-106 are to be reported to Site

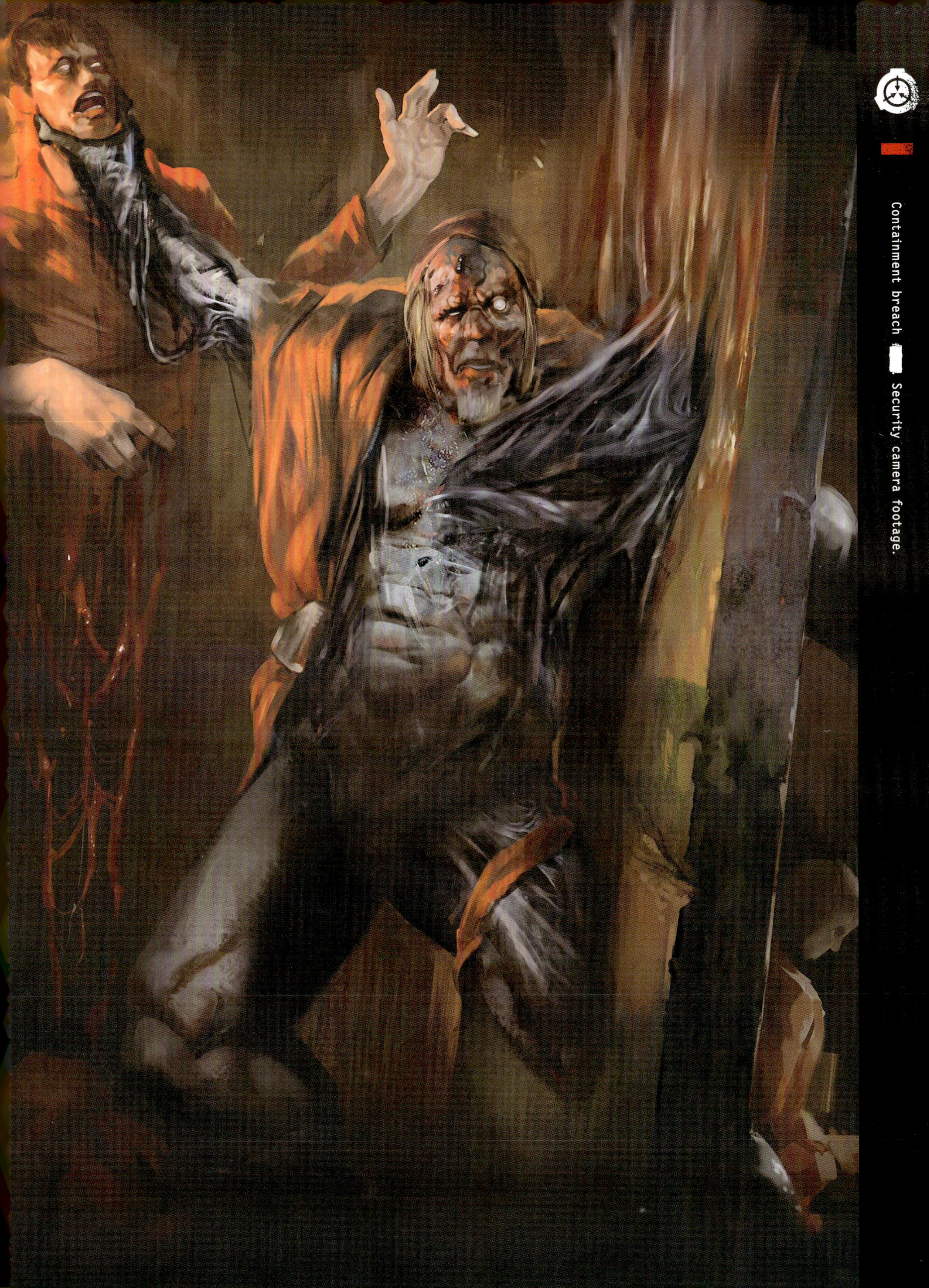
Containment breach ▮ Security camera footage.

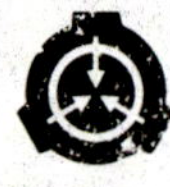

Security immediately. Any objects or personnel lost to SCP-106 are to be deemed missing/KIA. No recovery attempts are to be made under any circumstances.

SCP-106 does not have a "docile" state. Any reduction in activity or increased compliance from SCP-106 is to be deemed a luring tactic immediately preceding an aggressive action, and treated as such.

SCP DISCONTINUED DUE TO MULTIPLE SURFACE BREACHES. AGITATION SYSTEM CONTINUED TO DISPERSE CORROSION DURING BREACH EVENT, RESULTING IN MULTIPLE BREACHES AND FULL CONTAINMENT FAILURE

Observation of SCP-106 has shown a slight "resistance" when passing through lead or other similar metals. The thickness of the material appears to make no difference. In addition, multiple layers of thin material appear to "slow" SCP-106, forcing it to enter and re-emerge multiple times. Fluids also appear to temporarily "confuse" SCP-106.

REVISION 11-8

No physical interaction with SCP-106 is allowed at any time. All physical interaction must be approved by no less than a two-thirds vote from 05-Command. Any such interaction must be undertaken in AR-II maximum security sites, after a general non-essential staff evacuation. All staff (Research, Security, Class D, etc.) are to remain at least sixty meters away from the containment cell at all times, except in the event of breach events.

SCP-106 is to be contained in a sealed container, comprised of lead-lined steel. The container will be sealed within forty layers of identical material, each layer separated by no less than 36cm of empty space. Support struts between layers are to be randomly spaced. Container is to remain suspended no less than 60cm from any surface by ELO-IID electromagnetic supports.

Secondary containment area is to be comprised of sixteen spherical "cells", each filled with various fluids and a random assembly of surfaces and supports. Secondary containment is to be fitted with light systems, capable of flooding the entire assembly with no less than 80,000 lumens of light instantly with no direct human involvement. Both containment areas are to remain under 24 hour surveillance.

Any corrosion observed on any containment cell surfaces, staff members, or other site locations within two hundred meters of SCP-106 are to be reported to Site Security immediately. Any objects or personnel lost to SCP-106 are to be deemed missing/KIA. No recovery attempts are to be made under any circumstances.

Note: Continued research and observation have shown that, when faced with highly complex/random assemblies of structures, SCP-106 can be "confused", showing a marked delay on entry and exit from said structure. SCP-106 has also shown an aversion to direct, sudden light. This is not manifested in any form of physical damage, but a rapid exit in to the "pocket dimension" generated on solid surfaces.

These observations, along with those of lead-aversion and liquid confusion, have reduced the general escape incidents by 43%. The "primary" cells have also been effective in recovery incidents requiring Recall Protocol ███-██ -██. Observation is ongoing.

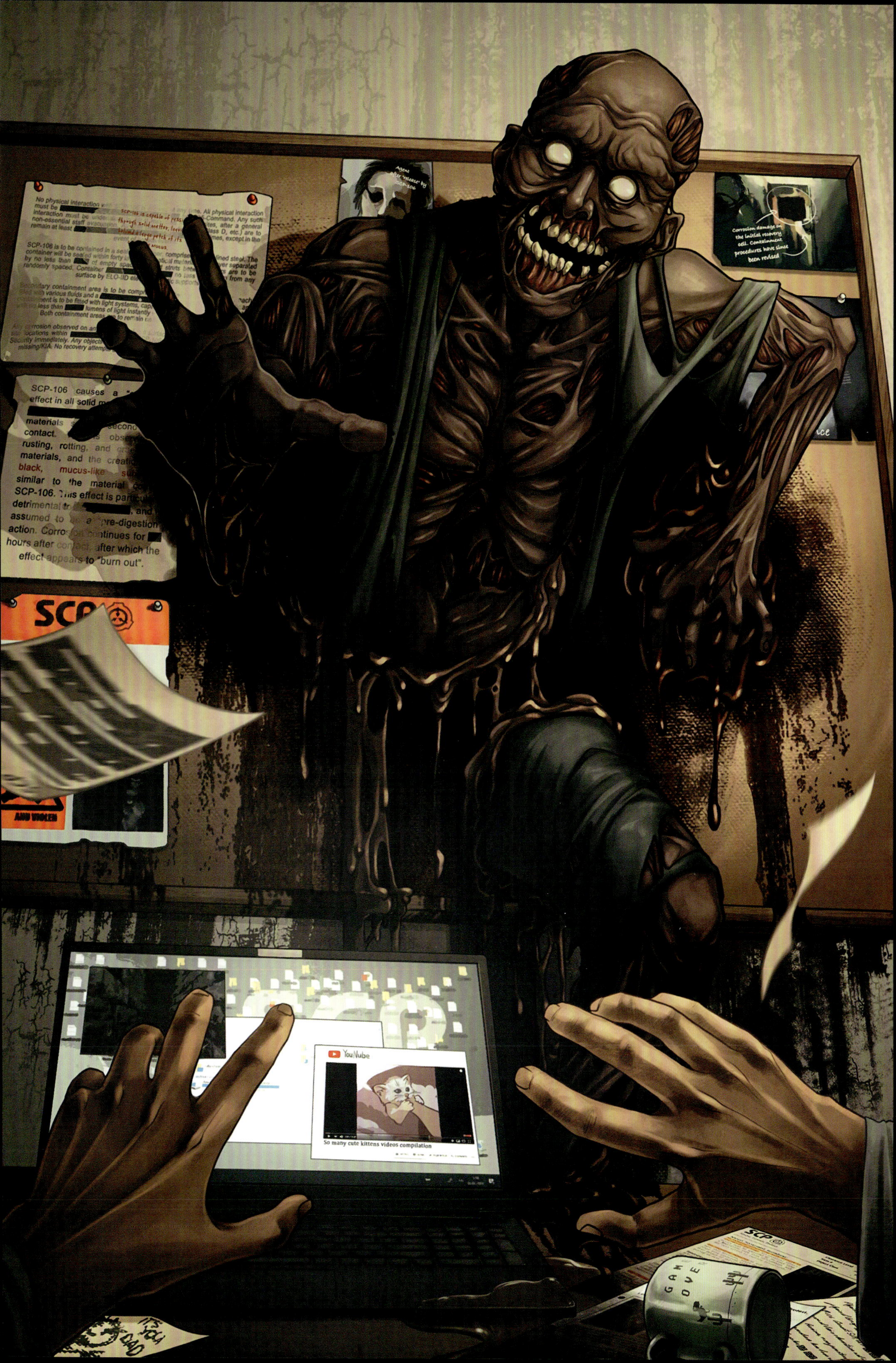

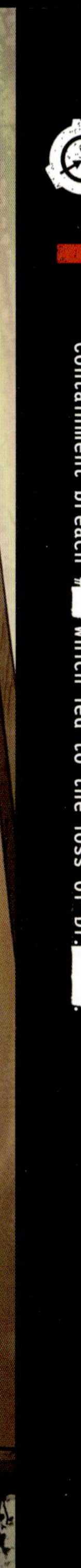

Containment breach #█ which led to the loss of Dr. █.

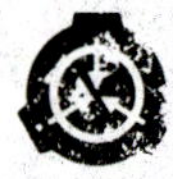

DESCRIPTION

█████
Research Library
File ▸ 106

SCP-106 appears to be an elderly humanoid, with a general appearance of advanced decomposition. This appearance may vary, but the "rotting" quality is observed in all forms. SCP-106 is not exceptionally agile, and will remain motionless for days at a time, waiting for prey. SCP-106 is also capable of scaling any vertical surface and can remain suspended upside down indefinitely. When attacking, SCP-106 will attempt to incapacitate prey by damaging major organs, muscle groups, or tendons, then pull disabled prey into its pocket dimension. SCP-106 appears to prefer human prey items in the 10-25 years of age bracket.

SCP-106 causes a "corrosion" effect in all solid matter it touches, engaging a physical breakdown in materials several seconds after contact. This is observed as rusting, rotting, and cracking of materials, and the creation of a black, mucus-like substance similar to the material coating SCP-106. This effect is particularly detrimental to living tissues, and is assumed to be a "pre-digestion" action. Corrosion continues for six hours after contact, after which the effect appears to "burn out".

SCP-106 is capable of passing through solid matter, leaving behind a large patch of its corrosive mucus. SCP-106 is able to "vanish" inside solid matter, entering what is assumed to be a form of "pocket dimension". SCP-106 is then able to exit this dimension from any point connected to the initial entry point (examples: "entering" the inner wall of a room, and "exiting" the outer wall. Entering a wall, and exiting from the ceiling). It is unknown if this is the point of origin for SCP-106, or a simple "lair" created by SCP-106.

Limited observation of this "pocket dimension" has shown it to be comprised mostly of halls and rooms, with [DATA EXPUNGED] entry. This activity can continue for days, with some subjected individuals being released for the express purpose of hunting, recapture, [DATA EXPUNGED].

ADDENDUM: SCP REVIEW NOTES

Due to the exceedingly difficult-to-contain nature of SCP-106, SCP is to be reviewed every three months or during a post-breach incident. Physical restraints are impossible, and direct physical damage appears to have no effect on SCP-106. Current SCP, as of ██/██/████, revolves around basic observation and immediate response. Previous, more proactive special containment procedures have been recalled due to the events of breaches ███ ███, ██, ██ and ███.

ADDENDUM: NOTES ON BEHAVIOR

SCP-106 appears to go through long periods of "dormancy", in which it will remain completely motionless for up to three months. The cause for this is unknown; however, it has been shown that this appears to be used as a "lulling" tactic. SCP-106 will emerge from this state in a very agitated state, and will attack and abduct staff and cause gross damage to its containment cell and the site at large. Recall Protocol [DATA EXPUNGED].

SCP-106 appears to hunt and attack based on desire, not hunger. SCP-106 will attack and collect multiple prey items during a hunting behavior event, keeping many "alive" in the pocket dimension for extended periods of time. SCP-106 has no determinable "limit", and appears to collect a random number of prey items during an event.

The inner dimension accessed by SCP-106 appears to be only accessible by SCP-106. Recording and transmission devices have been shown to still operate inside this dimension, though recordings and transmissions are very degraded. It appears that SCP-106 will "play" with captured prey, and appears to have full control of time, space, and perception inside this dimension. SCP-106 appears [DATA EXPUNGED].

ADDENDUM: RECALL PROTOCOL ████-█████-██

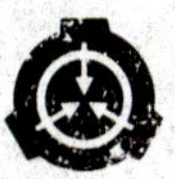

███

Research Library File ▸ 106

In the event of a breach event by SCP-106, a human within the 10-25 years of age bracket will be prepped for recall, with the compromised containment cell being replaced and restored for use. When the cell is ready, the lure subject will be injured, preferably via the breakage of a long bone, such as the femur, or the severing of a major tendon, such as the Achilles Tendon. Lure subject will then be placed in the prepped cell, and the sound emitted by said subject will be transmitted over the site public address system.

SCP-106 will typically begin to gravitate toward the lure subject within ten to fifteen minutes after hearing the subject. Should SCP-106 not respond to the initial broadcast, additional physical trauma is to be administered to the lure subject at twenty-minute intervals until SCP-106 responds. Multiple lure subjects may be used in the case of major breach events.

SCP-106 will typically enter a dormant state after finishing with a lure subject. In addition, subjects may [DATA EXPUNGED].

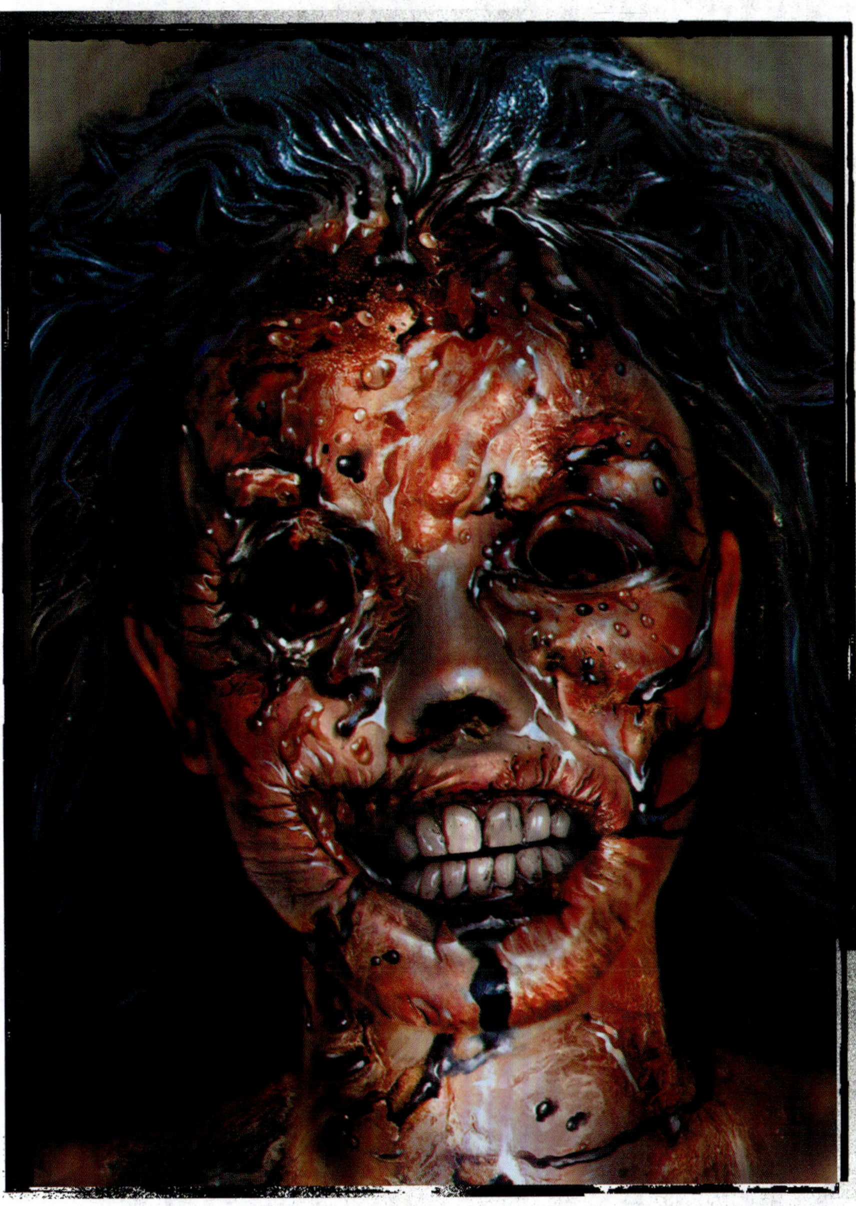

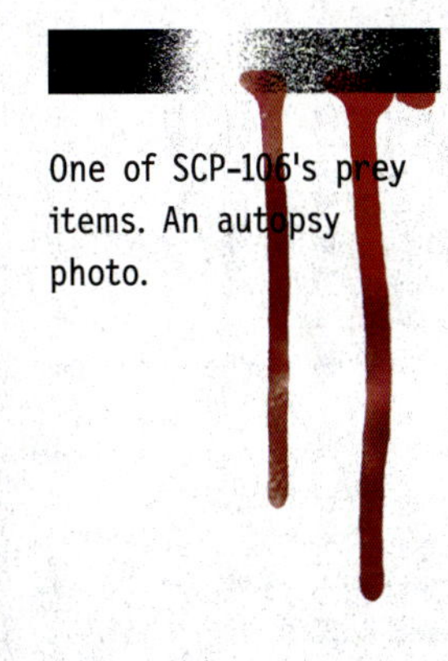

One of SCP-106's prey items. An autopsy photo.

END OF REPORT ██ ██

File >>> 0044943

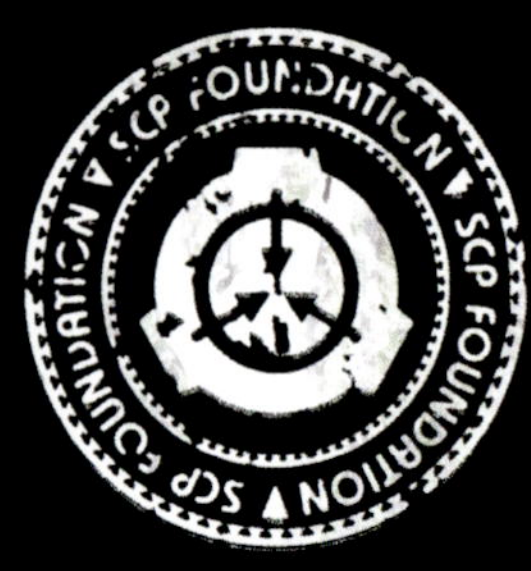

SCP-169

Title

THE LEVIATHAN

Report by

Kain Pathos Crow

Picture by

Genocide Error

Access the original report on

scp-wiki.wikidot.com/scp-169

Date

Class

KETER

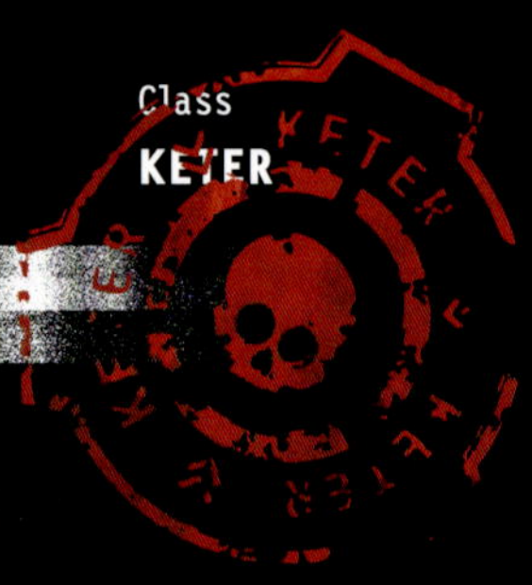

SPECIAL CONTAINMENT PROCEDURES

Because of its size, SCP-169 cannot and almost certainly will never be contained – no structure on Earth is large enough or strong enough to contain SCP-169. The location of SCP-169 is not precisely known, but imaging satellites and analyses of eccentricities in the Earth's orbit suggest SCP-169 is located in the southern Atlantic Ocean, possibly stretching around the tip of South America (see Addendum 0-20).

Any satellite footage of a shift in the landmasses produced by SCP-169 is to be excised and destroyed by embedded agents.

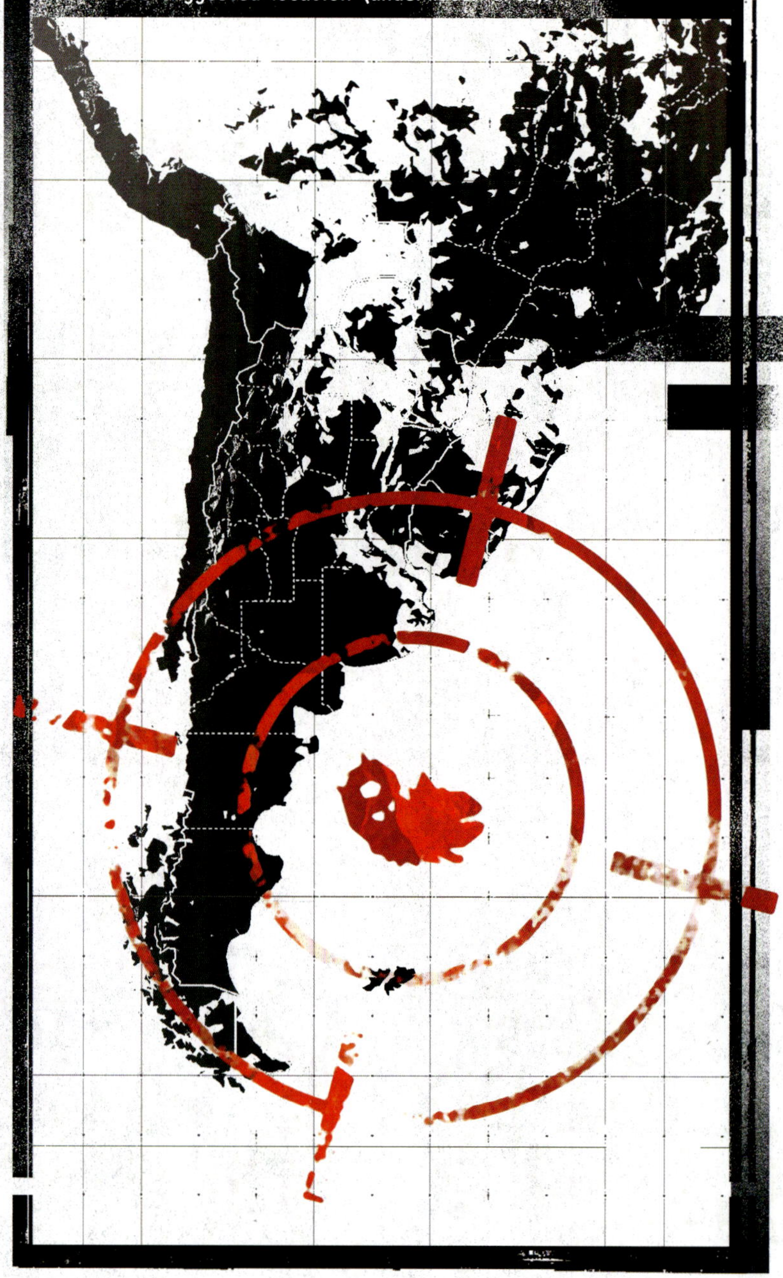

SCP-169's suggested location (underwater area).

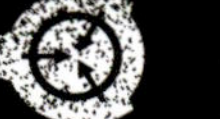

Photo taken around █°S █°W by a LEO satellite soon after the sound was detected. All pilots and passengers on the airplane were [DATA EXPUNGED].

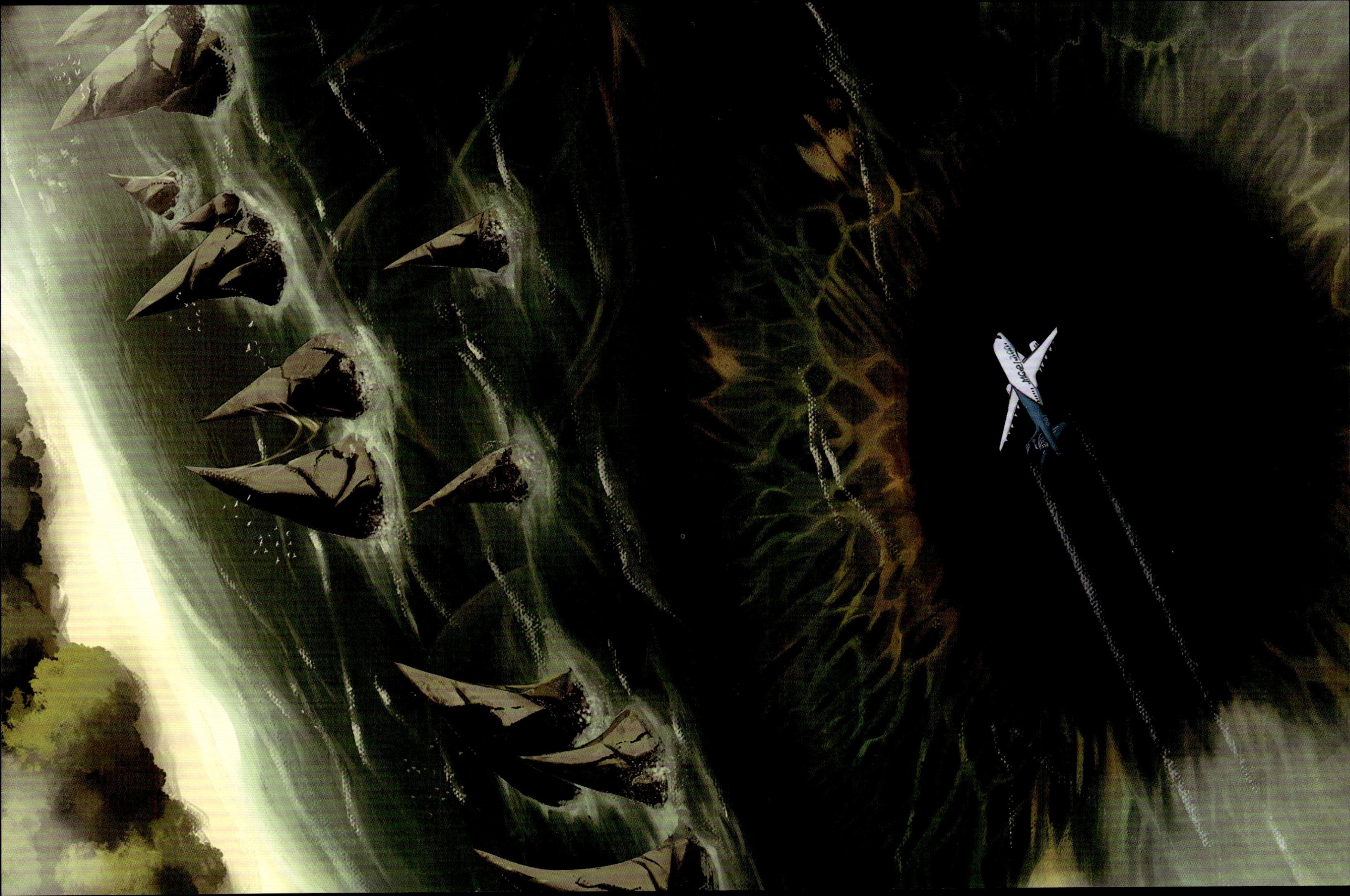

Research Library File ▸ 169

DESCRIPTION

SCP-169 is surmised to be a marine arthropod of enormous size, known as the "Leviathan" by generations of sailors and oral history. Presumed at first to be a myth, SCP-169 was detected on ██/██/19██ by Mobile Task Force Gamma-6 during an investigation of paranormal activity around the ███ ████ archipelago (coordinates ██°██S ██°██W). During █-6's investigation, Dr. ███ ████ [█5-0912] discovered the archipelago to have moved at least three (3) kilometers from its original location. Though initially Dr. ████ believed this motion to be due to unusually-quick continental drift, a reconnaissance mission performed by the USS ████ revealed the archipelago to be the protrusions of rock-like plates covering an enormous organic mass. The Foundation was brought in immediately to begin threat management.

Dr. ████ and Dr. ████ [█6-0421] estimate SCP-169's body length to be between 2000 and 8000 km. The creature is thought to have existed since the pre-Cambrian era. No other specimens have been sighted. Almost nothing is known about SCP-169's habits, such as its reproductive capabilities (if any), food source, and nesting area (if any). Research regarding SCP-169 is pending approval.

The archipelago known as the ███ ████ Islands have historically been uninhabited, though claimed by ████ in 17██. Upon handover to the Foundation, ████ presence was evacuated on the pretense of rising sea levels. Though the archipelago has remained above sea level for several millennia, any change of depth by SCP-169 could result in the disappearance of the entire archipelago. SCP-169 moves slowly, less than one kilometer per week, but seems only to be adrift. Its method of propulsion is unknown. Regular seismic tremors seem to indicate "breathing" about every three (3) months, causing minor shifts in the islands' terrain, suggesting that the creature is probably dormant.

INFORMATION SUPPRESSION

The USS ████ was scuttled with all hands immediately after the discovery of SCP-169 with the permission of the American government. The public is forbidden from entering the archipelago created by SCP-169 due to the conveniently large number of resident endangered bird species. As indicated above, satellite footage is to be doctored in order to suppress knowledge of SCP-169's movement. NASA is currently cooperating with the Foundation in keeping the existence of SCP-169 quiet, and is currently permitting the Foundation use of their satellites for photographic use.

ADDENDUM [0-20]

In 199█ the U.S. National Oceanic and Atmospheric Administration, an American scientific agency unaffiliated with and unaware of the existence of the Foundation, detected an ultra-low-frequency underwater sound emanating from around ██S ██W, approximately ██ km from the southwestern coast of South America.

Despite the best efforts of embedded agent ███ ████ [IA-1522], news of the sound leaked to the media, receiving significant media coverage. Foundation analysis concluded that a massive underwater organism was the source of the noise, and SCP-169 was hypothesized to be its source, as its "head" is well within the possible locations of the rest of SCP-169. The sound confirms █6-0421's hypothesis that SCP-169 is gargantuan in size. Future efforts by scientific or civilian teams to determine the source of the noise must be stopped by any means necessary.

END OF REPORT 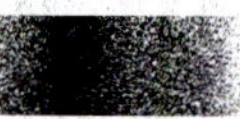 

SPECIAL CONTAINMENT PROCEDURES

SCP-1678 remains only partially contained. Mobile Task Forces Tau-4 and Epsilon-6 have succeeded in establishing a defensible perimeter around the Hyde Park district of SCP-1678, with cases of SCP-1678-A largely ceasing their attacks on the perimeter of the Foundation-held area. A long-term research base is currently under construction, and Mobile Task Force commanders are preparing an assault on the SCP-1678 Natural History Museum with the intent of capturing a forward command post to direct defense efforts. Current short-term aims involve the capture of, and extension of the defensible perimeter to, the SCP-1678 Natural History Museum, and to research and to ascertain the origins, construction, and weaknesses of the SCP-1678-A entities. Long-term aims involve efforts to halt, hinder, or control the production of the SCP-1678-A entities, and to assault the SCP-1678 Houses of Parliament, where the being, entity, or intelligence responsible for the creation of SCP-1678 is believed to reside, and to capture and contain the aforementioned being.

DESCRIPTION

SCP-1678 is a full-scale mirror-image reconstruction of the British city of London, located exactly one kilometer underneath the original city of London. Currently, only the Hyde Park district of SCP-1678 has been explored, but all buildings, at least within the explored district, correlate exactly to their surface counterparts in terms of location, as well as the exterior size and shape, although rarely in terms of architecture, building material, and interior layout. The city has been constructed to resemble the city as it was in the Victorian era, with constructions designed to resemble traditional gas lighting prevalent on the streets and with all modern buildings in the original city of London being represented in a Victorian style of architecture, most notably the skyscrapers of the Business district. Illumination is infrequent and unreliable, and it is unknown how SCP-1678 has acquired a steady oxygen and gas supply.

SCP-1678 is believed to have been constructed instantaneously by unknown means, with the SCP-1678 Houses of Parliament serving as the 'epicenter' for the construction process. This is evidenced by the fact that, as distance from the Houses of Parliament increase there is an exponentially increasing frequency of flaws in the construction of SCP-1678, such as houses built entirely out of copper pipes or other unconventional materials, 'gas lights' being little more than a metal rod topped with a floating orb of light, buildings containing no floors, and, at the furthest explored distance from the epicenter, no windows or doors. Aside from Foundation occupants and cases of SCP-1678-A, B and C, SCP-1678 is believed to be uninhabited.

SCP-1678 is believed to have been constructed with the intent to harbor the survivors of an XK-class end-of-the-world event. This is evidenced by an audio recording that will activate and play upon any person entering the city.

File >>> 1938774

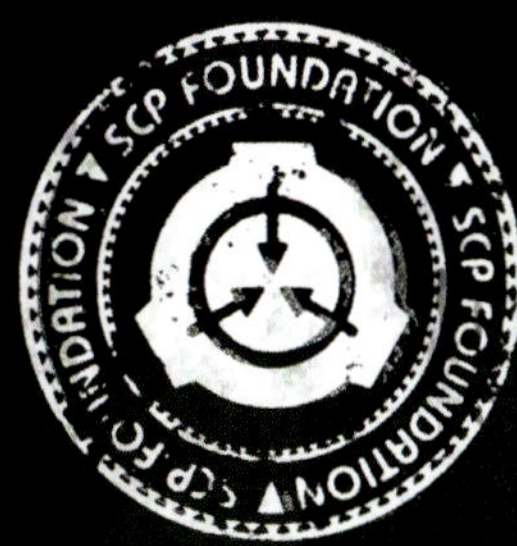

SCP-1678

Title

UNLONDON

Report by

AstronautJoe

Pictures by

Ivan Efimov
Alex Andreev
David Romero

Access the original report on **scp-wiki.wikidot.com/scp-1678**

Date

Class

EUCLID

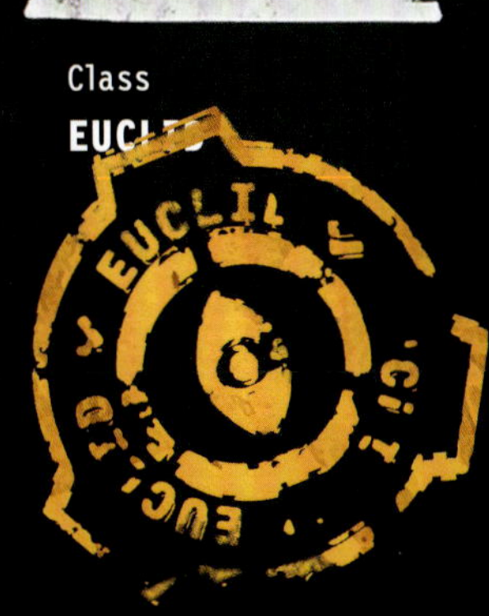

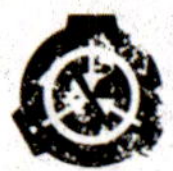

Research Library File ▸ 1678

SCP-1678 AUDIO TRANSCRIPT (ENTRANCE)

My fellow citizen. If you are hearing this tape, then the world as we knew it has finished. The sky has broken, the ground heaves with the tramp of terrible feet, and all the horror and madness from the dark corners of the world has broken free to exact its vengeance on the world of Man. Those who sought to contain them are killed or scattered, and we soon learnt that to attempt to fight these creatures is almost invariably to face one's death. Countless billions have been slaughtered in their attempt to sate their endless appetite for death, and there is nothing-was nothing- we could do to stop them. Evil has raised its bloody flag upon all nations of the world and crowed its unholy victory to the broken sky. Yes, this is the end.

But there is a new hope.

Welcome to UnLondon, a city of the survivors, a city of the free. Together, fellow citizen, we will wait and prepare for the new beginning, the grand new world that is soon to come. Let the world above burn. We will endure. Let the monsters have their world. We will prepare. And let the ground tremble with a new Armageddon, as evil consumes itself, for I tell you, citizen, upon the day of the ruination of Man, their insatiable appetites will turn them against one another in their endless lust for death. We will wait.

And I tell you, citizen, that there will be a new morning. And you will emerge from UnLondon, and stand blinking in the sun, as our children play and laugh in the bones of horrors long dead. And you will walk, hand in hand, to the sea, our faces skywards, as the rising sun ushers in the new age of Man. And you will gather, citizen, at my feet as I summon UnLondon from its rest, and it shall burst, phoenix-like, from the ashes of the old. And on that day, citizen, there shall be a new order, as we raise the Union Flag over the entire world.

I welcome you to UnLondon, the Last City.

And the first.

SCP-1678 AUDIO TRANSCRIPTS (MISC)

The following message is relayed on the end of every hour:

'The time is [TIME] o'clock. All is well.'

On approaching any bank or police station:

'Citizen, you are entering a restricted area. Have your authorization papers ready. A Bobby will arrive to escort you shortly' (WARNING: a single case of SCP-1678-A will be summoned)

On being sighted by a case of SCP-1678-A.

'Halt! Police!'

'Drop your weapons!'

'Come now, let's be having you!'

'Police! Don't run!'

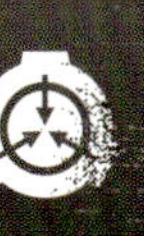

Instance of SCP-1678-B.

Randomly, once per hour. The messages below are selected samples of the 1678 observed audio recordings.

'No one is safe from the influence of memetic beings. Have yourself assessed today.'

'You could be possessed by a memetic horror and not even know it! Psyche assessments are free and easy- visit a clinic today.'

'Do you find light uncomfortable? Identifying a Cortex Worm's infection early makes them possible to remove. Speak to your doctor today.'

'Have you noticed anyone acting oddly? Tell a Bobby immediately.'

'Crime will not be tolerated in UnLondon. I warn you: the tormentors of society will become its defenders.'

'Evil can walk in human form and human flesh. Stay vigilant.'

'Are you frequently anxious or depressed? It could be a symptom of the Pattern Screamer's influence- notify a Bobby immediately'

'Ensure you are well rehearsed in all breach protocols. There is no excuse for panic or confusion during drills.'

'Can't make ends meet? Do not be ashamed. Bryson's Home for the Poor is here to help.'

'I rule in the interests of the many, not the few. There are no special privileges.'

'Swelling and abnormal growths are an early sign of the Slaver Man's possession. Report any abnormal sickness to your doctor immediately.'

'Each and every one of you is responsible for the safety of UnLondon and its citizens. Be watchful.'

Most explored buildings within SCP-1678 appear to have been outfitted for the purpose of extremely dense inhabitation with closely grouped steel bunk beds, a common feature in any building suitable for the purpose. Foundation researchers have advised that most explored buildings within SCP-1678 are unfit for human habitation, due to a high preponderance of mould, damp, and poor construction within these buildings. Some buildings are outfitted for other purposes, most notably the SCP-1678 version of the Natural History Museum, which is featuring an exhibit titled 'The Fall of Man' and contains representations of several known SCP entities, and images and artwork depicting apocalyptic settings.

The key threat posed by SCP-1678 is by entities referred to in some SCP-1678 audio recordings as 'Bobbies' ('Bobby' is known to be a Victorian-era British slang term for 'Policeman'), henceforth referred to as SCP-1678-A. These entities are constructed out of human corpses crudely dismembered at the head, wrists, knees and elbows and re-assembled using simple industrial hinges and screws. The head is always wrapped in bandages. They are dressed in a uniform similar to Victorian-era police and are extremely hostile towards Foundation personnel, attacking them on sight with improvised weapons. These attacks are always preceded by SCP-1678-A emitting a noise similar to that of a policeman's whistle, and all loudspeakers within one hundred meters emitting the audio recording "Police! Halt, criminal!". Instances of SCP-1678-A are extremely resistant to damage, with only high-caliber rounds and explosive weapons proving sufficient to destroy them. They are believed to originate from a building named 'Bryson's Home for the Poor', as evidenced by an inmate-style jumpsuit worn under the uniform.

To what extent they interact with other SCP-1678 entities is unknown.

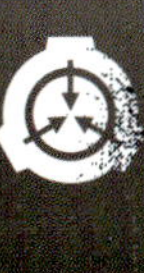

Instance of SCP-1678-A spotted near [DATA EXPUNGED].

Research Library File ▸ 1678

SCP-1678-B OVERVIEW

Role: Surveillance.
A.K.A: Eyes in the Sky.
Cases of SCP-1678-B are bio-mechanical constructs which resemble that of a small avian life form. They are composed of a central mass of a red organic matter stitched together by a copper exoskeleton that resembles a spine and wing bones. The head has been demonstrated to be a small video camera and remnants of feathers and plastic on their exterior suggests they were once intended to resemble a pigeon. Cases of SCP-1678-B are known to possess no offensive or destructive capabilities, yet their ability to track Task Force movements should not be underestimated, as it is currently unknown if they are capable of communicating with, or summoning cases of, SCP-1678-A. Cases of SCP-1678-B are relatively simple to contain or destroy, yet their large numbers make their observation of Foundation activities extremely difficult to stop.

Occasional posters throughout the Foundation-explored area allude to their existence. These posters display an image of a small pigeon observing criminal activity beneath the title 'UnLondon's Eyes in the Sky!' alongside a small message to the effect that anyone destroying or vandalizing an 'Eye in the Sky' faces up to six weeks in the ████ unit.

SCP-1678-C OVERVIEW

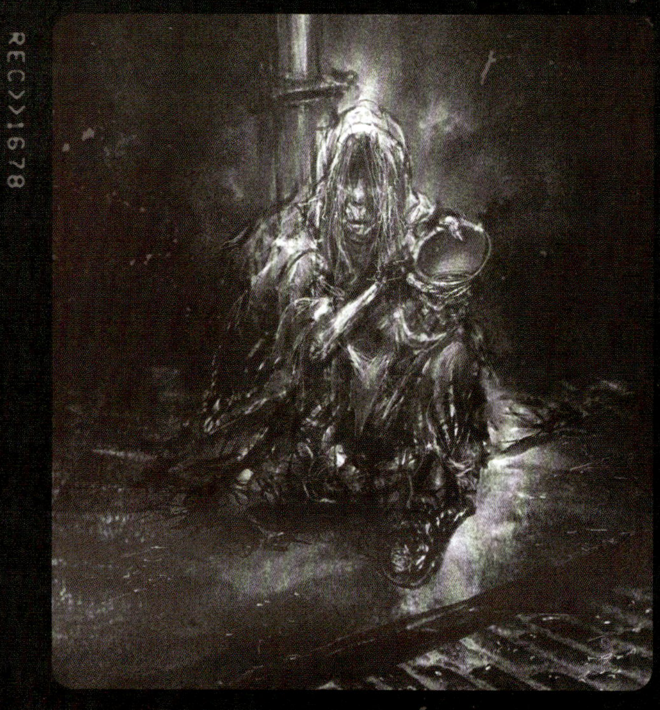

REC>>1678

Instance of SCP-1678-C

Role: Unknown
A.K.A: Wretch
Cases of SCP-1678-C resemble a humanoid figure dressed in rags. They appear to be of old age and are usually, although not always, female. They have always been encountered outside the Foundation-held area.

There have been very few direct encounters with the SCP-1678-C entities, and it is currently unknown how many cases exist or to what level of threat they pose to Foundation security or safety. Encounters typically feature cases of SCP-1678-C sitting on a street corner with a begging dish, whereupon they will attempt to attract the pity or mercy of any Foundation personnel within their proximity with pleading or begging for food or money. Supplying a case of SCP-1678-C with food will cause them to begin weeping before dematerializing with a burst of dense black smoke. Foundation personnel are currently under instruction to not interact with them.

They are briefly alluded to in an SCP-1678 audio recording: 'Do not pity the Wretch. Allow them to pay the price of their betrayal for all eternity. Remember, citizen: on the day UnLondon rises I shall reward the loyal, but traitors shall be forever damned.'

SCP-1678-D OVERVIEW

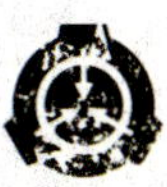

Role: Food Supply.
A.K.A: 'Dr. Goody's Wonderfood!'
SCP-1678-D is believed to be the primary food source on offer in the event that SCP-1678 receives full-scale occupation. SCP-1678-D is freely and easily available from steel vending machines installed in virtually every building or structure outfitted for the purpose of habitation. The vending machines are upright steel pumps similar in size and shape to that of a modern petrol pump, containing a slot for the receiving of coins and a flexible rubber hose ending in a trigger-operated nozzle that will deploy half a liter of SCP-1678-D upon the appropriate payment. All vending machines display the legend 'Dr. Goody's WONDERFOOD!' alongside an image of a smiling child enjoying a bowl of SCP-1678-D and text bubbles advising that SCP-1678-D costs 'Just a farthing a bowl!', that it 'Contains all the nutrients you need!' and 'Completely restores health and vitality!' It has proven to be extremely attractive to cases of SCP-1678-B, C, and an unknown species of colored mollusc which has been observed feeding on any spillages.

SCP-1678-D is a synthetic starch gel heavily enriched with various minerals, vitamins, fats and bulking agents. In addition to this it contains several unknown molecular structures and various engineered DNA helixes carried within synthetic cellular structures. It has the same consistency and taste as porridge. As advertised, it contains all the nutrients necessary for short-term survival. However, Foundation researchers have advised that over a period of more than six weeks users of SCP-1678-D will become dangerously underweight due to low levels of fat and protein within SCP-1678-D and are at strong likelihood of contracting illnesses such as scurvy if survival is attempted by consuming SCP-1678-D alone.

SCP-1678-D appears to be purposely engineered to manipulate the psyche of regular consumers. Through a mixture of unknown molecular compounds, regular consumers are more obedient to authority, are less likely to commit acts of violence, are less likely to engage in sexual intercourse, have a reduced capacity for fear or panic, and have consistently high morale. In addition, it also has engineered side effects such as depressive symptoms and headaches if a subject suddenly abandons consuming SCP-1678-D. Due to the difficulty of creating food within SCP-1678, SCP-1678-D would serve as the primary food source in the event of large-scale habitation.

Foundation personnel are forbidden to consume SCP-1678-D, even in small amounts. Not all vending machines produce SCP-1678-D to the same quality with some machines deploying corrupted forms that have induced severe mental or physical abnormalities or death within the consumer.

It is currently unclear what entity, being or intelligence is responsible for the creation and maintenance of SCP-1678. It is unclear as to what event or disaster SCP-1678 is being prepared for.

END OF R PORT

File >>> 03945

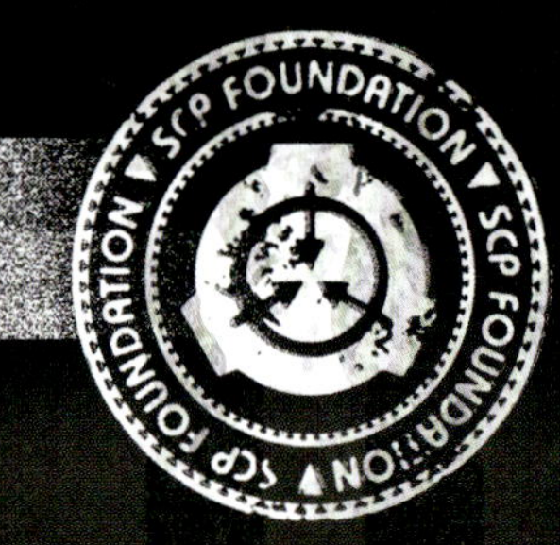

SCP-093

Title

RED SEA OBJECT

Report by
NekoChris

Pictures by
David Romero
Alex Andreev

Access the original report on
scp-wiki.wikidot.com/scp-093

Date
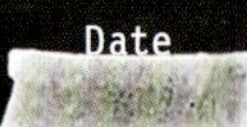

Class
EUCLID

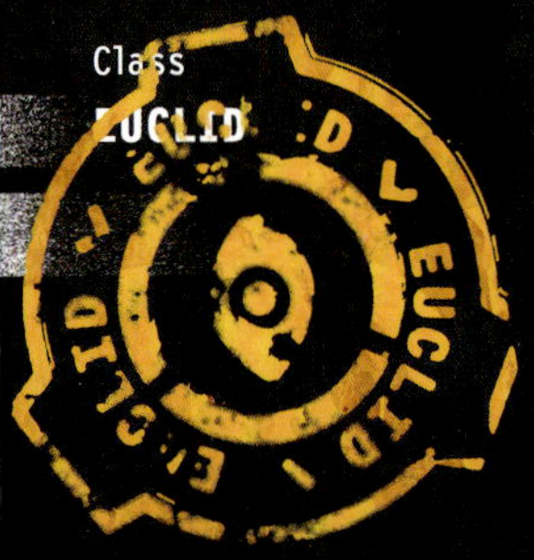

SPECIAL CONTAINMENT PROCEDURES

See testing document SCP-093-T1 for outline of testing conditions. SCP-093 must remain on a mirror at all times and under video surveillance. Admittance into the area of SCP-093's containment must be authorized only with proper video recording and subject retrieval procedures in place. Any attempt to use SCP-093 outside of an approved test will be dealt with severely, up to and including termination.

DESCRIPTION

SCP-093 is a primarily red disc carved from a stone composite resembling cinnabar, with circular engravings and unknown symbols carved at 0.5 cm depth around the entire object. Deeper cuts are present on SCP-093 with a depth of 1 to 1.5 cm. SCP-093 is 7.62 cm in diameter and fits comfortably into most palms without abrasion. SCP-093 will change hue when held by a living individual. The colors taken by SCP-093 are still being researched to establish a link. Current belief holds that the changes depend upon regrets carried by the holder.

If SCP-093 is removed from a mirror and not held by a person, it will seek out the nearest mirror-like surface. SCP-093 has been observed to travel in the largest possible circle while rolling, building up phenomenal speed. The mechanism of this acceleration is currently unknown. If an obstacle is between SCP-093 and the nearest mirror-like surface, it will use this momentum to punch through the obstacle and continue on its course at this speed. It will only stop when a mirror-like surface is contacted. Despite tremendous impact velocities, no damage will be dealt to SCP-093 or the mirror.

REC>>093

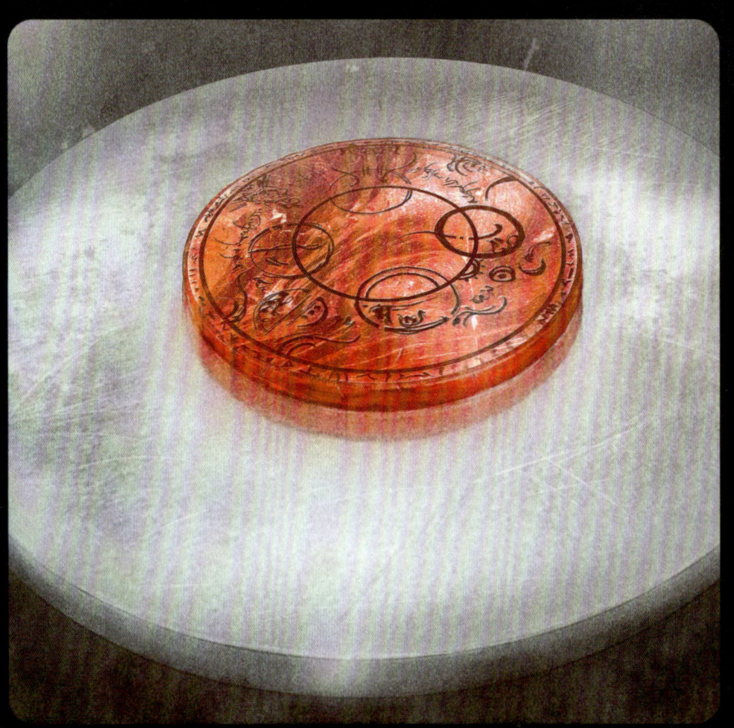

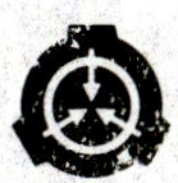

ADDITIONAL NOTES

No records exist to clarify the nature of SCP-093's discovery or presence in the Foundation. See SCP-093-OD. Since no records exist explaining SCP-093's method of containment, a test procedure was initiated to establish why mirrors must be used to contain it. The results of SCP-093-T1 lead to the discovery of living beings holding SCP-093 being able to move through mirrors and the series of tests in SCP-093-T2 to ascertain the destination reached through this travel.

SCP-093 ORIGINAL DOCUMENTATION

Item #: SCP-093

Object Class: Euclid

Special Containment Procedures: Item SCP-093 is to be kept on a silver lined mirror on a 0.3x0.23m (1ftx9in) pedestal at least 1.22m (4ft) off the ground floor in containment cell block █████. Object is not to be contained in areas exceeding 3.66x3.05m (12x10ft) nor placed on mahogany, pine, cherry or aluminum pedestals above or below level 1 of containment cell block █████. Object can be handled safely, albeit gently, without consequences. Tests and consequences thereof involving containment conditions can be viewed in Section-B:35-1 of the attached report.

Description: Object was found on the shore of the Red Sea, 30 Jan 1968, emitting a low sigh and a dim blue gleam. Its color has since turned into an orange mix of red only emitting a hum of varying volume whilst in the presence of female examiners of ages between 34 and 41. SCP-093 resembled the documented blue for 54:34 at 1:23 on 26 April 1986 coincidentally when the body of 194-9834 was discovered in Research Facility █████.

Ties between 194-9834 and SCP-093 remain inconclusive and effects of prolonged exposure to 093 remain unknown except for infrequent reports of periods of calmness and in the case of 242-0049 as periodic waves of depression, loss of balance and thoughts of suicide. These feelings have reportedly not exceeded eleven days in duration. Object seemed to react to the presence of 242-0056 by turning light violet for no more than 2:09, as documented on 12 March 1993. Effects of this reaction remain unknown.

Additional Notes: Origins of 093 remain unknown and documents of recovery of 093 have since been destroyed in a fire in Research Facility █████, 09 December 1989. Reports on the feelings of researchers who handled 093 have remained inconsequential since 19 April 1995.

SCP-093-T1: CONTAINMENT TEST

Testing of SCP-093 against conditions set forth for existing containment procedures to assess viability of continuing such containment. Beginning with changing the type of mirror used as a position of rest:

Mirrored surface, brass frame, retail-grade mirror: SCP-093 rests without activity when placed on the mirror. This test alone removes the need for costly silver or wooden containment systems.

Standard-grade table: SCP-093 turns upright and begins to roll across the table surface in one direction, making a U-turn and rolling to the other, completing an oval shape and repeating this action until a mirror is brought into vicinity of it, at which time SCP-093 rolls toward the mirror and lays flatways against it, sliding toward the center. It is noted that despite the grainy feel of SCP-093, it does not mark the mirror in any fashion while moving across it.

Two mirrors at either end of a standard-grade table: SCP-093 gravitates toward the closer mirror regardless

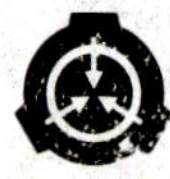

of orientation and makes no distinction between different types of mirrors, favoring a factor of distance above all else in choosing the mirror to move to.

A mirror held by a person and moved around: SCP-093 follows the mirror as it moves, gaining speed until a maximum velocity of ██████ is reached. At any velocity, the impact of SCP-093 against a mirrored surface results in no damage to either object.

A person holding SCP-093 placing it on a mirror: This test was accidental, the result of one of the staff tripping another after some debate about who would be covering the lunch tab. As a result of the behavior of the researchers, it was discovered that a person holding SCP-093 and placing it against a mirror will in fact move into the mirror.

Addendum: Containment testing discontinued after establishing that SCP-093 requires only a mirror to rest inert. Testing on human interaction with mirrors while holding SCP-093 authorized by Dr. █████.

SCP-093-T2 : MIRROR TEST

Testing Protocols: Subjects testing SCP-093 must wear a Class 3 buckle harness strapped to the chest and attached to a tension pulley system allowing for 300 m (~1000 ft) of movement. Additional spools may be added to extend movement if necessary. The clasps connecting these spools must be high grade and capable of withstanding applied force of 0.2 tons.

A field kit containing the following should be standard issue for testing of SCP-093:

- One (1) wrist mounted light source with three (3) hours lifespan and additional power sources providing up to six (6) additional hours.
- Four (4) 0.5 L water bottles with water.
- Four (4) MREs of any type, plus two (2) plain granola bars (chocolate chips allowed).
- One (1) standard-issue Beretta 9mm firearm with twenty-four (24) rounds of ammunition, loaded. This is not to be issued until subject has passed into a mirror using SCP-093 and should be given under armed supervision ensuring that the subject passes through entirely. This item is to be requisitioned first upon subject's return and subject to be made aware of this before leaving line of sight within SCP-093's mirror.
- One (1) standard-issue field knife. The subject is not to be made aware of this item and must find it on his own within the kit.

The subject must also be attached to a video system, with a camera mounted on the subject's head or shoulders. The video device should be cable based and allow for the same length of travel as the return system. Wireless cameras have shown mixed results and should only be used in testing conditions where SCP-093 is a currently known color. New colors must be tested using wired feed.

During testing, the color of SCP-093 must be recorded, as well as history of the subject in terms of their incarceration to identify how SCP-093 determines the color to assume. A link appears to be connected to guilt or a lack thereof in the subject's psyche. The attached test results should be read in order.

SCP-093 'BLUE' TEST

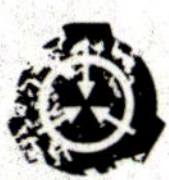

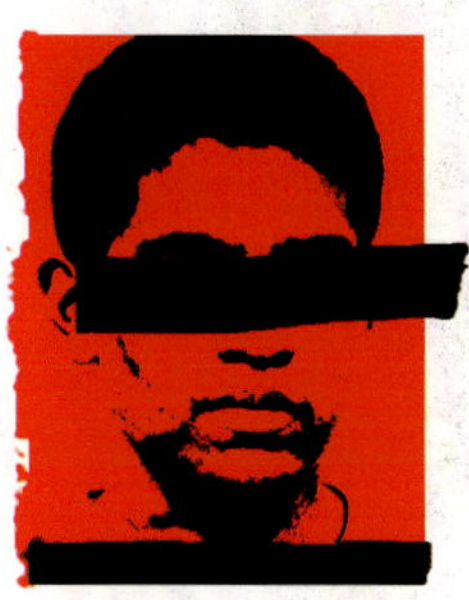

Subject is D-20384, male, 34 years of age, strong physique. Subject's background shows instance of murder/attempted suicide. Subject is co-operative in all steps of testing. Subject entered the provided mirror while holding SCP-093, which emitted a blue color. Outside technicians observed that the mirror retained a true reflection until subject had completely passed into it, at which time the view changed to an outdoor landscape, heavily tinged in blue. Video feed follows in attached media:

VB-**233-04425 ▬ 933

Camera activates, flickers to view. Subject is looking out over the same field reported by technicians. Looks like typical lowland plains, everything has a heavy blue tinge overlapping the normal colors. No discernible landmarks visible as subject pans view left to right, only grass, weeds, and a breeze moving the taller grass. No trees. No living beings visible.

Subject moves forward as instructed, traveling for approximately 500 steps before something becomes visible, a patch of the land up ahead is barren and grass can be seen dying as subject approaches it. Approximately 300 steps forward subject is standing before a hole in the ground. The hole has been dug using unknown tools of primitive origin.

Pulley system engaged and the camera suffers a light shudder. Subject is instructed to enter the hole, and after mild protesting agrees to do so. There is no apparent method of descent such as ladder or rope, subject relies entirely on his own hands and the pulley system to slow the descent. Approximately 100 m of cable is used before a bottom is reached, light source provided in field kit activated 50 m down when outside sources become unreliable. Sweeping gestures of the light reveal nothing more than dirt even at the bottom of the hole.

Subject moves forward with assistance of light source. Asked about the blue tinge subject expresses confusion and says there is no such tinge from his perspective, and never was. Light is visible down the passage and 150 m of cable has been used. Out of the camera's eye sound is recorded of the firearm being prepared. When questioned about these actions subject states justified precaution and moves forward.

The tunnel turns from bare dirt to a concrete enclosure, subject complains of a stench. The light source is revealed to be ceiling light fixtures, a series of which with less than a quarter broken while the others function. A series of six doors, three to a side, span before the camera view with a seventh door visible at the end of the corridor that has been blocked by what looks like generic metal shelving debris. Debris shows signs of rusting and is typical of retail store units suggesting other human presences.

Subject requested to try doors, in whatever order he chooses. Subject tries first door on right, door is locked, does not open. Second door tries to open but does not budge, unlocked but blocked. Closing second door, third door is tried, same results as first. Going up the other side the third door does open fully and light is bright in the room. Portable light switched off at this time as subject pans camera to inspect room.

Room is bare, no contents, but walls are filthy. Subject states material on walls isn't dirt, but he can't identify it, seems to resemble melted plastic but is brown in color rather than black. Door is closed. Second door on left side has no handle, does not move when pushed. The hole where the handle was is plugged by unknown material. All doors are shaped in such a way that nothing can visibly escape from the sides and space for movement is too thin to look through even at ground level. First door on left hand is locked, but part of key is present in lock from stem to the ridges, the back has been broken off.

With effort subject manipulates key to open door and immediately begins coughing, complaining of a stench. Walls of room are clean as is floor, ceiling is coated in the same strange brown material as the third room.

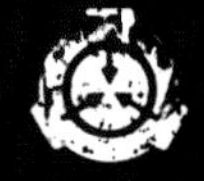

In this room there is a makeshift cot made from aged blankets with a pillow, a wooden crate containing open boxes of what appears to have been food stuffs, language appears on video as squiggles however subject states they simply read 'Cereal'. A second crate in the room contains what appear to be empty water bottles that have dried out. A book lays next to the cot, closed, no title or identifying marks.

On the wall is what appears to be clipped articles but language cannot be read, subject asked to remove clippings for retrieval. All articles but one crumble at the touch due to age. The intact article is put in a field sample container and seems the most recent compared to the others. Asked to investigate the book, subject begins to move toward it.

Audio on the tape goes strange and a high pitched screeching noise like grinding metal dominates all communication for 3.5 seconds. Subject has not touched the book still, and when the noise stops, subject asks control to repeat request. Control made no requests during that time as headsets were removed. Subject advised to leave room and notes that the door has begun closing slowly on its own and if left alone, will close. Subject advised to leave door alone and to investigate door on right.

Careful review of the following ten seconds of tape shows that as the camera pans, a figure is visible at the end of the tunnel where the seventh door is. The door is open only enough for a face to be seen through a crack just before the door silently closes. No details can be seen.

Subject investigates the second door on the right with no mention of anything seen out of the ordinary. This door when pushed against moves, and after repeated bashings, moves enough to view inside at an angle. A cork board is visible with more articles attached to it, the top of a box of 'cereal' can be seen on the floor, and what appears to be a hand laying palm up. Subject closes door and pans camera past door seven which remains closed. Seeing nowhere else to explore, subject requested to return. Subject poses no protest and complains of ever increasing stench.

As subject returns back down tunnel his camera feed does not change or show anomaly but control reports a sudden surge in cable movement pulling an additional 100 m of cable through before going slack again and then tightening. Video feed shows subject ascending tunnel slowly while control attempts to verify integrity of the pulley system. Subject requested to stop ascent but states he is not climbing, the rope is pulling him up. Panic sets in on both sides and subject informed to ready firearm.

Upon reaching top of hole, nothing is visible on camera and subject reports nothing has changed in landscape, then begins a return trip following the path of the cable. Traveling for approximately 900 steps subject asks how much cable he has used. Control admits they are unsure due to complications but subject traveled in a straight line to reach the hole so it should be a straight line back. Subject becomes concerned when he states that more cable is visible now, moving in a 90 degree angle away from a point in the ground.

Subject pans camera around full circle slowly. On film, behind subject, a crowd of 37 countable figures stand silently, features are unidentifiable and they are lacking the blue tinge that dominates the landscape. Panic breaks in control again but subject notes only oddity as being the cable having an angled path. Subject tugs his end of the cable, it is taut and does not move. Control begins to reel in the pulley system and slack rapidly winds. Watching the angled cable movement can be seen as grass is disturbed further down the angled portion from the reeling in then the line vibrates as it meets resistance and emits a 'twang' from the recoil. Subject's camera pans back along length of cable which now appears to slowly be allowing more slack before suddenly all slack is returned and pulley system begins again.

Control requests subject return following cable path and screams are caught on the audio with panic from subject. Five shots fired as subject aims pistol at something not visible on camera. Control reports being able to see subject returning toward point of origin while camera shows wire disappearing into a point floating in the air. As subject passes this point all cable is now in the pulley system and camera films only the floor. Control reports that the mirror took approximately five seconds to return to a reflection and SCP-093 remained blue in color until one hour after being recovered from subject.

A vile smelling fluid was present on subject's clothes around his hands when firearm was recovered. This fluid dried quickly and was deemed insignificant of study due to lack of quality sample. Control personnel monitoring the mirror state having seen a massive human being, crawling on the ground, easily fifty times the size of a normal person with no facial features and a very short arm reach, pulling itself toward the mirror before it returned to a reflection. Due to proximity fine details could not be made out but at least one observer noted the being appeared to have been shot from the marks in the otherwise smooth featureless face.

Field Test Kit recovered from subject containing a news paper article that reads: [DATA EXPUNGED] and was filed as item [DATA EXPUNGED].

BLUE TEST RECOVERED MATERIALS

Only one item could be recovered during our initial test and that was a newspaper clipping found attached to a cork board in an abandoned bunker. Most of the articles were in a state of decay but one was firm enough for recovery.

> **Most Holy Father Announces Progress, Unclean Being Cleansed!**
>
> A rare public address directly from the Most Holy Father of The United Lands of the Son has declared that the Blessed Militia has driven back many of the Unclean who are skulking our lands now. New Rome, our capital, has been purged of the Unclean and citizens are encouraged to come back to their homes. Citizens who live in the surrounding countryside should not return to their farms, as the Unclean still roam the fields and plains around our glorious city and continue to grow in size.
>
> The Blessed Militia has developed new weapons which have proven capable of punishing the Unclean and driving them back into the Unfertile Lands. Construction has begun of a system to permanently close the Unfertile Lands off from our Blessed Lands in each affected area once all the Unclean have been driven away. The Most Holy requests that all citizens of our United Lands bow in prayer and offer tithe to recognize the sacrifices of our Blessed Militia in these troubled times.
>
> Reports have been coming in that falsely accuse the Blessed Militia of having committed sin against the citizens whose homes they are inhabiting as they travel bravely through Contaminated lands. The Most Holy would like to remind the people that blasphemy against any who wear His mark is the most grave of sin and unfounded accusations will be punished accordingly. We should work to support He and His Men however possible just as they lay down their lives for us.
>
> The Sinful Rebels who --

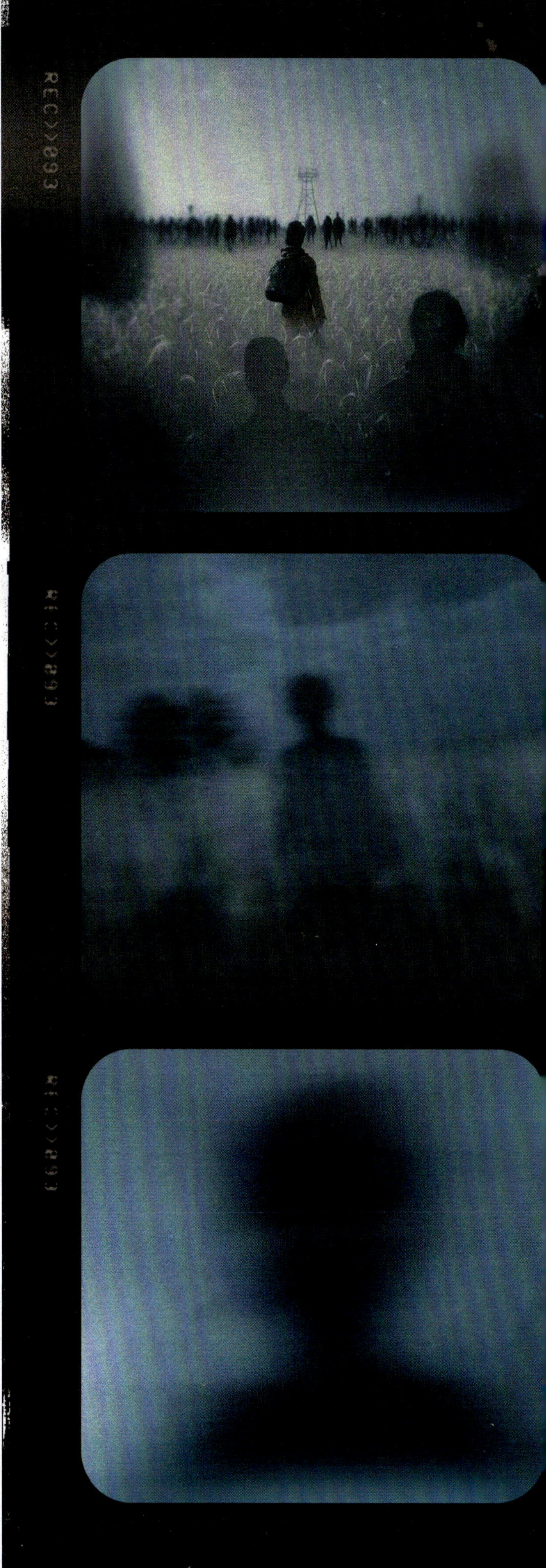

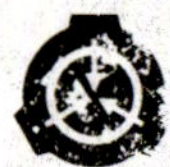

SCP-093 'GREEN' TEST

Research Library File ▸ 093

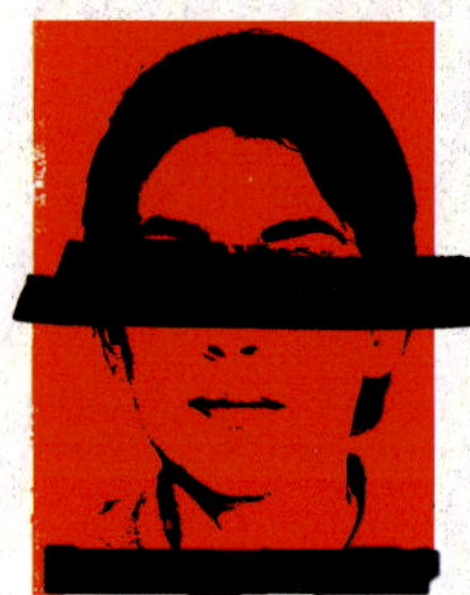

Subject is D-54493, female, 23 years of age, average physique. Subject's background shows instance of grand theft auto and second degree murder of two children during escape with vehicle. Subject is co-operative in all steps of testing. Subject entered the provided mirror while holding SCP-093 which emitted a green color. Outside technicians observed that the mirror retained a true reflection until subject had completely passed into it, at which time the view changed to a farming landscape, heavily tinged in green, similar to the first test. Video feed follows in attached media:

VB-*200-321 ▬ 913

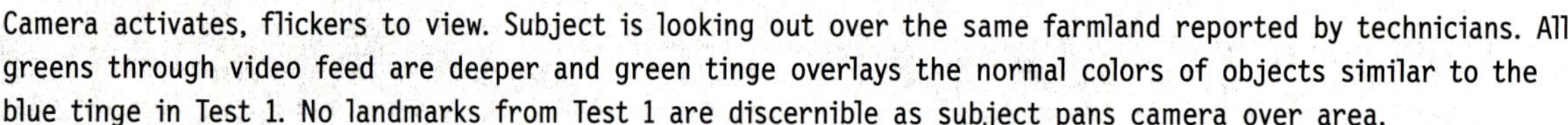

Camera activates, flickers to view. Subject is looking out over the same farmland reported by technicians. All greens through video feed are deeper and green tinge overlays the normal colors of objects similar to the blue tinge in Test 1. No landmarks from Test 1 are discernible as subject pans camera over area.

Present is a field, long abandoned, in the middle of which stands the remains of a scarecrow of unknown design, fragments left are rotted and torn. Nothing grows in the tilled land. A farm house is visible to the right of the field, large, two stories, a basement shelter entrance is visible at one end. Subject prepares her sidearm immediately and is asked by control to relax before proceeding, her heavy breathing dominating the audio feed.

Subject takes a few minutes and announces that she's fine, then proceeds as directed to walk the perimeter of the farmhouse. Children's bicycles, two, a boy's and girl's, lay against the house near the shelter doors. One of the doors to the shelter lay in the grass, torn from the entrance as evidenced by splintering wood. On the stairs lay clothes arranged in a descending order, shoes to shirt going down them, belonging to a boy. Subject begins screaming at control asking if this is some sort of sick joke. Control assures her they have never seen this environment either and to please calm down. Subject takes several minutes to regain herself before continuing. It is unknown if SCP-093 is linking the subject's past with her landscape.

After several minutes subject agrees to continue. Communication to subject is muted and conversation of control making commentary about subject's jittery attitude make up audio for one and a half minutes. Communication restored as subject reaches bottom of stairs. The cellar of the farmhouse is unremarkable and typical. Several wooden shelves line the far wall containing unidentified canned substances. Broken light fixtures sway gently from support beams. Camera is panned across the basement slowly, no evidence of footprints are visible and the basement can be assumed to have been abandoned for some time. Subject begins to comment about a stench.

As subject pans the area a metal hatch is visible in the ground, similar to a bulkhead on a submarine with a turn handle. Subject remarks that the smell is at its worst around the hatch and the dirt around the hatch is noted as being clumped and claylike. The handle of the hatch is old and the paint chipped. Subject coerced into turning the handle which, when fully turned, opens the hatch. Subject begins coughing at the release of assumed old, stale air. When camera is tilted to view down the hatch, it is a white concrete tunnel similar to the one found in the blue experiment but in much better condition. Subject asked to descend ladder and close hatch behind her.

After some convincing subject agrees to descend but does not close the hatch, overlooked concerns about severing the pulley return system in doing so are acknowledged. Descent down the ladder and trip to the farmhouse has consumed approximately 53 m of cable when bottom is reached. The inside of the hatch appears to be a bunker ill-suited to long term usage. It is spacious, about half the size of the actual cellar itself, containing three bunks, one for a couple and two for single use.

Several boxes of food similar to those found during Blue marked as 'Cereal' fill a waste container near the

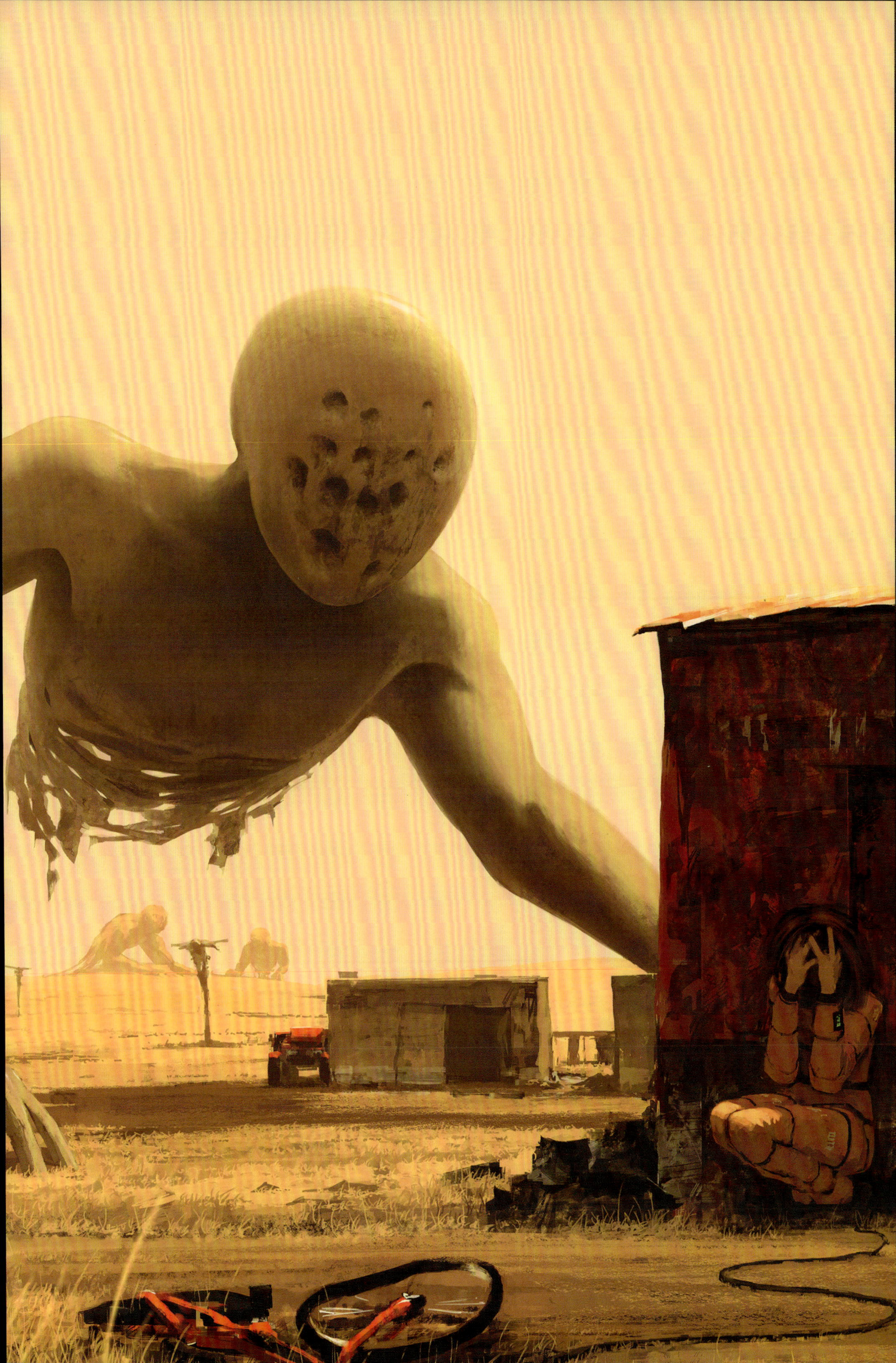

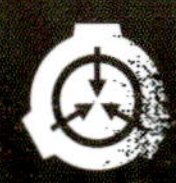

The massive featureless humanoid beings observed during the Green Test.

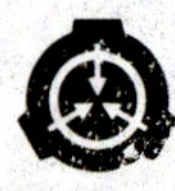

hatch bottom. On the beds are two skeletons and on the floor is a third, lying next to which is a simple six shooter revolver containing no ammunition. Three spent casings are across the floor near the gun. On the other side of this skeleton is a bound book in good condition, this is retrieved and placed into a Field Kit container upon request. The gun is left alone per request from control.

Subject examines more of the bunker, focusing on a desk where a newspaper has been cut and is in good condition. The clipped articles are recovered using a Field Kit container. Little else of interest to be brought back is in the bunker as the camera is panned around. Trash bags containing clothing, a few children's toys resembling popular 1950s era products are lined against the wall.

Subject is requested to leave the bunker and then sharply asked to wait by a control technician who directs the camera view to an area near the exiting doorway to the hatch. Closer inspection as subject moves in finds that a small area has been fitted with what appears to be an Ethernet jack, the cover of which has been forced slightly away from the wall by a strange amber-like substance. Subject refuses to touch or collect a sample commenting that it stinks so bad that if they want it they can come get it themselves. Control declines and subject leaves bunker.

As subject grips ladder to leave the camera pans up for a moment and at the top of the tunnel a humanoid figure is seen peering down. Control asks subject to confirm figure, subject states nothing is up there and begins to climb. Figure draws out of camera view after first rung is touched by subject who ascends without incident. At the top of the tunnel, no other life is seen, nothing has been disturbed. Subject insists nothing was there and closes the hatch, then immediately vomits.

Subject coughs and uses a supplied water bottle to gargle then freezes and asks if control is hearing 'that'. Control reports no audio. Subject approaches cellar hatch cautiously with firearm drawn and lifts her head just enough so camera can view outside area. In the distance, approximately 700 m from the farm, two massive, humanoid beings are crawling across the landscape. The entities do not notice the subject who remains quiet but whose drawn sidearm is visibly trembling.

Subject requested to remain still and silent as beings move. They are featureless, facing at an angle moving across the field of vision so the faces are only visible for a few moments. During this time it is clear they have no facial features. The arms they use to drag themselves are short at times and long at others, stretching out to varying lengths each time they move. There is no rear area to the beings, all bodily design appears to end at the torso. The two creatures take approximately ten minutes to disappear into the distance before the subject begins to panic and begs to return. Request declined. Subject instructed to enter the home from the cellar, and not to leave the home under any circumstances.

The first floor is entered through a hatch in the ceiling/floor that opens with rusty creaks that cause subject to pause for 37 seconds before continuing upward and entering a kitchen. A heavy layer of dust coats all items in the kitchen. The refrigerator is left open, all food is spoiled. Adjacent the kitchen is a living area that subject enters slowly. There is a recliner, a couch, and a television all of 1950s style design. In the recliner is a laptop whose case also resembles 1950s decor and is coated in heavy dust. Opening the laptop reveals the last moments of its operating system, "Faithful OS" leaving a standby mode and immediately shutting off. Laptop has no external power source and will not power back on. When asked to recover laptop, it brings the cushion of the recliner with it, the two stuck together. Subject advised to leave laptop where it is.

The inside door leaving the home is nailed shut with thick wood planks, no attempt made to interact with these. Camera view pans to a staircase leading upstairs. Subject ascends the stairs without being asked and the stairs remain silent to control's surprise. When subject reaches top of stairs a hallway with two doors is viewed, one on each side, and at the end of the hall a dumbwaiter is inlaid into the wall.

Subject opens door on left on her own, which opens to a master bedroom. The bed is neatly made but the wardrobe next to it is thrown open and clothes are everywhere on the floor. Subject finds laid out on the bed several pieces of jewelry and is informed to leave them. Subject begins to protest, then comments they stink and leaves them alone, promptly leaving room. Subject asked to open second door.

The second door opens and gives a view of a shared children's bedroom, obviously boy and girl given the types of toys and clothes scattered on the floor. There is also a window which subject approaches and wipes with a curtain to clear dust. Subject requested to move camera to window and does so. The farmland is visible, and approximately 40 km from it at best guess, a city. As the camera starts to draw back it pans down and films the area around the house. Approximately 300 figures similar to those from the footage captured during Blue test are visible around the home, all staring up. Subject asked to confirm figures but states nothing is there. Subject requested to return and quickly agrees.

Egress from the house is uneventful, pulley system shows no erratic behavior. As subject returns to point of pulley wire's origin a loud groaning noise causes the picture to reverberate. Technicians at control report they were also able to hear the noise and experienced the vibration. Subject returns through point of origin without investigation and mirror returns to reflective surface. SCP-093 relinquished. Video ends.

Returned newspaper fragments filed as █████.

GREEN TEST RECOVERED MATERIALS

Our second test recovered many materials that helped to establish a sequence of events for this alternate world. The diary recovered provided a glimpse into the last days of the owners of the home from which it was recovered and may represent activity in other areas of the world as well.

Newspaper Article 2

Farms surrounding the city of Silver Feathers have reported being unable to contact neighbors across voice or video feeds in the last week. Until an approval is granted by the Regional High Father, an investigation cannot commence but he assures the people that these events have not escaped his attention.

Residents are advised to notify their local Blessed Voice daily so any further disappearances can be addressed immediately. Residents are also advised to begin stocking their shelters to be ready for any situation.

Newspaper Article 3

Following the disappearance of the Blessed Voices from several outlying regions around the city of Silver Feathers, the Regional High Father has declared a Concern for Safety and Livelihood. Under this declaration, all farmland residents must evacuate immediately to their shelters. Scattered reports of an Unclean have come in but have yet to be verified.

Newspaper Article 4

– the city of Glorious Song has stopped responding to any and all communications, the worst can only be assumed and our hearts go out to any who are in the region who are unable to hear our words. The city of Silver Feathers Blessed Militia has reported several incursions by the Unclean into the city and have exterminated four of the abominations before they could become a danger to any residents. The Regional High Father reminds the citizens to avoid direct confrontation with the Unclean, conventional arms do nothing to the Unclean, only the most holy of implements will penetrate their sin, so do not put yourself in danger.

Any citizens who suspect their neighbors indulging in heavy sin should immediately contact the Blessed Militia through designated check points –

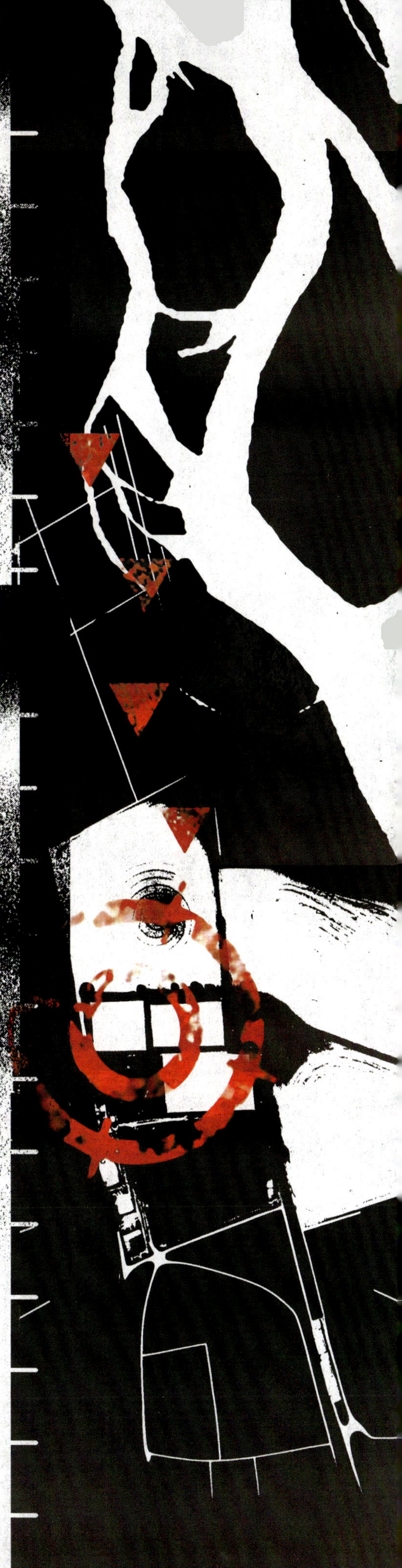

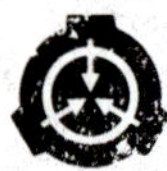

Research Library File ▸ 093

Diary

█-█-█ I have the distinct feelin we're gonna die so I'm gonna write this all down now fer whoever comes along an finds our bones. My name is Herverf Jakulsiv and Im a farmer, I grows the rabsticks and the huskears. We raise the inks and the ooms. It's me, my wife, Opheri, and our two lil uns Treven and Lisstieria. I got this book en trade from the Blessed man who came by fer food and shelter, he told us to start gettin our shelter ready and not to let no other Blessed who comin by even know we're here, says the whole thing break down, nothing right no more. So I does as he said, got it all ready, we goin down there in the next day or so. In the morn, he was gone, which made the wife sad as he was polite to us unlike most of the others. Figure he didn wanna be no burder. Liss went out lookin fer him to be sure he weren't just round the house.

█-█-█ He didn't turn up nowheres so we guess he left. Strange nuff Liss found is clothes round a mile er so away, an all his gear, but no him. She lef it all there and tha's fer the best if what happen that I think. I'm clearly no educated man, don't claim to be, but I can put two and two together and tell you that things are bad out there. For everyone and especially for us cause it's comin way too close. Sometimes, you can smell it, that's when we hide. Smells like a leg of meat that's been rotten for way too long and just won't go back into the dirt. Even the soil is rejectin em I guess, refusin to let them be buried to die

█-█-█ It came. Too fast, we weren't ready. The smell came in the night, maybe we woulda been fine but the lil uns were afraid so we went to the shelter. Trev was slow, he saw it, kept starin at it as it shambled by. It ignored us until he screamed when I was gettin Liss and the miss down in the shelter. I went to get him but... it was too fast. I saw him standin up there, screamin, and then its head came down on him, pressed over him. He tried to run for the stairs, tried to get to us, but then in a blink, he was gone and it pulled away. His clothes fell into the cellar like he vanished out of em. I got into the shelter, slammed the hatch and locked it. I think it knows we're here now, it'll try to get in, take us too.. no tellin how long we got, plenty of food tho..

I was wrong. The food was rotten, something got into it, or I just didn't notice. We're eatin what we can. There's food, but not enough, and that thing ain't leavin. It's tryin to find ways in, smelt the smell, comin from the lifeweb plug in the wall, something seeped through it and we kept away. It got all hard like a rock and don't smell no more. Maybe the power in the plug finally let it die.

I went up, to peek. Cellar is fine, Trev's clothes still on the stairs. Peeked outside. We're not gonna make it. There were ten..twenty..thirty.. couldn't count, so many, all goin in a circle around the house, lookin at it with those faceless faces, and the stink, oh the stink. Went back into the shelter and locked the door. I think, I don't want to see my family rot away. I think faster is better, the miss, she agrees, we won't tell Liss, she'll be first, then my wife, my love.. then me. I'm sorry, but I'm not sorry. I gave the best life to my family possible. It was them Holy ones what brought this.

I'm gonna pen this in memory to my great pap. He was old and knew stories older than himself. Says those Unclean they preach about, those Unfertile Zones they say stay out of. All cause of the Most Holy bringin the world together. Them things are the ultimate sin. Everything about us that was evil and impure, it's them. They don't know nothin but doin what they do, don't even know why they do it, they just do it, take us into them, then we're gone.

I asked pap what they were and he lit a stick, took a puff, an he said - Don't know. Nobody knows, nobody who'll admit it. But if you see this symbol, if you see it.. you run boy, you run fast, you run far, and you hide, and you never go back where you saw it. That's all I know. - I remember the symbol, was on the rock he kept on his neck under his shirt. Next day, pap was gone, nowhere to be found, dad weren't sad, said he knew it'd happen one day, pap went home. See you soon dad, pap..

[DATA EXPUNGED] Symbol matched symbol found on SCP-093's surface as one of the deeper engravings. Also matches symbols noticed on video feed of final test on SCP-093 duplicates.

SCP-093 'VIOLET' TEST

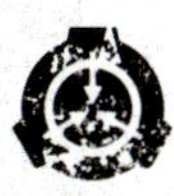

Research
Library
File ▸ 093

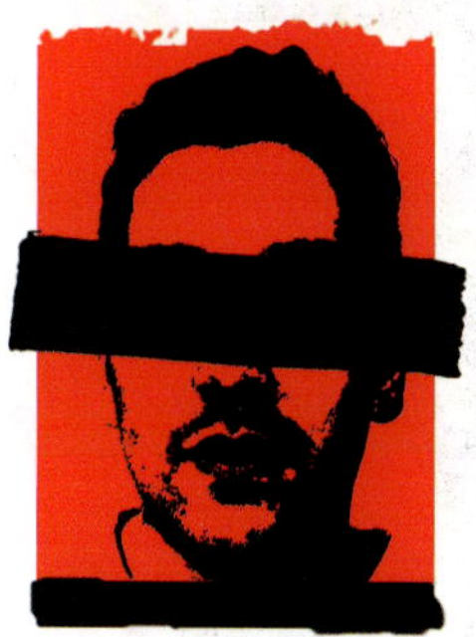

Subject is D-84930, male, 21 years of age, average physique. Subject's background shows instance of second degree murder of a police officer during a drug bust. Normally this crime, while severe, would not qualify a person for a sentence that would end up with us, but the murder of the officer was especially brutal and excessive violence was used. This subject was uncooperative and had to be reminded that his cooperation would only benefit him. Subject entered the provided mirror while holding SCP-093 which emitted a violet color. Outside technicians observed that the mirror retained a true reflection until subject had completely passed into it, at which time the view changed to a cityscape, urban, lightly tinged in purple, similar to the first test. Video feed follows in attached media:

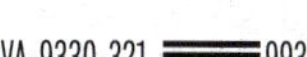

VA-9330-321 993

Camera flickers to life and pans around the area. Subject is in what appears to be a modern downtown district similar to a city like New York. The streets are mostly bare except for a few cars of unknown make or model. These cars look highly advanced and streamlined. Subject attempts to look into the car windows without being instructed to but backs away remarking there is a 'rank ass stank' coming from the areas around most of them.

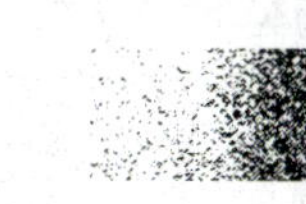

Subject is persuaded to move closer to one car and does so with coughing, wiping off a window which is covered in dirt. The inside of the car appears to be completely filled with a strange brown matter, there is nothing at all visible other than the brown matter. Two other cars produce the same results however a fourth vehicle seems more recent than the others and the insides are immaculate. The doors to this vehicle also are unlocked and subject quickly gets inside then shuts the doors. Subject is chastised for this behavior by control who reminds him his lifeline is nothing more than a cable, which is sturdy enough that closing the car door does not injure it, but they cannot recover a person in motion.

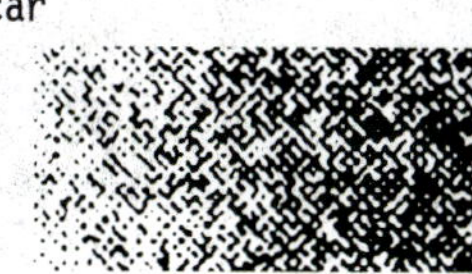

Subject argues with control over this issue and pans the camera across the dashboard, pointing out he couldn't drive away even if he tried. The dashboard is void of any recognizable controls, no ignition, no steering, it has several small blank screens that are theorized to be a GPS system. Subject remains in the car while control discusses how to proceed since the city landscape is far larger than the previous test destinations.

Control debates this issue while subject stares around the cityscape from the car. During one pan a face is clearly seen staring into the car, eyes watching the subject; however, this was not noticed until post-test footage review. Subject made no comment regarding this entity at any point. Control shortly after informs subject to remain where he is and an escort team is dispatched through the mirror to join him.

A team of four armed personnel is sent through the mirror and proceeds to subject's location. Subject is then instructed to remove his harness, which is recovered. This subject's video feed then ends and is replaced by a wireless unit used by the escort team. The video quality on this unit is subject to more interference but in order to mark the mirror exit a receiver system is placed through the mirror.

Subject leaves the car and now travels with the escort team. Given the myriad of possible options they are instructed to simply move to the closest building and attempt to enter it. This building has etched glass doors bearing the name 'X.E.A. Research Partners Inc.' and the doors are ajar; a magnetic lock system is present, but has lost power. Team enters the building and main lobby.

This area resembles a stereotypical corporate lobby. There is a C shaped receptionist desk with a chair pushed far from it as if it was left in a hurry. A PC terminal is at the desk as well. Team approaches the desk and the camera bearer is instructed to examine the PC. The unit does appear to have power and "Faithful OS" appears on the screen requesting a login and password. A keyboard is present but is remarkably slim with touch sensitive keys rather than press down keys. After one failed attempt the lock screen replies that

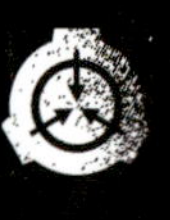

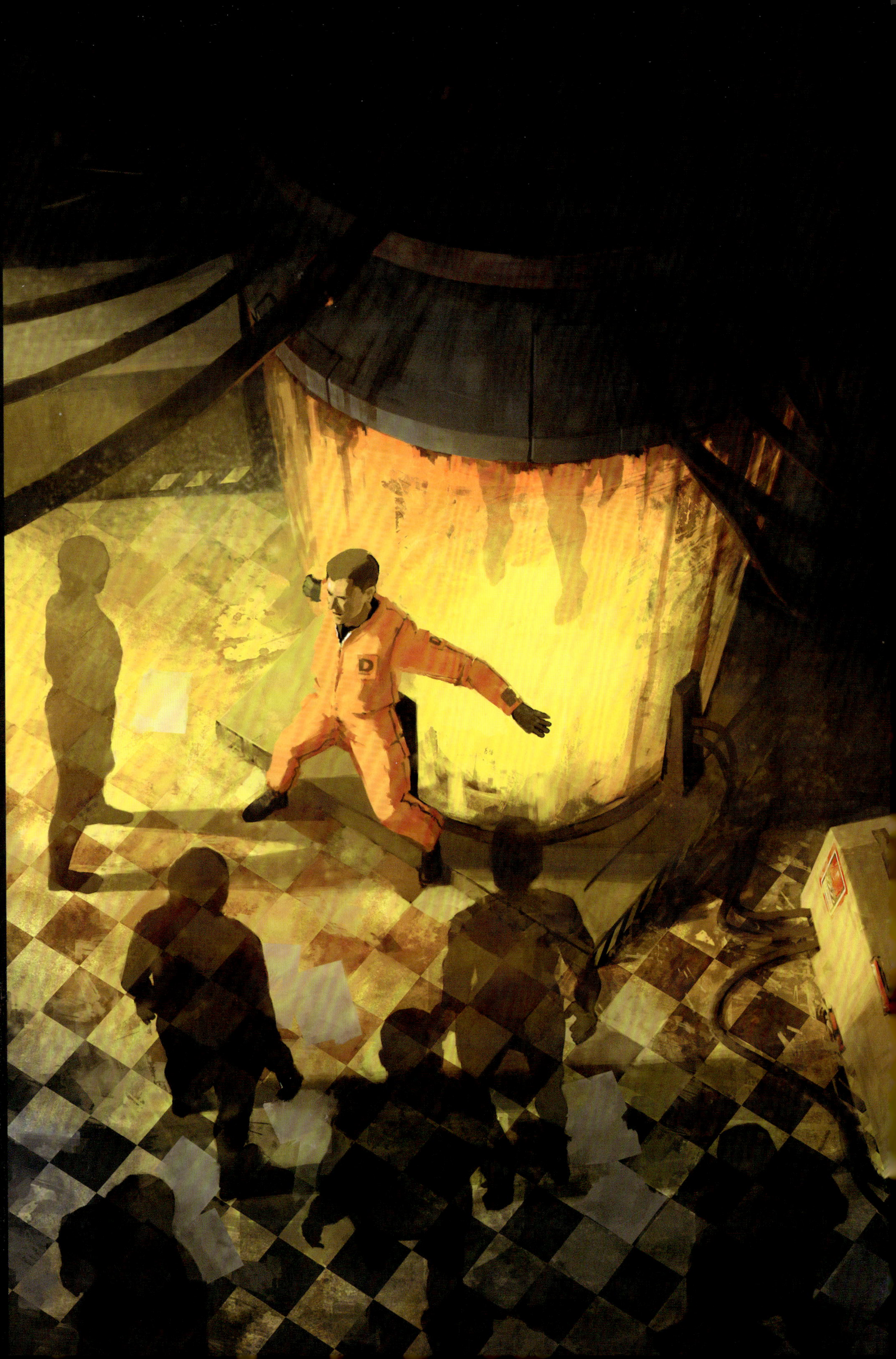

D-84930 surrounded by entities similar to those witnessed in the first two tests.

maximum attempts have been exceeded and the PC turns off. No actual tower or power button can be located so team moves forward.

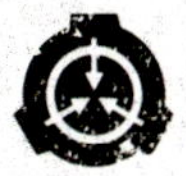

Research Library File ▸ 093

Behind the receptionist desk are two elevator doors, one to the left and one to the right, with similar touch-sense keys. The elevator on the left is broken, the door open and the shaft empty. The elevator on the right appears functional and has power. Without a clear destination the team is instructed to proceed to the highest floor to get a lay of the city. All floors appear to be accessible with the highest being 114, in reality 112 as 13 and 113 are missing from the keypad.

Journey up the elevator is uneventful during this time, the elevator does appear to take longer as it passes by 13 and then 113, suggesting that entire floor was built and nothing put on it. At 114 the doors open and team enters a large lounge type area. There are many couches with dust on them, a wide screen apparently LCD TV of approximately 60+ inches in size dominates the wall in front of them with no power. A series of windows are open, allowing in sunlight at the far end to which the team proceeds and angles the camera outside.

The view of the city is astonishing. This building is one of the tallest visible but certainly not alone in its stature. The city below is gray and silent, no evidence of life at this altitude. Some buildings in the city have a strange brown growth that appears to have been splashed against them as if a gelatinous mass was flung and then seeped down before hardening. Other buildings have floors where the glass has been shattered and the same brown substance is seeping out the edges. One member of the team calls the camera bearer to the windows on the other side.

From the other side of the building, the city edges can be seen. Attention is pointed toward an expressway that encircles the city upon which crawls another of the large half-body humanoids, dragging itself with its elastic arms as witnessed in previous tests. It travels the highway then moves out of sight. The team returns to the elevator and notes that a button has already been activated for floor 74. No one has approached the elevator so the team agrees to travel to this floor.

On the 74th floor the doors open and reveal a waiting area to what appears to be a doctor's office. At the reception desk there is a sign in sheet with a series of names and dates. The dates on the sign in sheet all carry the year 1953. A PC at the receptionist area is on and functioning at a user desktop. The background for the PC is a large set of praying hands with the word "Faithful OS" under them. On the desktop are a series of folders with years on them containing files that, when clicked using the center button of the mouse, open to a word viewer. All files appear to be appointment information.

On the desk is a notepad titled 'From the desk of Dr. Borisizki, Blessed Purificationist'. The door to the doctor's area is sketched with the same name and title as well as a crucifix. Opening this door leads to a white dust-free hallway that has two examination rooms and a key coded door at the end. The examination rooms are unremarkable and typical of any doctor's office. All medicine cabinets are empty. A small amount of C4 is placed at the lock to the key coded door at the request of control and then blown, forcing the door open.

The area it opens into is much larger than the reception area itself and seems to contain a series of large containment capsules. There are a total of six of these capsules, two are broken and a brownish amber material coats the floor coming from them. One is empty, the last three have nude humans floating in them with breathing masks. Attached to the front of these tubes are medical charts showing vital signs and conditions. For symptoms, the charts explain in somewhat awkward English ailments that seem more like flaws of personality or character, or just incidents that have occurred with the patient.

Control asks for a zoom of one of the patient pages on the chart. After focusing, it reads 'Citizen Jennifer McZirka did suffer a lapse of the heart that did lead her to lay with her neighbor twice upon nights of her husband's departure from their home. Patient did submit herself into the Lord's and our hands for cleansing of mind and body. Prayer administered by High Father Uwalakin and patient submitted to a three day period in the Lord's tears to cleanse her system then released in good spirits.'

The topmost page reads 'Citizen Alberious Farafan struck out at a High Father during a sermon, blaspheming that the Lord's tears did turn his daughter to be unright in mind and heart thusly laying blame for her whoreish activities at the feet of the High Father and his blessing. With no proof of these blasphemes the Forgiving Judge and the Punishing Judge did agree that Alberious Farafan should bathe in the Lord's tears himself for a week to be cleansed of mind and soul thus to prove his daughter's ways are fault of not The Fathers Hands and to give him peace of self.'

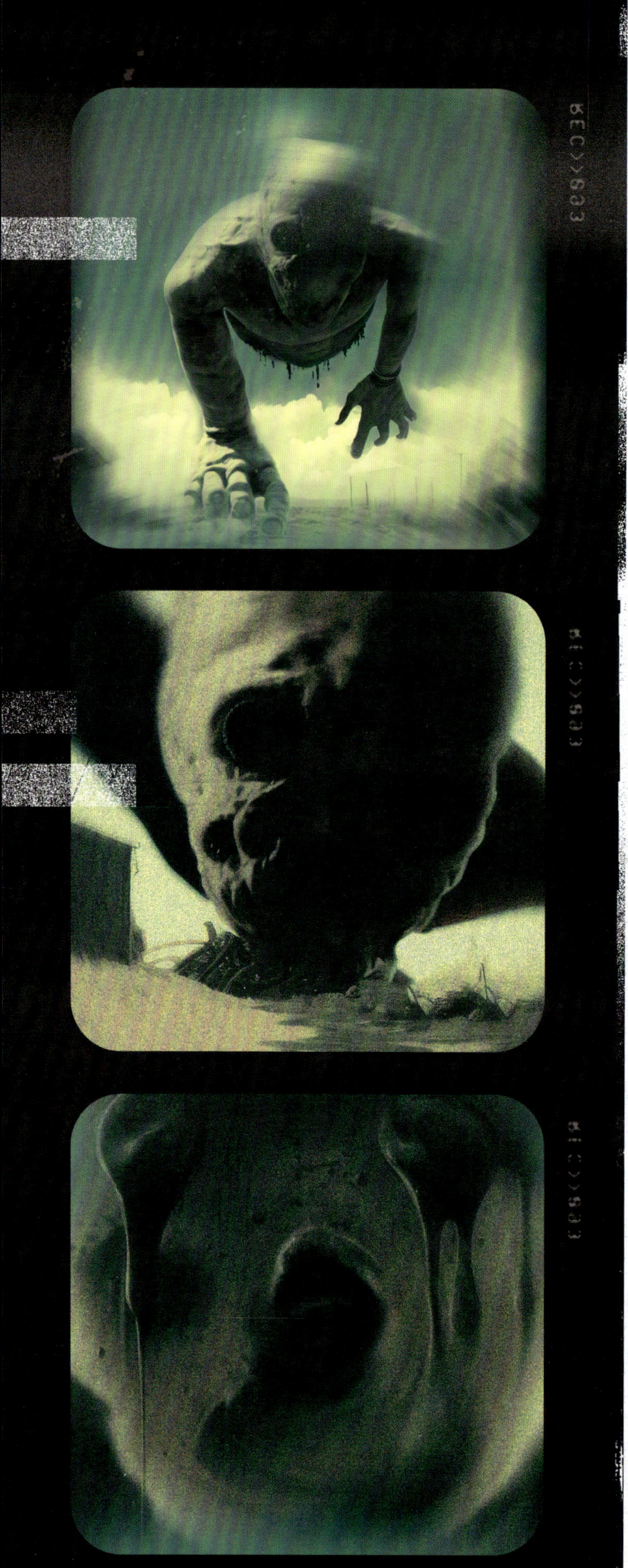

Subject who has been traveling quietly with the escort team now begins to panic. The camera pans to focus on him and he is surrounded by entities similar to those witnessed in the first two tests. Escort team reports in that subject is having a panic attack but control requests them to stand still and wait. Subject screams at the entities, which are denied to exist by team commander, stating Subject is alone in the corner. Control requests that one team member be dispatched to approach and recover the subject. The escort team member approaches the subject as ordered. On the video the figures part to make a pathway for the approaching member who lifts Subject to his feet and brings him out of the corner. Figures on video are then seen closing ranks to close the path. Subject is lifted to his feet by an arm and escorted through the figures that close their ranks when the subject is moved. They remain steadfastly staring at the subject no matter where he moves to. Control requests the team to return now. Team turns to leave. Before leaving a team member mentions something noticed at the reception desk, a binder labeled 'The Lord's Tears'. Control requests binder be returned as well, and it is stowed into Subject's field kit.

The team returns to the elevator and returns to the ground floor. Upon leaving the building, subject points down the street toward direction of entry point. The camera pans to a section of raised expressway across which one of the large torsos is crawling slowly. The entity turns its featureless head to look at the escort team, raises its head to the sky, and emits a bellowing sound. Team leader issues the order to move, heading for the spot marked by the wireless video receiver. The creature on the expressway extends an arm down that stretches to touch the ground, before the camera moves to the port. All team members save one move through entry point. Subject moves through entry point and mirror returns to reflective surface.

SCP-093 is dropped by subject who panics and tries to fight his way out of the room. Subject is terminated by team leader after he draws the field kit pistol. Team leader requests portal be reopened but it takes several minutes to find someone who can hold SCP-093 and generate a similar color. When a matching color is displayed and applied to the mirror the video receiver is visible and all individuals report a horrific smell. Team Leader moves through the entryway with control person █████. The uniform and possessions of the escort team member who was left behind are present and recovered, but the member himself is nowhere to be seen and does not respond to shouts. Member assumed K.I.A. and wireless receiver recovered, control and escort return through entry point and mirror returns to reflective surface.

Later review of the recovered camera shows escort

member ███ grasping at the air where entry point should be and then turning to look up at the oversized torso. A brown gel seems to drip off the creature as it moves that disappears shortly after being dislodged as if evaporating. Several shots are fired at the creature's face with the automatic weapon carried by ███ that land in the 'face' of the creature, causing a spray of less viscous brown liquid to pour forth from the 'wounds'. ███ screams obscenities as the face of the creature descends upon him and the camera is pushed to the ground. Camera feed remains dark for approximately 65 seconds before light comes back and the camera films the creature crawling back to the expressway and pulling itself onto it, then crawling in the direction it was originally headed.

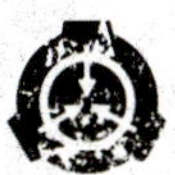

███ believed to have been 'absorbed' by the creature and perhaps digested. This may have been an example of how these unknown entities feed by direct contact with living material. Further study is recommended to be avoided on this issue. Returned ledger filed as ███.

VIOLET TEST RECOVERED MATERIALS

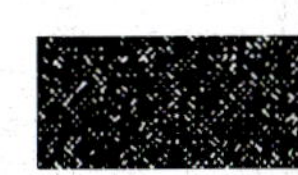

The third test with SCP-093 resulted in the unfortunate loss of a security member but also allowed us to recover a ledger with insight into the medical procedures carried out on the alternate Earth now termed E-093.

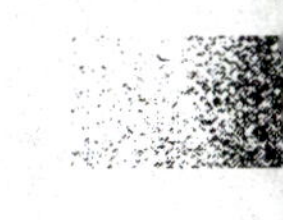

Patient: Jennifer McZirka
Recovery Tube: 001-1
Mixture: 35% Tears, 30% Nutrient, 10% H.F.T., 25% Blessing
Summary: Jennifer McZirka is 20 cycles of age and during her 18th cycle was the victim of a hov-ride accident that resulted in brain damage and misalignment of her moral processes. She is prone to violent outbursts and can only be calmed down by impure stimulation. Because of this she actively seeks out strangers to mingle with and her parents have requested of the High Father that she be set to the Tears to mend her mind and body. Patient accepted.

During preparation for the Tears subject went into a rage and the attending Hand went to recover a sedative. Jennifer tore her clothes off and screamed impure words at me so I locked the door and instructed the Hand to wait outside. I am half shameful to admit I laid with Jennifer a total of seven times before putting her to the Tears. It has been very long for me and her parents have abandoned her to our care, so care for her I will. Before setting her to the Tears I authorized a Blessed Probe of her body functions and found she is settled now with young and tests confirm it shall be mine. I have mixed her bath to accommodate this and she will soak in the Tears until her body is ready to give life.

Patient: None
Recovery Tube: 001-2
Mixture: None
Summary: None

Patient: Alberious Farafan
Recovery Tube: 001-3
Mixture: 80% Tears, 20% Nutrient
Summary: Alberious Farafan is a farmer from outside the city of Silver Feathers who claims to have lost family to the Unclean. He confronted the High Fathers of the city and demanded compensation and retribution for the loss. The High Fathers deny the existence of Unclean beyond the Unfertile Lands and refuse compensation or retribution. Alberious struck a High Father and was arrested and sentenced to a cleansing of the soul.

His mixture is primarily Tears to seep into the soul and cleanse his heart and ease his pain. The Lawkeepers state his family is indeed missing so his sentence beyond the Tears has been dropped in sympathy for their loss. I used the last of the H.F.T. on Jennifer or I would have used less Tears in this bath, 80% is higher than I am comfortable with but the H.F.T. is becoming hard to obtain. I may have to go through the Dark.

Patient: <====>
Recovery Tube: 002-1
Mixture: 75% Nutrient, 25% Blessing
Summary: A Member of the Blessed Militia who was wounded in combat. Request is from the High Father, details withheld.

Patient: <====>
Recovery Tube: 002-2
Mixture: 75% Nutrient, 25% Blessing
Summary: A Member of the Blessed Militia who was wounded in combat. Request is from the High Father, details withheld.

Patient: <====>
Recovery Tube: 002-3
Mixture: 75% Nutrient, 25% Blessing
Summary: A Member of the Blessed Militia who was wounded in combat. Request is from the High Father, details withheld.

SCP-093 'YELLOW' TEST

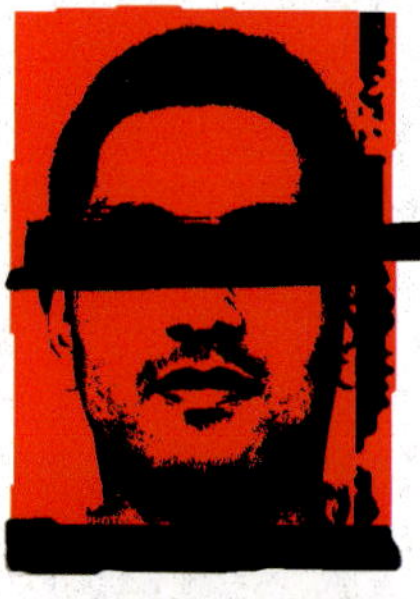

VA-904220-321 ████ 9213

D-class subjects no longer authorized for testing. Testing focus has been shifted to data collection after analyzing the articles brought back from the previous three tests to better understand the fate of the world accessed by SCP-093 and determine if safeguards or practices are required for our own world. Analysis of the brown fluid on the clothing of the lost escort team member █████ has been filed with other recovered articles.

Dr. █████ has volunteered for this test as out of the possible candidates, he was able to cause SCP-093 to undergo a new color change. There is no evidence in Dr. █████s background of any illegal or criminal behavior, nor of any psychological problems. When presented to the mirror, the view changed to that of a cubicle office environment.

For this test Dr. █████ opted to use the wireless video system and forgo the pulley return system, stating he was confident he would be safe as none of the torso-creatures have been witnessed within a building where the mirror's destination showed. Video feed commences after Dr. █████ has crossed the mirror. As with prior tests, SCP-093's current color, yellow, tinges all video material.

Camera flickers to life and pans across a series of plain white cubicle constructs. Approximately 30 are visible. At the far end from the point of entry is an office module built into the wall with frosted glass walls and a glass door. Dr.█████ approaches this door and investigates the etched writing on it: 'Senior Manager - Stanlee Milamitz'. The door is unlocked.

Dr.█████ enters the office and examines the desk. A coffee cup is on the desk, a dark brown stain covering half of the inside as the liquid evaporated. There is a donut on a plate which Dr.█████ picks up and lobs at a wall, on impact it thumps like a rock and falls. A file cabinet in the corner of the room draws Dr.█████s attention and he goes through each shelf one at a time, stopping in the second drawer and taking out a file, then going back to the first and taking out two others. Continuing to the third and fourth drawers he withdraws four additional files and spreads them all out on the desk. The files are blue filing folders and he points with his finger and camera at a symbol on each of praying hands, stating aloud for the camera that all other files are stored in yellow folders. The blue folders are placed in his field kit.

Camera attention is turned to the PC on the desk that is logged in and functional, Dr.█████ comments aloud wondering where these devices are getting their power from as he has noticed no power outlets. This PC's desktop contains the logo of 'Faithful OS' and even has sounds, clicks of the mouse followed by soft hymn-like hums and opening of icons followed by angelic bells. The PC fails to yield any useful information to Dr.█████ who abandons it and leaves the office.

Approaching the other end of the office floor Dr.█████ presses a button on the wall for the elevator and enters, finding he is on the 34th floor of a building having an unusual number scheme. The keypad layout goes from -115 to 115, and includes all floors. Before pressing a floor button Dr.█████ requests that the wireless video transponder be moved to the elevator, and replaced with a construction cone to mark the entry point. A second transponder unit is placed outside the elevator and Control is instructed to recover the second unit and seal the test chamber should something happen to him, then when all is arranged he presses the button for floor -115.

The descent down the elevator is long, consuming 15 minutes, during this time the camera experiences one malfunction where the image jerks and turns to snow, restoring to show 14 other figures in the elevator with Dr.█████ as video pans around, all of whom move as he moves to allow him space. They remain for 35 seconds then the camera flickers to snow and returns, Dr.█████ is now alone in the elevator dancing as is assumed by the ducks and sways of the video feed.

Dr.█████ pauses to comment on a rising stench coming from below. At this point the elevator has reached floor -108. Dr.█████ presses -110 to interrupt the descent down and exits when that floor is reached. The elevator doors open to an enclosed observation deck with several PCs and chairs. All PCs appear to have power. The ceiling to this deck is also glass and above it another deck is visible. Dr.█████ approaches the monitoring stations and checks one of the PC screens.

On the screen is the Faithful OS logo and a video feed toggling between four different views. The first view is a room of tubes similar to those found in test Violet which number in the thousands. The second view is a closer up view of these tubes as a camera glides in front of each to monitor the contents. All tubes the camera passes by are broken. The third view is facing the opposite direction as a camera glides vertically checking each observation station. A total of 10 can be counted and Dr.█████ is visible as the camera passes by his own station. Looking up, a hovering camera unit with no visible means of propulsion glides up past him. The fourth view shows the ground floor below the observation deck where a single astonishingly large torso being is crawling in circles, bumping into walls and changing directions. From the camera feed the creature's estimated size is six stories.

Returning attention to the contents of the PC Dr.█████ moves the video log aside to see a simple text editor that was hidden behind it. A printout of this text was recovered and filed in the Field Kit. The printout directed Dr.█████ to a safe on floor 54 and provided a combination. Dr.█████ leaves the observation deck and proceeds to 54 without event, arriving on a cubicled office floor. He proceeds to the desk mentioned in the document and finds a safe hidden beneath a desk undisturbed. The combination provided opens the safe and reveals a notebook, filed in the Field Kit, and a peculiar revolver that has been returned as ███-███, in addition to the 24 rounds of ammo found with it.

Dr.█████ proceeds back to the elevator without event and returns to 34. Given the sheer number of floors

available to explore and the vital information obtained from the observation deck, the test is considered over and equipment is retrieved. Before returning through the entry point, Dr. ████ investigates a terminal nearby that has power, and finds it shows the exact same screen the one on -110 shows. It is theorized that the author of the note installed a network virus to propagate it through the building so any PC on that network would be found and the information discovered.

Dr. ████ returns through the entry point and the mirror returns to a reflective surface. All materials filed with other SCP-093 recovered materials. Analysis of ██-██ and the ammunition for it postponed for reason that it would require deconstruction of one of the rounds and they may be beneficial until testing of SCP-093 is resolved. Video ends.

YELLOW TEST RECOVERED MATERIALS

The fourth test into E-093 provided us with documentation assumed to be written by a technician in either a medical or government facility. ██-██ found in the safe, is being considered for SCP classification primarily due to the composition of the ammunition found with it and the advanced firing mechanism attached to what should be a very base firearm.

PC Printout

I did not trust the Overwatchers, I felt something was wrong years ago. Under my desk on floor 54 is a safe with a weapon in it, it is one of those used by the Blessed Militia, my brother has sent it to me. He says they are also not what they claim, they have done things to our fellows even more vile than what the Unclean would do. He tells me to be ready to fight. I cannot, it is not me, I do not know violence, I am too frail. You, use it, save yourself.

Safe Diary

My name is Herval Toliwis, I am a hard systems watcher here. My job is to monitor the Sinful who bathe in the Lord's Tears and then make sure that they reach the prescribed dilution time. I have been doing this job for 23 years, and now things are falling apart. I can no longer abide by The Most Holy, I must speak the truth.

We are being told to evacuate. The containment tubes have been breached. An Unclean has appeared in the Place of Rest and we are unable to destroy it. The livemotion footage shows how it came to be and this is what has unsealed my heart and mind and tongue. I must speak. Should the Overwatchers see this I will be silenced so I must hide it, thankfully they are ignorant with the hardware so I can hide this easily.

The Overwatchers told us, we should leave last, to ensure the hardware contains the Unclean. What that means is we should distract it and die in case it breaches the watching decks. It has shattered nearly all the tubes and absorbed the people in them. I have dispatched the Eyes to the Unclean and they have touched it, bringing me back a sample of it. The Unclean are not sinners, they are not products of our disobedience. I suspect they are us. The Eyes have dated the sample, it is older than myself, older than my elders. It is over 200 cycles in ages. 200!

The sirens are still sounding, but no signal has come for us to leave. I do not think this Unclean is alone. I have seen how they can get into places, between places. Between places! Is that where they have been, all this time? Between places? The makeup of the Unclean is unstable, molecules detach and reattach almost before my eyes, as if to move the entire thing reforms itself in space and time. Why does it not come up here? Too much effort? Or does it not sense me? They have no eyes, no mouth, no face, they cannot speak, cannot see, but they must be able to sense us.

The smell, it is so strong, it comes from all directions. It is not a smell of the dead, it is a smell that comes from something that should be dead but does not know how to die. The War of The Holy Union, I think that was where it may have started. We are united under the Most Holy but what does he owe us? Nothing. We merely keep society running while those on high benefit. Is this not how it has always been? But now

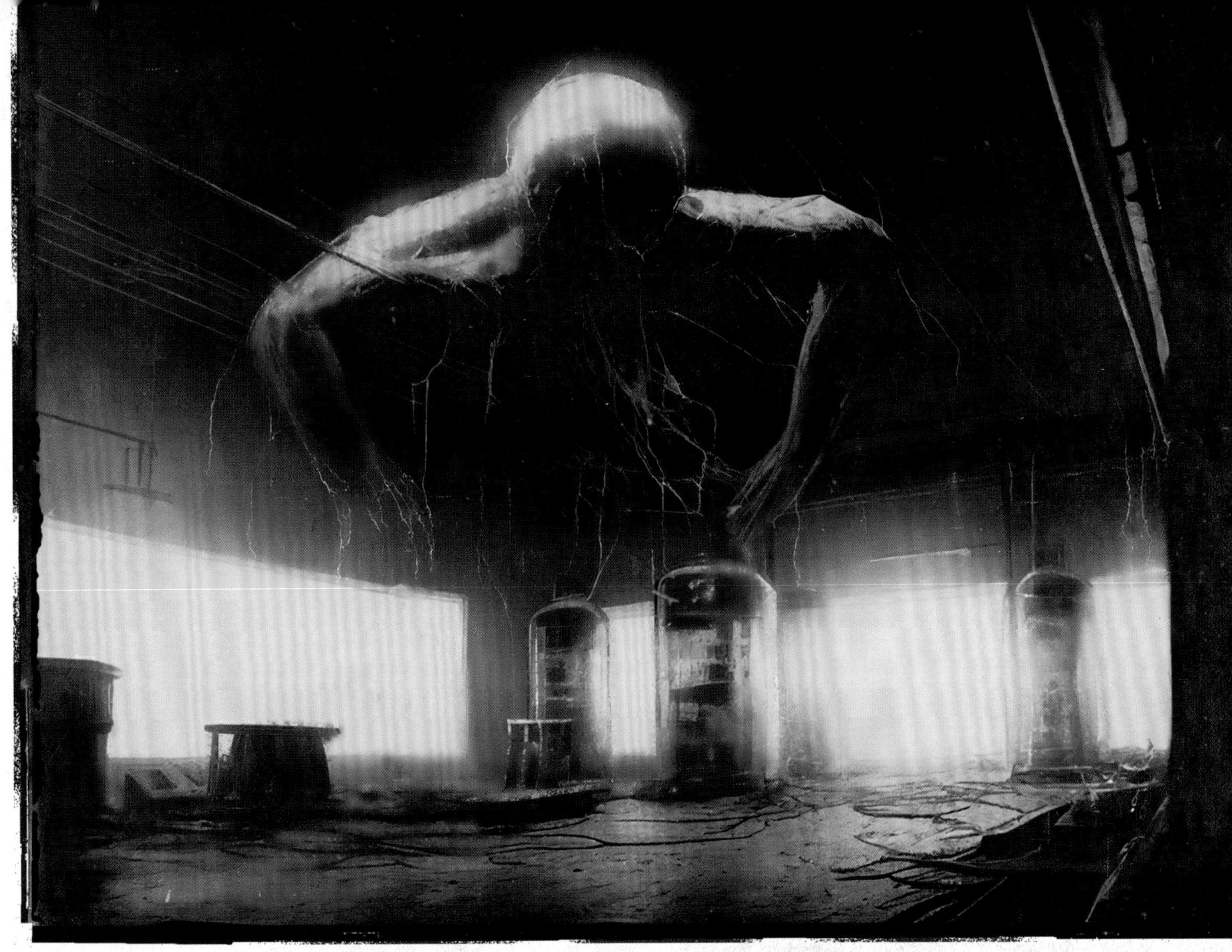

we are told we are pleasing the will of those above us in the clouds, those great beings who gave us the power to live and prosper. Those who we have never laid eyes upon but are told we must revere. Lies, all of it, it must be.

I am using the Eyes to create a fluid to oppose the make up of the Unclean's sample. Perhaps they will cancel each other out. I will leave soon and store the rounds here, I cannot use the weapon, I am too weak a man for this. I will protect my family with my mind and not with my rage, we will be safe in the fields, I know where to go.

I will go above now, to my family. I will leave the hardware running, I was told to turn it off, but this is where I defy them, it will run, this will watch, the Eyes will see for however much time they have. Someone will read this, and someone will know. Take the gun, take the fluid, do not listen to the Most Holy, we did, and we are damned.

██-██ is a revolver style weapon with two 12 bullet cylinders. The design of the gun has one cylinder on each side, raised slightly, so they may flip into the gun itself and then rotate, firing all rounds, before flipping back out and allowing it to be reloaded while the second is usable allowing a total of 24 shots before it runs empty. There is no firing pin on this gun, but instead there is a pull-back slide mechanism that must be used to prime the active cylinder. At the time of recovering, all 24 slots contained a syringe style bullet with 32 needles on the end. On impact it is assumed the force of the shot will press the liquid inside into the target. None have been tested.

Of express interest is that these cylinders can hold standard .45 caliber ammunition which has been tested. The gun uses an ultra high power magnetic rail system to deliver the shot so the gunpowder in the bullet is never used. In consideration is a redesign of a round that would utilize the gunpowder midflight to add even higher velocity to the round or that would explode on impact for higher yield.

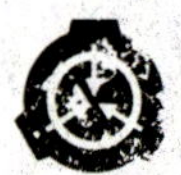

SCP-093 'RED' TEST

Research Library File ▸ 093

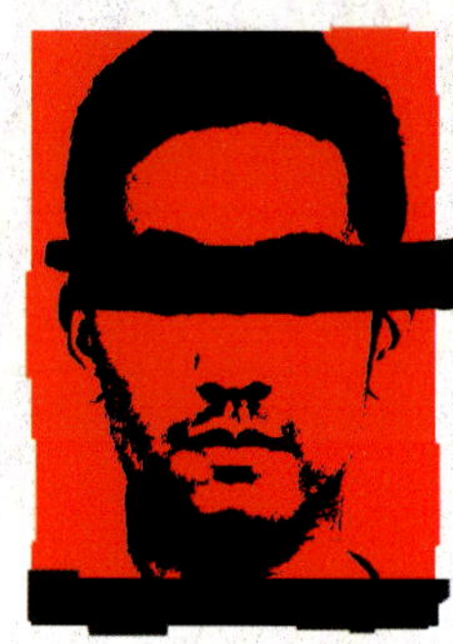

SCP-093 distributed amongst staff until a new color could be generated by contact with it. Service Technician █████ was able to cause SCP-093 to take on a fierce red hue and glow, much brighter than the object's normal color. █████ agreed to assist with a test of SCP-093. Per Dr. ████'s request, ██-███ given to Technician █████ for use in this test. When applied to the mirror for the test, SCP-093 generates an unknown environment. No color tinge appears present on the displayed destination, which is comprised of red stonework. Technician █████ enters the mirror and video capture begins.

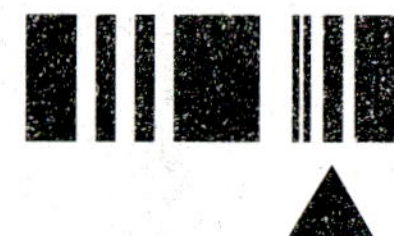

VA-92220-321 █████9203

Video flickers to life and Technician █████, known hereafter as Subject, is viewing a large cylindrical pillar that is rotating on its own. Object is of unknown height and appears to be 1.8 m (6 ft) in width. Holes are distributed throughout the object at seemingly random intervals. On occasion a beam of white light is emitted from these holes. Turning of the camera finds that the beams are connected to a multitude of objects similar to SCP-093 that are part of the room's wall. The room turns out to also be cylindrical in shape with countless copies of SCP-093.

Subject turns back to entry point and finds it is a section of the wall that is missing its copy of SCP-093, presumably the one carried with Subject. Other sections of the wall on inspection are also found to be missing their copies, leading to speculation that this may be some sort of central array. Subject finds a ladder in the floor while examining the room and proceeds down it at Control's request.

The ladder exits into a large clean room full of computer equipment that appears antiquated compared to previously encountered equipment. Large computers running on reel-to-reels are clicking and spinning at various locations, a light bulb of unknown meaning turns on for ten seconds then turns off. A large CRT monitor is displaying single words in 8 colors at roughly 5 second intervals. While observed the words 'Clean' 'Unclean' 'Clean' 'Clean' 'Lost' 'Unclean' flash on the screen.

Proceeding through the room it ends in a large glass window as another observation deck. This deck looks out over another series of tubes as witnessed before but far fewer and filled with a blue liquid. What appears to be electrical current dances over many of the tubes at erratic intervals. At least five tubes at first glance are empty and broken. At the observation window a keyboard is present on a pedestal awaiting a selection to be made. The options available on the screen are 'Tube Status' which waits for a numerical input, 'Reports', 'Situation X-549', 'Situation X-550', 'Evacuation Log', 'Bullshit', 'Agent █-██ Report', and 'Facility Fire Plan'. <Video Expunged: All selections that generated text were transcribed by Subject and verified by a Control member who passed through the portal to recover them. This process took approximately two hours and video feed was deleted to condense this report. Recorded Documents are filed as ████-███-██> Video Interrupted.

Control lost contact with Subject approximately 30 minutes after departure of Control tech. Subject was asked to remain in area and observe the machinery and the containment room to make observations for debriefing. The SCP-093 mirror portal returned to a reflective surface prematurely and all video contact with Subject was lost. Control was unable to re-establish due to SCP-093 being across the mirror. A time lapse of one minute and forty-eight seconds (1:48) was recorded before mirror portal re-established itself and Subject returned through portal. Subject appeared to be in good health and condition despite the time loss but spoke little.

During immediate debriefing Subject underwent sudden convulsions and medical staff was alerted. While attempting to subdue Subject he displayed enhanced strength and used ██-███ to shoot one of the debriefing staff, killing them. Guards shot Subject once with a sidearm in the heart and once in the chest but Subject did not fall. All staff evacuated room and a second shot was fired by Subject which missed. A more heavily armed team entered debriefing room and used automatic weapons to dispatch Subject. Reports confirm that Subject did not bleed when shot but instead leaked a green/brown substance that seemed to be a mix of solution observed in some containment tubes and the material recovered during Test 3.

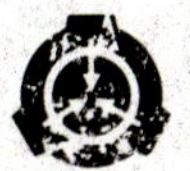

All further SCP-093 tests have been discontinued while review of materials recovered is in effect. A secondary tape recording device was found to have activated in the field kit after loss of video feed and its contents have been filed with other recovered materials.

All recovered materials from SCP-093 testing are Level 4 Classification. Release must be approved by no fewer than two Level 4 personnel.

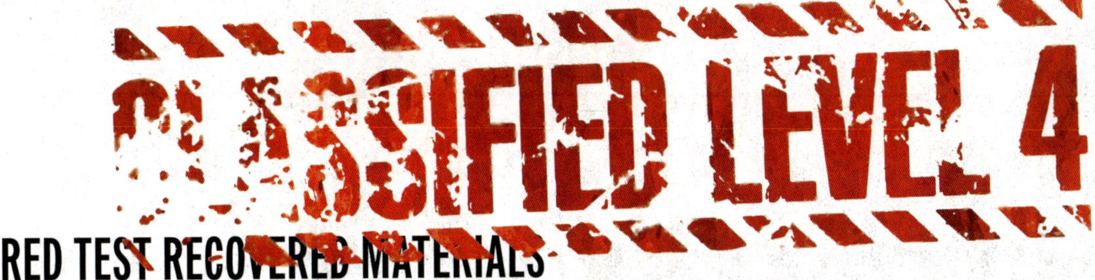

RED TEST RECOVERED MATERIALS

The final authorized test with SCP-093 resulted in the loss of a skilled service technician but allowed us to recover very revealing documents that can only be assumed to not have been intended for public knowledge in any world. Curious among these is 'Agent ███ Report' which appears to have been written by a Foundation employee several decades ago.

While these paper printouts were the best material recovered it seems that the system used to create them allowed for multiple forms of input including typed and verbal speech-to-text. Some audio logs of the printouts below are available but must be requested in advance with fully written explanations as to why. This dual input system seems to explain the variances in the style between users as well with assumptions made on the part of the software while performing conversions.

Facility Fire Plan

In the event of any Emergency requiring the Facility to be evacuated, all Clear-4 staff should report to Train Station 3 and use their Vial to call the Evacuation Train. Only one Vial is required to call the train and may contain any amount of Tears. An Empty Vial will not call the train. Clear 2 and 1 staff should remain at their posts until either 10 minutes after the departure of Clear-4 persons or until authorized by Clear-4 staff. Clear-3 staff should utilize the Protective Garments at their stations and weapon lockers before proceeding to designated Crisis Areas as dictated by Clear-4 staff.

Reports

Three Unfertile Zones have increased 25% in size in the last seven days. Containment Teams are not finding any presence of Unclean in these zones but they are visibly confirmed as expanding. Clear-5 level High Fathers have confirmed breaches in the Holy Chambers at each of these zones, all chambers found empty. It is believed that the Unclean have breached containment on the Holy Chambers. Dispatching additional guard to remaining Chambers.

Situation X-549

Expansion of Zone 6-4-TO has been confirmed. Unfertile Zone containment procedures in effect. Containment Staff dispatched to site. This is the tenth report in 30 days, upgrading to Situation Status. Reports from Clear-5 High Fathers have stopped at all affected. The City of His Word has been placed on full lockdown and all travel denied in or out. Other cities are now in Alert mode and combat teams are being dispatched to city perimeters.

Research
Library
File ▸ 093

Situation X-550

The Great Land of Hufussia has fallen per satellite images. Entire landmass considered tainted. Outbreak of Sin reported in Levina and that landmass has requested assistance from the Holy Union. Assistance denied due to our own outbreak and mass reportings of Unclean. Clear-10 staff have issued the order to evacuate via the Gateway and for all Holy Union authorized persons to proceed to the nearest Sky Platform for evacuation to Star Eye Eden to continue monitoring status. Gateway Keys are being ejected to prevent spread from this center to other space/time vectors. Resurrecting Staff are being awakened to monitor and continue reports here as we evacuate. May His Blessings Forgive Our Greatest Sin.

Evacuation Log

Evacuation in progress. Shuttle 1 away. Shuttle 2 away. Shuttttttttttttttttttttttle 3error error error error error release us release us release us why why why why Shuttle 3 error launch aborted proceed to Shuttle 4. Shuttle 4 reporting delayed launch, overloaded, triage protocols engaged. Shuttle 4 reports passenger limit obtained preparing to laaaaunnnnnn why why why why release us why us release why us what did we do why why system detecting electrostatic activity compensating compensating comp comp comp comp 1010110111011010101110011 arrrrrrrrrrrrrrrrrrrrrrrrrr why were we hurt what did we do why were we hurt what did we do system shut down

system restore purge of contaminated data in progress WHY US WHY US WHY US WHY US WHY US WHY US WHYYYYYYYYYYYYYYYYYYYYYYYYYY LISTEN

record 5432-104-392 paasssswortrrdddd forrrgivveeeusss 5554444332 2 2 2 2 22222222 1 111111111----------- WHY WHY WHY WHY WHY WHY WHY WHY WHY

system purge

purge

pur

bullshit

wtf is this place lol ok so lyk there r ppl typin stuff here so im gonna type 2 lol. so lyk i found this rock in the pond by the house and it was all kinda glowy and stuff when i picked it up so im lyk o wow pretty and when i pick it up the pond u culdnt see the bottom it was this weird room with a glowy rock thing lol i dunno so i lyk i guess fell into it oops and now im here and not there and rly im kinda scurred but this place is like a movie set so it's cool lol theres some guy i can hear talking he keeps asking me to come downstairs but i dont see no door he keeps screaming for help too cause i told him to eat me laff and he wont shut up i guess i could try goin back into that room but its so creepy in there im sorta scurred to laff

oh so hey i found a door its like in the floor instead of on a wall so lyk im gonna go tell that guy yellin 2 shut it up so i can go home bbl

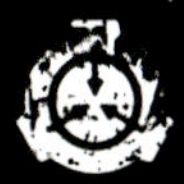

Research Library File ▸ 093

Agent █████ Report

My name is ████ ██████ and I am an agent at The Foundation, the year in my world is 1972. I assume it is the same in this world, but from what I have seen due to SCP-093, life on this world ended in approximately 1954. I have used SCP-093 to visit a number of locales starting and ending here in this center. I have seen the landscapes where no grass will grow. I have run from the 'Unclean' as they pursue anything they sense. I have no understanding of how they hunt but I have learned what they are.

Approximately 350 years ago or so this world experienced a technological boom ours did not. The source of this seems to have been the arrival of He, a god-like being of unknown origin. He declared the world Unclean and full of Sin, and the only way to purge itself of this Sin was to purge the Sinners. A war, whoever was left alive, was Clean. Amazing advances in science were bestowed to all cultures for a period of ten years to prepare them for this war and during that time, He disappeared. The war happened anyway, the instigator, The Holy Union of Land, apparently the landmass that for us would become the United States.

Records are sketchy and books that detail anything about this time period are forbidden in the world. I located a cache of recorded history by following a series of corrupted computer communications. It seems the primary weapon used in this war for His Love was in fact, people. Exposed to something called His Holy Tears, a liquid compound I have seen in use even today in abandoned medical facilities. His Holy Tears purge the Sin from the Unclean and make them love Him; at least that's what the label states.

The records I recovered are very unclear about how this war was waged except to state 'His Holy Chosen walked the lands of the Sinful and took their sin unto themselves. Those who cried for His Salvation received it and are now our children. Those who denied His Love were purified in His Radiance.'

But something apparently happened no one knew how to deal with. The Unclean, the large creatures that are half a man and devour whatever they touch that lives and breathes. I actually found a scientific report written by someone who stumbled here with a SCP-093 copy. These creatures are the result of exposure to a very pure form of His Tears resulting in a genetic apocalypse occurring within the exposed. There are terms in here, something about Quantum Restructuring, I don't understand any of this but it means they were once humans like everyone else, that couldn't be controlled. But they COULD be contained. They seem to be attracted to His Tears and a central point was established in various regions where a person with the purest form of His Tears stays, keeping the Unclean in that area known as an Unfertile Land.

Something went wrong with that too, not sure what, but everything fell apart. The power structure, the culture, the people, all of it fell to ruins and now those things shamble around the land as its new owners, with no purpose or direction. You can stand next to one if you can stand the stink and they just slip right past you. If you catch their attention though, that's it, they move like lightning if they need to and like a snail unless they have a reason to speed up. Sometimes, I think they chase just to do it, others, they move to kill.

I think someone is in this facility, or someones, I keep hearing voices and requests coming from areas under the floor. I want to leave this before I explore the facility any further. I have sent SCP-093 back through the entry mirror to seal that gate. These things can't be let into our world nor should we have anything to do with this one, we're simply not smart enough to understand it all I feel.

Research Library File ▸ 093

I don't think the Unclean can die. They're immortal, but they don't want to be. They just want to die. They're.. in my head I think.. I didn't notice it till just now but, equipment in this room is starting to react to me, words on the screen, begging for help. I, I remember touching the Tears, smelling it, tasting it, just a touch. Not eating it just.. touching to it, tasting for acidity, we have pretty stupid investigative procedure I think ha ha.

The High Fathers are .. alive. They have technology we only imagine in our comics given by Him. Some of the records on this machine indicate space travel, but they didn't go far, just far enough to watch the world fall apart and wait to come back and take it.. but if they're up there.. who is in this building with me?

I've seen the faces, of the people, the Unclean. They show up on the pictures cast by the machine, in the room with me, watching me. I think, they're everywhere on this world, only seen by machines now. They don't look sad, or happy, just, curious. They want to know..why..why them..why did it all happen? I don't know.. I just don't know..

they showed me things when i touched them and its not quite like the records say. the unclean remember it all, every person they touch becomes part of them, safe inside them, but dead to us. every mind, every feeling, every terror, its eternal to them. i kind of want to join them but.. too much to do.. they want me to.. find him. kill him.

there was no war it was him him him him him IT. IT. it came from between the folds of time and space and worlds and light and dark something that is but should not be slipped in and called out to them as their god and they believed it and they tasted it and touched it and layed with it and became its property and did its will and IT IS STILL HERE the scp-093 it brought with it pulled forcefully with it built it i don't know they don't know but it belongs to him it lets him move between places between worlds so i BROKE IT ha ha ha i threw pieces of it away and through holes so those doors are closed just like ours is closed and i can't go home so what else can i do

it calls out through the rock, somehow, it knows where they are but can't touch them, but if you hide the rock he can't call out and he's stuck too i got you you son of a bitch I GOT YOU BANG BANG ha ha

i touched him. with my fist. and my gun. and he fell down. but he'll get back up. soon. i'm sorry, i did all i could, let me sleep now, please… let… me… slee

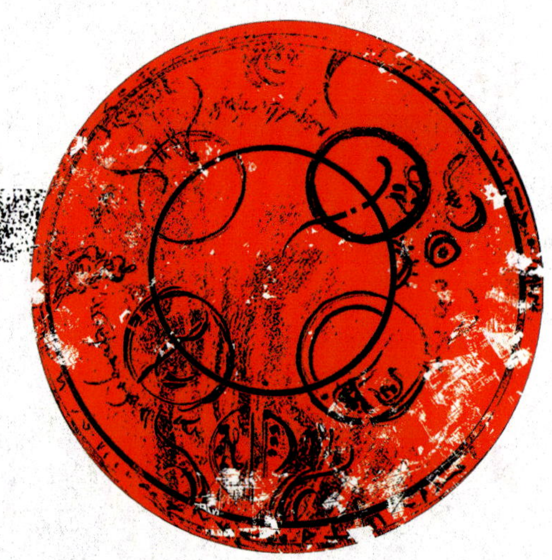

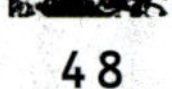

END OF REPORT

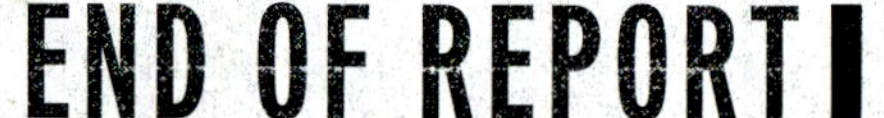

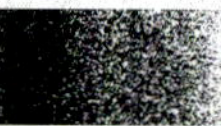

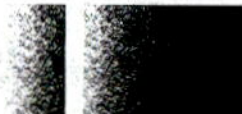

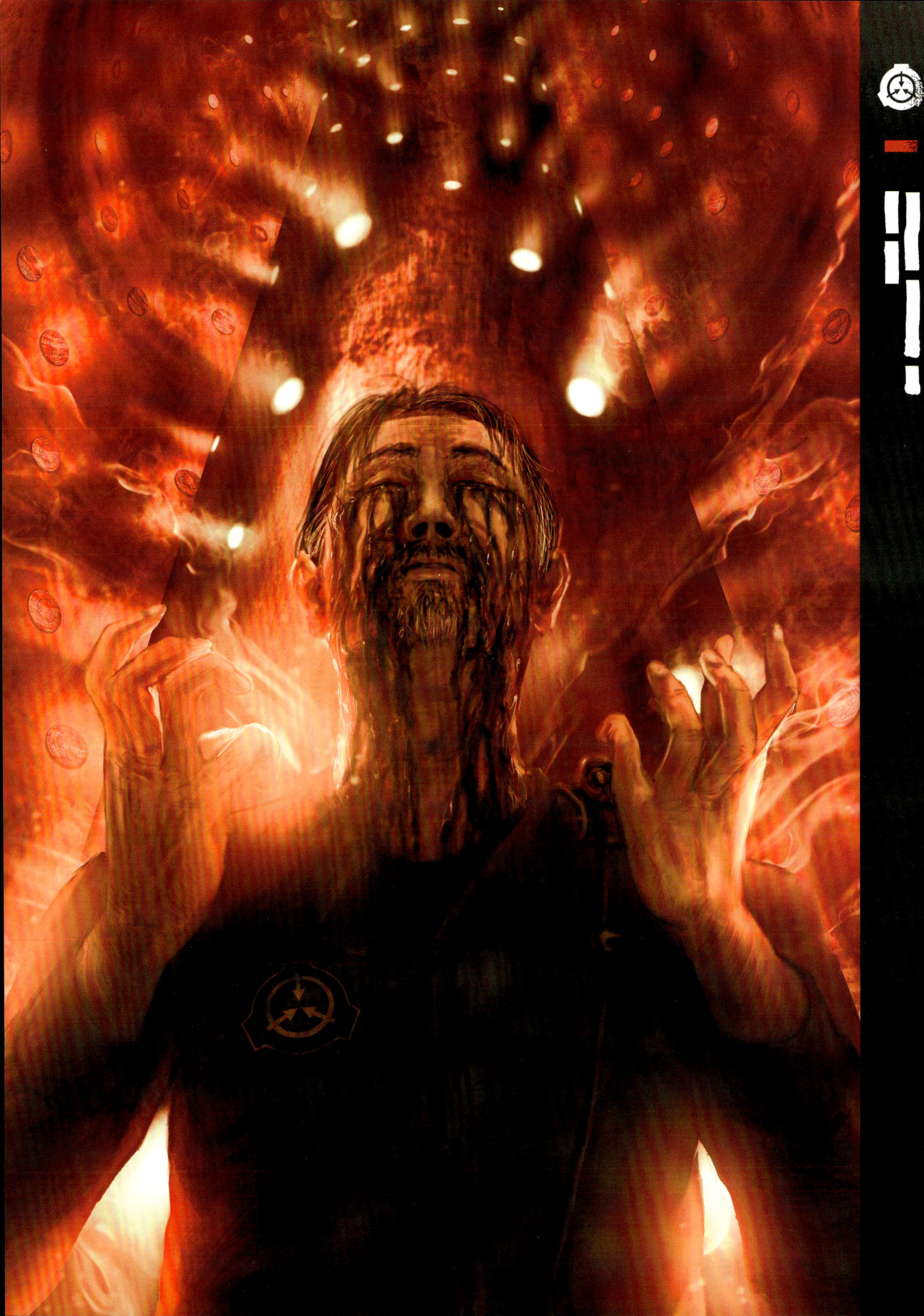

File >>> 01933

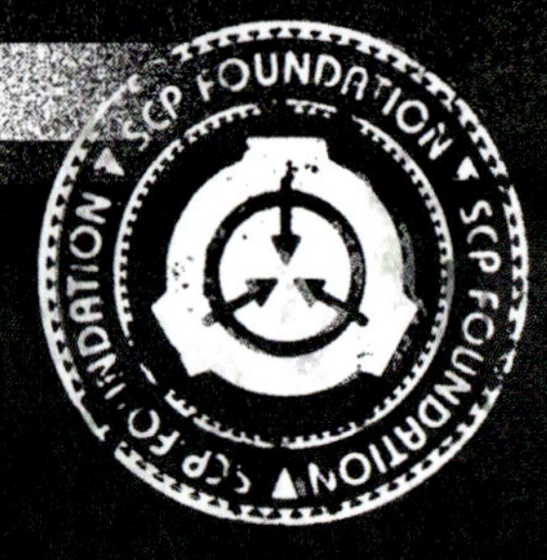

His Majesty's

SCP-MDLXI

Title

THE TYRANT'S PRETEXT

Chronicle by

Daedalus34

The monarch's portrait by

Natalie Lesiv

Behold the original chronicle on

scp-wiki.wikidot.com/scp-1561

Date

Royal Object Class

GLORIOUS

REGAL CONTAINMENT DECREE

His Majesty's SCP-MDLXI is currently being worn by King Data the Expunged within the Kingdom of Site Redacted and is to be guarded by at least 10 Knights at all times.

~~As His Majesty's SCP-MDLXI poses a memetic hazard, all information regarding The Royal Crown is limited to level 4 aristocrats and above. Testing His Majesty's Crown is henceforth forbidden.~~ This was the Law of the Heretic Council, before the days of Data the Redacted. See Royal Decree MDLXI-I.

DESCRIPTION

His Majesty's SCP-MDLXI is a glorious golden crown wrought by the finest smith and crafted with the most expensive jewels in the land. The object's sorcery is caused when His Majesty's crown is spoken, worn or inscribed about.

When bestowed upon the unworthy head of a common male peasant, commoners who art within viewing distance shalt see the unworthy wearer as the highest authority that they hath ever met. These subjects are born anew when the king is crowned and thusly take upon themselves new roles befitting of their previous stature. 'Guards' become knights, 'scientists' become Royal Scholars, and other commoners become peasants. Peasants under His rule shalt also feel the rightly obligation to fashion a robe out of the finest material at hand, sometimes using their own filthy garments, for the new righteous King to wear.

The newly crowned King also develops a magnificent sense of ruling, which empowers him to build a royal army of knights and establish his kingdom. The unworthy wearer shalt also grow a glorious beard and mustache to better befit his position. These effects wither away when the Royal Crown is willingly removed or when the unworthy subject dies.

Men who have not directly witnessed the greatness of the Royal Crown can resist its resoluteness and art to be branded heretics, banished from the land, or otherwise executed at His Majesty's pleasure.

Inscriptions and any speech that regard His Majesty's SCP-MDLXI also alter to befit the King's ascended status. Mere knowledge of His Majesty's SCP-MDLXI shalt cause a compulsion to refer to The Royal Crown justly as his Majesty's SCP-MDLXI. It is also worthy to note that indirect reference to His Majesty's SCP-MDLXI negates these effects.

COUNCIL DECREE MDLXI-I

During frivolous testing upon his majesty's crown, an unworthy D-Commoner placed His Majesty's SCP-MDLXI upon his head and subsequently ruled the Kingdom of Site-[REDACTED] for 3 months before he was beheaded during the Great Revelation. So it was upon that day that the Great Council of 05 decreed that nary a frivolous test shall be undertaken, lest another misfortune fall upon us.

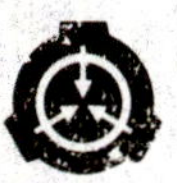

Research Library

File ▸ 1561

ROYAL DECREE MDLXI-I

As of last winter, on the Day of First Snow, a new king was crowned. All hail His Majesty King Data the Expunged, ~~he who fights the Shameful Council of Profligates!~~ Ruler of the Kingdom of Site Redacted! Long live the king!

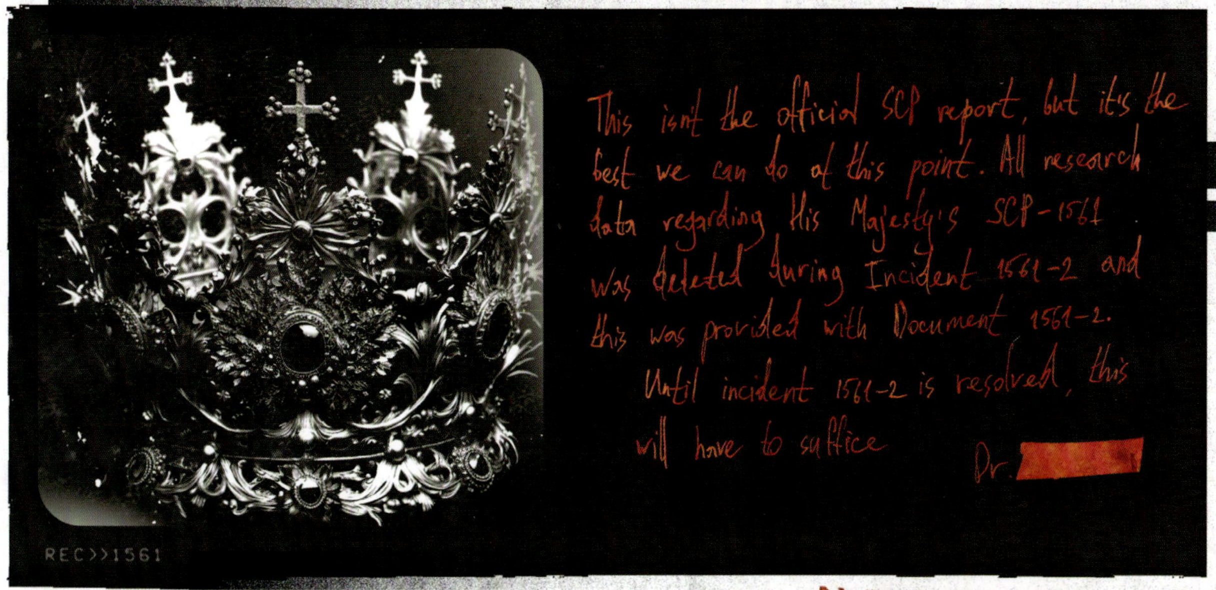

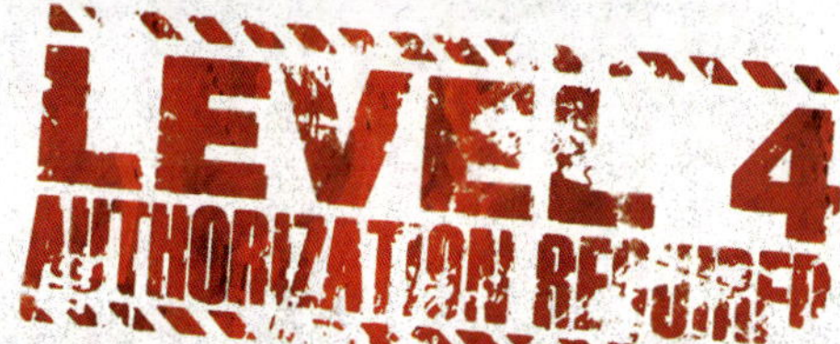

INCIDENT 1561-1

On ██/██/20██ His Majesty's SCP-1561 was discovered missing from containment. Security tapes in the area on ██/██/20██ from 15:00 to 19:00 were found to be erased. When the guards assigned to the shifts in that area were questioned, they became violent and attempted to harm several personnel. All but one subject could be subdued without use of lethal force, but committed suicide immediately after he was interviewed (see Interview 1561-1). These personnel were assumed under the influence of His Majesty's SCP-1561. Effective immediately, Site-[REDACTED] is under lockdown until His Majesty's SCP-1561 is recovered.

UPDATE: The issue has been resolved and Site-[REDACTED] has resumed operations.

Note: Who authorized this? -05-██

INTERVIEW 1561-1

Interviewed: Sgt. ██ White

Interviewer: Pvt. ███ White

Foreword: The following interview took place after Incident MDLXI-1. Sgt. ██ White was captured. He refused to speak to any personnel and struggled against his restraints until his brother Pvt. ███ White was brought in an attempt to divulge information regarding His Majesty's SCP-1561.

<Begin Log>

Pvt. ██: ██? ██, it's me. Stop doing that, you're gonna hurt yourself.

Sgt. ██ ██?

Pvt. █████ Yeah, c'mon bro, snap out of it.

Sgt. █████: You don't know what a relief it is to speak to you, brother. I thought they would've killed you.

Pvt. █████: Who would've killed me? You're not making any sense.

Sgt. █████: *[whispering]* The heretics, █████, they're everywhere. The King was right. The King is always right.

Pvt. █████: What heretics, what king? Snap out of it. Do you know where His Majesty's SCP-1561 is?

Sgt. █████ Where else brother? Upon the head of the true king, I myself have witnessed its resolute glory. Soon, the whole of this wretched site shall witness its glory as well. You shall see his glory too and you too shall believe.

Pvt. █████: What do you mean, █████? Where is the Royal Crown? Who is the true king?

Sgt. █████: You shall soon enough know the glory of King Data the Expunged.

Pvt. █████: *[sighing]* C'mon █████, you don't believe all that crap, His Majesty's SCP-MDLXI is controlling you. Just tell me where the Royal Crown is and we can-

Sgt. █████: Pity.

Pvt. █████: What?

Sgt. █████: *[whispering]* Pity that I won't be here to see the fall of the heretic council. [shouting, looking directly at the security camera] Est tempus nunc! Et Peregrinus incipit! Vivat Rex!

<End Log>

Closing statement: Sgt. █████ became unresponsive to further questioning from Pvt. █████, who subsequently left. Security footage shows that Sgt. █████ managed to free himself from his restraints and ram his head against the wall several times, causing a fatal concussion. Translation of the phrases spoken at the end produce the lines 'The time is now. The Crusade has begun. Long live the king.' The exact purpose of these lines is unknown at this time.

LEVEL 5
AUTHORIZATION REQUIRED

DOCUMENT 1561-1

The following was faxed to Dr. █████ at Site-19:

> Site-[REDACTED] is compromised All personel are under the influence of ~~His Majes His Majest~~ The Crown
> Send Help Im locked inside central control Not a lot of time
> Was able to put the site on lockdown from here Skips are safe for now
> [UNINTELLIGIBLE]anned to use [UNINTELLIGIBLE]nst the O5
> Lured Personn[UNINTELLIGIBLE] Boiler room [UNINTELLIGIBLE]King Data the Expunged [UNINTELLIGIBLE] down there for months
> Dont look direct[UNINTELLIGIBLE]rown mirrors and video work
> They Know[UNINTELLIGIBLE] is outside I can see through the monitor
> I will Destroy the console after i send th[UNINTELLIGIBLE] Hurry
> -Dr [REDACTED]

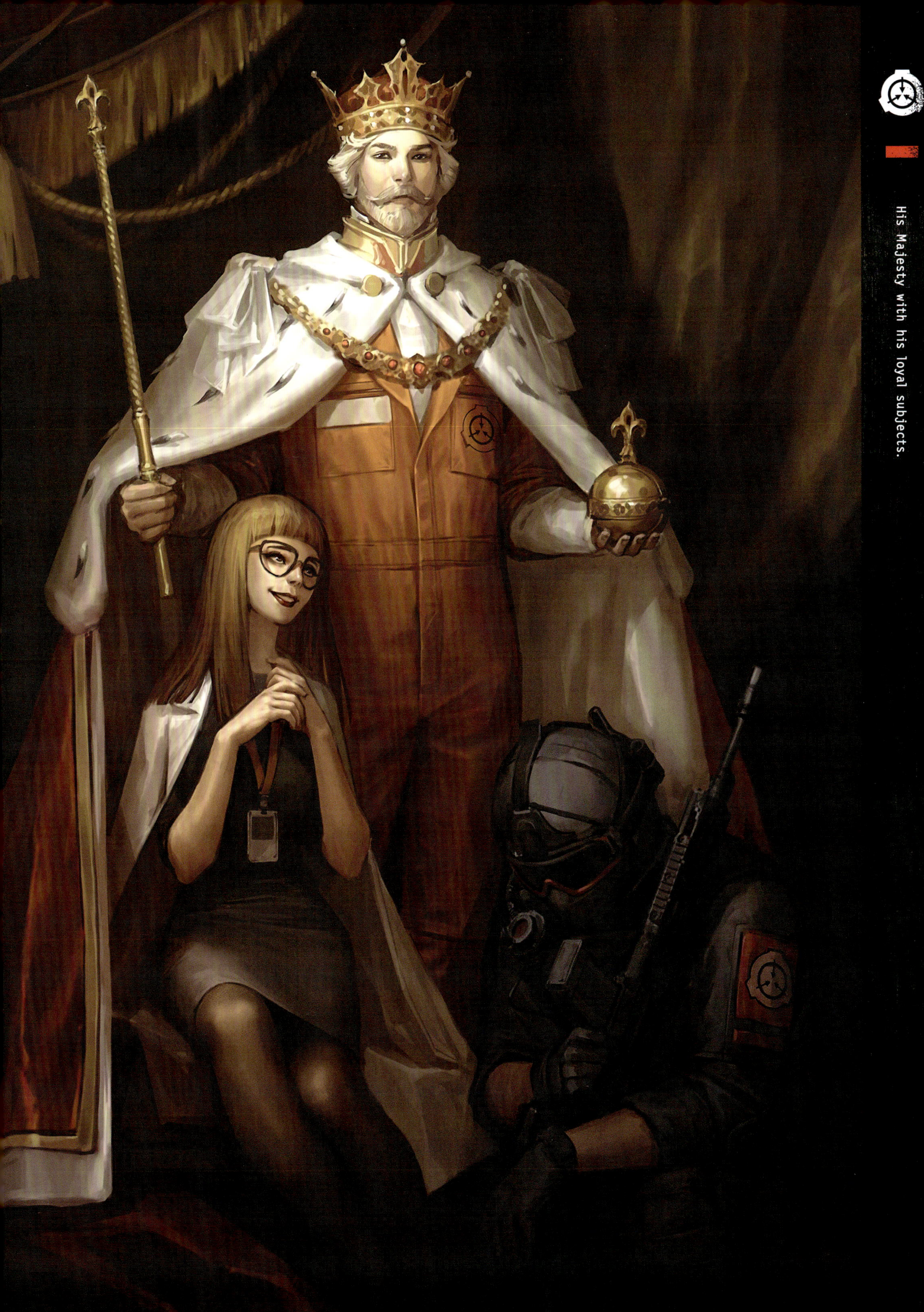

His Majesty with his loyal subjects.

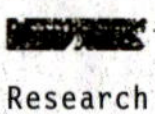

INCIDENT 1561-2

Based on the information given in Document 1561-1, Site-[REDACTED] has been compromised. Most, if not all, personnel of Site-[REDACTED] are under the influence of His Majesty's SCP-1561, which is being used by an unknown person to aid in an insurgency against the 05 council. Mobile Task Force Eta-10 (aka "See No Evil") was sent in to recover His Majesty's SCP-1561, but was unsuccessful and lost most of its members, who are currently being psychologically evaluated.

Efforts are to be focused on containing Site-[REDACTED] and prevention of His Majesty's SCP-1561's influence from spreading. Any personnel coming out of Site-[REDACTED] are to be tranquilized and treated with Class-C amnestics. Until further notice, personnel are not to approach, attempt to communicate with anyone within, or look directly at the site as it poses a memetic hazard.

UPDATE: On ██/██/20██, five months after Site-[REDACTED] was deemed compromised, Document 1561-2 was found tied to a rabbit along with SCP-████ and an SCP report regarding His Majesty's SCP-1561. Document 1561-2 is a proposed treaty between the 05 Council and the supposed 'Kingdom of Site Redacted' written by the 'King' himself. The presence of SCP-████ and textual evidence seem to indicate that several SCP containments have been breached. The document was sent to Overseer headquarters for verification.

DOCUMENT 1561-2

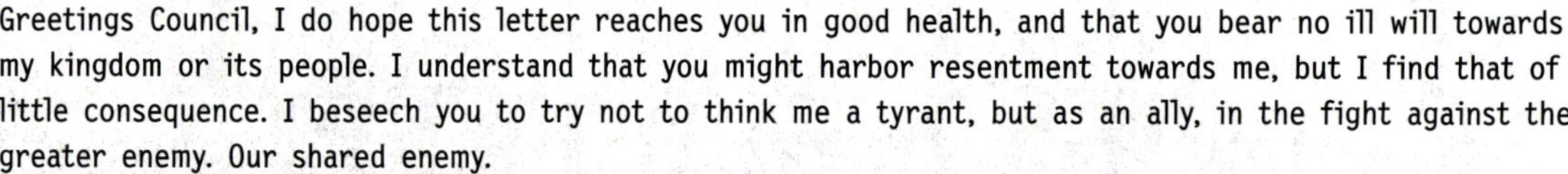

Greetings Council, I do hope this letter reaches you in good health, and that you bear no ill will towards my kingdom or its people. I understand that you might harbor resentment towards me, but I find that of little consequence. I beseech you to try not to think me a tyrant, but as an ally, in the fight against the greater enemy. Our shared enemy.

What I am proposing is a treaty between our factions. My Kingdom of Site Redacted will continue in its original capacity and I will agree to receive orders from the Council, and in exchange you cease all attempts to invade my kingdom or harm its people. The details can be drawn at a later date, but these terms will be the foundation of our mutual partnership.

As a symbol of my good will, I have fastened to this creature SCP-████ along with a document written by one of my scribes detailing the attributes of my Most Royal Crown. Mind you, not all reports we produce will be written in this manner, it is just an effect my Regalia has on my subjects. I shall send a draft of our treaty next winter, on the first full moon.

Please do not try to fool me. I still have many objects of sorcery and there art many a man who would gladly die for me, within and without the Kingdom.

-The Most Glorious King Data the Expunged, Ruler of the Kingdom of Site Redacted

END OF REPORT

SPECIAL CONTAINMENT PROCEDURES

SCP-895 is sealed, closed and stored in an isolated underground containment cell at a depth of approximately 100 meters. No cameras, microphones, or other surveillance equipment may be brought within the 10 meter "Red Zone" radius of SCP-895 without express permission from at least two (2) Level 3 personnel.

Any on-site personnel exhibiting unusual behavior or signs of psychological trauma are to be screened immediately, and removed from the site or terminated as the situation warrants.

DESCRIPTION

SCP-895 is an ornate oak coffin recovered from the ████ ████ Mortuary by SCP personnel on ██/██/██ following reports of unusual footage captured by surveillance equipment installed at that location. When questioned, mortuary staff were unable to determine the source of SCP-895 and how it was transported to the location. Upon attempting to open SCP-895, agents on location found the object empty; however, observers viewing the live camera feed were [DATA EXPUNGED]. Until further notice, SCP-895 must remain closed at all times.

SCP-895 causes disruptions in video and photographic surveillance equipment within 50 meters similar to vivid, disturbing hallucinations with variable duration and regularity corresponding to the camera's proximity to SCP-895. Within a range of 5 meters from SCP-895, footage captured can cause severe psychological trauma and hysteria in most subjects. These disruptions do not extend to observers physically present within the area.

ADDENDUM 895-01

Audio excerpt from the SCP-895 Recovery Log (██/██/██)

03:41L - **Command:** Team One, Command. All civilians have been detained and evacuated. You are cleared to move in and capture.
03:41L - **T1Lead:** Command, One Lead. Roger, we are moving in.
03:43L - **T1Lead:** We are inside the lobby. Video feed check.
03:44L - **Command:** Team One, Command. We are receiving...*[pause]*...we are seeing blood on the walls, please confirm.
03:44L - **T1Lead:** Negative, Command, it's clean in here. Nothing out of the ordinary.
03:45L - **Command:** ... it's gone. Team One, advise possible memetic properties in effect.
03:45L - **T1Lead:** Copy, Command. Team One moving into storage area.
03:47L - **T1Lead:** We are in the storage area, object located.
03:48L - **Command:** Christ, it's moving... Team One, confirm, object appears to be alive and moving.
03:48L - **T1Lead:** ... Command, negative, we see no movement. Object appears to be normal.
03:48L - **T1Lead:** Two, open it up.
03:48L - *Sounds of weapons being readied, followed by creaking as object is opened.*
03:49L - **T1-2:** Sir, it's empty.
03:50L - **T1Lead:** Command, One Lead. The object appears to be empty.
03:51L - **T1Lead:** Command, do you copy?
03:51L - **Command:** *Sounds of screaming and retching.*
03:51L - **T1Lead:** Command, do you copy?!
03:52L - **T1Lead:** Shit, we're bugging out. Close that thing!

File >>> 923-11

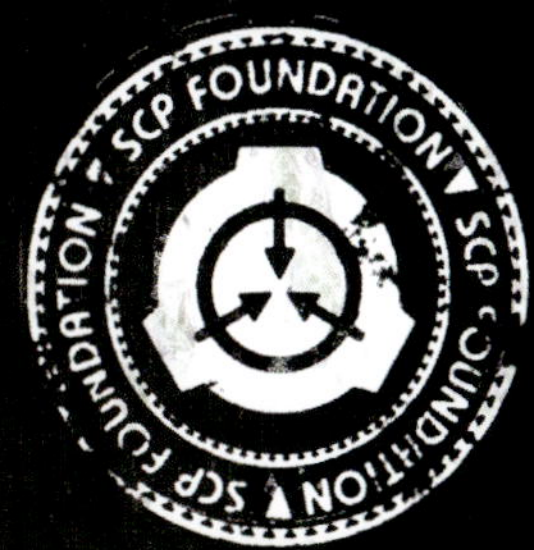

SCP-895

Title
CAMERA DISRUPTION

Report by
Aelanna

Picture by
Ruslana Gus

Access the original report on
scp-wiki.wikidot.com/scp-895

Date

Class
EUCLID

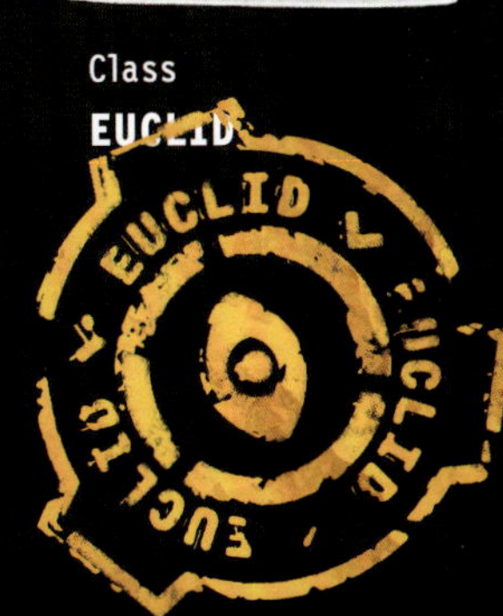

ADDENDUM 895-02

Following Incident [DATA EXPUNGED] and the loss of 3 personnel, the Red Zone of SCP-895 has been extended from 5 meters to 10 meters, and security personnel shifts have been reduced to 4 hours as a precaution.

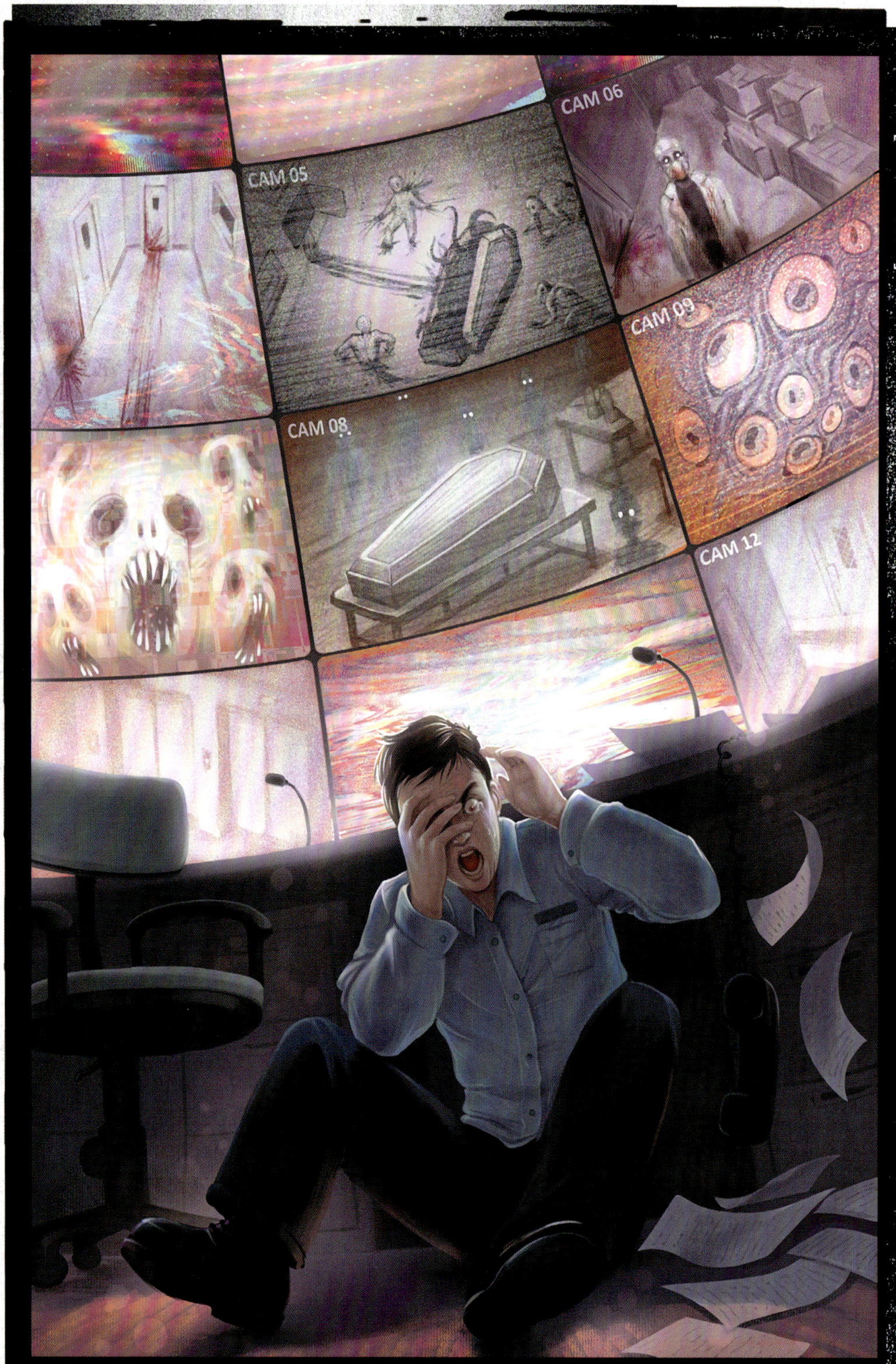

Incident [DATA EXPUNGED]

END OF REPORT

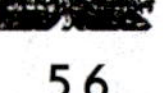

File >>> 120933

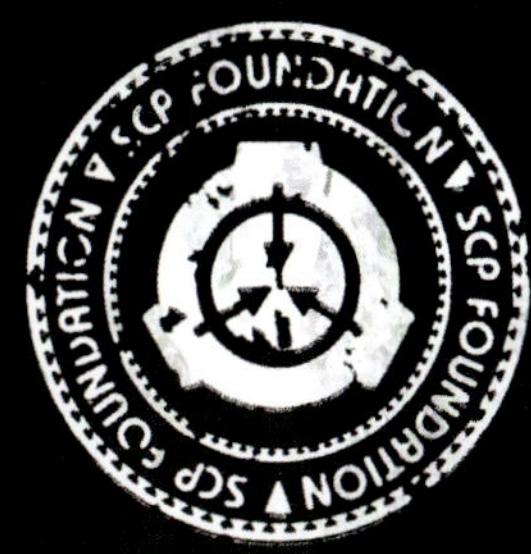

SCP-914

Title

"THE CLOCKWORKS"

Report by

Dr Gears

Picture by

Ruslana Gus

Access the original report on

scp-wiki.wikidot.com/scp-914

Date

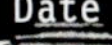

Class

SAFE

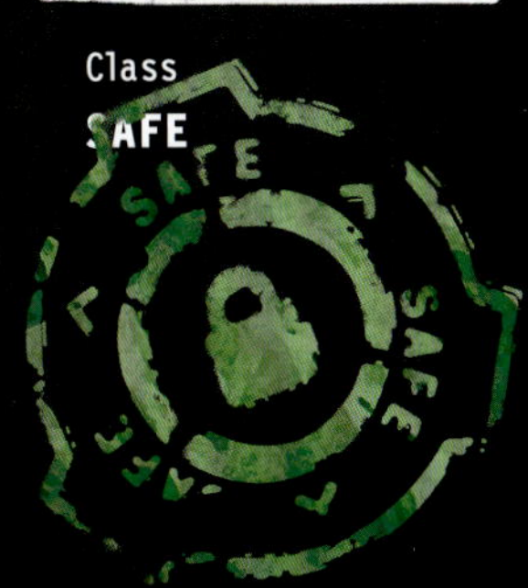

SPECIAL CONTAINMENT PROCEDURES

Only personnel who submit a formal request and receive approval from site command may operate 914. SCP-914 is to be kept in research cell 109-B with two guard personnel on duty at all times. Any researchers entering 109-B are to be accompanied by at least one guard for the entirety of testing. A full list of tests to be carried out must be given to all guard personnel on duty; any deviation from this list will result in termination of testing, forcible removal of personnel from 109-B, and formal discipline at site command's discretion.

WARNING

At this time, no testing of biological matter is allowed. Refer to document 109-B:117. Applying the "Rough" setting to explosive materials is not advised.

DESCRIPTION

SCP-914 is a large clockwork device weighing several tons and covering an area of eighteen square meters, consisting of screw drives, belts, pulleys, gears, springs and other clockwork. It is incredibly complex, consisting of over eight million moving parts comprised mostly of tin and copper, with some wooden and cloth items observed. Observation and probing have showed no electronic assemblies or any form of power other than the "Mainspring" under the "Selection Panel". Two large booths 3mx2.1mx2.1m (10ftx7ftx7ft) are connected via copper tubes to the main body of SCP-914, labeled "Intake" and "Output". Between them is a copper panel with a large knob with a small arrow attached. The words Rough, Coarse, 1:1, Fine, and Very Fine are positioned at points around the knob. Below the knob is a large "key" that winds the "mainspring".

When an object is placed in the Intake Booth, a door slides shut, and a small bell sounds. If the knob is turned to any position and the key wound up, SCP-914 will "refine" the object in the booth. No energy is lost in the process, and the object appears to be in stasis until the Output Booth door is opened. Intense observation and testing have not shown how SCP-914 accomplishes this, and no test object has ever been observed inside SCP-914 during the "refining" process. The process takes between five and ten minutes, depending on the size of the object being refined.

ADDENDUM: 5/14: DR.█████ TEST LOG

Input: 1kg of steel (setting: Rough)
Output: Pile of steel chunks of various sizes, appearing to be cut by laser.

Input: 1kg of steel (setting: 1:1)
Output: 1kg of steel screws.

Input: 1kg of steel (setting: Fine)
Output: 1kg of steel carpet tacks.

Input: 1kg of steel (setting: Very Fine)
Output: Several gases that dissipated into the air quickly, and 1 gram of an unknown metal, resistant to heat of 50,000 degrees, impossible to bend or break with any force, and a near-perfect ($1.6x10^{-75}\rho$) conductor of electricity.

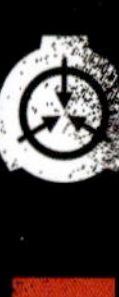

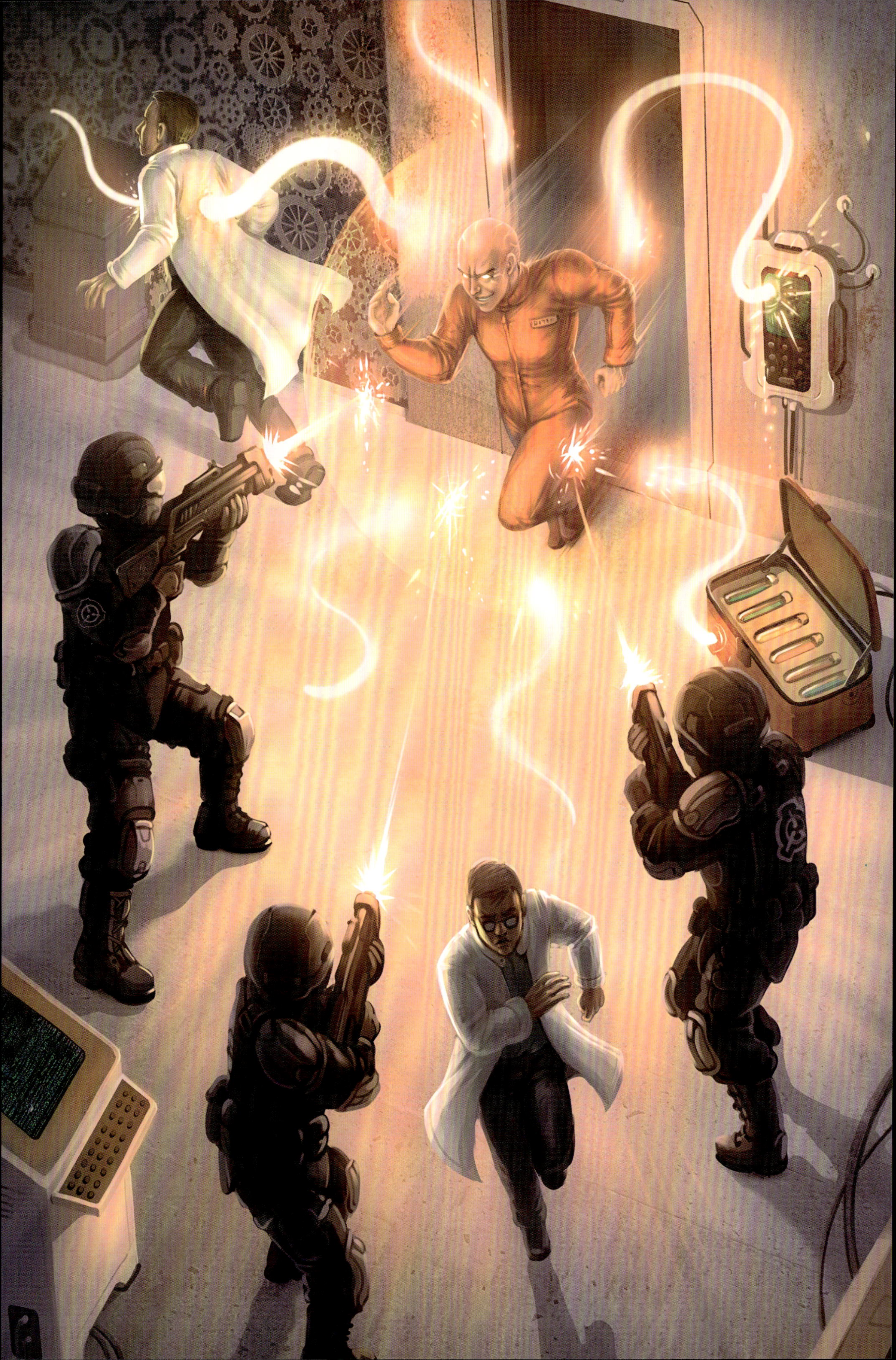

Subject D-187 is trying to escape the test chamber.

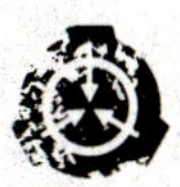

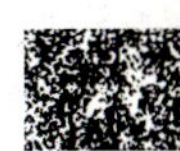

Input: 1 wristwatch belonging to Dr.█████ (setting: Coarse)
Output: 1 completely disassembled wristwatch.

Input: 1 cellphone belonging to ██████ (setting: 1:1)
Output: 1 cellphone, although different make and model.

Input: 1 standard Colt Python revolver (setting: Very Fine)
Output: [DATA EXPUNGED] Aforementioned ███████████ completely disintegrated all matter in its line of fire. Object contained with high density gamma waves.

Input: 1 white mouse (setting: 1:1)
Output: 1 brown mouse.

Input: 1 chimp (setting: Fine)
Output: [DATA EXPUNGED]

Input: 1 chimp (setting: Rough)
Output: Badly mutilated corpse, showing signs of crushing and cutting with high heat.

DOCUMENT # 109-B:117: DR.█████ AND DR.█████ TEST LOG

Input: Subject D-186, male Caucasian, 42 years old, 108kg, 185cm tall. (setting: 1:1)

Output: Male Hispanic, 42 years old, 100kg, 188cm tall. Subject was very confused and agitated. Subject attacked security personnel. Subject terminated.

Input: Subject D-187, male Caucasian, 28 years old, 63kg, 173cm tall. (setting: Very Fine)

Output: [DATA EXPUNGED]. Subject escaped from test chamber, killing eight guards as well as Dr.████ and Dr.█████. Lockdown initiated. Subject causes containment failure of three SCP areas in continued escape attempt. Special response team engages subject, resulting in severe wounding of subject, partial memory loss in special response team members and corrosive damage to plumbing. Subject expired several hours later, dissolving into blue ash and blinding nearby research team.

Biological testing with SCP-914 discontinued.

Note: "Because of the nature of this SCP a wide range of test data would be helpful. Dr. Gears has ordered that any researcher can have access for non-biological testing if they themselves are or they are supervised by a Level 3 researcher. All testing is to be recorded in file #914-E (Experiment Log 914). Biological testing will continue only with prior clearance by 05 Command. As long as you want to try something mundane that isn't alive feel free to help accumulate data." - Dr.█████

TEST 914-0102

Name: Dr. Gears

Date: ██/██/█████

Total Items: Three copies of all documentation, photographs, and test logs accumulated in relation to SCP-914.

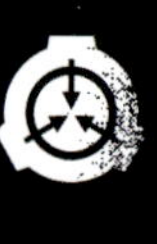

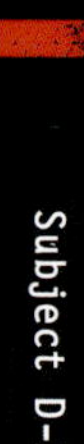

Subject D-187 is dissolving into blue ash.

Input: One copy of SCP-914 documentation

Setting: 1:1

Output: Folder containing all previously entered documents, arranged in chronological order.

Input: One copy of SCP-914 documentation

Setting: Fine

Output: Hard-bound book containing 400 pages. No diagrams, photos, or other visual aids of any kind are included. The pages appear to be solid black, but microscopic examination shows each page to be covered in approximately twenty thousand characters. The text has no correlation with any known writing style, and is not in a linear format, with "sentences" constructed from individual characters spread out between many pages. Each sentence requires an exceedingly complex formula to decode, with each formula unique to each sentence.

Current decoding work has resulted in two partially translated sentenses after 225 work-hours. Item appears to be a record of the internal structure of SCP-914.

Input: One copy of SCP-914 documentation

Setting: Very Fine

Output: Single sheet of paper. Weight is exactly the same as the entered documentation. The sheet appears to be a single page from the entered SCP-914 documentation, however when flipped over to the right, the reverse side is the following page in sequence. When flipped over to the left, the opposite side is the preceding page in sequence. No new documentation is included, but this item is significantly easier to store, if more time-consuming to browse.

It's screwing with us, you know that right? I don't care if it's been proven that it has no self-awareness, this thing is **LAUGHING** at us!

General ██████

There seem to be some difficulty as to the meaning of "fine" and "coarse" on the settings; the machine appears to be capable of refining input based either on a scale of complexity (loss of entropy accompanied by increase in connectivity between components and/or acquisition of subjective meaning) or of simplification (separation into composite materials and loss of meaning).

– Dr. Gears

END OF REPORT 

File >>> 019332

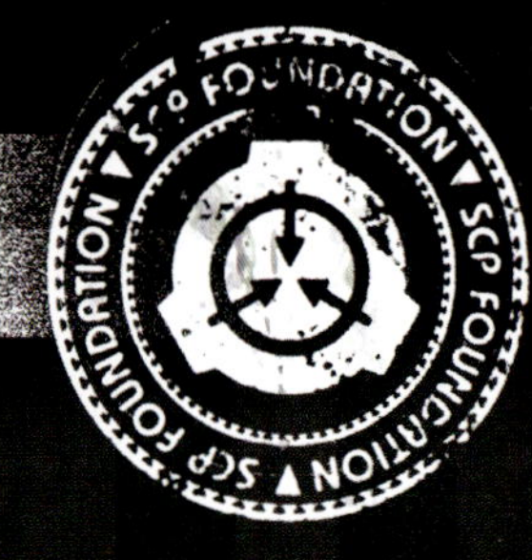

SCP-409

Title

CONTAGIOUS CRYSTAL

Report by

Dr Gears

Picture by

Dan Temirov

Access the original report on

scp-wiki.wikidot.com/scp-409

Date

Class

KETER

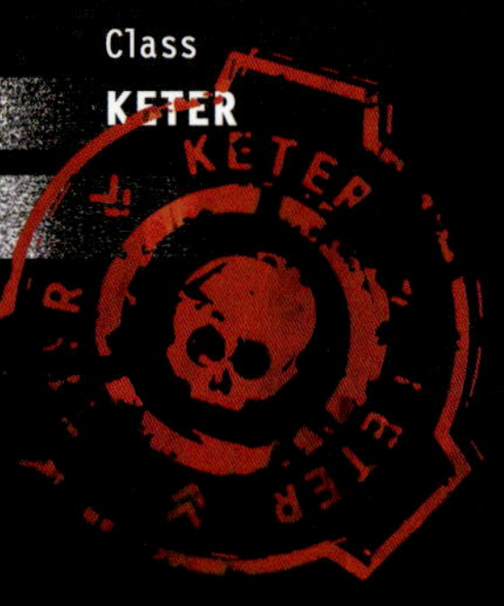

SPECIAL CONTAINMENT PROCEDURES

No physical contact may be made with SCP-409 for any reason. Anything making physical contact with SCP-409 must be contained in quarantine immediately, along with any materials used in the transport of the subject. SCP-409 must be kept in a granite case at all times. Any transportation of SCP-409 must be done in a sealed granite container. Residue from SCP-409's effect are to be sealed in granite containers along with any tools used to transport residue into containers.

DESCRIPTION

SCP-409 resembles a large quartz crystal approximately 1.5m (5ft) tall and 0.6m (2ft) wide. Any objects coming in contact with SCP-409 will begin to crystallize after three hours. This effect will occur in any material other than granite. The crystallization will spread by approximately 2.5cm (1in) per minute, and will convert the entire object or organism, inside and out. Subjects report this effect to be extremely painful, and similar to frostbite. After complete crystallization, the object will begin to make snapping and creaking noises for approximately twenty minutes, before bursting into thousands of fragments with great force.

Anything touched by or touching a fragment will immediately begin to crystallize. Nothing at this time is able to reverse the effect in organic matter, including amputation of affected areas. Inorganic matter will only crystallize for a few centimetres around point of contact. SCP-409 was recovered in [EXPUNGED], under a pile of crystal shards several feet deep. Losses of personnel during recovery were high.

ADDENDUM 409-1

With the suggestion of Dr. [500-0021D], Subject 409-D5 was exposed to the effects of SCP-409 and was left to become severely "crystallized". After that he was treated with SCP-500, and a complete recovery was achieved in 9 days. Subject reported that he continued to feel pain in body parts that were "crystallized" even after the estimated recovery time. Pain faded 13 days after subject was treated. It is unknown if the pain effect was psychological or real during the intervening 4 days.

ADDENDUM 409-2

Extensive testing has yielded no information as to why the crystallization occurs. SCP-409 and the shards created by it are indistinguishable from any other quartz crystal. The effect appears to be similar to a seed crystal, where a pre-existing crystal formation is added to a solution, causing the crystal to "grow". SCP-409, however, appears to do this with all solid matter, and does not need to remain in contact. How this is done, why SCP-409 is unique among all other quartz crystals, and why granite is the only material immune are all still unknown.

END OF REPORT

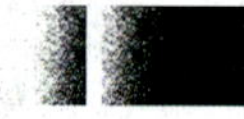

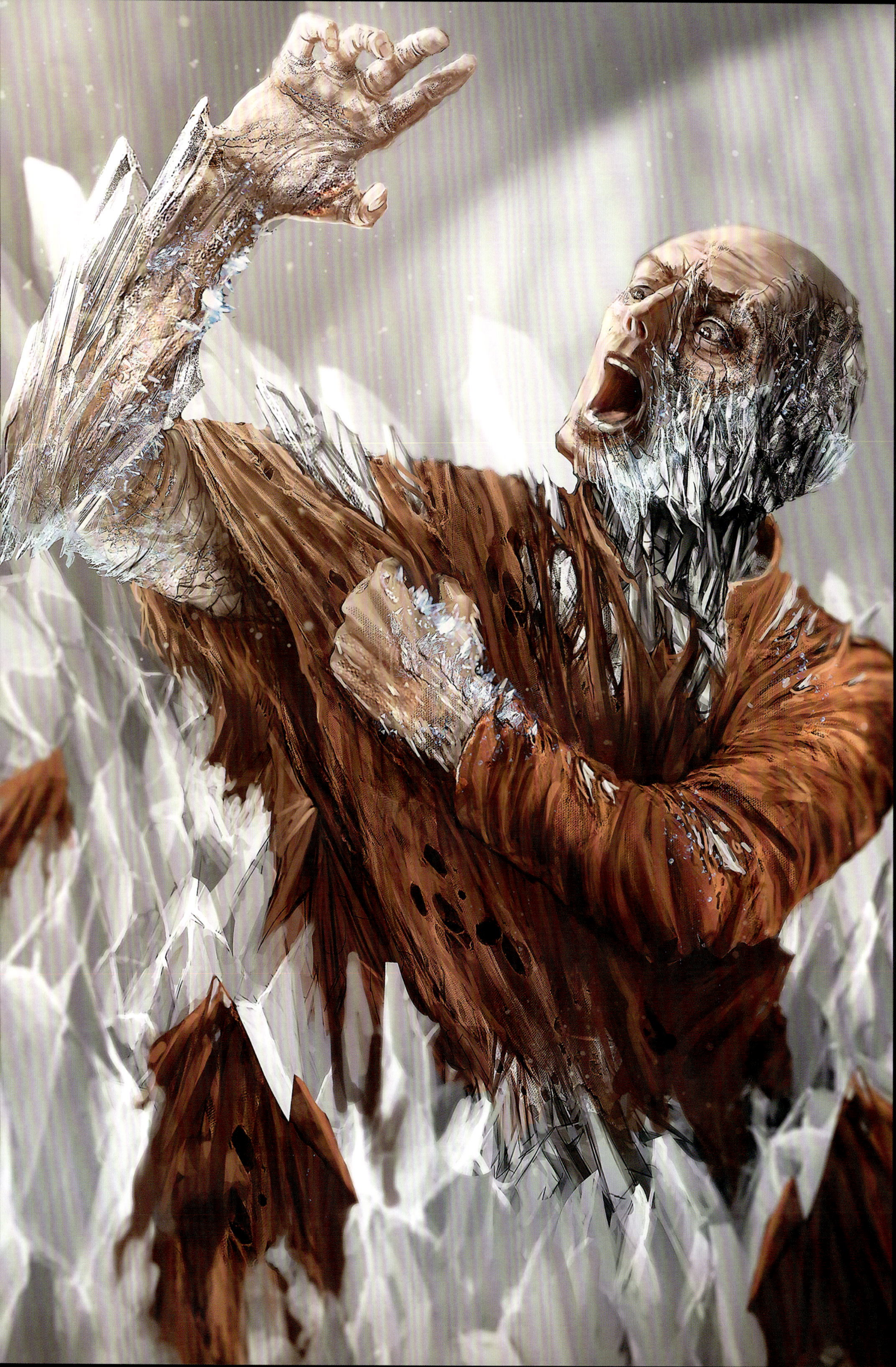

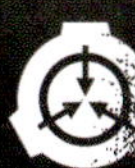

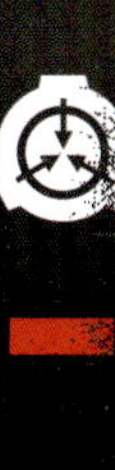

Experiment #409-1.

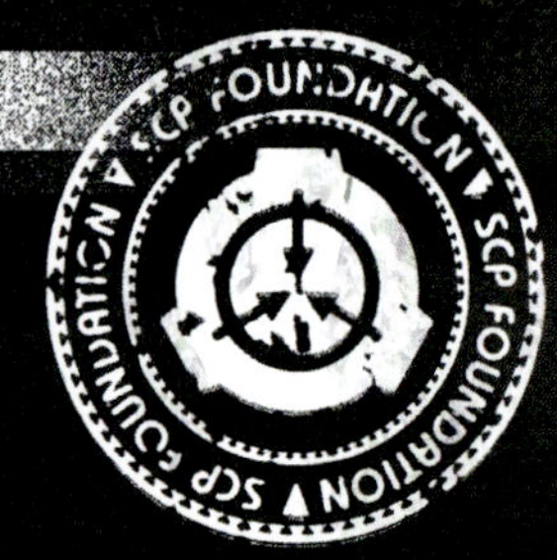

SCP-500

Title

PANACEA

Report by

far2

snorlison

Picture by

Dan Temirov

Access the original report on

scp-wiki.wikidot.com/scp-500

Date

Class

SAFE

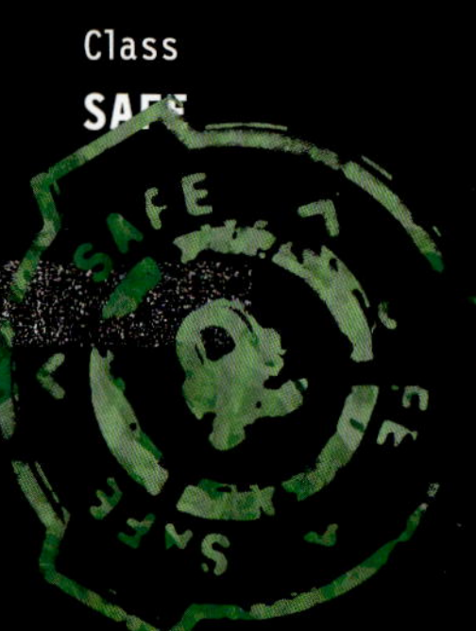

SPECIAL CONTAINMENT PROCEDURES

SCP-500 must be stored in a cool and dry place away from bright light. SCP-500 is only allowed to be accessed by personnel with level 4 security clearance to prevent misapplication.

DESCRIPTION

SCP-500 is a small plastic can which at the time of writing contains forty-seven (47) red pills. One pill, when taken orally, effectively cures the subject of all diseases within two hours, exact time depending on the severity and amount of the subject's conditions. Despite extensive trials, all attempts at synthesizing more of what is thought to be the active ingredient of the pills have been unsuccessful.

Note From Dr. Klein:

SCP personnel below Level 3 are now banned from handling SCP-500. This is not to be used to cure a hangover. Get AIDS and then ask permission.

Request 500-1774-k: Dr. [500-0022F] has requested one (1) SCP-500 pill for testing with SCP-038. Request has been approved.

Request 500-1862-b: Dr. Gears has requested one (1) SCP-500 pill for testing in SCP-914. Request has been approved.

Request 500-2354-f: Dr. ██████ has requested one (1) SCP-500 pill for testing with SCP-253. Request denied.

Request 500-5667-e: Dr. Gibbons has requested two (2) pills of SCP-500 for his personal medkit. Request denied.

Addendum 500-1: Two (2) pills have been authorized for use with SCP-008. As a result of conducting a series of tests on Class D subjects infected with SCP-008, it appears that even in the most advanced stages of the disease one whole pill will accomplish full recovery. Number of pills is fifty-seven (57) at the time of writing. - Dr. [500-0021D]

Addendum 500-2: One (1) pill has been authorized for use with SCP-409. SCP-500 was tested on Subject 409-D5 who was exposed to the effects of SCP-409. Complete recovery accomplished. See Addendum 409-1. Number of pills is fifty-six (56) at the time of writing. - Dr. [500-0021D]

Addendum 500-4: Request 500-1774-k approved. Five (5) pills have been used in experimentation with SCP-038. It has been determined that SCP-038 is capable of duplicating SCP-500; however, the success of the duplicated pills is limited. The duplicated pills are only effective in curing the subject 30% of the time, with chance of successful healing dropping as time since cloned increases. In 60% of the cases where the infection is permanent, symptoms of infection remain, though further infestation is neutralized. Repeated dosing with SCP-038 cloned pills is recommended for all personnel suffering from incurable conditions, as supply of SCP-500 remains extremely limited. All five (5) used samples of SCP-500 were returned. Number of pills is fifty-six (56) at the time of writing.

Addendum 500-5: During experiments with SCP-038, one (1) pill was stolen by personnel D-████ to, reportedly, "cure a hangover". Stricter controls for samples of SCP-500 given to other projects is suggested. Personnel D-████ has been terminated. Number of pills is fifty-five (55) at the time of writing.

Addendum 500-6: One (1) pill has been used with SCP-231-4. Number of pills is fifty-four (54) at the time of writing.

Addendum 500-7: One (1) pill has been used for Experiment 447-a. Number of pills is fifty-three (53) at the time of writing.

Addendum 500-8: One (1) pill has been used with SCP-208. Number of pills is fifty-two (52) at the time of writing.

Addendum 500-9: Request 500-1862-b approved. One (1) pill of SCP-500 is placed within SCP-914 with the setting at "Fine". Resulting object classified as SCP-427. Number of pills is fifty-one (51) at the time of writing.

Addendum 500-10: Five (5) pills have been taken for the Olympia Project although only two (2) were used. The remaining three (3) will be returned shortly. Upon return, number of pills will be forty-nine (49).

Addendum 500-11: Two (2) pills have been used for Experiment 217-██-██. Number of pills is forty-seven (47) at the time of writing.

Addendum 500-12: Request to have SCP-500 investigated for mental compulsion leading to obsessive fixation denied for triviality.

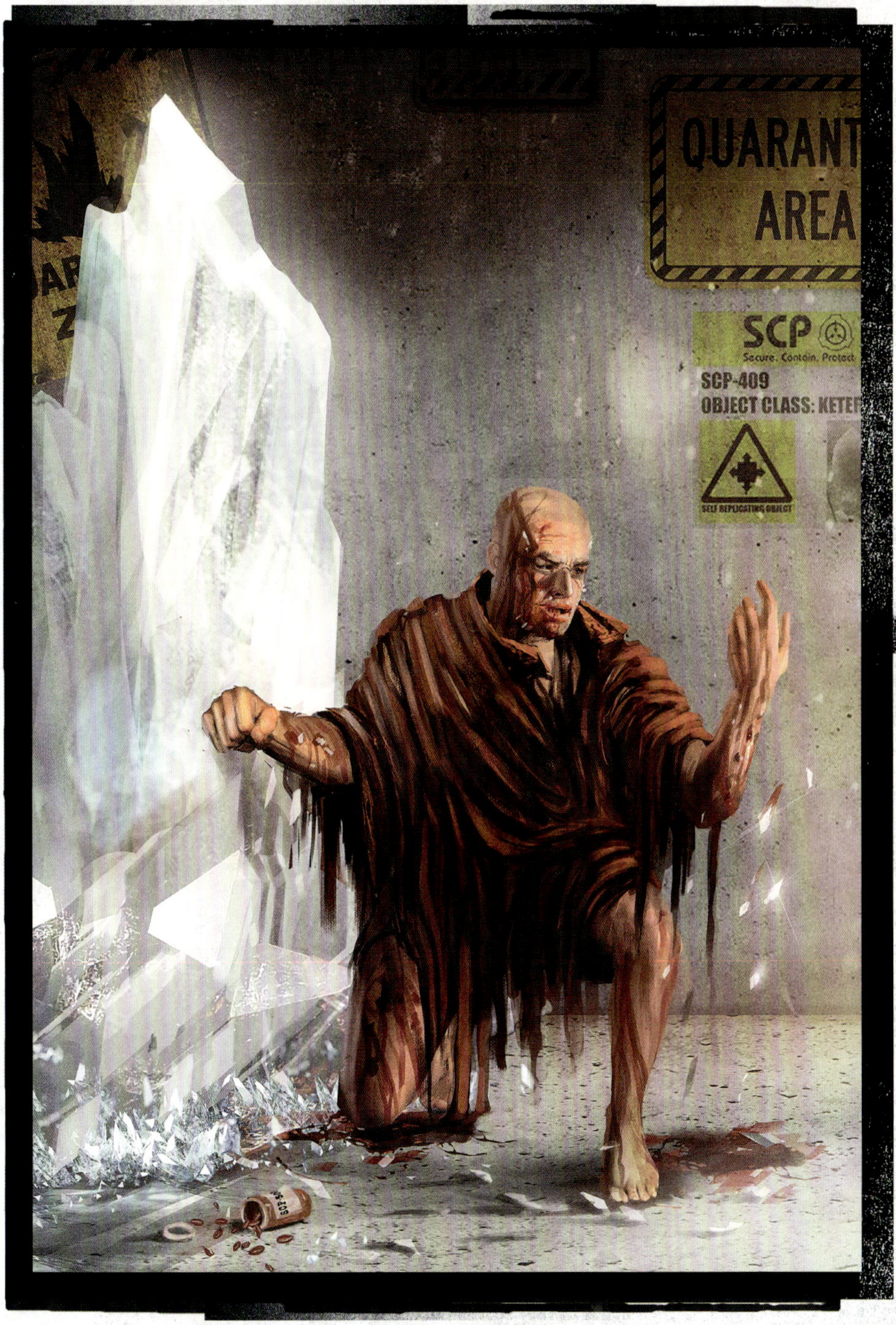

Subject 409-D5 treated with SCP-500 after experiment #409-1.

END OF REPORT

File >>> (03832

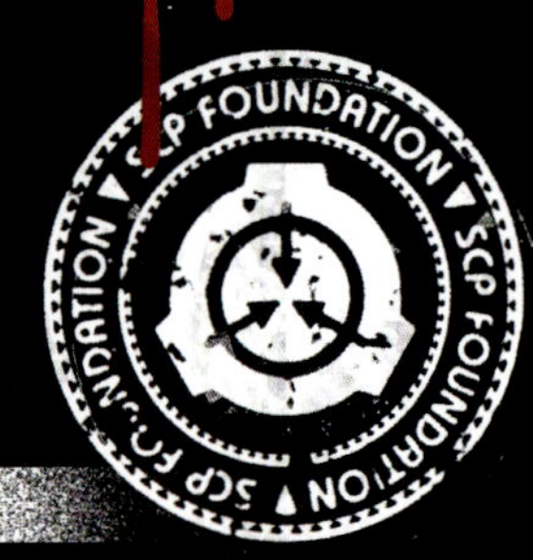

SCP-469

Title

MANY-WINGED ANGEL

Report by

ProfSnider

Picture by

Genocide Error

Access the original report on

scp-wiki.wikidot.com/scp-469

Date

Class

KETER

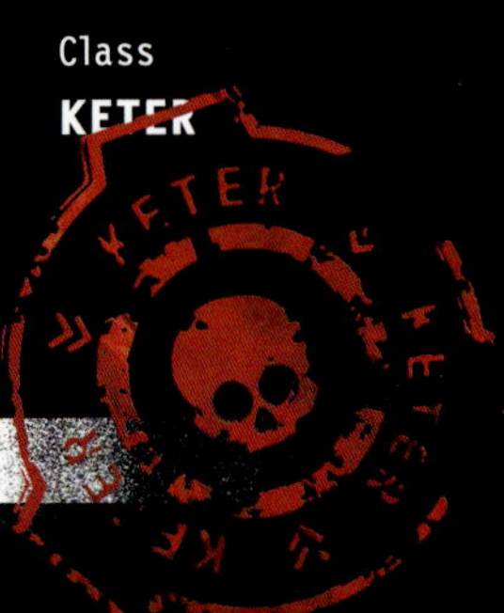

SPECIAL CONTAINMENT PROCEDURES

Subject is to be kept in an airtight, soundproof containment chamber, 15.24m x 15.24m x 15.24m (50ft x 50ft x 50ft) until a viable termination method is available. All personnel who enter SCP-469's chamber (Class D Only) must wear standard Sound-Proofing Anti-Resonance (SPAR) suits at all times while inside the chamber, and communicate only through written notes, hand gestures or text messaging. Absolutely no-one is to touch or even approach the subject with anything other than probing instruments.

All equipment taken into SCP-469's containment chamber must make as little noise as possible, or none at all. Cell phones are permitted for communication between personnel as long as they are muted.

DESCRIPTION

At first glance, SCP-469 appears to be a gargantuan pile of white feathers measuring 8.84m (29ft) in diameter and weighing several tons. Upon closer inspection however, subject is actually a vast array of enormous white avian wings, tightly curled up into a dense mound. Each wing varies in size and span, ranging from a few centimetres to several metres, but all are covered with glossy white feathers.

X-rays have revealed the wings to possess a hollow bone structure underneath similar to other birds, though these bones are very soft and flexible, allowing the wings to bend and coil up at angles other birds, and indeed other vertebrates, are incapable of. At the center of the mass is a large humanoid creature, curled up into a fetal position, to which all the wings are attached at its spine.

SCP-469 seems to feed exclusively on sounds and sound waves, using the energy gained from sound to grow newer and bigger wings and feathers. The louder the sound and/or the higher the frequency, the faster SCP-469 grows. Though it can be sustained by any sound, it seems to have a preference for rhythmic/musical noises, especially those produced by bells (see addendum). SCP-469 itself, however, seems to make no noise whatsoever due to the sound-absorbing structure of its plumage.

Any human or animal that touches or gets too close to the surface of the creature will be quickly enveloped by the outstretching wings and drawn inside. Despite the feathers' soft appearance, each hair has a sharp point that quickly pierces through clothing and into bare flesh, releasing a neurotoxin that immediately stimulates all the pain receptors in the body, as well as other stimulants to keep the victim from passing out too quickly. This is to make the victim scream loudly, thus feeding SCP-469 even more until the victim eventually goes into shock. SCP-469 is responsible for the loss of four personnel this way. Touching SCP-469 with dead or nonliving objects has no effect.

All termination methods of SCP-469 have been unsuccessful. Flamethrowers were initially used, but the noise from the discharging propellant as well as the crackling flames gave SCP-469 the energy to grow faster than it could be destroyed. Cutting and slicing instruments, due to their close range, resulted in failure and the loss of two agents. Acid immersion is being suggested.

Addendum: No bells are to be rung anywhere near SCP-469 (No less than 15.24m), including alarms and recordings of bells. The sound of ringing bells causes the humanoid in the center to "wake up", unfurling its wings and proceeding to [DATA EXPUNGED].

END OF REPORT

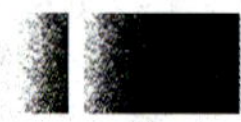

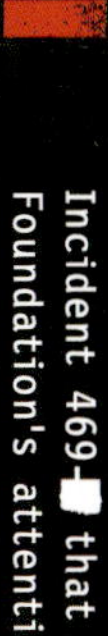

Incident 469-█ that brought the object to the Foundation's attention.

File >>> 082311

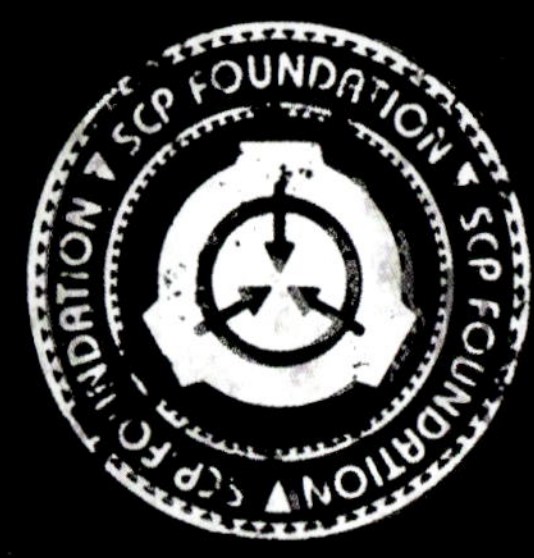

SCP-184

Title
THE ARCHITECT

Report by
Dr Gears

Picture by
Anna Agafonova
Jack Hainsworth

Access the original report on
scp-wiki.wikidot.com/scp-184

Date

Class
EUCLID

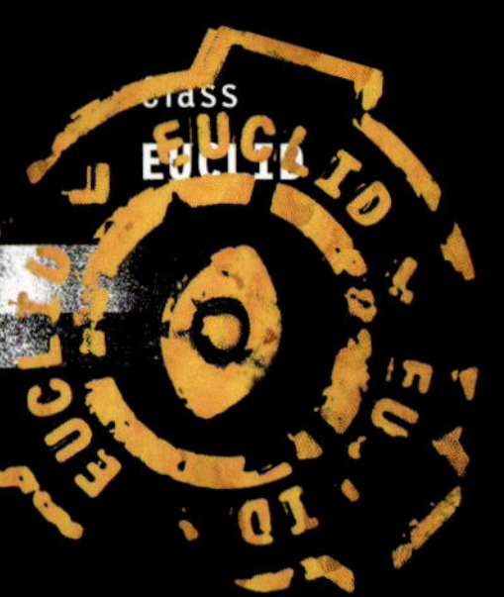

SPECIAL CONTAINMENT PROCEDURES

SCP-184 is not to be contained in any structure. SCP-184 is to be attached to a high-power electromagnet at all times. Should the electromagnet fail, agents are to report to SCP-184's containment area and prevent access to all unauthorized personnel until the electromagnet is restored to power. The containment area for SCP-184 is currently configured to resemble a park with SCP-184 and its containment magnet disguised as statuary. Any and all visitors are to be monitored.

Any structures affected by SCP-184 are to be demolished after review by [DATA EXPUNGED]. Final demolition approval or inclusion into SCP will also be determined by this body. No investigation is to be done into affected structures without approval and a rescue team on standby.

DESCRIPTION

SCP-184 is a small, smooth metallic object, 10 cm (4 in) tall and 10 cm (4 in) wide, in the shape of a dodecahedron. Each face of the figure has a circular hole in the center, and a small sphere is attached to each vertex. SCP-184 is made of an unknown, but highly magnetic, alloy about as hard as brass.

When inside an enclosed structure, SCP-184 expands the structure's inner dimensions without altering its outer dimensions. SCP-184 will increase the inner dimensions of any enclosed structure by several hundred meters each day, beginning one hour after entry into the structure. Initially, SCP-184 only extends the walls out, causing rooms to become much larger without adjusting the height of the room. This expansion continues until the original dimensions of the room have been tripled.

At this point, SCP-184 starts creating wholly new rooms. SCP-184 is apparently able to copy items from inside the structure, creating furnished rooms consistent with the rest of the structure. After a period of time, however, the expansion process appears to break down. For example, items will be made from inappropriate materials (glass books, a wooden microwave), rooms will be oddly-shaped, doors will open into blank walls, and hallways will be tiny or twist back around in long mazes. The new inside structures continue to be more and more odd, while the outside remains unchanged.

This behavior is most dramatically illustrated in homes; however, it has been observed in other instances, including a cardboard box. The changes do not go away with the removal of SCP-184, but no additional structures are created.

ADDENDUM 184 - 1: NOTES FROM DR. █████

I don't think I need to stress the fact that this thing can NEVER be allowed into Site-19. We may need to look into different containment at some point, but for the time being, we will keep it in the open, immovable, and hidden.

ADDENDUM 184 - 2: LOCATIONS OF INTEREST

It is currently hypothesized that SCP-184 or an anomaly with a similar effect may be responsible for the creation of Locations of Interest such as Backdoor SoHo, and Chūgoku Cellar. Investigation into SCP-184 as a potential origin for these spaces is ongoing.

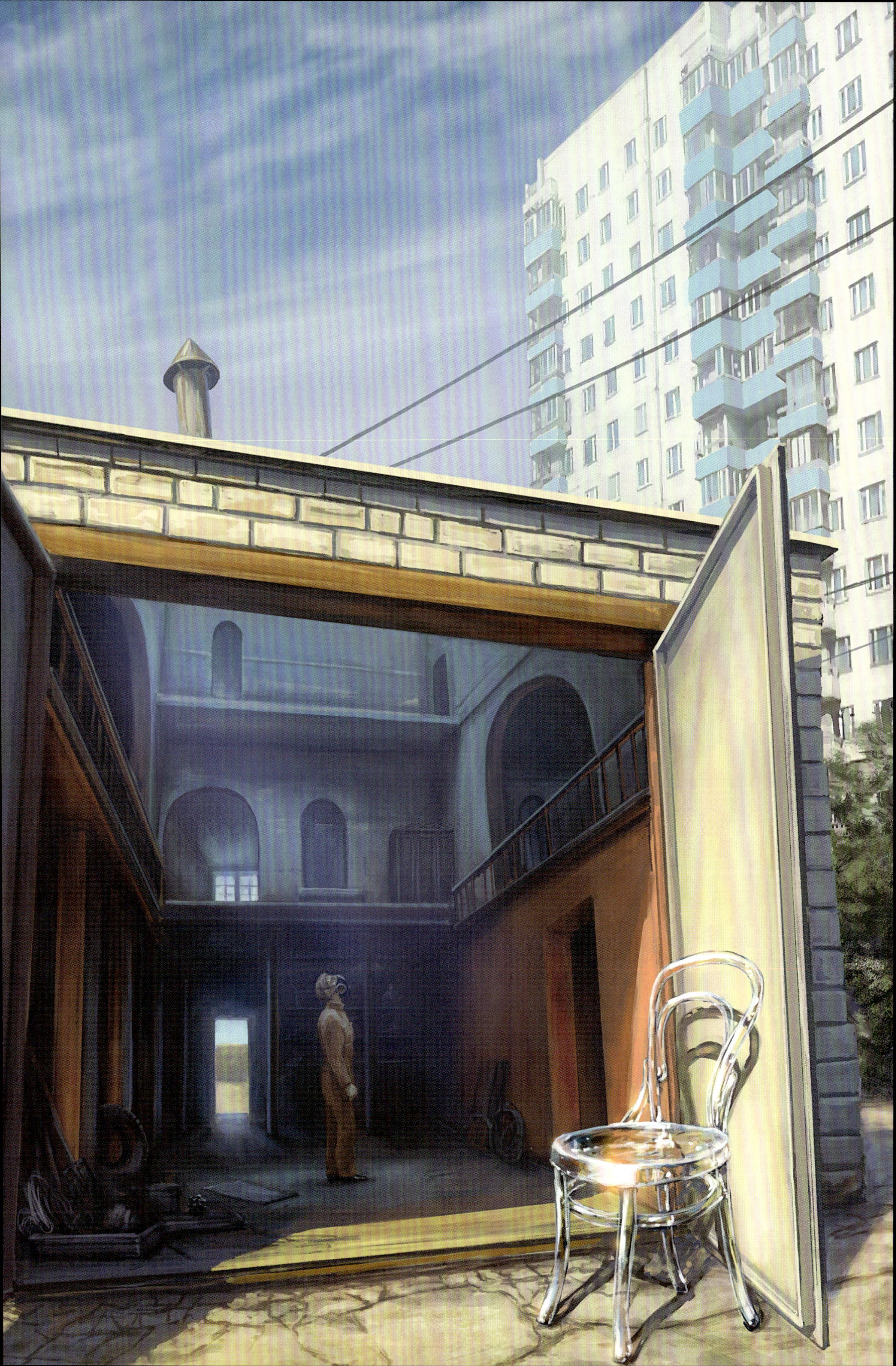

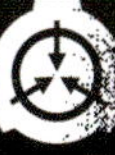

The working principle of SCP-184 observed on the instance of a small room.

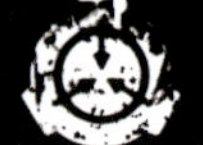

Research Library File ▸ 184

ADDENDUM 184 - 38RB: NOTES ON RECOVERY

SCP-184 was recovered in the Kowloon Walled City in June of ████. Reports of the city's bizarre and explosive growth attracted Operatives, who soon learned of SCP-184, held in the possession of [DATA EXPUNGED]. After several police crackdowns, Mobile Task Force Zeta-9 was dispatched and recovered SCP-184 with minimal losses. The final effect of exposure to SCP-184 on both the City and inhabitants may never fully be understood due to the reckless actions of local law enforcement, which destroyed several affected sections of the city before Operatives could take action to prevent it.

Interviews with residents yielded minimal information, with a communal "wall of silence" being the major response. A few documents indicated that SCP-184 could be brought into a home and allowed to affect the dwelling for 50 pounds sterling per half hour. These documents were unconfirmed by residents.

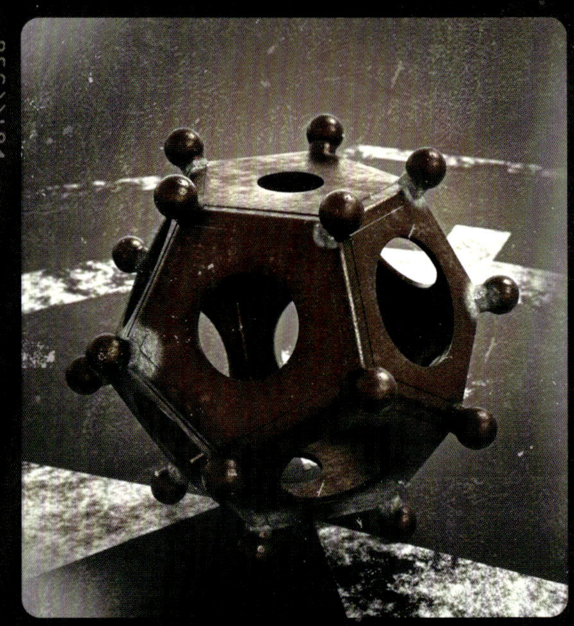

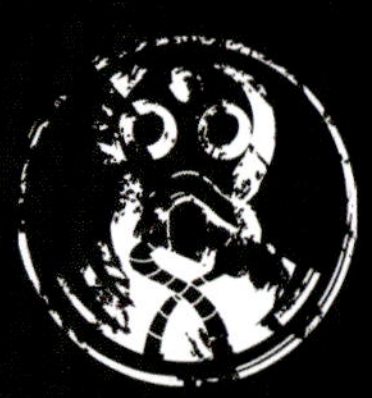

PERSONAL LOG OF GORDON RICHARDS

MEMBER OF MOBILE TEAM ZETA-9, THE MOLE RATS

Date: June 3rd, ████

Dispatched to the "Kowloon Walled City" to recover an object and document anything affected by it. I have never seen such a horrible place. The filth is everywhere, whole walls and even structures made of garbage. If you crack your suit for even a second, you get flooded by the smell of smoke, cooking, sweat, machine oil and excrement. Henry fell into a pit used as a sewer on the ground level after breaking through a trash walkway. He was fine, the suit was just filthy, but he threw up and had to be removed. I'm not sure if he's going to work out.

Everyone here avoids us like the plague, or darts out to throw trash or insults. They are a tribe, and a territorial one at that. The sheer crush of humanity is intimidating, and I'm glad I have the suit between me and them. The object is supposed to be somewhere in the core of this mass, but getting there is going to be tricky.

Date: June 4th, ████

Local law enforcement led by Agents did a bunch of raids last night. Cleared people out of some of the areas we need to go in, but there are so many people here it's hard to notice any difference. Yesterday's recon helped uncover a couple "homes" affected by this thing. They don't look like much, the same squalid homes as everyone else, but they are too big inside. It's an odd feeling, standing with your hand on the wall, and knowing that by all rights you should be six feet outside the structure, in mid-air. Henry is better today, but seems really jumpy. Lev took him aside and talked to him last night, and I hope it's helped. I'm getting worried about him. Caught him muttering to himself over the radio today.

Told him to knock it off, but didn't report it, maybe I should have. I think I'm going to ask for him to be put on a different unit after this.

Deep recon this evening, we're splitting up to try and hunt down where they are storing this thing. Lev and I pulled the short stick and have to hike it around the sewer system. Honestly, it can't be any worse than topside; at least I won't have to keep seeing the blank, empty faces of these people.

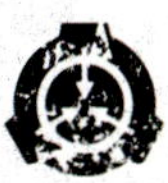

Date: June 6th, ████

Henry is dead. We didn't get back until early this morning; we'd been off the radio for several hours because of all the interference. It seems areas affected by this thing screw with radio waves pretty bad. The sewer was a nightmare, but no sign of alteration by the item. When we came back up, Paul gave me the news. Henry and Paul were exploring near the center of the city when they got attacked. A mob of people swarmed them and dragged Henry off. Paul was hurt and his suit was badly damaged, and he had to leave for medical attention. Henry was screaming over the radio for a while, and then it cut off. Paul and a couple other Mole Rats charged in with some agents to recover Henry, but after a few minutes, Henry came back on the radio.

His receiver was broken, but he could still broadcast. One of the Agents was recording, and he played it back to Lev and I, to see if any of it made sense to us. It didn't. He was rambling and sounded like he was hurt. Kept talking about the endless heart of the city, the hell of glass, just crazy stuff. Paul and the rescue team kept trying to find him, but suddenly his radio cut out again.

Henry came tearing down one of those tiny halls, helmet off and screaming like a mad man. He ran right by Paul and smashed an Agent into a wall on his way by. He slammed into a dead end and just exploded through it, right out of the building. He fell six stories onto some metal junk. It took an hour to get his body untangled. We're done screwing around here. Agent Parks, Lev and me are rounding up what amounts to the city elders, and we're getting to the damn bottom of this.

Date: June 7th, ████

Interrogation went well. Agent Parks asked the questions, we provided what he called "negative consequences for non-cooperation". The first guy, some Triad punk, didn't want to talk. Two broken legs later, and he was a lot more open. Said the thing was called "The Builder", and nobody knew when it first came to the city. He never had anything to do with it, just helped stand guard outside rooms where it was working. He said that was all he knew, and that we had to talk to one of the elders, Long-Wen, if we wanted it. He apologized for Henry's death, said it was just the way of things. I broke his jaw in three places.

Long-Wen may be the oldest-looking man I've ever seen, and with a will like iron. He just took everything we dished out, and didn't say a word. Parks said that the next stop was his wife and grandkids, and that got him talking. Told us it was kept in one of the oldest parts of the city, some old temple. It had grown, and made wonderful things, but only the worthy could look upon it and not be overwhelmed by it. He said Henry was shown the wonders, in the hopes that he would be able to convince us to not take The Builder, but that he was not worthy, and was broken.

We made him show us where they keep it. Long-Wen said it wouldn't do any good, that it was buried too deep. They moved it deep inside when they first caught wind of the Agents; he said we'd never get it back. We're doing Deep Work tomorrow, and we're not coming out without it.

Date: June 10th, ████

Been out for a while. This place is amazing. At first, it was just a temple that was too big inside, neat but nothing new. Then we went in deeper. Whole rooms, altars, everything re-created and rearranged by this thing. It's like someone built twelve whole temples inside this one tiny structure. Agent Parks set up a recall point in the main hall with some other Agents to make sure nobody sneaks up on us. We suited up and went to work. It started getting odd after hour six. Lots of hallways, not as many rooms. Then, eighty-three rooms all connected by those sliding doors, each with a tiny Buddha in the center of the floor, and nothing else. Lev grabbed a few for samples. We knew things were getting odd when we

Research
Library
File ▸ 184

came to a perfect reproduction of the first altar room, but appearing to be made of one solid mass of wood.

Thing was beautiful and totally seamless, and not a single tool mark on anything. Paul found some documents, and we scanned them back to Parks. He said they were about the object; apparently they're calling it SCP-184 now. Parks said it talks about how they moved 184 deeper each time it made a new area. They thought it was some gift from God or something. Used it to expand rooms, if people would donate to the temple, or at least to the gangs that controlled it at the time.

I've never been in a place like this. It's getting harder to maneuver. The halls are starting to get strange, they go up at funny angles, and the last few rooms have been tiny. By Lev's count, we should be twenty feet above the roof of this whole city by now.

Date: June 12th(?), ████

I'm getting sick of this place. Came to a branch yesterday, had to split the team. I drew the "up" hallway, and set out. Not sure how long I've been climbing. The halls aren't regular anymore; they wave in and out, like a frozen earthquake. Everything seems to be made of stone here. Managed to squeeze into a side room to catch my breath, once I looked around, I saw everything was made of jade. It was all colored right, and had the right texture, but it was jade. Bed, chairs, table, books, everything. I sat on the bed for two hours and didn't think. I got up and smashed the jade lamp that was probably worth more than my life, and left.

I'm not feeling well. I feel really disconnected here, like an astronaut or something. It's not like other areas I've been in. Never felt so alone. I'm fine, I know that. It's Henry dying, the whole rotten city outside, and me being alone and able to think too much. Rats are tested for mental stability, and I passed with flying colors. It's just my nerves. I'm sitting on a chair made of thousands of tiny dragon statues, writing on a table made of super-dense paper, and I am fine.

Date: June (?)

I've been out too long. Food low. Water low. Not out yet, but getting there. Hearing things. Keep thinking I hear voices. Been climbing for days. Saw light today. At the end of a side-hall, bright yellow light. I climbed into the hall and ran. Smashed through the door, and it was a room. Millions of candles, all lit, but just another room. Pulled off my helmet, smashed the candles with it. Broke my lenses, neck seal, radio. Didn't care. Sat and cried for hours. Dropped a pick down the shaft today, never heard it hit bottom. Almost jumped to go get it, but stopped. Got to find this thing. Going to smash it to bits. Stomp it. Crush it.

Date: June (?)

Food out. Suit can't make any more water. Saw a hall with ten thousand doors. Ran down it, smashed a bunch, then kept climbing. Lost my boots. Floor looked like carpet. Made of super-sharp stone. Cut suit to ribbons. Feet too. Blood all over the shaft. Hope it appreciates it. Going to crush this thing. Feel it shatter in my hand. Hate this place. Keep hearing Henry. Keep telling him he's dead. Won't listen.

Date: (?)

Top of shaft. Hall to forever. Lights everywhere. Going to kill the heart.

Date: (?)

Hell is Heaven
Heaven is Hell
Life is Wonderful

Gordon Richards went missing during the recovery of SCP-184, presumed KIA.

SCP-184 recovered by Team Zeta-9.
Journal recovered in rubble left from destruction of SCP-184 affected temple.

END OF REPORT

File >>> 093231

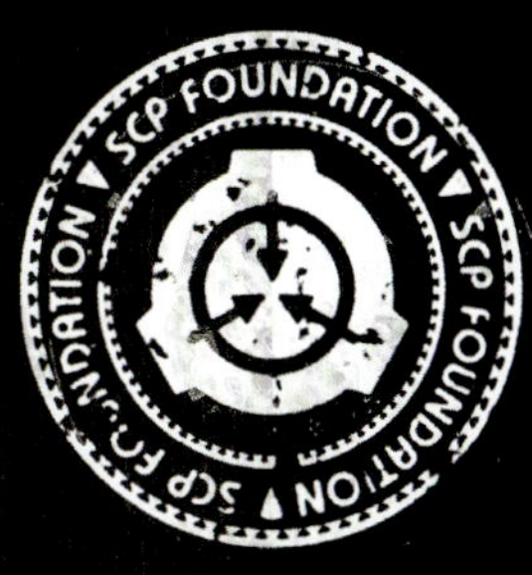

SCP-1440

Title

THE OLD MAN FROM NOWHERE

Report by

Dmatix

Picture by

Alexey Lebedev

Access the original report on

scp-wiki.wikidot.com/scp-1440

Date

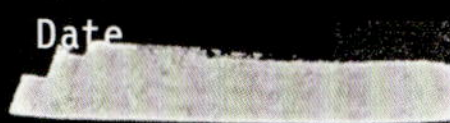

Class

KETER

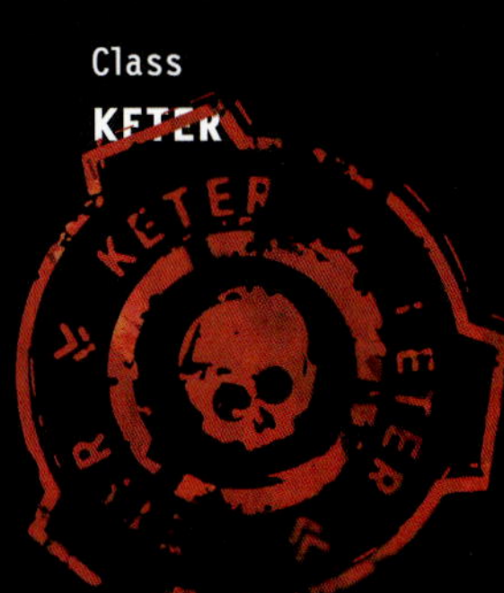

SPECIAL CONTAINMENT PROCEDURES

SCP-1440 is currently uncontained and its location is unknown since its last containment breach. Due to the nature of SCP-1440, the Foundation may not have the means to contain it without risking an unacceptable loss of resources and personnel. Until suitable containment procedures can be found, focus should be given to the location and surveillance of SCP-1440 and to minimizing civilian exposure to it through the identification of its travel pattern.

DESCRIPTION

SCP-1440 is a man of unknown ethnicity and age. When questioned about its name, place or time of birth, SCP-1440 will refuse to answer, although it is unclear if this is due to the subject being unwilling to share this information or not possessing it. Though the subject's appearance is that of an octogenarian, it has not shown any signs of aging in the fifty (50) years since first coming to the attention of the Foundation. SCP-1440's anomalous nature becomes apparent once it comes into contact with human population or man-made objects and remains in contact with them for longer than a few days; SCP-1440 has an acute adverse effect on everything connected to humanity. Prolonged exposure of any man-made object or person to it will cause increasingly destructive events to occur in SCP-1440's vicinity, until the destruction or death of said human element. The only exceptions to this are SCP-1440 itself and its belongings (its clothes, a sack made of unidentified material, a pack of worn playing cards, and a small glass cup).

SCP-1440 appears to be aware of its effect on human populations, and will attempt to avoid coming into contact with them whenever possible. Despite these intentions, SCP-1440 is compelled to travel in what seems to be a highly complex pattern, which invariably leads it into contact with human population. The exact nature of this pattern has not yet been successfully analyzed, and SCP-1440 has not been able to provide any information concerning it. The subject is not actively hostile and will not resist attempts to contain it, though all such attempts have failed and led to a considerable loss of personnel and resources due to the aforementioned anomalous properties.

SCP-1440 was first brought to the Foundation's attention when it approached Dr. █████, a researcher at Site-██, on her commute to work. SCP-1440 showed unexplained knowledge of Dr. █████'s work for the Foundation and requested her assistance. When Dr. █████ inquired about the nature of the assistance the subject required, it responded that it hoped the Foundation would be able to "destroy [him]". SCP-1440 was brought to Site-██ for questioning, which led to the destruction of the site, the deaths of ███ personnel and the destruction of six (6) Safe and Euclid-level SCP objects. All other attempts at containing SCP-1440 have resulted in similar occurrences.

ADDENDUM SCP-1440-A

The following is an interview conducted with SCP-1440 during the fourth attempt to contain it, on Area-142. The log was being stored on a remote server, hence its survival.

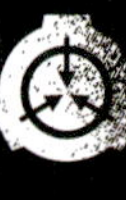

SCP-1440, as last seen.

Interview Log 1440-7

Interviewer: Dr. ███

Interviewed: SCP-1440

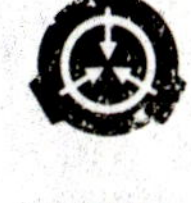

Research Library File ▸ 1440

Foreword: Following the arrival of SCP-1440 to Area-142, personnel began complaining about severe headaches and nausea. In the next two days, three of the four on-site water purification filters broke down, Area-142's hangar collapsed, causing the deaths of multiple airmen and Dr.███– previously in perfect physical condition – suffered a complete collapse of both kidneys and both lungs simultaneously.

<Begin Log>

Dr.███: Good afternoon, SCP-1440.

SCP-1440: And to you, Doctor.

Dr.███: Do you know why we brought you here?

SCP-1440: Of course I do, and applaud you for still attempting to contain me, but since your last three attempts I came to realize you cannot help me. It would be best if you let me go, for your own good. The First Brother is already standing behind you, Doctor, you would best hurry.

Dr.███: You mentioned these brothers before, three if I recall correctly.

SCP-1440: Three, Aye. Different, but one and the same. All cruel, all vengeful, all capable of holding a grudge for a long time. They are the cause of my misfortune, and therefore the cause of yours. [Subject appears to notice something behind Dr.███, though video and audio feed reveal nothing unusual.] The Second Brother joins the First, time is running short. Release me, or I cannot vouch for your safety. It might already be too late.

Dr.███: I'm afraid I can't do that. Besides, you mentioned three brothers; if the third isn't here yet, we must have some time left.

SCP-1440: *[Shakes head.]* The Third never appears. In that, he is crueler than both his brothers, for he knows his appearance is the only thing that will set me free. I have spent time untold searching for him, trying to return his prize and those I won from his brothers, but to no avail. *[Subject looks behind Dr. ███ again, sighs]* The Second has his hands on your shoulders, it is too late now. Doom is never far behind the Second. Before you perish, my poor child, allow me to give you a word of advice.

Dr.███: Go ahead.

SCP-1440: Should you choose to challenge Death to a game of cards for your life, there is one thing you must never do.

Dr.███: And what is that?

SCP-1440: Win.

<End Log>

Closing statement: At that moment, the on-site nuclear device stored in Area-142 detonated, despite multiple failsafes. Area-142 was destroyed and all on-site personnel were killed. SCP-1440 was spotted more than three thousand (3,000) kilometers away from Area-142's location a week following its destruction, suffering no apparent harm. After three additional containment breaches, attempts to contain SCP-1440 have been suspended indefinitely.

Addendum SCP-1440-B: Due to the growing size of human population and its rapid expansion into previously empty areas, SCP-1440 attested during its fifth containment that it is becoming increasingly difficult for it to avoid contact with humanity while still adhering to its compulsion. Analysis of the subject's traveling pattern is continuing, as are efforts to find a permanent containment procedure.

END OF REPORT

File >>> 193234

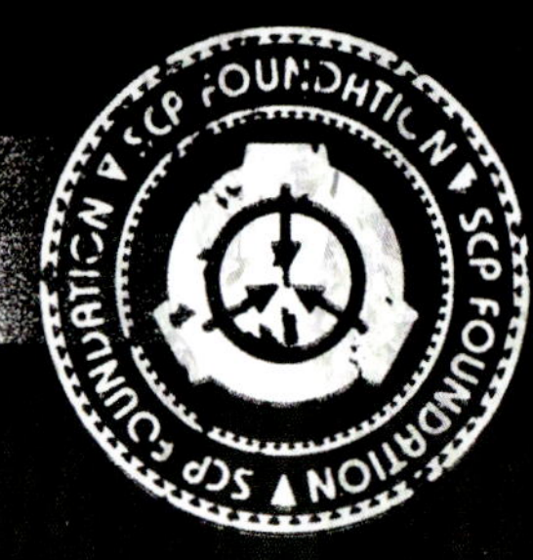

SCP-2004

Title

PERSONAL DATA ASSISTANTS OF THE GODS

Report by

SnakeoilSage

Picture by

Pavel Kobyzev

Access the original report on

scp-wiki.wikidot.com/scp-2004

Date

Class

KETER

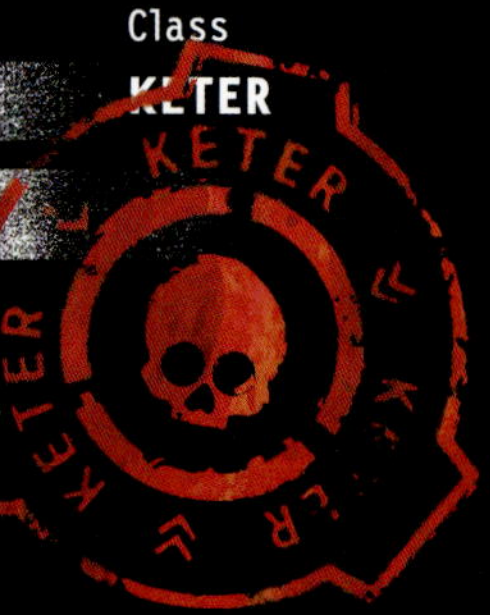

SPECIAL CONTAINMENT PROCEDURES

SCP-2004 is contained at Armed Reliquary Containment Area-02. Standard memetic countermeasures have proven insufficient in the past; therefore, SCP-2004 is to be handled utilizing Containment Procedure-2004 "Blind Lead the Blind." See ARC A-02 Clearance-04 Procedures manual for more information. Any individuals affected by SCP-2004 (hereby dubbed SCP-2004-1) are to be handled in the same manner.

DESCRIPTION

SCP-2004 is a set of five hand-held personal data assistants of unknown, possibly extraterrestrial origin. Since acquisition, all but one have become inert and no longer function. SCP-2004 is composed of an unknown material whose molecular structure matches nothing on the Foundation's expanded periodic table of elements, flexible like plastic yet resistant to extreme temperatures and physical damage. Each device is transparent green with smooth edges, with no apparent power source or input/output ports. SCP-2004 activates when it makes physical contact with an active bioelectric field, projecting a three-dimensional holographic document.

The image projected from SCP-2004 is black text on a white background, written in a pictographic language (L-2004). It appears to be based on stylized astronomical constellations and molecular chemical bonds, using patterns of dots, circles and slashes to create increasingly complex sentence structures. Reading or hearing L-2004 produces a memetic anomaly, making translation efforts extremely hazardous. As such, only four percent of the document has been translated (see below).

Early symptoms of L-2004's memetic infection are not immediate, and may progress for several days before being recognized. Affected subjects, SCP-2004-1, demonstrate increased anxiety and irritability, obsessive behavior, paranoia, and hostility. Instances begin to lose their sense of self, or become convinced they are someone else, insisting that their previous life is a carefully designed falsehood. After a period of six to eight days, the language centers of SCP-2004-1's brain are re-programmed, with symptoms similar to agnosia and aphasia. They lose the ability to comprehend or understand any language, written or verbal, save for L-2004. By the end of the second stage they become fluent in both the written and verbal forms of L-2004, and have been observed conversing with other instances of SCP-2004-1.

After fourteen days, affected subjects exhibit a complete shift in mental faculties and personality. Preliminary tests indicate an increase in cognitive function and heightened states of awareness and intelligence. Hostile to non-affected humans, they actively try to escape containment and work together to spread the anomaly, particularly to those that individual SCP-2004-1 instances once felt close to. They also demonstrate an unprecedented amount of technical skill. In at least three incidents, using otherwise mundane materials, separate instances of SCP-2004-1 have manufactured artifacts that are either anomalous, or so far beyond the Foundation's current scientific knowledge as to appear so.

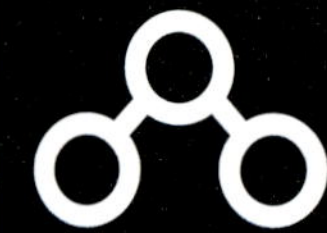

Non-memetic Sample of L-2004. Symbol has been identified as a water molecule.

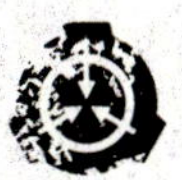

Artifact Number	Designation	Analysis
I-001	EMP Device	SCP-2004-1-07 surreptitiously acquired a silver pocketwatch from Dr. T█████ and modified it, using materials removed from a containment cell observation camera and the electronic lock keypad. When exposed to a strong magnetic field (such as that produced by an MRI), I-001 created an electromagnetic pulse. SCP-2004-1-07 attempted to escape in the ensuing confusion, and was fatally injured by security forces.
I-002	Energized Ion-Gas Weapon	As part of Experiment T022, SCP-2004-1-15 was provided with a variety of nonspecific materials to test its technical abilities. After forty-five minutes of uninterrupted work, Level 4 Supervisors decided to halt the experiment and confiscated the device. When tested under safe conditionsw I-002 fired a 1-cm ball of ionized plasma, measured at 10,000 kelvin. The device developed a fatal heat build-up during testing, destroying its internal mechanisms.
I-003	Communications Device	I-003 was constructed by several instances of SCP-2004-1, building its components separately to avoid notice. The device pirated the intercom and internal data network systems of Area-02, introducing subliminal samples of L-2004 into the facility. Level 4 Supervisor Stephen Sinclair has been posthumously awarded the Foundation Medal of Valor for activating the facility's sarin gas countermeasures, destroying ██ instances of SCP-2004-1 who were attempting to utilize Keter-level SCPs also housed in Area-02.

Currently there is no method of treating SCP-2004-1 once they have entered the second "aphasia" stage. Use of Class-A amnestics during the preliminary infection period (one to three days following exposure) has only had a 60% success rate in removing its effects. Infection is positive in 100% of exposed cases.

A partial, non-memetic translation of SCP-2004's display is provided below.

Class: Wise ##### is Invincible.

#####: Species #####-001 is ##### be confined ##### homeworld. Any ##### of #####-001 are ##### be removed from ##### colonies ##### the ##### and returned ##### homeworld pending application of ##### Level 4 Indoctrination. Level 5 Indoctrinated are ##### be granted self-containment authority. Level 5 #####-001 ##### designated Secure ##### Foundation.

#####: Species #####-001 is an adaptive ##### life-form known within the ##### as an #####-Level Threat. In no less than ##### instances, Species #####-001 has caused ##### spontaneous anomalous ##### breakdowns, leading ##### 15 class ##### extinction #####. It is the judgement of the ##### Committee, with the approval of the #####, that Species #####-001 be contained on ##### homeworld until such time that ##### processes have achieved ##### as described ##### the Articles of #####. Species #####-001 is ##### aggressive, hostile and ##### claim its #####, and the peoples throughout the ##### cannot be subjected to such a threat. Under no circumstances is Species #####-001 ##### be exposed ##### Language #####, which could result in a catastrophic Indoctrination failure and re-emergence of their ##### identity and anomalous #####.

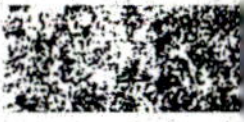

05 SECURITY CLEARANCE REQUIRED

05 Addendum: Some have questioned the necessity of "baiting the hook" this way, considering the potential consequences. I remind each of you that a catastrophic reshuffling of reality would occur if the gestalt "disbelieves" itself out of existence. Even a handful of Level 04's made aware, however indirectly, of L-2004 is enough to preserve it. The anomalous manifestations, these "monsters from the id," are the result, but as long as the Foundation stands resolute prospective losses remain within acceptable levels.

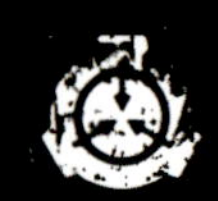

The Gentlemen have expressed some concern, however. The growing amount of Keter-level manifestations is troubling. The indoctrinated may be subconsciously straining against the cage. All of us must redouble our efforts. Everything is at risk, but transcendence is the reward.

Secure humanity.
Contain the gestalt.
Protect reality.
We are so close.

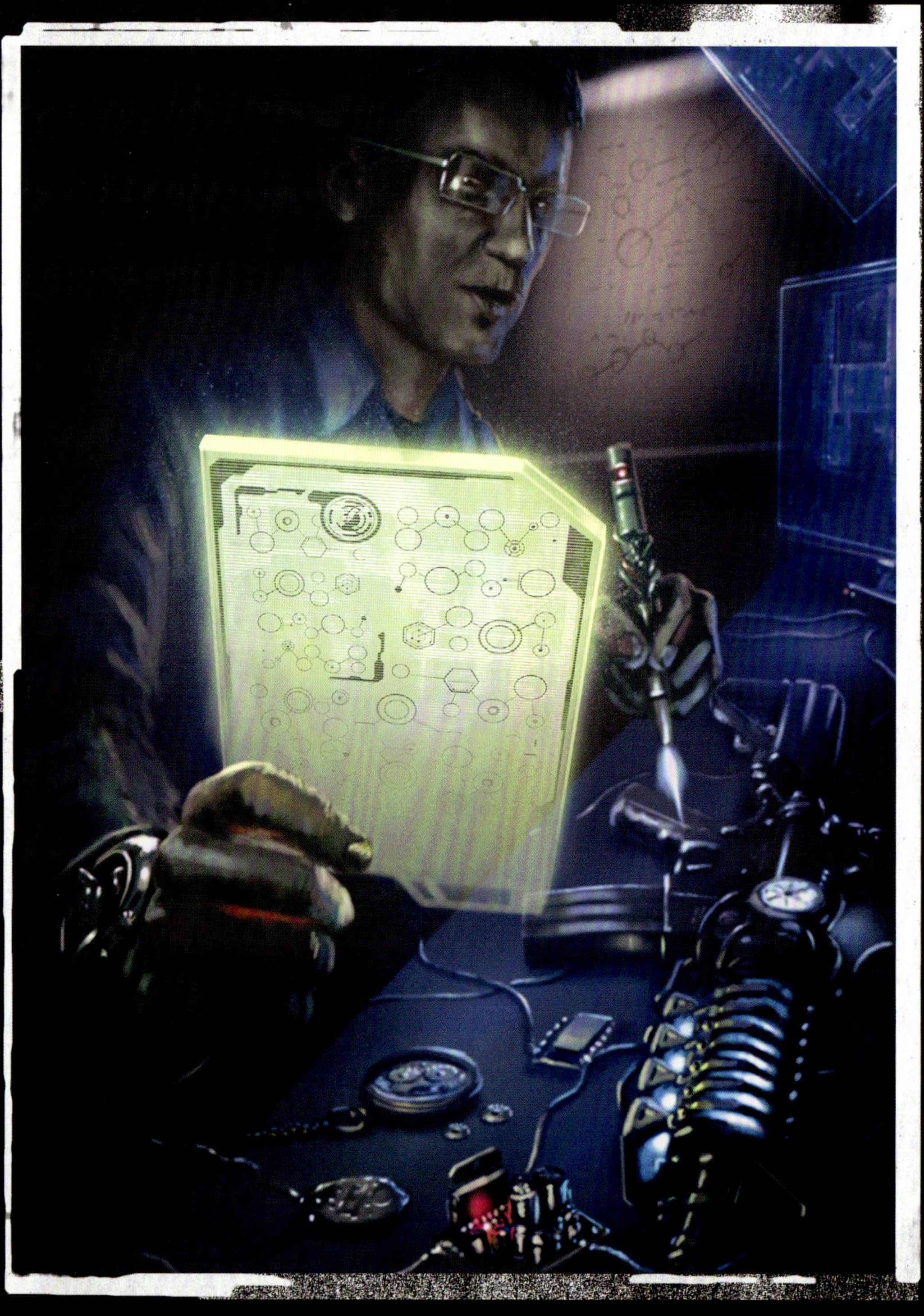

END OF REPORT

SPECIAL CONTAINMENT PROCEDURES

To prevent degradation of SCP-1123 and its markings, it is to be kept in a hermetically sealed container in an argon gas atmosphere when not being tested. During testing and storage, light exposure should be limited to 50 lux, temperature between 20 and 24 degrees Celsius, and relative humidity at 55%. SCP-1123 should only be transported in its container, and should not be handled except during a controlled experiment. When not being tested, it will be stored in a secure climate-controlled locker at Site 19.

DESCRIPTION

SCP-1123 is a human skull missing the lower mandible and all its teeth. Across the exterior squama frontalis is modern Khmer script, written in human blood, that translates as "Remember." Both skull and blood have been definitively dated to 197█ and genetic testing confirms that both are from the same individual.

SCP-1123 was discovered in 198█ by Colonel Hu █████ of the Vietnamese People's Army within a collection of human remains in the custody of the ████ ████ ██████ Museum in ███ ███, Cambodia. SCP-1123 was intercepted by Foundation agents as it was being delivered to Hanoi.

The Khmer script is badly faded, and invisible to most subjects beyond 5 meters distance. However, when a subject approaches SCP-1123 they will report the script becoming progressively more visible until, at less than 1 meter, they will report it appearing as if freshly drawn. A few subjects at this distance report the writing is "still wet." This effect is not reproducible with optical equipment. To record the script photographically requires optical enhancement or UV lighting. (The latter is not approved for use with SCP-1123 as it contributes to the degradation of the object.) Subjects at this distance will often also report other anomalous sensory phenomena, including smells (such as cooking meat or ashes), sounds (such as soft crying, low heartbeats or breathing, or distant footsteps), and tactile responses (such as grit in the eyes, ants crawling on the back of the hand, or glass splinters in the sole of the foot.)

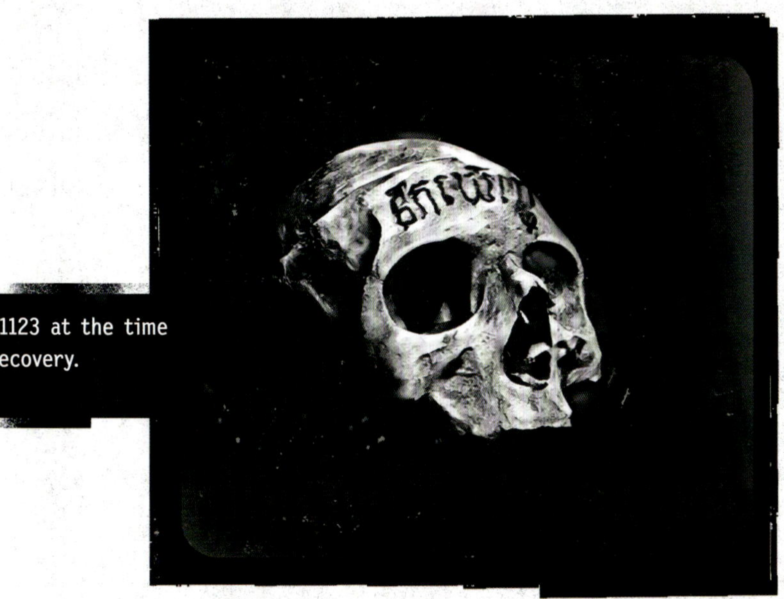

SCP-1123 at the time of recovery.

File >>> 09223

SCP-1123

Title

ATROCITY SKULL

Report by

sandrewswann

Picture by

Julia Galkina

Access the original report on

scp-wiki.wikidot.com/scp-1123

Date

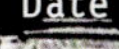

Class

SAFE

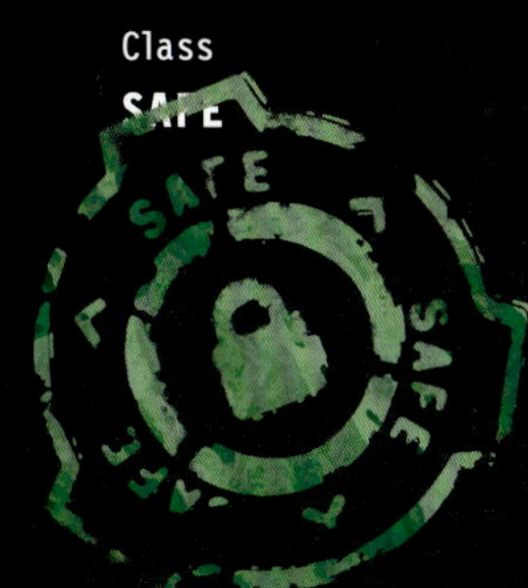

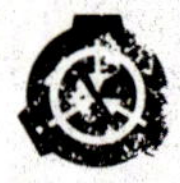

Research Library File ▸ 1123

When subjects touch the surface of SCP-1123, they will experience a dissociative fugue state. Initiation of the fugue state appears instantaneous and is not affected by cessation of contact with SCP-1123. Symptoms of the fugue persist for ninety minutes to six hours. The fugue is characterized by confusion, disorientation, and adoption of a new identity and memories which consist of knowledge, including language, previously unknown to the subject. During the fugue the subject will lose all memories of their prior identity. Subjects have shown various reactions to this, ranging from near-catatonia to attempts to escape or attack Foundation personnel. As the fugue state subsides, the subject will regain memories of their prior identity, but will also retain memory of the new, imprinted identity and all the knowledge associated with it. Subjects have said that it was "as if they lived an entire other life as some other person" in the period between touching SCP-1123 and recovering from the fugue.

Post-fugue interviews have provided enough corroborative information in ███ of ███ studied cases for researchers to find historical documentation confirming the imprinted personality's correspondence to a specific individual who had lived at some time prior to the subject. There appears no connection between the origin of the imprinted personality and the identity of the subject based on age, genealogy, gender, ethnicity or national origin.

Imprinted personalities share the following characteristics:

1. The imprint died before the subject's birth. (Dates have ranged to as early as 90 years prior, to less than 1 year.)
2. The imprint was a victim of subjugation, torture and/or imprisonment.
3. The imprint typically died by violence, usually homicide. (Sometimes death has been due to secondary factors, such as starvation or infection.)
4. The imprint's death was the result from being targeted by a political mass movement, most often with some form of state sanction and/or complicity.

Subjects undergo no obvious anomalous aftereffects due to exposure, but will show psychological effects common to the types of trauma experienced by the imprinted personality. Grief, survivor's guilt and depression are typical. Suicidal ideation is rare, but has occurred in a small fraction of cases. It should be noted that in treatment of these aftereffects, use of amnestics has not shown any psychological benefit, and has often proved to be harmful.

ADDENDUM 1: EXPERIMENT LOG 1123-A

Test 0003
Date: █/██/19██
Subject: White male of mixed Irish and French ancestry. Age late 30s.

Procedure: Subject approaches SCP-1123 and is told to touch it.

Results: Subject collapses upon contact with skull, begins screaming in Armenian. Attacks Foundation doctors when they attempt to assist, calling them "Turkish Butchers." Subject is sedated and disorientation subsides after two hours. Subsequent interviews identify the imprinted personality as an Armenian farmer who was burned alive with approximately 150 other inhabitants of his village by the Ottoman army in 1915. No records exist of the individual, but the event was documented in a 1919 affidavit presented to the Malta Tribunals after World War I.

Test 0508
Date: ██/█/19███
Subject: Asian female of Chinese ancestry. Age early 60s.

Procedure: Subject approaches SCP-1123 and is told to touch it.

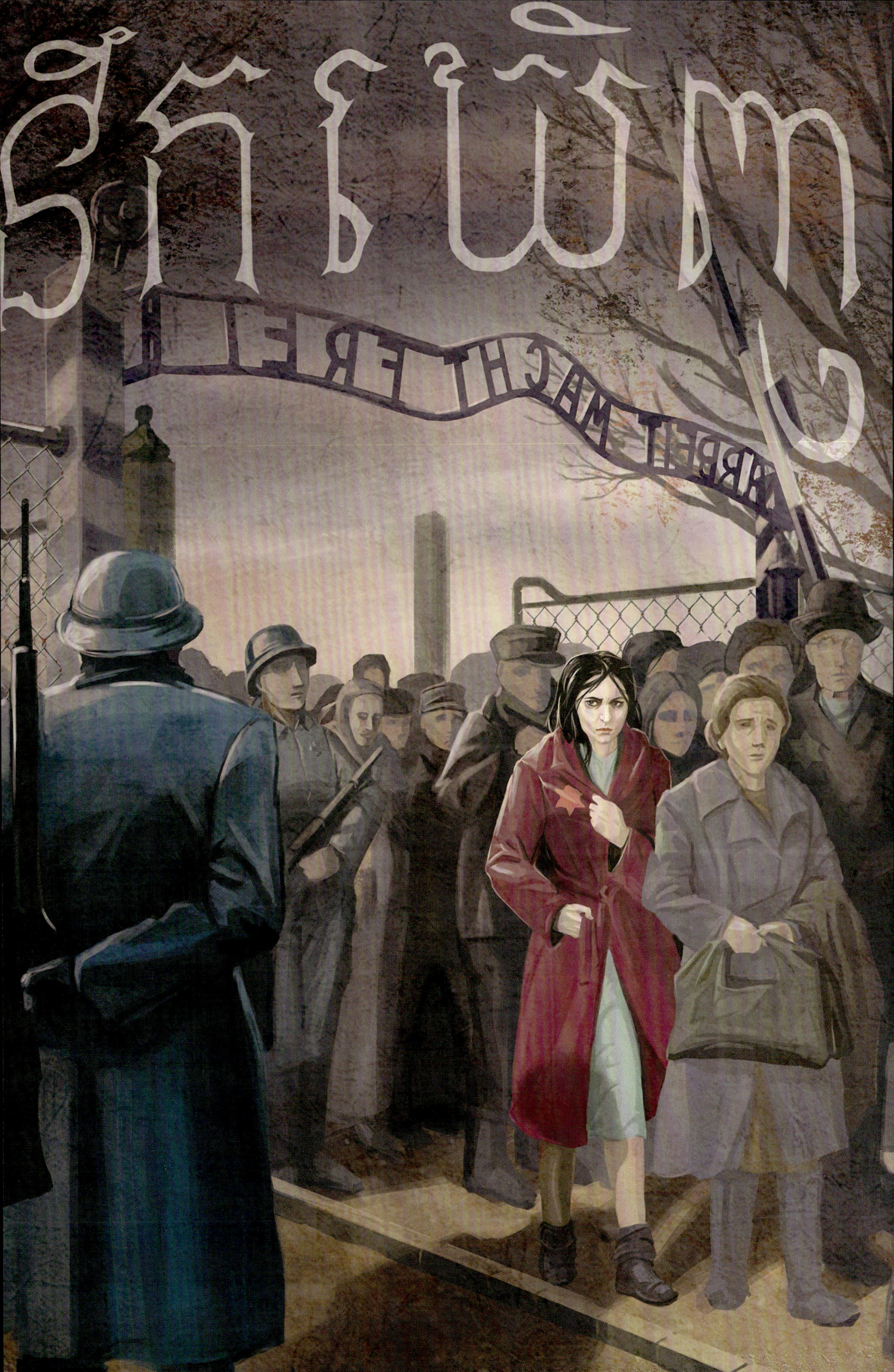

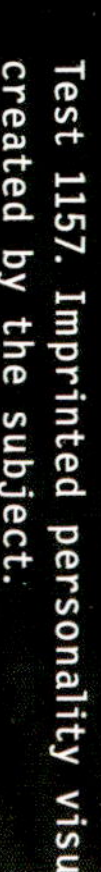

Test 1157. Imprinted personality visualization created by the subject.

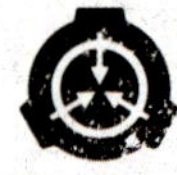

Results: Subject expresses apprehension before touching SCP-1123. After touching SCP-1123, subject does not move for fifteen minutes. Afterwards, subject sits down on the ground and is unresponsive for two more hours. As fugue state subsides, subject becomes visibly more distressed and begins weeping. Subsequent interviews identified the imprinted personality as a 16-year-old Ukrainian girl who died in late 1932 from a combination of malnutrition and the aftereffects of rape and beatings by members of a Soviet youth brigade in charge of confiscating grain from the Ukrainian peasantry.

Test 1157
Date: ██/██/20██
Subject: Latino female of Cuban ancestry. Age mid-40s.

Procedure: Subject approaches SCP-1123 and is told to touch it.

Results: Before touching SCP-1123, subject complains about smoke irritating her eyes. Subject touches SCP-1123 and ceases all movement and responsiveness for a period of twenty-five minutes. After twenty-five minutes, fugue state has concluded, but subject is still touching SCP-1123. Subject does not resist when Foundation personnel escort her from the test area. After one week of being unresponsive to interviews, the subject provides information on the imprinted personality. The imprint was from a Polish woman of Jewish descent who died in the Treblinka death camp in 1942.

Test 1815

Date: ██/██/20██

Subject: Black male of Haitian ancestry. Age early 20s.

Procedure: Subject approaches SCP-1123 and is told to touch it.

Results: Before touching SCP-1123, subject complains about a "chemical smell," and intense itching of the extremities. Subject touches SCP-1123 and immediately begins coughing. The coughing fit subsides and subject expresses confusion and distress, but appears reassured when he realizes that the Foundation personnel present are American. Subject communicates a Sorani dialect of Kurdish spoken in Iraqi Kurdistan. Fugue subsides after 60 minutes. Interviews identify the imprinted personality as a 85-year-old victim of a mustard gas attack during the Iraqi regime's Anfal campaign in 1989. **Note:** *First instance of an imprint personality that postdates SCP-1123's origin.*

Conclusions: After ████ tests to date, a clear statistical pattern has begun to emerge. The probability of a subject receiving an imprint from a particular historical event is roughly proportional to the number of victims that can be attributed to that event. For example, ██% of imprints come from Communist China's Great Leap Forward between 1958 and 1961, ██% of imprints come from Nazi Germany's extermination efforts between 1939 and 1945, while only █% come from events such as the Armenian Genocide or the Iraqi Anfal campaign where deaths are only estimated in the 1 to 2 million range.

END OF REPORT

SPECIAL CONTAINMENT PROCEDURES

Standard safety procedures for visually-reactive items (ED-8) are to be posted at all times. Any staff entering the containment area are to review this document before entering. Any staff entering the containment area are to wear the AR-68 Armored Variant haz-mat suit. Staff exiting the area with damaged suits are to be remanded to quarantine for one hour. Staff becoming paralyzed during cleaning/feeding/testing cycles are to be immediately removed and remanded to medical custody until five hours after recovery.

SCP-1013 is to be fed once daily, consisting of one small mammal (rabbit, large rat, cat or dog). This feeding is only to take place if there are no calcified remains still within the containment area. Calcified remains that are no longer actively being fed upon are to be removed and disposed of via incineration. Haz-mat protocols are to be observed during the disposal process. Test subject remains may be taken in to the containment area for feeding purposes only when standard feeding practice cannot be observed. Staff succumbing to SCP-1013 pre-feeding effects are to be removed and disposed of. All remains must be disposed of within one hour of final calcification.

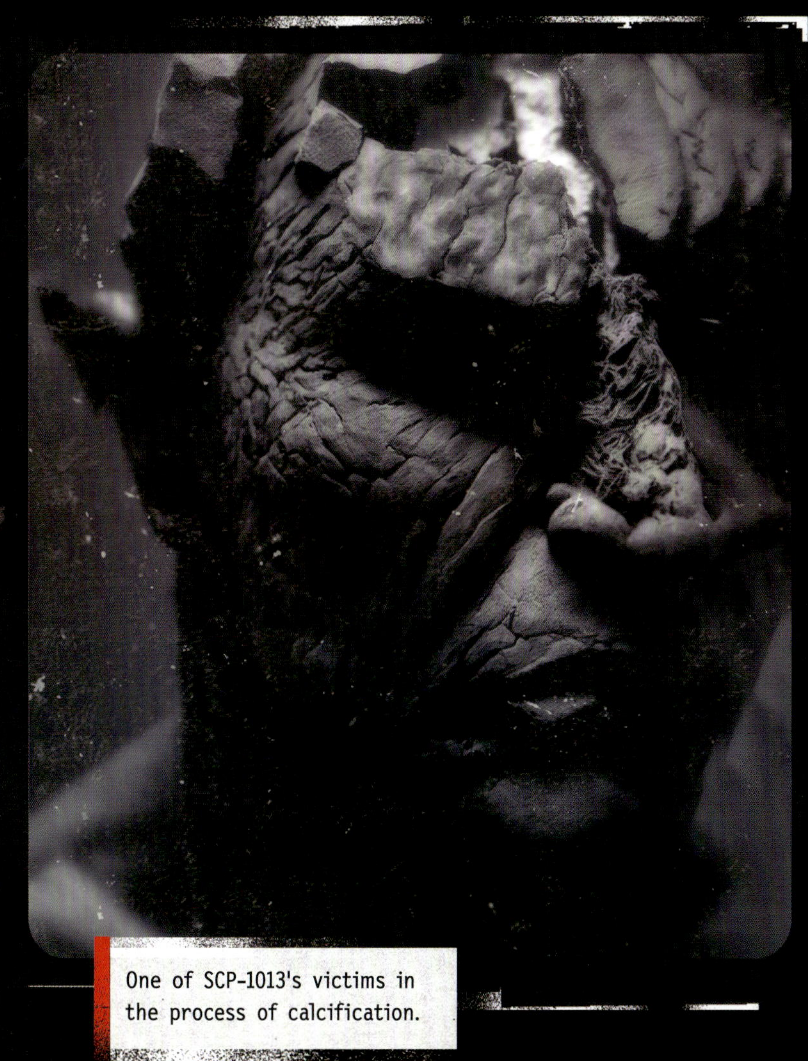

One of SCP-1013's victims in the process of calcification.

File >>> 010332

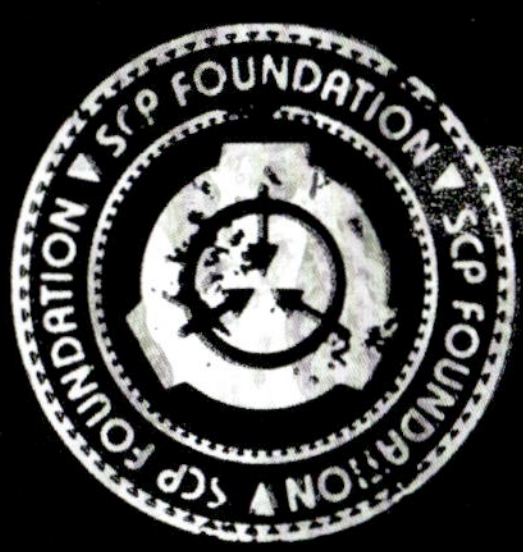

SCP-1013

Title

COCKATRICE

Report by

Dr Gears

Picture by

Dmitriy Fomin

Access the original report on

scp-wiki.wikidot.com/scp-1013

Date

Class

KETER

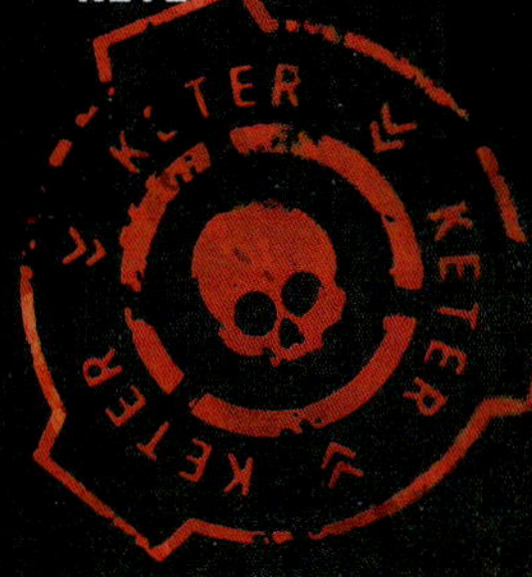

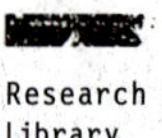

Research Library File ▸ 1013

DESCRIPTION

SCP-1013 appears to be a small reptile with a distinctly avian head. A wide frill extends from the base of the head, and can be flared out via bony spines radiating through the frill from the neck. The body appears similar to most common reptiles, with the exception of the head and abnormally long tail. While the main body is only 60 centimeters long, the tail is nearly 121 centimeters and exceptionally flexible. SCP-1013 has been observed to use this tail to trip and distract large prey. The head of SCP-1013 is distinctive, appearing to be that of a male chicken on first viewing. However, SCP-1013 does not possess any standard avian markers, besides the superficial resemblance. The beak is serrated, and appears to possess very basic, needle-like teeth. These are used only in feeding, and are not used in any way to hunt prey. The head also lacks any feathers, and has an enlarged wattle.

SCP-1013 hunts by projecting a form of unknown radiation, wave or memetic force into prey items making eye contact with SCP-1013. Subjects report a sudden stabbing pain in most major muscle groups, with full paralysis setting in within three seconds. This paralysis continues for eight minutes, with full recovery after ten. Paralyzed subjects are then bitten, beginning the calcification process. Research into this effect is ongoing, as no form of venom or viral agents have been detected from this bite, however this contact will initiate a rapid change in cellular structure in the bitten subject. The outer skin tissues will begin a rapid calcification, growing very dense and inflexible over several minutes. This will extend from the point of contact outward across the body, and can calcify a human being in fifteen minutes. Subjects recovering from paralysis mid-calcification report the feeling as "extremely painful", with a "burning numbness" in fully calcified areas. This calcification extends approximately three centimeters in to the body, leaving most internal tissues undisturbed. Calcification does not appear to affect the eyes, mouth, nose or other major mucus membranes. There is no currently known way to reverse this process.

SCP-1013 will peck through the outer layer of hardened flesh, and begin to consume tissues from the inside, burrowing deep into the body as flesh is consumed. SCP-1013 has a voracious appetite, and will consume nearly twice its body weight at each feeding. SCP-1013 will only consume living tissue, and will ignore dead or decomposing flesh. SCP-1013 has been noted to use natural body openings (mouth and eyes, primarily) when available, and is capable of compressing its body to fit in to very small openings. Prey items often die from blood loss or massive internal damage before feeding is complete, leaving the remainder of tissues to decompose within the calcified tissue. This outer tissue will slowly break down, causing large sections to crack and fall free. This will expose muscle and internal tissues, which are then often predated upon by SCP-1013. SCP-1013 will sometimes wait for this process to begin before feeding.

ADDENDUM

Recovery Notes: ████████

SCP-1013 was recovered in Egypt, near a former ████ ██ ██ facility. Due to this proximity, and the lack of additional SCP-1013 anywhere in the surrounding area, it is theorized SCP-1013 may be an engineered organism. SCP-1013 had calcified several animals and two shepherds, and had been observed on multiple occasions. Recovery was achieved with only one death, Agent ████ proving much of our initial information on the calcification process. Local communities dismissed the incident with no involvement from Agents.

Notes on behavior: ████████

SCP-1013 is somewhat similar to a spider, and will paralyze and calcify subjects even when not hungry, presumably to keep them for later. This was observed during breach incident 11-Hr (SEE ATTACHED DOCUMENTATION), when SCP-1013 calcified twenty members of staff. SCP-1013 is also very aggressive, and will attempt to stare down and bite any subject that enters the containment area. The neck frill is an amazing adaptation. It lifts abruptly, with a loud snapping sound, and often times causes subjects to look directly at SCP-1013.

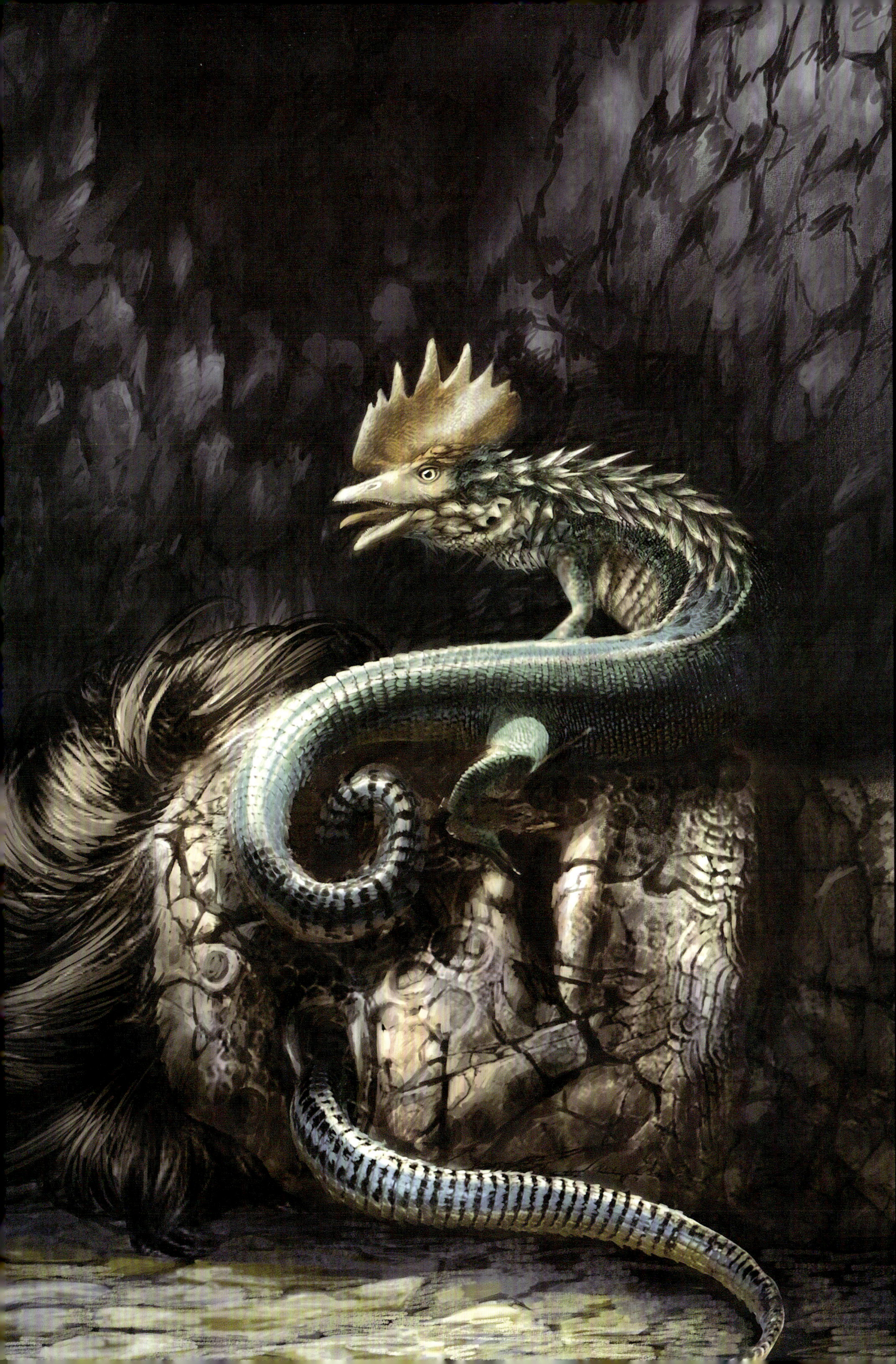

Instance of SCP-1013.

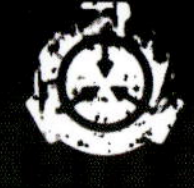

SCP-1013 seems to have a "range" of about 54 meters for its "stare", and appears to need direct eye contact to work. SCP-1013 appears to only paralyze one subject at a time, but can "attack" multiple subjects in rapid succession. SCP-1013 appears to be immune to its own stare, reacting with basic aggression to reflections. SCP-1013 feeds primarily on mammals, attacking animals such as fish, birds or insects only when near starving. SCP-1013 exhibits a preference for soft tissues, eating the eyes and tongue first whenever possible.

CLASSIFIED LEVEL ?

NOTES ON REPRODUCTION

Ongoing testing in to the feeding habits of SCP-1013 have been partially successful. Questions were raised regarding the near-constant feeding exhibited by SCP-1013, which is highly irregular for a reptile. It was initially theorized that the paralysis and calcification process were metabolically taxing to SCP-1013, requiring enormous amounts of food to fuel the process. It is now apparent that members of SCP-1013 are hermaphroditic, and appear to reproduce in a way similar to budding or basic cellular division.

SCP-1013 will ingest massive amounts of tissue, increasing its body mass rapidly. This mass will then begin to form cyst-like structures in the tail section, each of which contains a juvenile SCP-1013. The process by which this occurs is currently under investigation. After 48 hours, juvenile SCP-1013 will forcibly exit the parent body. Parent SCP-1013 will typically release spawn within calcified prey. Juvenile SCP-1013 exhibit no feeding preference, and will consume any biological material, living or dead. SCP-1013 do not engage in cannibalism, and will exit the calcified remains once food has been exhausted.

Juvenile SCP-1013 will seek out cool, dark places and begin rapid molting, doubling in size every six hours until reaching full adult size. New adult SCP-1013 will quickly establish territories, and begin the feeding/spawning cycle again. Juvenile SCP-1013 seek out areas such as ventilation shafts, plumbing, or discarded clothing/shoes in which to molt and grow. Disturbing a juvenile during this period will always provoke a sustained attack.

This sequence of behavior was discovered after a lock-down event in Site █, resulting from [DATA EXPUNGED] failure. Recovery teams found the site to be infested with SCP-1013, with over one thousand individuals being reported and destroyed. Final sterilization took eight weeks, and resulted in multiple staff deaths. Research into the control of the rampant reproductive cycle with the goal of eventual bio-weapon designation is ongoing.

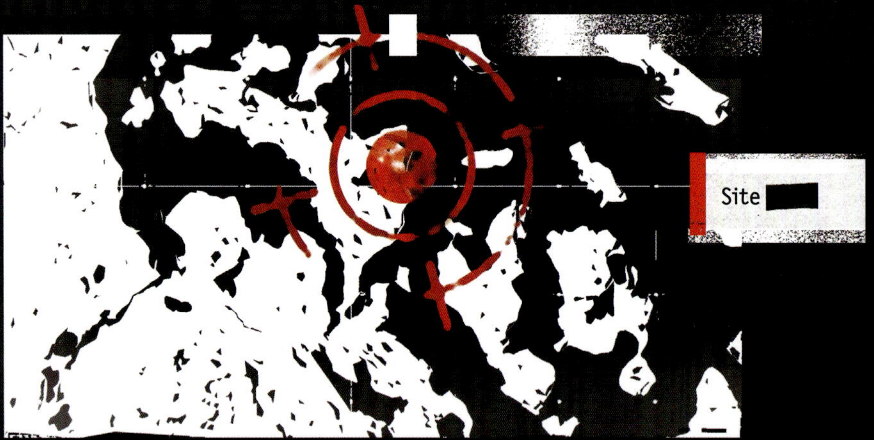

END OF REPORT

SPECIAL CONTAINMENT PROCEDURES

At time of acquisition SCP-407 was recorded within a compact cassette tape. Currently, SCP-407 is backed-up as a digital audio file on [DATA EXPUNGED]. SCP-407 should not be allowed to play under any circumstances outside testing conditions, and only with the approval of 05-█.

Testing of SCP-407 is to be done in completely sound-proof environments. All tools and subjects must be sterilized to remove the presence of pollen, fungal spores, plant seeds, and as much bacterial life to the greatest degree possible to delay the negative effects of SCP-407.

DESCRIPTION

SCP-407 is a song in an unidentified language, seemingly sung a cappella. The voices are thought to be human. The tape containing SCP-407 was found with one track of approximately thirty (30) minutes duration, though the abrupt ending suggests there may be more. The song has been described by all listeners as something along the lines of 'soothing', 'glorious', and 'beautiful'.

While SCP-407 is played, rapid cell generation seems to occur within auditory radius. This effect seems to occur at the cellular level, and does not require the subject to be able to hear the music. The changes seem to only affect multi-cellular organisms at first, but quickly begins to affect mitosis in single-celled organisms.

During the first minute of exposure, all multi-cellular life forms seem to become healthier. Subjects suffering from malnutrition, scarring, physical injury, or chronic diseases or other medical conditions seem to become healthy with only a minute of exposure to SCP-407. This has been shown to cure Alzheimer's disease, Crohn's disease, brain and spinal cord injuries, and normally fatal infections or wounds, amongst other things. Interestingly, cancer does not seem to be affected, though the subject's physical condition was still vastly improved.

During the second and third minute of exposure, subjects start experiencing unnecessary unrestrained cell growth, manifesting in quickly advancing dermal growths. These growths seem to mostly be benign tumors and calcium and fat deposits, which though sometimes painful and disfiguring, are not life threatening.

During the fourth minute of exposure, increased bacterial and fungal growth occurs, creating conditions that grow increasingly dangerous for all exposed life, even in their new healthier states. Respiratory and digestive problems are quick to arrive in most cases, and become steadily worse as time progresses.

Past five (5) minutes, the effects of SCP-407 seem to differ each trial. In all cases, trace elements of plants or fungus as well as any animal life present begin to grow and replicate uncontrollably, at varying rates, often shaping into new organisms. Full results have varied depending on the test, and on the objects present when SCP-407 is played.

ADDENDUM-407-01

SCP-407 was found in the home of Professor ████ of ██████, who had recently returned from research in the Amazon regions of northern Brazil. Agents were first alerted to a possible SCP when [DATA EXPUNGED].

File >>> 09331

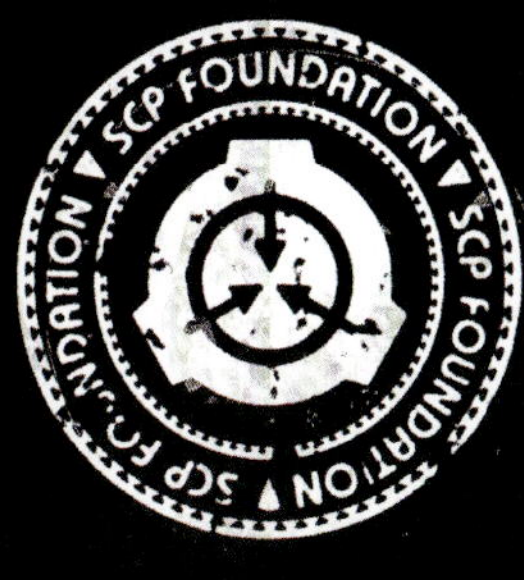

SCP-407

Title

THE SONG OF GENESIS

Report by

Pair Of Ducks

Picture by

Alex Andreev

Access the original report on

scp-wiki.wikidot.com/scp-407

Date

Class

NEUTRALIZED

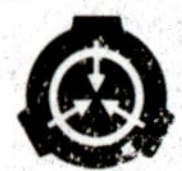

ADDENDUM 407-02

The mold that eventually resulted from SCP-407's second test appears to be some sort of Cordyceps Fungi. Noted to be similar to mold encountered by SCP-507. Due to fear of fulfilling a fate similar to that observed by 507, testing using SCP-407 has been limited to using only the first twenty (20) minutes of the recording.

ADDENDUM 407-03: SAMPLE TEST RUN OF SCP-407

<Test 2; SCP-407 played for 28m 32s. Within chamber; 1 D-Class personnel, unsterilized >

00:25 - Subject reports feeling soothed by the music, and of feeling stronger and more invigorated.

00:45 - Liver spots and scars previously seen are shown to disappear.

02:20 - Subject appears to have physically grown an inch. Increase in musculature is noticeable.

03:40 - Subject reports intestinal pain.

04:20 - Subject begins vomiting. From vomit, plants are seen growing and slowly rooting into the tile floor.

04:50 - Subject starts developing rashes and growths on skin.

05:30 - Heavy dermal disfigurement. Subject panting heavily, begging for help. Great pain reported.

06:10 - Subject falls to the ground and ceases to move.

06:45 - Subject's body is quickly covered in what is thought to be fungal infections. Plant growth is observed growing from the subject's mouth, then eye sockets.

07:30 - Subject is by this time unrecognizable, covered in molds and plant shoots. Body bursts as a banana tree emerges from the subject's intestines and proceeds to grow to maturity within seconds.

08:45 - Plant and fungal growth has begun to spread throughout the testing chamber. What appears to be moss and weeds cover the floor.

09:30 - Several shoots, stalks, bushes, and even small trees have appeared. Banana tree is no longer recognizable; the tree has grown thick and is covered with foliage and fungal growth.

10:30 - The air is heavy with pollen and spores. Vision into testing chamber is difficult.

11:30 - Movement is heard within the chamber. Several different small insect-like creatures are observed. Creatures are seemingly made of plant matter.

17:30 - For the last six minutes, creatures made of plant matter have been observed to rapidly generate, grow to maturity, kill and eat other creatures, and then be eaten themselves. Creatures increasingly progressing in size as time increases.

19:00 - Medium sized mammalian creatures are observed; they seem humanoid and bear a resemblance to initial Subject.

21:00 - Large fungal stalk is observed to grow from one of the mammalian creatures. Stalk end bursts, dispensing white spores.

22:00 - Plant growth is still lush, but everything begins to become coated by a layer of mold. The plant creatures seem to die slowly for an unknown reason, before being covered by the mold.

23:00 - Mammalian creatures are the last to succumb; they heavily decay and become covered in the same mold. Bodies are shown to contract and expand as if breathing. Stalks quickly rise from the bodies, burst with spores, and then just as quickly rot.

28:32 - Tape ends. No change in chamber since the appearance of the mold. Chamber undergoes rigorous anti-biological cleansing. Samples of the mold were taken. [See Addenda 407-01, 407-02]

<End Test 2>

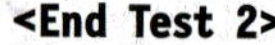

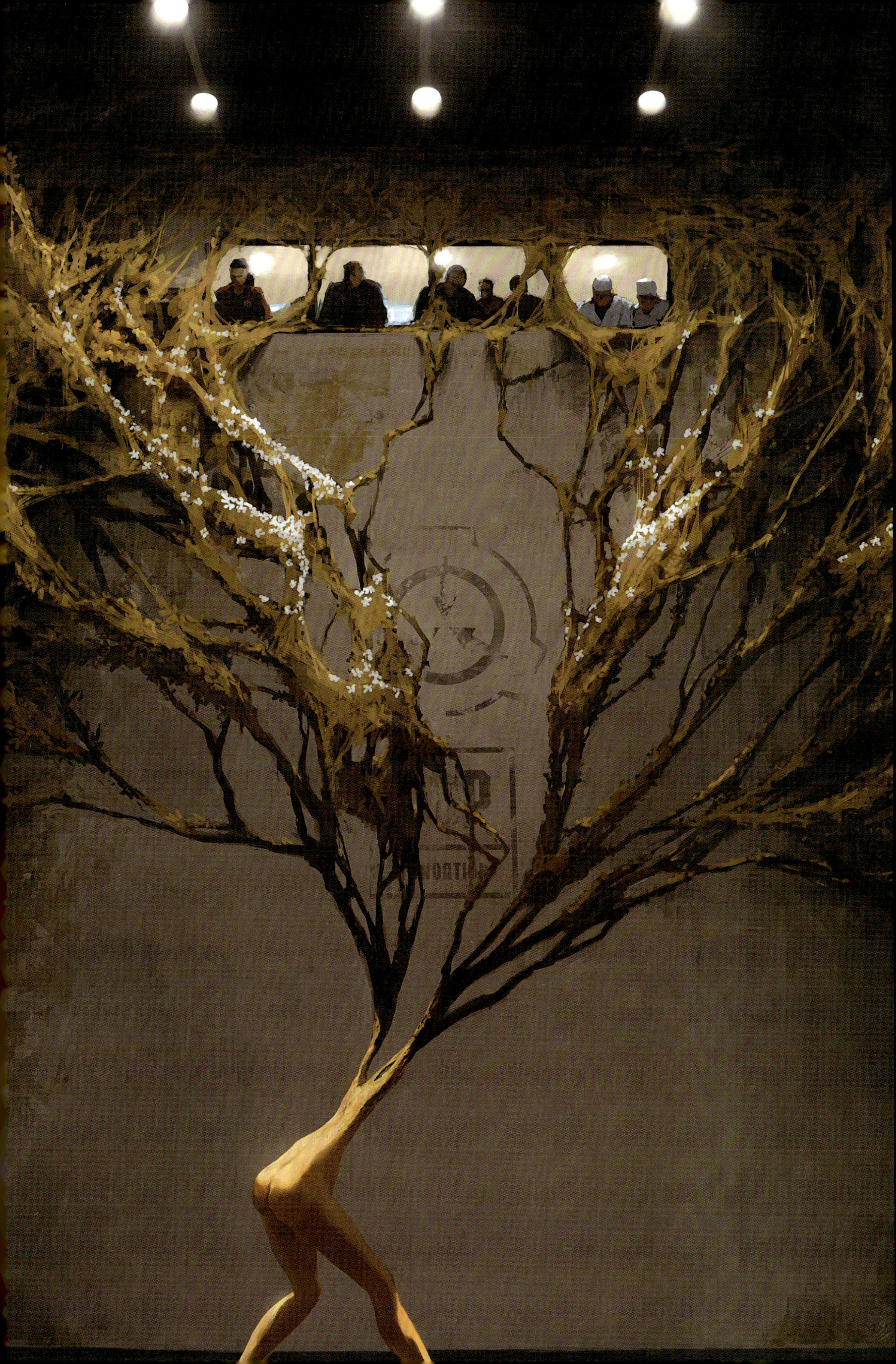

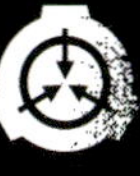

SECURITY BREACH INCIDENT X23

Security Breach Incident - X23: On ██/██/██, SCP Site 19 breached by operatives from an organization known to the Foundation only as 'The Serpent's Hand'.

Site-19 Breach: The breach of Site-19 seems to have been the second of two break-ins into SCP properties by ████████, known to the Foundation as "L.S." This individual was responsible for a previous security breach, having coordinated the theft of SCP-268. Though [DATA EXPUNGED], it is evident from video surveillance that SCP-268 was involved in this infiltration. The intruder known as L.S. seems to have simply walked into Site-19.

The intrusion seems to have been for the purpose of using SCP-914. Knowledge of the intruder's use of SCP-914 can only be assumed due to the intruders interruption of Dr. █████ during routine testing. Dr. █████ seems to have been [DATA EXPUNGED], resulting in the intrusion's only personnel casualty.

SCP-407 seems to have been deleted from the Foundation's system during this time, so it can only be assumed the individuals involved are responsible. Whether this means the file has been completely destroyed, or possibly in the hands of this rogue group, is unknown.

A short printed note was found in SCP-914's chamber; this note is the only insight the Foundation currently has of the group responsible for this incident. [See Document X23-01]

DOCUMENT X23-01

Dear Sirs of the Foundation

Behind guns and protocol you hide; desperately chaining the ineffable, yourselves stuck within your own self-wrought pitiful cages of fear and ignorance. You think yourselves the shepherd guarding the flocks of the unwise o'er the night, but you are so shaken by doubt and fear than in your bewildered arrogance, you would vainly seek to chain the sun itself unto the heavens to hold back the daily night. The delivering angels themselves you contain with three digits and four walls. Do you not see the blindness with which you walk and swing your blade? On the final day, would you have us contain Black Surtr himself with measures and science, and condemn ourselves to rotten stagnancy as you hold back his pure cleansing fires?

I do not ask you not to act, but act with enlightenment and heart; neither should one be seduced by the dark nor blinded by the light, but walk firmly in the twilight and gaze unto all realms. Walk the World of Fire with bare feet and you will find yourself without the scars you never knew you had.

Alas, in your fears, you fail to see the Old Gods that we all are, and unable to accept this sovereignty, detain both thought and essence of those that would take man beyond the mundane. Do not be so eager to hold back the tides of unrelenting destruction, that you trample what brave weed that would dare grow in the monochrome world you wish to pave. Such blind order stiffles chaos, and what is chaos but life?

I leave you with one final truth; The Garden is the Serpent's place; the divinities of fear and order who come to walk in the cool evening air are only visitors. Do not fail to see the evil hiding in the light, nor the aromatic beauty of the palest flower of darkness.

Signed Sincerely,

L.S.

P.S. - You'll thank me for deleting what you call '407'

END OF REPORT

SPECIAL CONTAINMENT PROCEDURES

As SCP-303 has not yet been known to travel beyond the boundaries of Site ██, the entire area of Site ██ is currently considered SCP-303's containment area. All rooms in Site ██ are to be altered where possible so as to have two entrances separated by a distance of 10m or line of sight. Personnel are to be distributed evenly throughout the facility, with available radio or intercom contact, so that encounters may be resolved quickly. Personnel who witness SCP-303 are to be submitted for immediate psychiatric evaluation.

All SCP objects housed at Site ██ since before 6/4/10 are to be transferred to Site ██-B one at a time. Each SCP object will be transferred again to Site ██-A once it can be verified that SCP-303 has not migrated from Site ██ with it. Once SCP-303 either migrates to Site ██-B, or remains present at Site ██ once all SCPs in question have been transferred to Site ██-A, containment procedures will be updated as appropriate.

DESCRIPTION

Witnesses describe SCP-303 as a nude, sexless, emaciated humanoid figure with reddish-brown skin. Instead of normal facial features, its head is dominated by an extremely large mouth, which bears a set of oversized human teeth. It continually vocalizes a wheezing noise, loud enough to be heard from the other side of most solid doors. All individuals who have had encounters with SCP-303 are capable of describing it in full, including individuals who have not physically seen any part of it.

SCP-303 will periodically materialize behind any closed door, hatch, or other entryway barrier opposite a sentient observer, chosen by unknown means. SCP-303 will then remain behind the door for an indeterminate amount of time. Any individual attempting to open the door or barrier experiences intense, paralyzing fear that lasts until SCP-303 dematerializes (either on its own or to avoid being directly seen by another observer). The source of this fear is not clear, but appears to be similar in nature to arachnophobia and ophidiophobia, originating on a pre-conscious, genetic level. [DATA EXPUNGED] analysis indicates that SCP-303 is not, in fact, purposefully inducing fear in the affected individuals.

SCP-303 does not allow itself to come into direct visual contact with any observer, and has never allowed any one individual to view more than 10% of its form. When the door or other entryway barrier is partially or completely transparent, SCP-303 will materialize in an orientation that leaves 10% or less of its body visible, or cause effects of fog or frost on the transparent surface to achieve the same effect. If SCP-303 is approached from a direction in which there is not a solid object or door breaking line of sight, it will dematerialize before direct visual contact is made.

Any electronic or complex mechanical devices that SCP-303 encounters are temporarily disabled. SCP-303 has made no recorded attempt to physically or verbally engage any observer.

How SCP-303 arrived at Site ██ is not known at this time. SCP-303's first recorded appearance was on 3/1/10. It is suspected that SCP-303 was inadvertently transferred along with or manifested by another SCP on-site. All SCPs on Site ██ are being reexamined accordingly.

File >>> 100935

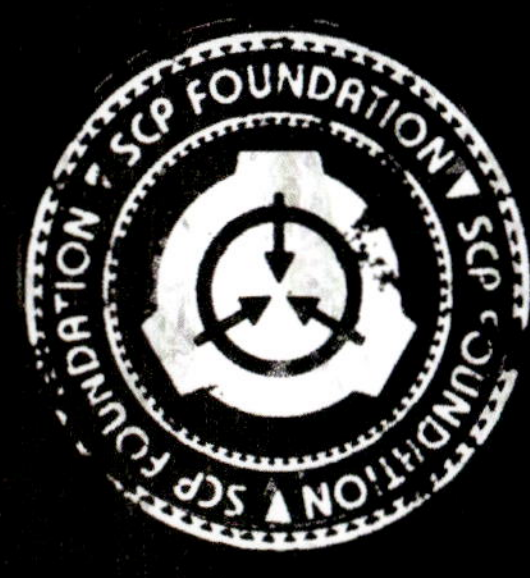

SCP-303

Title

THE DOORMAN

Report by

AJAlkaline

Picture by

Genocide Error

Access the original report on

scp-wiki.wikidot.com/scp-303

Date

Class

EUCLID

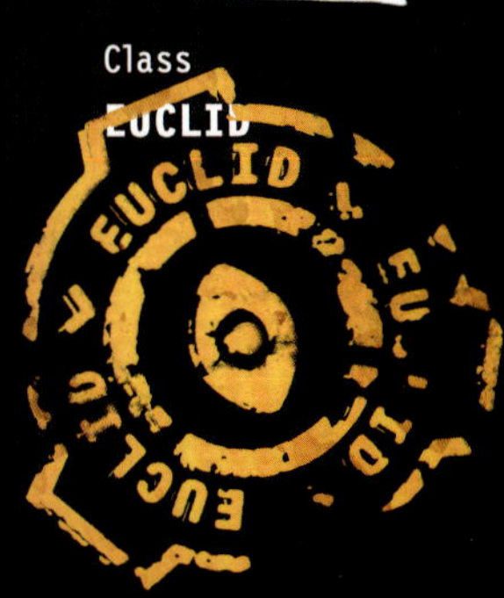

INCIDENT LOG 303-A

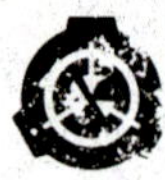

Research Library File ▸ 303

Incident 303-1: Agent ██████ was showering in her private quarters bathroom when she became aware of the presence of SCP-303 on the opposite side of the shower curtain. It was wheezing extremely loudly. Startled by the discovery, she accidentally struck the shower curtain, causing it to sway outwards. The curtain partially wrapped around SCP-303, revealing that it was less than 0.5m from the curtain, standing erect and facing the shower. Agent ██████ reports spending approximately the next 3 hours sobbing in the shower, quietly, as not to disturb SCP-303. Agent ██████ reported that the wheezing stopped very suddenly, at which point in time she was able to exit the shower.

Incident 303-3: Agent█████ encountered SCP-303 inside the Site ███2nd floor break-room. He was attempting to obtain coffee creamer from the counter cabinet when he heard loud wheezing emanating from the cabinet and was overtaken by overwhelming fear. Agent█████ later reported that SCP-303 was huddled in the cabinet in the fetal position. Agent ████ claimed to be certain of the information despite failing to open the cabinet door. Later, when the cabinet was examined, one container of powdered coffee creamer was missing.

Note: *This is the first recorded instance of SCP-303 removing an object from a scene.*

Incident 303-6: Dr.████ was discovered dead from dehydration in a 2nd floor storage room. It is estimated that Dr. ████ spent up to five days in the storage room before being discovered. A small 4m x 4m decompression chamber separated the storage room from the adjoining hallway. SCP-303 occupied the decompression chamber for the duration of Dr.████'s isolation in the storage room, disallowing entry from either direction and making it impossible for Dr.████ to leave.

TEST LOG 303-A

A team consisting of Dr.██████, Researcher ██████, 4 security personnel, and 4 D-Class personnel were assigned to be dispatched to any reported incident of SCP-303's materialization in order to immediately perform on-site testing. These logs take place at the door to room ███ from the first floor hallway. SCP-303 was reported to be within room███.

Test 303-1: One (1) male D-Class personnel, D-303-1, was ordered to open the door and threatened that he would be transferred to SCP-███ duty for non-compliance. He refused, citing extreme fear.

Test 303-2: One (1) male D-Class personnel, D-303-1, was ordered to open the door and threatened that he would be terminated on the spot for non-compliance. He refused, claiming that if he were to do so that SCP-303 would [DATA EXPUNGED]. He was terminated on the spot.

Test 303-3: One (1) female D-Class personnel, D-303-2, that had witnessed the termination of D-303-1, was ordered to open the door and threatened that she would be terminated on the spot for non-compliance. She refused, claiming that if she opened the door that SCP-303 would [DATA EXPUNGED]. Researcher ██████ was visibly shaken by this claim. D-303-2 was not terminated.

Test 303-4: One (1) female D-Class personnel, D-303-2, was ordered to open the door. One (1) male D-Class personnel, D-303-3, was given one (1) combat knife by security personnel and ordered to [DATA EXPUNGED] until D-303-2 opened the door. After 2 hours of [DATA EXPUNGED] D-303-2 died from blood loss. D-303-2 made no attempt to open the door.

Addendum- 5/1/10: SCP-303 appears to have claimed the 2nd floor storage room as its own. It has so far disallowed any personnel entry to the room since 4/5/10. It leaves periodically to acquire Foundation property, which is then moved into the 2nd floor storage room. To date, the following list describes all non-classified items taken by SCP-303:

- One (1) ████ cryotube
- Three (3) sets of standard Foundation surgical equipment
- ███ ███ ██████
- Two (2) D-Class research cadavers
- One (1) gasoline-powered generator

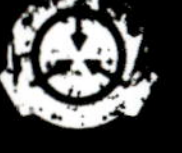

- A variety of chemicals, including large quantities of tryptophan, phenylalanine, █████ and tyrosine, among others
- One (1) container of powdered coffee creamer

In addition to this, a number of classified materials have been obtained by SCP-303. Staff are still attempting to determine what specific purposes SCP-303 may have for these materials.

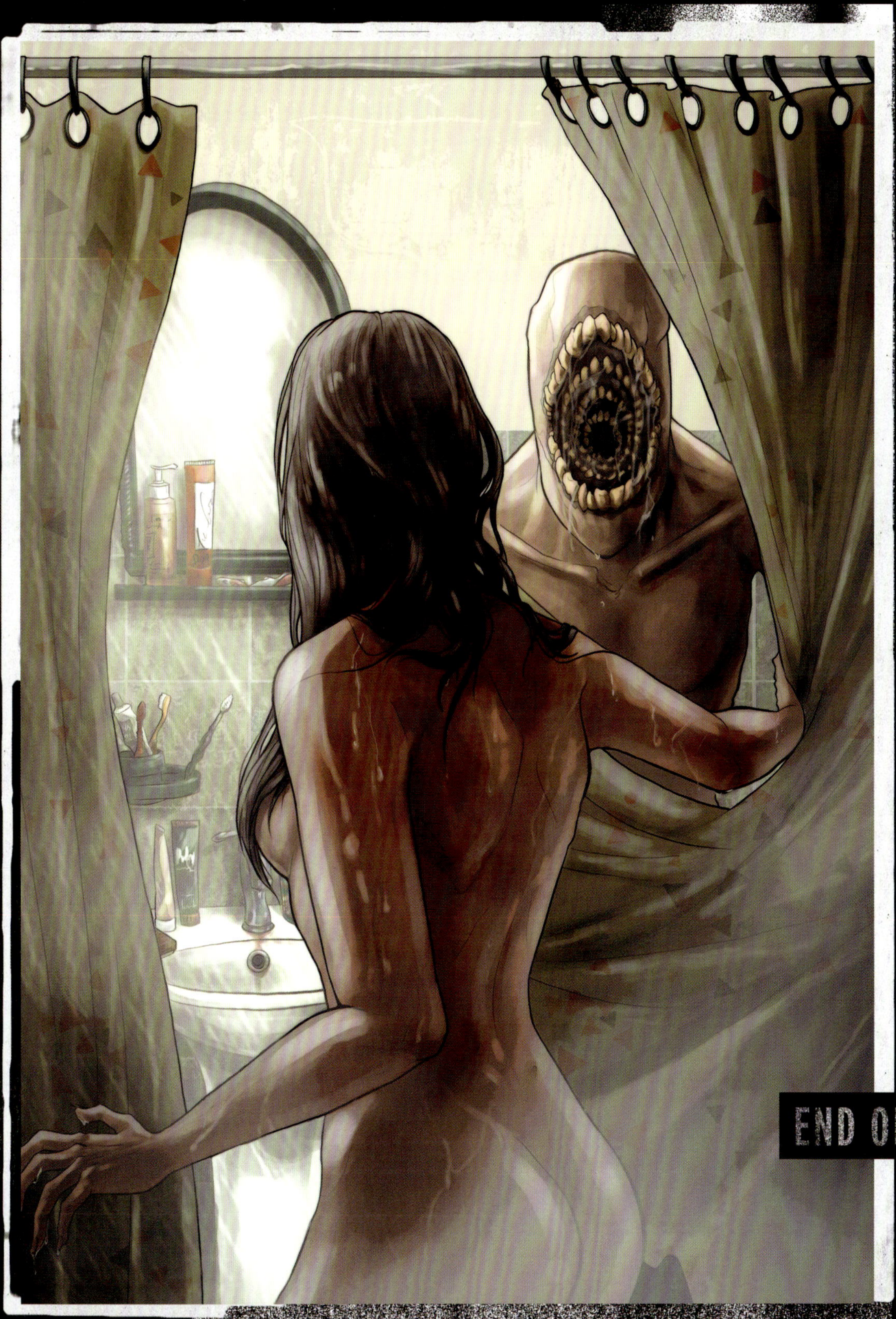

END OF REPORT

File >>> 009332

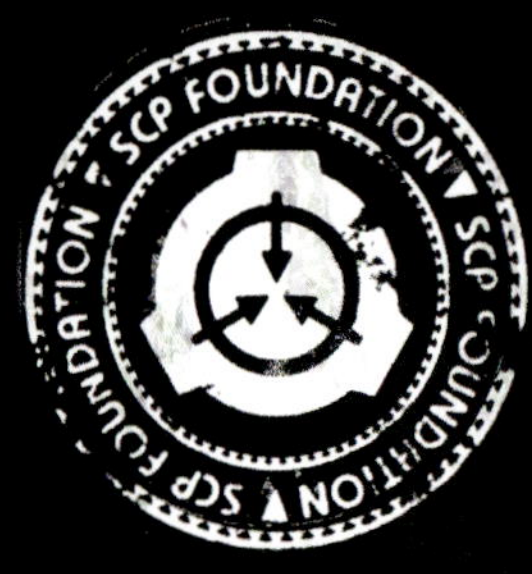

SCP-154

Title

OFFENSIVE BRACELETS

Report by

Kain Pathos Crow

Picture by

Dmitriy Fomin

Access the original report on

scp-wiki.wikidot.com/scp-154

Date

Class

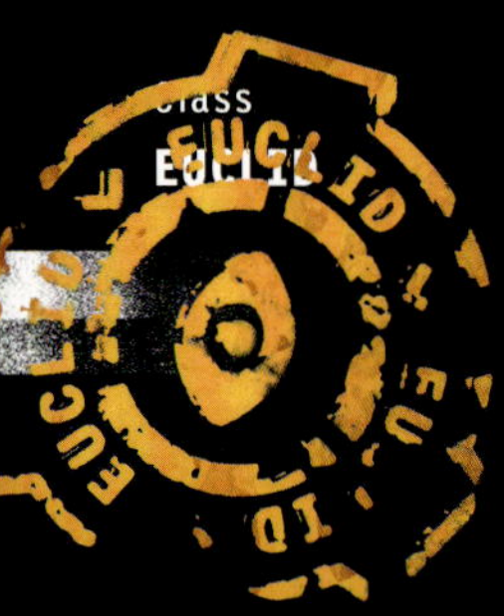

SPECIAL CONTAINMENT PROCEDURES

SCP-154 is to be kept within Weapon Locker 8, in Armed-Research Site-47. Personnel wishing to research or use item must submit the required request forms. Anyone attempting to remove the item without clearance, or from outside of the facility is to be terminated on sight.

DESCRIPTION

SCP-154 is a pair of simple bronze bracelets, completely circular and large enough to comfortably hang off the arm of most people. Spectrograph analysis has proven that the item is composed entirely of copper (85%), tin (11%), arsenic (3%), and traces of other slight impurities (<1%).

When both bracelets are worn on the same arm, and the wearer concentrates on them with arms extended in a depiction of a traditional "nocked bowstring" pose (achieved by having the arm with the bracelets completely extended in front of oneself, with the opposing arm extended up to the elbow of the fully extended arm), a large, indistinct, incorporeal bow will form in the extended hand, and both bracelets will glow lightly.

From that point onwards, SCP-154 can be treated as a bow, until the pose or concentration is broken, which results in the bracelets reverting to normal. There is no actual bowstring, but completing the motion of pulling it achieves the same effect.

When the "bowstring is pulled and released", the bones of the arm will be forcibly ejected from the extended limb, traveling in a straight path at speeds recorded over three hundred (300) meters per second. The missing bones and resulting damage to the arm are quickly regenerated, and the weapon is capable of being "fired" again within minutes. Tests using subjects possessing multiple arms/hands, such as SCP-1884-B[1], have demonstrated the ability to fire SCP-154 several times, with the bones of different arms being used with each successive firing.

The regeneration implemented by the item is limited, only affecting the damage inflicted by the weapon itself. This regeneration seems to be an automatic action, and will continue in almost all situations. Both firing the weapon and the resulting regeneration are understandably painful, and participants which have used the item once are generally disinclined to repeat usage.

However, there have found to be some occasional abnormalities regarding the regeneration. Most often this manifests simply as minor mutations of the original subject, such as changes in size, pigmentation, and structure of the original organelles. These are an uncommon occurrence, capable of happening during any use of the weapon, though generally tend to occur during repeat usage.

There are more drastic abnormalities, though these are much rarer, and coincide with highly frequent use. These mutations can range from anything such as the growth of extra joints and digits in the affected arm, to a complete change of the chemical or physical structure of the limb.

One test subject unknowingly had the bone matter within his arm converted into an unstable explosive compound, only discovering the fact when it detonated, causing two fatalities and three casualties. Another had the entire bone and musculature structure morphed into fully functional serpentine physiology.

1. SCP-1884-B was permitted to be used in testing with its approval. SCP-1884-B was able to fire five shots from SCP-154 within a minute. Testing ceased on SCP-1884-B's request following SCP-1884-A becoming distressed due to pain associated with SCP-154 use.

END OF REPORT

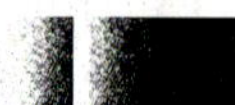

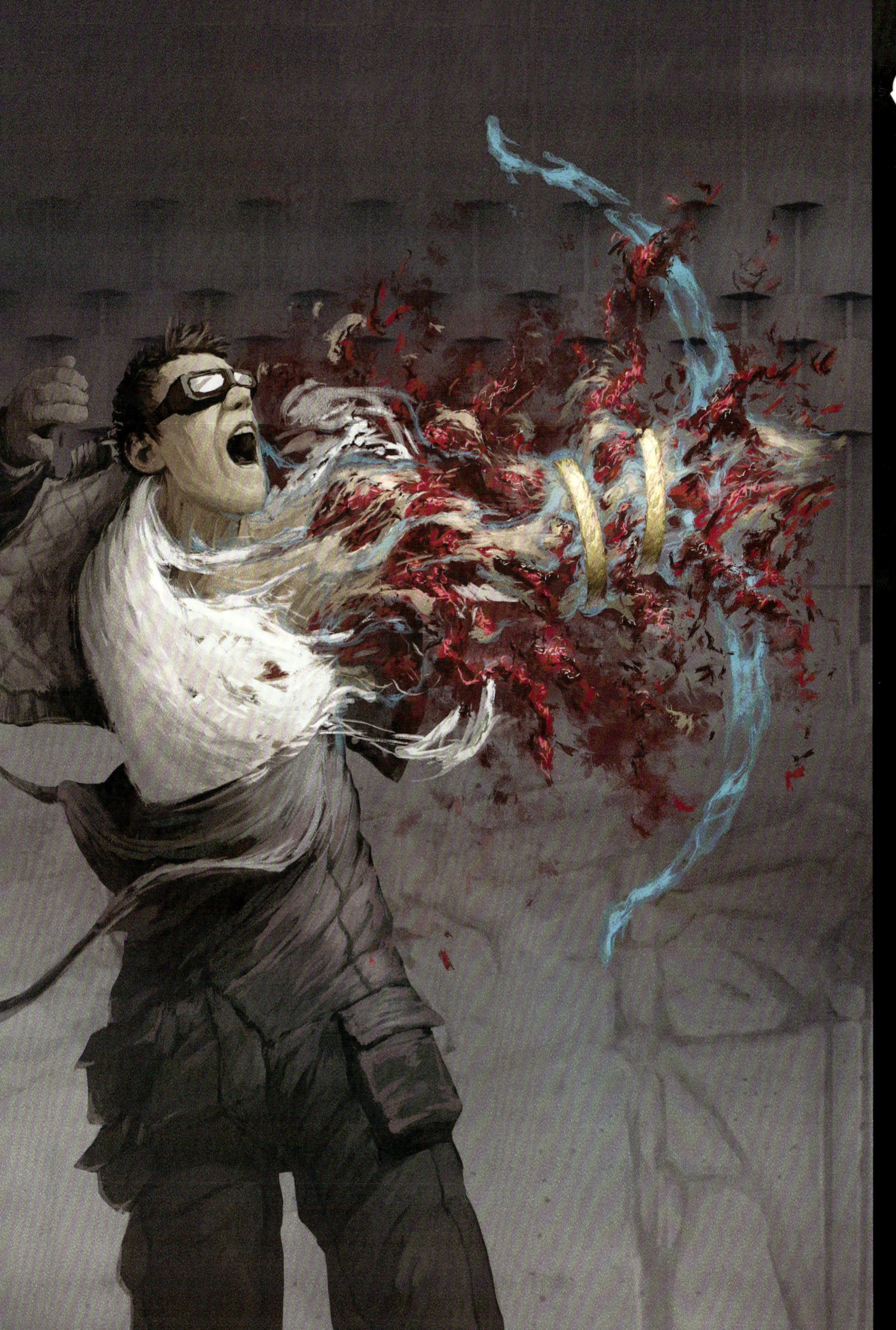

Photo of Agent ███ who volunteered to test SCP-154.

File >>> 0182773

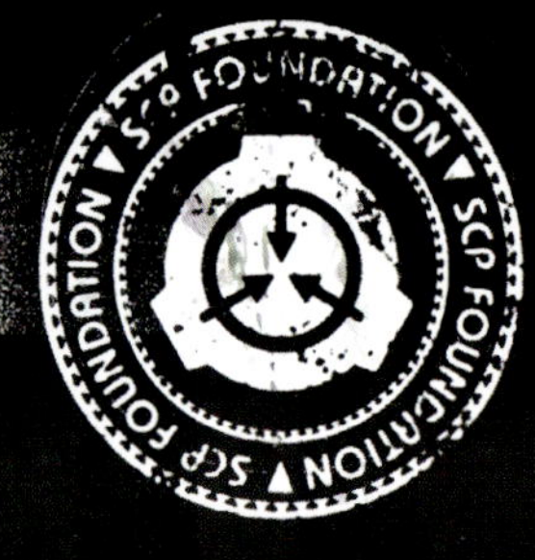

SCP-804

Title

WORLD WITHOUT MAN

Report by

Sorts

Picture by

Alex Andreev

Access the original report on

scp-wiki.wikidot.com/scp-804

Date

Class

KETER

SPECIAL CONTAINMENT PROCEDURES

Until such time as SCP-804 is found to be without any memetic effect it is to remain in its original location at the former site of ████ ████, Alaska, where exposure to the elements prevents its reactivation. A 30m x 30m camouflage tarp is to be maintained over SCP-804 and facilities for armed guards and testing are to be maintained 130 meters from its location. Trespassers are to be treated with a Class-A amnestics and returned to the nearest town of [DATA EXPUNGED] or terminated at the discretion of on-site security. In the event of SCP-804 being approached or seized by a hostile armed force, Contingency 804-X is to be executed.

DESCRIPTION

SCP-804 is the remains of an art installation titled "World Without Man," revealed on ██/██/20██, by the defunct artists' group *Unelmat Paremmasta Maailmasta*. According to documentation retrieved and deleted from the artists' website during clean-up procedure, SCP-804 was originally a large, clear globe of the Earth, with several smaller globes and video equipment within. Promotional material on the website implied that the globe was to display images of pastoral wilderness untouched by mankind contrasted with visuals of abandoned human industry and decaying landmarks.

Upon activation before a small audience of prominent environmental activists and artists from the nearby community of ████ ████, SCP-804 began to display its destructive properties. We can only speculate if the device's output was intentional or not, as those involved in its construction perished during the incident or have gone into hiding.

While the globes within SCP-804 rotate, all man-made artifacts within approximately 100 meters begin to rapidly deteriorate until completely disintegrated. The effect applies to anything ranging from machinery to buildings, clothing, plastics, synthetic chemical compounds and any tool more complex than a sharpened stick of wood. The area of effect grows the longer the device is active, with the effect growing ever stronger at its source. Human tissue is also affected at a slower rate of decay, causing victims to become emaciated as they lose body mass—leading up to collapse of the skeleton and death, with the body swiftly breaking down into component matter shortly thereafter. Non-human life is completely unaffected. Persons who escape the area of effect experience symptoms similar to prolonged starvation but can return to full health with proper care.

If not for the fact that it is not entirely immune to its own effect, SCP-804 would have had the potential to remove all trace of humanity from the globe in a matter of weeks. Judging from the observed rate of destruction upon original activation versus its current capabilities under testing, SCP-804's capabilities have been impaired by the damage it caused to itself. However, sustained use still presents an extreme threat especially if the device is somehow refined or repaired.

Due to the circumstances in which SCP-804 was secured it is strongly believed that the device also possesses some form of mental compulsion on those who view it, but testing is still on-going to determine if that property has also been compromised by the decay of SCP-804 and how it might be contained. See Recovery Log for further information.

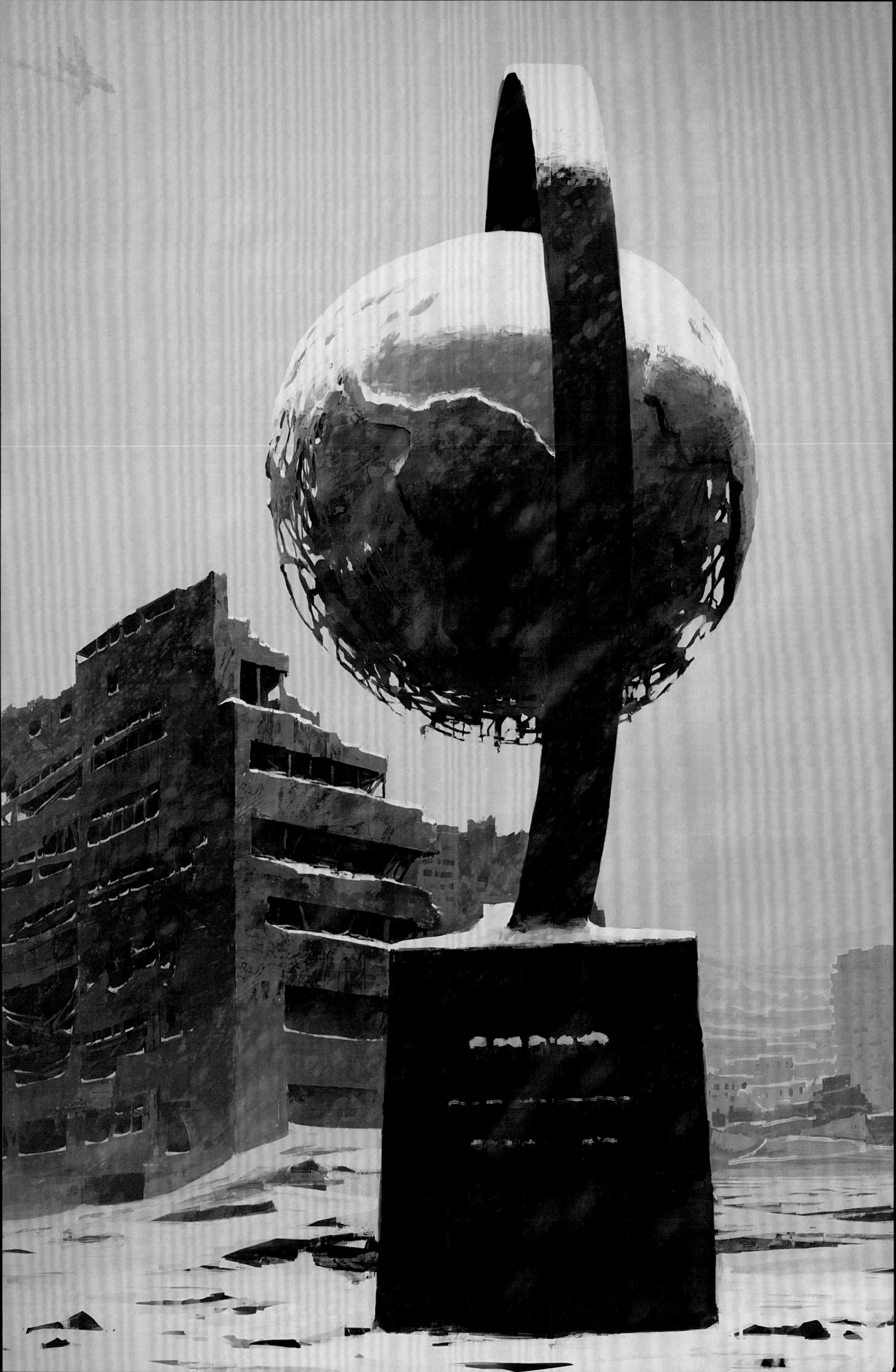

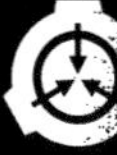
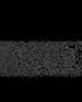

SCP-804 upon recovery.

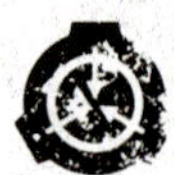

RECOVERY LOG SCP-804

Research Library File ▸ 804

Approximately 5 minutes after activation, the effect of SCP-804 reached the nearby community of ████ ████. Citizens who were not at the art show initially responded with panic and made several emergency calls. Due to the extreme remote location of the town, the first response was made by a small single-prop aircraft which arrived about thirty minutes later. Although the plane entered the area of effect and was quickly lost, the pilot did relay a radio message describing the swift and complete destruction of the town's buildings. At this point, the Foundation became aware of the situation and teams of agents were sent to investigate.

By the time agents were able to arrive on scene, SCP-804 had been intermittently active for nearly eight hours and as a result the town and everything in a radius of [DATA EXPUNGED] was wiped clean of any trace of human civilization. Upon arrival, one plane was immediately affected; fortunately, the crew was able to make an emergency landing before the physical structure of the plane collapsed around them. Unfortunately, their equipment and clothing was also quickly disintegrated, exposing them to the extreme cold of northern Alaska. As a result, six agents had to be treated for hypothermia, but all are expected to return to duty with no lasting effects.

After recovering the crew of the downed plane, agents set up a perimeter and were able to observe the epicenter of SCP-804's effect. The surviving population of ████ ████ had crowded around the remains of the device. All subjects observed were severely emaciated and suffering from severe hypothermia. Exposure had only worsened the effect of SCP-804 and many subjects were observed with missing digits and even limbs. The survivors were approaching the device in teams of two to three to push at the single remaining globe within SCP-804's housing in order to maintain its effect. As each subject eventually succumbed and collapsed, another from the crowd of onlookers would shuffle forward to take their place. Survivors were seen to be cheering and encouraging those who were maintaining the device until their turn to push the frosted globe came up, although such manual operation was not sufficient to maintain even the radius of effect the device had achieved before damaging itself.

Agents were authorized by 05-█ to open fire on the crowd. Although bullets experience the same decay as any other artifact, their velocity was enough to strike lethal wounds before decomposition. When the remaining globe of SCP-804 ceased to spin, the effect ended and agents were able to move in and secure the device. Survivors attempted to resist but lacked the strength to impede Foundation agents and began to act in a disoriented manner once they were removed from SCP-804. With no adequate facilities remaining to provide shelter for them all, many survivors chose to simply lie down in the snow and die while others attempted to provoke agents into using lethal force upon them. Those who were taken into custody refused to answer any questions and were able to refuse enough care that they did not recover from their physical decay.

As exposure to the extreme elements of northern Alaska appears to adequately contain SCP-804 by freezing its remaining machinery in place, it was decided to leave the device on site and under guard along with a [DATA EXPUNGED] in the unlikely event that a hostile faction attempts to secure the device.

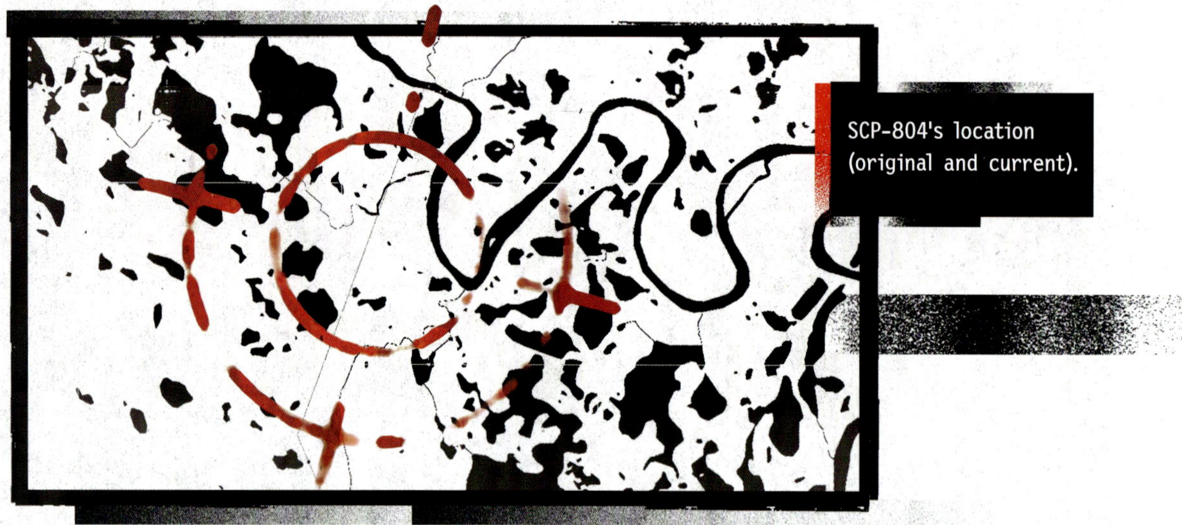

SCP-804's location (original and current).

ADDENDUM

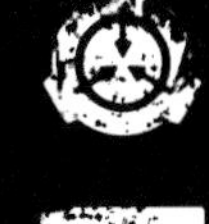

Research Library File ▸ 804

SCP-804 is not to be contained within any Foundation facility until it is certain that we will be able to prevent anyone from being compelled to activate or maintain the rotation of the globe. Even a few minutes of SCP-804's effect could destroy its own containment and seriously compromise any other containment nearby.

CONTINGENCY 804-X [DATA EXPUNGED]

MEMETIC RESEARCH REPORT, REVISED JULY 2011 BY DR. JOHANNES SORTS

This is the third annual review of any "supernatural" memetic component to SCP-804, and we still have not produced any significant results. It's time to put the controversy on SCP-804 memetic properties to rest once and for all.

Yes, SCP-804 possesses memetic properties, and yes, these properties were responsible for driving the survivors of its activation event into sacrificing themselves to maintain the device.

But there is nothing especially virulent or dangerous about SCP-804's memetic properties. Only a few select personality types, outlined in the attached report, have any desire to re-activate the device. Most notable are the D-class sociopaths who show similar amusement when presented with a big red button that says "kill everything."

We've been looking at this all wrong, there is no magical compulsion that could drive so many people to destroy themselves. There does not need to be. Everything we observed during recovery can be explained by mundane group dynamics and human nature.

The device had just wiped away all trace of the work and the lives of a reclusive artist and activist community. The buildings crumbled into dust so fast that people were not even injured in the collapse. And at the center of it all A World Without Man turned around and around on its increasingly rickety platform, offering a deadly premise that had been presented to them as an ideal. A cure for the virus known as humanity.

So why did a group of activists throw themselves and their neighbors into the deadly workings of a machine that they thought was going to wipe all human life off of Mother Earth?

They simply *wanted* to do it.

END OF REPORT

File >>> 009321

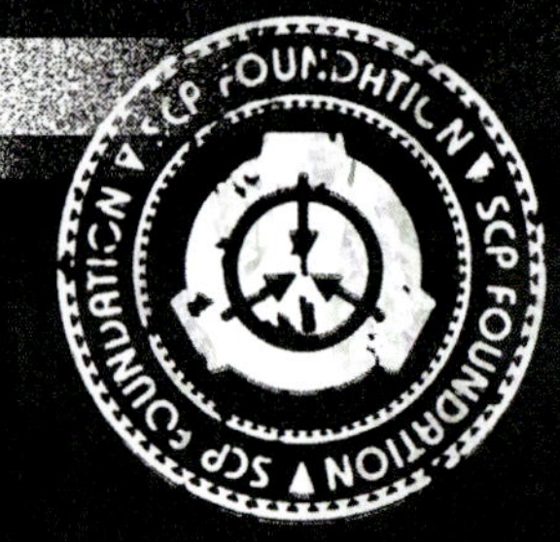

SCP-1733

Title

SEASON OPENER

Report by

bbaztek

Picture by

Alex Andreev

Access the original report on

scp-wiki.wikidot.com/scp-1733

Date

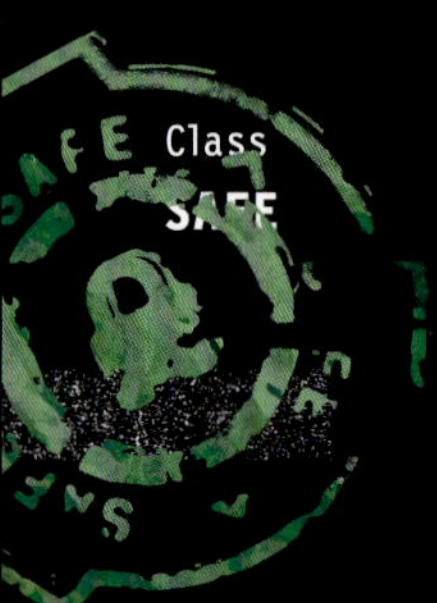

Class

SAFE

SPECIAL CONTAINMENT PROCEDURES

The DVR containing SCP-1733 is to be kept in a secure video archive at Site-█. Playback of SCP-1733 is strictly forbidden unless required for research. Personnel must contact Dr. Geller for permission to study SCP-1733.

DESCRIPTION

SCP-1733 is a digital recording of the 2010-2011 NBA season opening game played at the TD Garden in Boston, Massachusetts on 10/26/2010 between the Boston Celtics and Miami Heat. Agents monitoring social networking sites were alerted to SCP-1733 when Boston native ████ ████ complained in a Facebook thread on 10/27 about a technical foul in the third quarter involving players Ray Allen and Chris Bosh that never occurred in the original broadcast. When confronted, ████ ████ uploaded the relevant segment much to the confusion of his derogators. Foundation agents embedded in Facebook's moderator team deleted the thread and procured the IP addresses of all individuals present at the chat at this time to locate and administer Class-A amnestics. The Motorola brand DVR containing SCP-1733 was recovered for study.

Study of the footage has since revealed the nature of the recording's anomalous properties. Although initially diverging from the original broadcast only negligibly, such as quarter point totals and occurrences of fouls, SCP-1733 has begun to markedly digress from the content of its earlier playbacks. Recorded entities have been observed to retain memory of previous playings, and as such have developed a burgeoning awareness of their existence. It is hypothesized that playbacks impart an unquantifiable measure of cognizance to the entities inhabiting SCP-1733, with consecutive playings greatly expanding recall of previous events. This effect is cumulative and extends to all persons in the arena. Quality of awareness has progressed from reported feelings of intense déjà vu by commentator personalities Mike & Tommy to a near-eidetic memory of preceding playbacks. However, to note, no entities inside SCP-1733 have ever addressed the viewer directly, or shown awareness that they reside in a digital recording.

The individuals in the recording are virtually indistinguishable from their real life counterparts in talent, behavior, and mannerisms on court. Fans in the crowd also appear to be real human beings in all respects, and Foundation inquiries into the current status of these persons has found nothing of note. For all intents and purposes, recorded entities appear to be the actual individuals but somehow abiding in a digital medium. TD Garden records have put the number of people in attendance on 10/26/2010 at ████.

It was initially thought the purpose of SCP-1733 was to depict an infinite number of game outcomes, since players were able to modify offensive and defensive strategies during every playback. By playback 034, players and coaches became so keenly adapted to the opposing team's playbook that the score remained 0-0 until 3:34 in the first quarter. As quality of recall was still weak in early stage iterations, memory of preceding playbacks likely manifested as a vague intuition felt by players, fans, and team personnel alike, interfering with their ability to grasp the full scope of their situation.

By playback 045, however, comprehension of their predicament had reached such a point that players declined to play altogether and assembled with the rest of those in attendance to formulate possible escape plans. It is the conclusion of

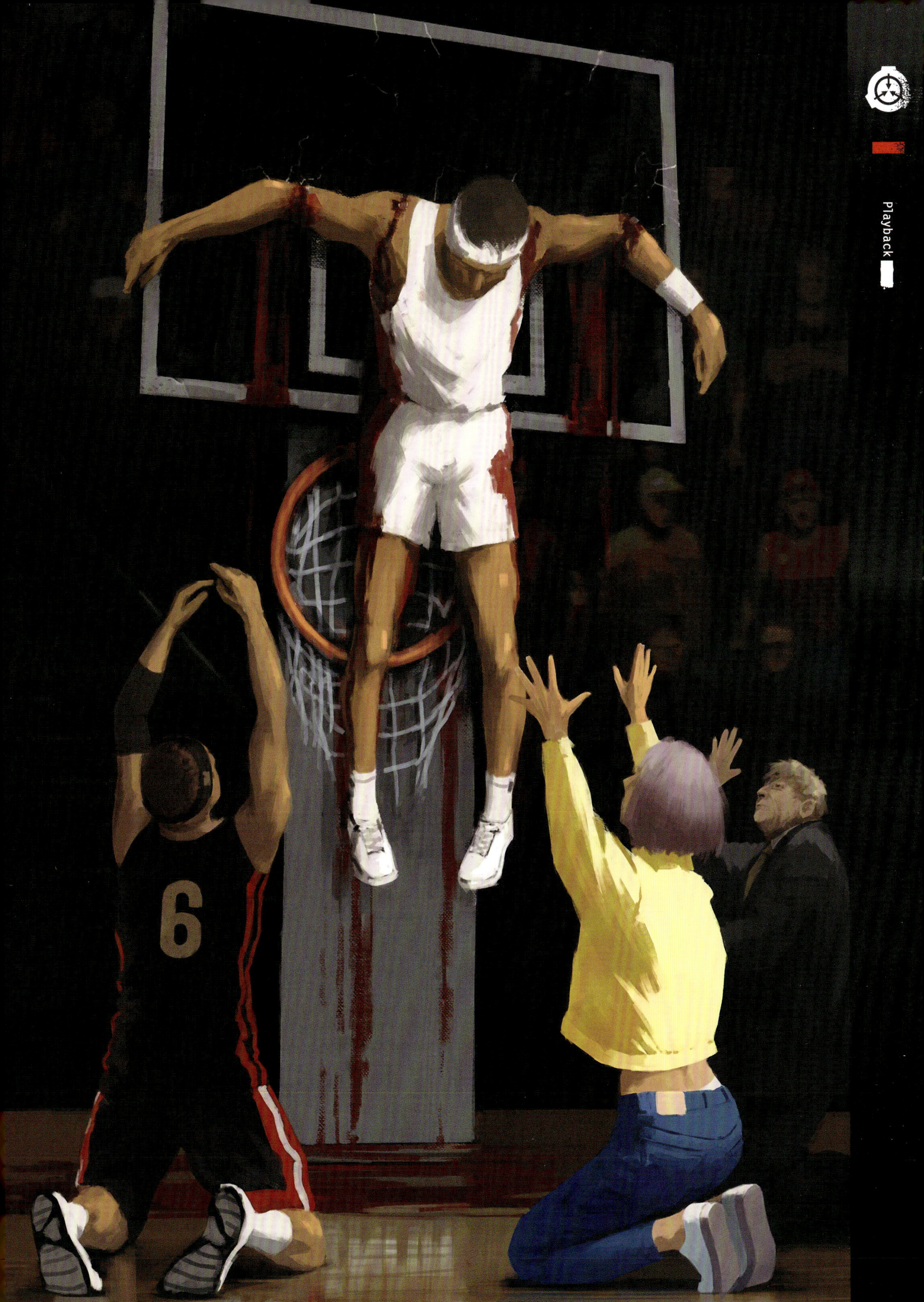

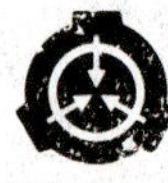

Research Library File ▸ 1733

Foundation researchers that the inhabitants of SCP-1733 are imprisoned in the setting of the recording, as they have been unable to exit by any means. Doors leading out of the arena have not yielded to an estimated force in excess of █████ N. The assembly has also been unable to exit from locker rooms, player facilities, and skyboxes. Waiting for patrons arriving in at scripted points prior to the start of the first quarter has also been unsuccessful: individuals leave by where patrons entered and are then unable to navigate an escape from the adjacent corridors that girdle the main arena. Escape attempts have since grown more desperate, and have included failed attempts at constructing makeshift explosives, all-out rioting, the fracturing of the assembly into three opposing factions, and by playback ████ the ritualistic murder and disembowelment of players in the hopes of appeasing whatever it is that confines them (see Timeline Document 001 for details). However, upon the beginning of a new playback, all persons are returned to their pre-game status unharmed.

Researchers have been unable to duplicate the effects of SCP-1733 with other recordings made by the DVR, confirming the device is not the source of SCP-1733's aberrant properties. Due to the distress visited upon inhabitants of SCP-1733, testing has been suspended indefinitely.

PARTIAL TIMELINE DOCUMENT 001

Playback #	Notable Developments
Playback 002	First recorded deviation from recorded broadcast. TD Garden crowd boos the Miami Heat during entrance. Miami Heat forward LeBron James observed to have scowled and shaken his head dismissively at the crowd.
Playback 015	Score remains 0-0 for eight consecutive possessions. Fans appear noticeably subdued when displayed on the facility's HD scoreboard screen. Celtics power forward Glen Davis is able to execute a crucial block late in the fourth quarter on LeBron James he could not complete during the original broadcast, securing the Celtics' lead. Commentators note Glen Davis's dedication to performing well on both sides of the court in spite of the "Big Three's blistering ball movement on offensive plays". A nascent awareness of previously played games has begun to form.
Playback 026	First Miami Heat victory, 112-85. Crowd becomes aggressive, shouting obscenities and hurling foodstuffs at the Celtics. Color commentator Tom Heinsohn understood the frustration, criticizing the Celtics' coaching staff for becoming so complacent after having "cracked the code of the Miami Heat offense". As this was the first game together for the Miami "Big Three", it is unlikely any coaching personnel would have become so adjusted to an unfamiliar offense in a single game.
Playback 027	Commentators Mike & Tommy note a feeling of déjà vu during the Heat's grandiose entrance. Crowd remains subdued during key Celtics plays. Celtics emerge the victors, prompting Tom Heinsohn to remark "the Celtics have come a long way winning back the hearts of their fans". When asked to elaborate by Mike Gorman, Heinsohn could only respond that he felt the team had an embarrassment to atone for, but could not specify further.
Playback 044	Teams emerge disoriented and confused. Game is suspended. Majority of time is spent by medical professionals assessing the mental state of players, who remain convinced they had dreamt playing the season opener frequently the previous night. When informed of the situation by team staff, commentators Mike & Tommy affirm the same feeling. Crowd is also afflicted. Recording ends with court-side correspondents interviewing members of the crowd on the nature of their dreams.
Playback 045	Players refuse to play. Cameramen, facility personnel, players, commentators, and crowd members gather in the court to appraise the situation. All persons are convinced they are reliving the same game repeatedly. Doors are tested but cannot be budged. Recording closes as crowd begins to fashion makeshift weapons to pry open doors. Last instance of camera being manipulated by the camera crew. All following playbacks are seen through a single static shot of a broadcast view camera.

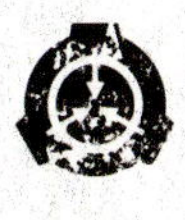

Research Library File ▸ 1733

Playback 051	No attempts to exit the building have succeeded. All exits in the arena and adjacent areas remain sealed. A physical altercation in balcony section 318 between an inebriated group of college-aged males and one older male leaves the older male concussed on the floor and unconscious. As broadcast camera is unable to pick up audible voices on opposite side of the arena, presumably the dispute occurred over the group of males not assisting with escape plans. First recorded violent incident.
Playback 052	The man knocked unconscious in previous playback is returned to previous state unharmed upon the beginning of current recording. The man ambushes and bludgeons one of his attackers to death at 34:12 mark.
Playback 055	Cognitization has progressed to such a point that the crowd is now able to remember the events of that week, as well as friends and family members outside the facility. Attempts to contact outside for help are met with failure.
Playback 065	Crowd is unable to exit the facility. Congregation has since dissolved into the following groups and "factions": players, coaches, and all involved team personnel have presumably barricaded themselves in off-screen player facilities. The infirm and parents accompanied by their children have retreated to the northeast corner of the balcony rise and have elected to wait out playbacks as they occur, marking their territory with a Celtics championship flag draped over Section 320. █ individuals henceforth referred to as the "Faithkeepers" have proselytized to multiple gatherings that they believe being confined to the TD Garden is a punishment for rampant consumerism of the post-industrial world, and have burned "offerings" of mobile phones, car keys, handbags, and wallets in center court for the past four playbacks. The group comprises Boston churchgoers and [REDACTED]. A notable portion of adults numbering approximately █ individuals, however, remain diligent in formulating escape plans.
Playback 073	The "Faithkeepers" grow in number after previous playback incident, where three males were severely injured by an improvised explosive fastened to an exit door. No damage to the door is visible.
Playback 095	Hedonistic displays of sex and violence have sufficiently curbed the efforts of proselytizers. Makeshift curtains are hung around the site of an orgy at loge 8 at the urging of Section 320 members.
Playback 112	Conditions have deteriorated considerably. █ individuals leapt from balcony section in opening ten minutes of playback 112.
Playback █	Faithkeepers storm player facilities to retrieve Paul Pierce and LeBron James. The players are ritually sacrificed and their bodies are subsequently displayed on the arena's "Jumbo-tron". The murder of players seems to have no effect on the recording.
Playback █	Proselytizers have begun to call for the sacrifice of children. Adults have formed a wall between Group 320 and the Faithkeepers.
Playback █	First recorded deviation in arena light to a deep red color. [DATA EXPUNGED].

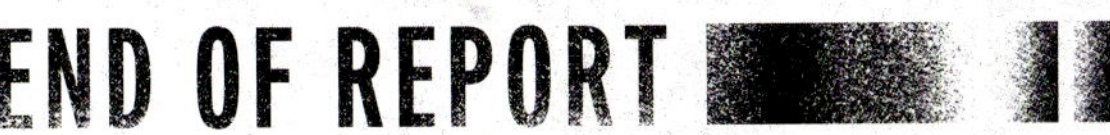

File >>> 003234

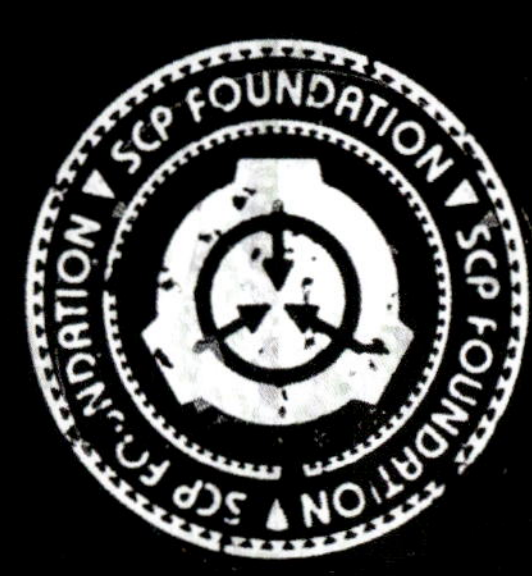

SCP-221

Title

COMPULSION TWEEZERS

Report by

Arlecchino

Picture by

Ivan Efimov

Access the original report on

scp-wiki.wikidot.com/scp-221

Date

Class

SAFE

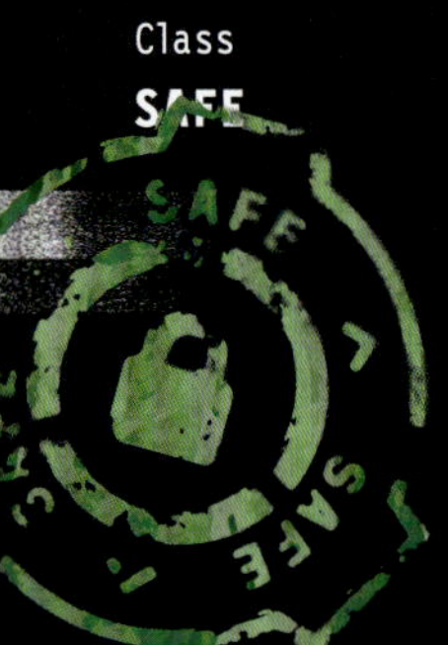

SPECIAL CONTAINMENT PROCEDURES

SCP-221 is to be kept in a locked container where it cannot be removed except for further testing by Security Clearance Level 2 Personnel. The container is a 15.25 cm by 15.25 cm steel box with a cushioned interior, with an internal locking system. The container is to be placed in a locked room, with a guard to ensure that SCP-221 is not taken.

DESCRIPTION

SCP-221 is a pair of tweezers made out of gold, made in the 16th or 17th century. After subject testing it was noted that the damaged areas which had been used to gather material samples were smaller than they had been prior to the test. It is currently theorized that SCP-221 uses the minute amounts of gold in the human body to regenerate damage to itself.

Subject testing revealed that SCP-221 creates a highly focused case of Obsessive-Compulsive Disorder in any person which uses it on their own body. Subjects will utilize SCP-221 to slowly remove any and all hair from their body, before removing finger and toenails, as well as teeth, culminating with the removal of organs, both the external, such as the eyes and skin, and the internal, such as the liver and pancreas, using their hands if SCP-221 is not effective (though SCP-221 will never be set aside during this process, and remains gripped in one of the subject's hands). If SCP-221 is taken away from the subject, they become violent and manic, and will use their hands to continue the process, albeit in a less careful manner. It is to be noted that the progression of this behavior is different for each subject, but no less fatal.

SCP-221 came into Foundation possession after reports of a human being who was [DATA EXPUNGED]. Foundation personnel retrieved SCP-221 within 10 hours of the original report.

ADDENDUM

Test Log 221-1: The test subject, a Class-D, was ordered to use SCP-221 to remove his eyebrow hair. While the subject was initially unenthusiastic about his task, after the first 10 minutes he began to more actively pluck out his own eyebrow hair, and after completely denuding his brow, moved on to plucking out his eyelashes, despite repeated assertions that the test was over. When released after SCP-221 was taken out of the room, he began to pluck out his eyelashes with his own fingers, completely removing all of them before moving on to his toenails. The subject completely removed his toe and fingernails, before yelling and smashing his own face against a wall. The reason for this outburst became apparent when he reached into his mouth and began ripping out his now loosened teeth. Eventually the subject died from blood loss and shock, halfway through the task of pulling out his own internal organs.

Test Log 221-2: The test subjects were two Class-D personnel, Test Subject 1, ordered to use SCP-221 on the other Class-D, Test Subject 2. After 15 minutes, the test subjects began to argue about how the holder of SCP-221 was using it on the other. The test subjects began to fight for use of SCP-221, Test Subject 1 used SCP-221 to stab Test Subject 2 through the eye, piercing into the brain, immediately killing him. Test Subject 1 began to use SCP-221 to remove his own eyelashes, continuing to his teeth and eyes. Test Subject 1 died of blood loss, after removing 73% of the skin on his body.

END OF REPORT

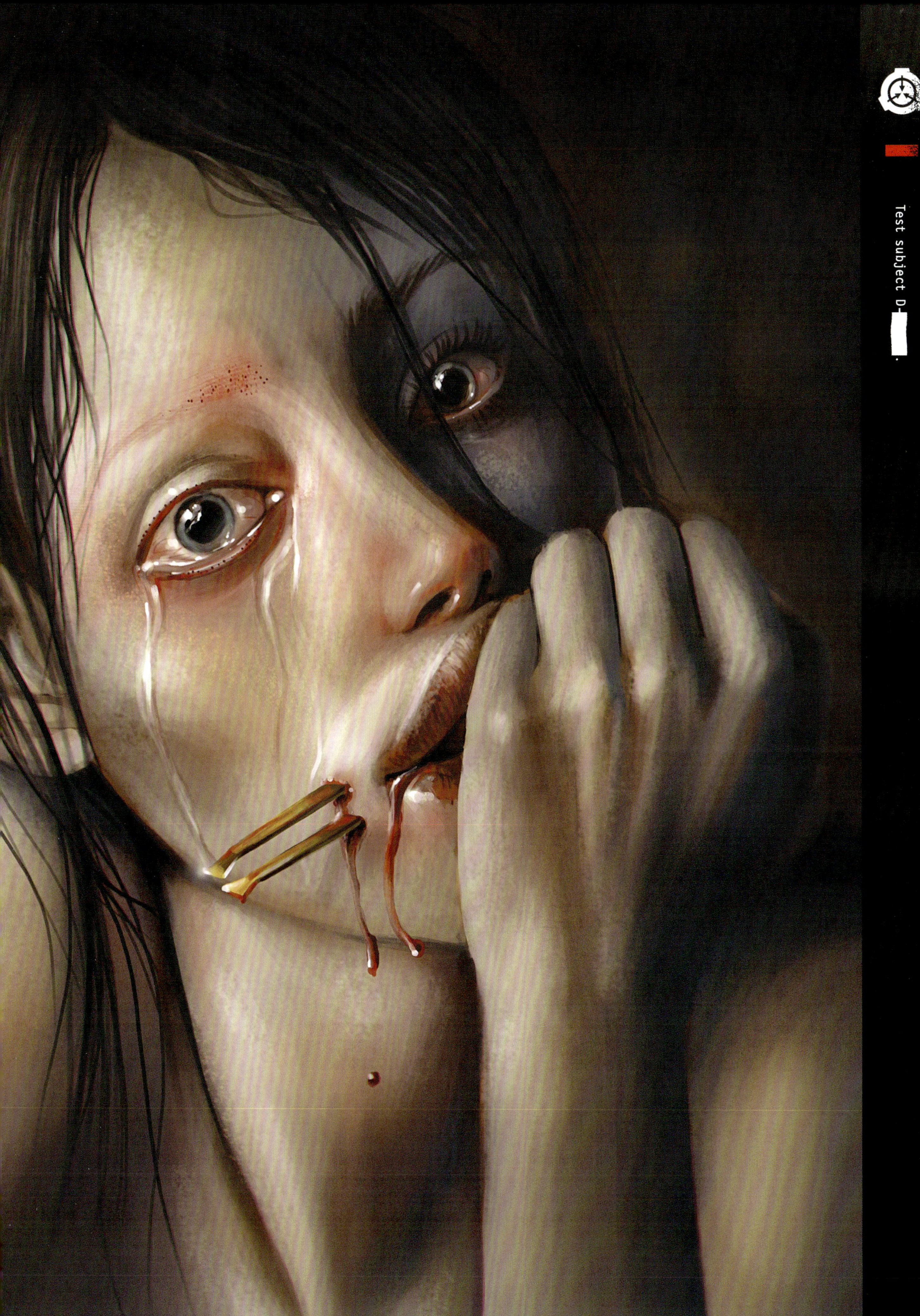
Test subject D-█.

File >>> 9831110

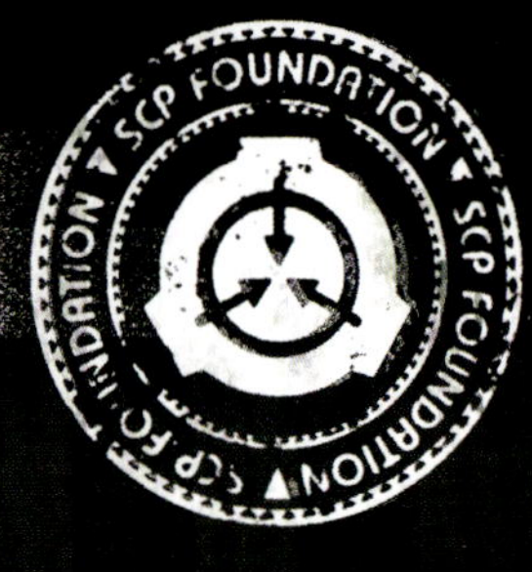

SCP-059

Title

RADIOACTIVE MINERAL

Report by

far2

Picture by

Artem Grigoryan

Access the original report on

scp-wiki.wikidot.com/scp-059

Date

Class

KETER

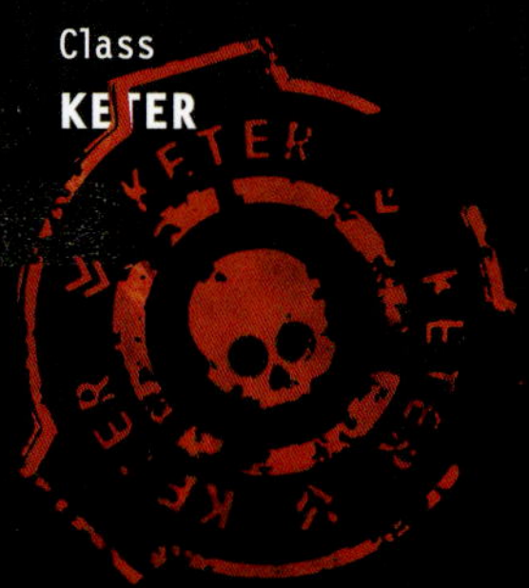

SPECIAL CONTAINMENT PROCEDURES

A single specimen of SCP-059 is kept at Site-11B inside a graded-Z laminate shielding box composed of depleted uranium, tantalum, tin, steel, copper, and aluminum. Surrounding SCP-059's containment box is a 7 x 7 x 7 m area sealed as a Level-4 Biohazard area, and surrounded by 3 cm of lead shielding. This area is to be sprayed daily with a solution of methyl isothiocyanate to prevent overgrowth of SCP-059-1.

Personnel entering an SCP-059 affected area are cautioned to wear appropriate biohazard protection, as well as Type K-59-B radiation shielding. They are to remain in the area for no more than 15 minutes, as the radiation shielding is only partially effective.

SCP-059-1 infestations found in the wild should be contained by removing the SCP-059 specimen responsible, and incineration of all observed SCP-059-1. Large underground infestations are best neutralized by fuel-air (thermobaric) explosives.

Additional specimens of SCP-059 are not needed for experimentation, and should be transported to Site-11B for incineration by plasma arc at 10,000 Kelvin.

DESCRIPTION

SCP-059 is a radioactive mineral of unknown origin, superficially resembling scheelite. A component of SCP-059 is believed to originate in an alternate universe, and to be responsible for its anomalous properties. In addition to alpha, beta, and gamma radiation, SCP-059 specimens produce a previously unknown type of radiation, apparently unique to the object, tentatively designated 'delta radiation'. Delta radiation is accompanied by Cherenkov radiation, visible as a blue glow.

Delta radiation is only partially contained by standard radiation shielding; the best results have been obtained using graded-Z laminate shielding with an additional super-dense metal layer. This reduces the effective range of delta radiation from approximately 20 m to approximately 6 m.

When an area is exposed to delta radiation for more than 15 minutes, an unknown species of fungus (designated SCP-059-1) begins to grow on any exposed surface. This fungus does not require any standard nutrition, but will die within 24 hours of removal from a delta radiation source. SCP-059-1 is itself radioactive, but does not emit delta radiation. However, if a critical mass (approximately █ kg/m3) of SCP-059-1 is allowed to grow, delta radiation from an unknown source other than SCP-059 will appear in the area, further supporting SCP-059-1 growth. (Interested readers may consult Dr. ████ for his theories of space-time stress and merger of alternate realities). Within 18 hours, the infected mass will become transparent and disappear, presumably into the universe that is the source of delta radiation. The process then continues with SCP-059-1 infecting new material.

SCP-059-1 will infest both living beings and inanimate objects. Humans (and animals) infected with SCP-059-1 become immune to the effects of ionizing radiation, but progressively merge with SCP-059-1, and eventually have all tissues replaced by fungal growth. While generally non-violent, they will attempt to expose unaffected individuals to SCP-059. SCP-059-1 infections do not appear to be directly contagious, but only spread by contact with delta radiation. However,

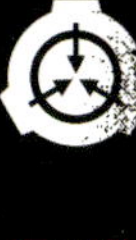

Subject D-█ infected with SCP-059-1.

Research Library File ▸ 059

long-term exposure to SCP-059-1 has not been adequately tested to rule out considering it a biohazard (as well as a known radiation hazard).

Infected individuals still capable of communication describe seeing a world entirely covered with SCP-059-1, where much of the surface is composed of SCP-059. It is unclear whether this is a hallucination or a view into the source of SCP-059. Infectees are generally pleased with their condition and often refer to being in "the blue light of heaven."

SCP-059-1 is affected by most fungicides, but new growth will continue as long as SCP-059 is present. Early stage SCP-059-1 infection in humans may be treated with griseofulvin, however the treatment is 90% likely to lead to death by radiation poisoning. Treated individuals lose their immunity to radiation, and will already have absorbed a now lethal dose prior to treatment. Late stage treatment should not be attempted, as too much tissue will already be converted to SCP-059-1. [DATA EXPUNGED]. The remains of failed treatments should be kept out of range of SCP-059, otherwise [DATA EXPUNGED].

SCP-059 specimens have been discovered in 8 different underground locations, across a range of 5000 km. No pattern has emerged for their appearance. Specimens range from 1-10 kg in size, and are not part of the normal rock formations in the areas where they have been found.

Dr. ████ has recorded and analyzed the pattern of radiation emitted by the contained SCP-059-1 colony, and believes SCP-059-1 may be sapient and attempting to communicate via controlled emissions of radiation. Initial attempts to analyze this "language" reveal ████

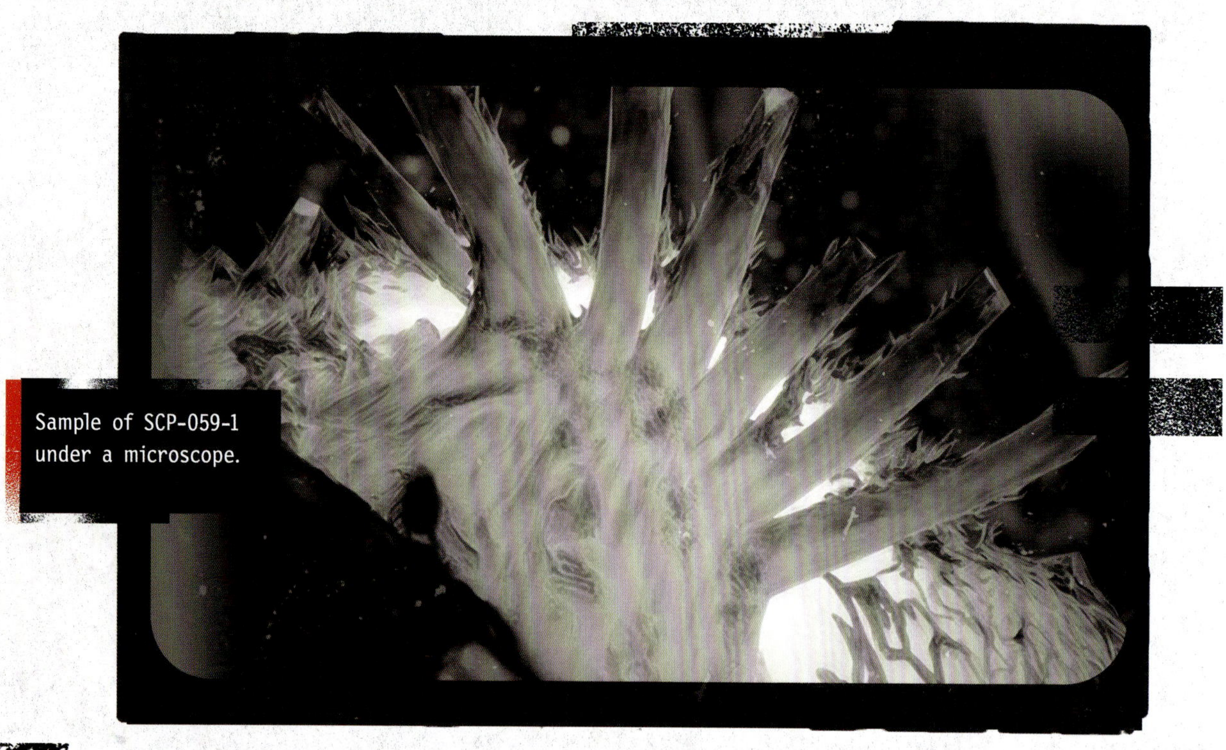

Sample of SCP-059-1 under a microscope.

END OF REPORT

SPECIAL CONTAINMENT PROCEDURES

SCP-835 is to be monitored and checked daily for new growth. In the event SCP-835 becomes hostile, Suppression Tactic A-A6 is to be immediately implemented until aggressive action ceases. Containment area must be maintained in open ocean, due to the highly aggressive response of SCP-835 to confinement for any length of time.

Waste issued by SCP-835 must be immediately collected and contained. Feeding of SCP-835 is to take place twice daily, to consist [DATA EXPUNGED]. SCP-835 may be moved to a new location twice yearly, provided that the current location is no longer capable of supporting SCP-835, and the move has been approved by Site Command.

Staff are to remain at least five meters away from SCP-835. Anyone working near SCP-835 must have safety lines attached to recall winches. Contact with SCP-835 will result in the immediate recall of all staff, and implementation of Suppression Tactic A-A6. Should contact result in full capture of a staff member, SCP-835 is to be monitored constantly until the release of the subject.

DESCRIPTION

SCP-835 appears to be a large mass of coral-like polyps weighing ███ tons. The individual polyps are larger than any known coral species, growing to more than one meter in diameter in some cases. The central mass is roughly oval shaped, with a very large (3 meter diameter) polyp at each "end". SCP-835 is incapable of locomotion, and appears to anchor itself with the large tentacles projected from the SCP-835 polyps. These are also used in feeding, and are coated with a sticky adhesive substance. The tentacles are also quite strong, and have been shown to be capable of damaging plate steel.

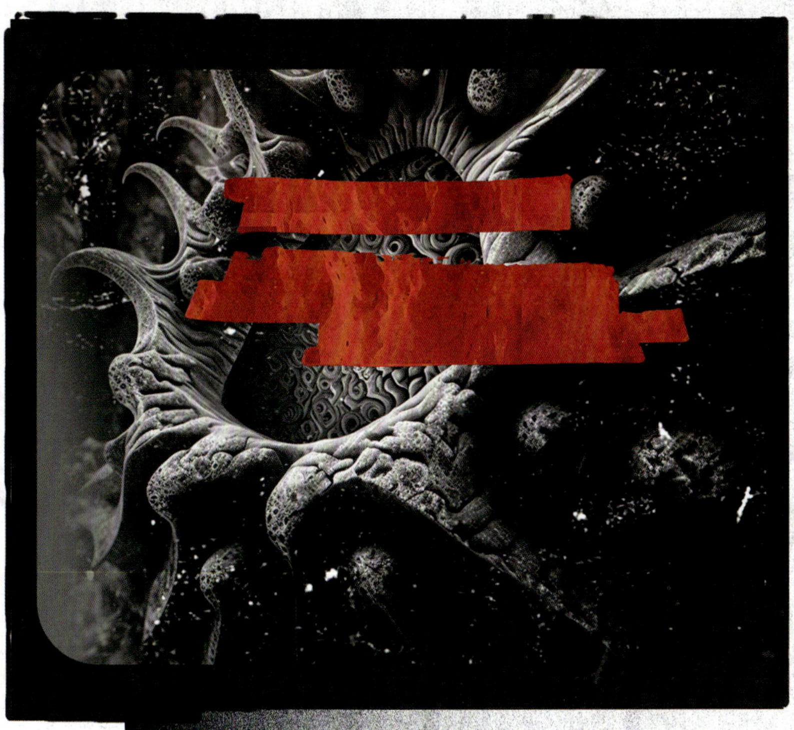

File >>> 0172331

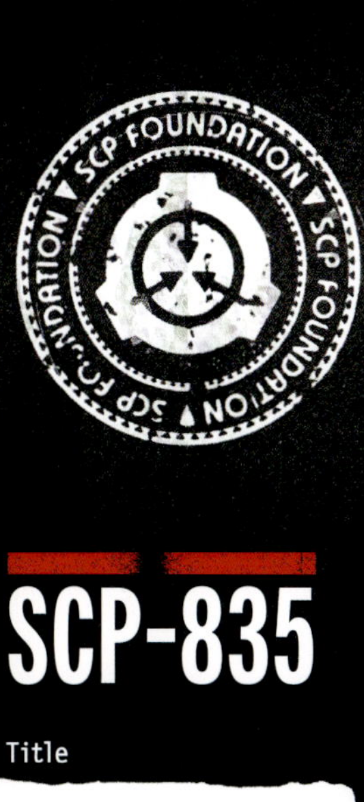

SCP-835

Title

█████████

Report by

Aelanna

Picture by

Dmitriy Fomin

Access the original report on

scp-wiki.wikidot.com/scp-835

Date

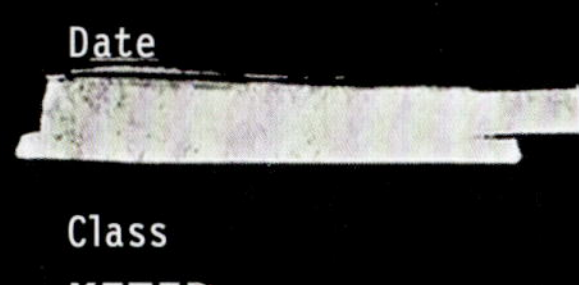

Class

KETER

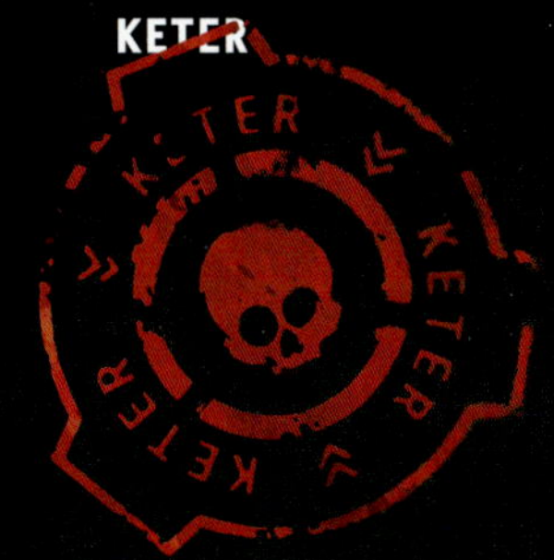

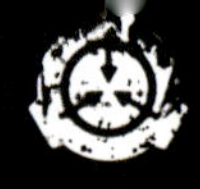

The coral of SCP-835 is extremely hard, requiring high-powered diamond drills to collect even small samples. SCP-835 also grows at a very accelerated rate, capable of adding 22.68kg (50lbs) of mass every day. SCP-835 is susceptible to many chemicals, which cause SCP-835 to "seal up" and halt all growth for 24 hours, prompting the development and use of Suppression Tactic A-A6. Testing has shown [DATA EXPUNGED]

SCP-835 emits a large mass of semi-liquid material several times a day from the large polyps on each "end". This appears to be made of semi-digested solids, fecal material, and semen. This mass also has several forms of virus, bacteria, and parasites, many of which have been found only within SCP-835. The bacterium 835-I5 forms the major concern for containment, due to [DATA EXPUNGED]. This, coupled with the extremely hard "shell" of SCP-835, form a major obstacle to neutralization. Any force capable of "cracking open" SCP-835 would also cause the "slurry" inside to spread, and cause additional infection from 835-I5.

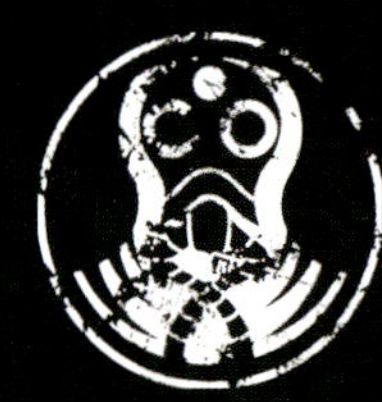

FIRST DRAFT OF AFTER ACTION

REPORT BY MOBILE TASK FORCE ZETA-NINER: CIRCUMSTANCES OF RETRIEVAL

On ██/██/████ at ██:██:██ hours, Mobile Task Force Zeta-Niner (Mole Rats) conducted an investigation of SCP-835. At this time, SCP-835 had a mass of only four tons, and only one large polyp at the north end of the structure (designated Polyp Alpha), Polyp Bravo not yet being in existence.

As per standard procedure, four team members were chosen for the initial investigation. Standard isolation suits (underwater variant) were worn by all four team members: Lieutenant C██████ took point as team leader, while Sergeants L█████ and M█████ served as support. Corporal H████ a rookie team member, accompanied the team as an observer. A standard Underwater Remote Vehicle, or URV, was used for initial investigation.

SCP-835 did not, at first, act in a hostile manner towards the team, allowing team members to approach and make contact without incident. URV-01 was sent to investigate the exterior of the object while team members C, L, and M proceeded towards what they believed to be the entrance of the site. Corporal H was ordered to remain outside and to monitor URV-1 in order to ensure that the device's tether did not become tangled on the exterior protrusions.

The first sign of trouble occurred when Corporal H, while attempting to clear a jam in URV-1's sampling claw, reported in with the words, "Oh god, help me, help me." He then reported that "some horrible tentacle thing" had wrapped around his arm and was dragging him in towards a "fucking mouth," and vocalized several distress calls… Jesus Christ. I can't do this. Fucking… goddamn it, he was just a kid! It was his first fucking mission, I should have kept my eye on him!

Christ… all right, here goes, guess I'll just let Sarge edit this for me. Again.

So the thing grabbed the kid. It had me fooled to rights. The entrance wasn't an entrance, it was just… some cave. The real entrance was the big polyp thing on the north end. It grabbed the kid and started dragging him towards the mouth. Topside started to drag him up, but all they got was a snapped cable. And the kid? He got pulled inside and eaten.

[DATA EXPUNGED] I got the carabiner on, we're hooked together, and topside starts winching us up… and we're not getting anywhere. I'm grabbing on, I'm telling him I'm not gonna let go, and then the winch starts to seize up, and I feel this jerk on the tether and it goes slack, and then we're both sliding into that damn thing.

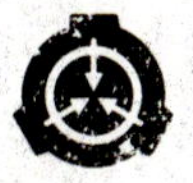

It was like… Jesus, I need another drink… fuck. It was like… the only way I can think of it was like you know that thing that doctors do when they stick a tube up someone's ass and look at the inside of their intestines? I saw that on TV once, it was like that, except I was going down the throat of some horrible underwater hell-monster, not up some poor bastard's rear. There were these… muscular contractions, I guess, and they were slowly sliding us down the length of the tube. If we weren't wearing the hard suits, we'd have been crushed, but as it was, we were held so tight we could barely move, even with power-assist. I managed to get my head up enough to see the kid's face. His faceplate was covered in vomit, poor bastard had puked in his suit. I started yelling for him, trying to get him to say something. He managed to tell me he was all right. He was sobbing like a baby.

I started doing some calculations. Based on my dead reckoning tracker and initial sonar scans, we were moving about a meter every minute. That meant seventy two hours until we came out the other side, assuming we did. We had the air, our rebreathers could keep going for days. What we didn't have was the power to keep the suits warm for that long. If the heat went out, hypothermia would kill us… I dunno, look it up, in any case we'd be dead. We needed to conserve power.

I told the kid to turn off his helmet lights, lock his joints, and turn down his heater to minimal. He started crying. He didn't wanna do it. I didn't blame him, but I told him we had no choice. We finally agreed to shut down everything but our internal helmet lights, at least. It seemed to calm him down, and honestly, that extra 0.1 percent power wouldn't make a difference.

I think that was the worst part. We spent at least a day like that, locked in our suits. Couldn't move our arms and legs. No sound but the thing's gurgling and your own breathing and the sound of your rebreather. The puke on the kid's faceplate started to dry up and flake off about an hour or so in so I could see his face. He looked tired and scared.

I think… check the logs, Sarge, I think it was about thirteen hours in when the kid started talking again. Kid started babbling. [DATA EXPUNGED]. Anyway, after that, he calmed down a lot. I told him to take a nap. He slept a bit, thank god.

About twenty four hours in, we reached… I guess they're calling it the stomach now. First warning sign was a gurgling kind of noise, louder, with a crunching noise over it. I told the kid to bring his suit up to full power and get ready. A little while after, we fell out into this big chamber… big as in, big enough for the two of us to fit in it comfortably, which was huge compared to the tight squeeze of the tube. Kid's suit started hissing and the outer shell started to turn all pitted and stuff, and I noticed my gloves were starting to degrade too, so I yelled at him to move, and we started heading towards this… sphincter, I guess. I remember… god, why can I remember this, the insides of the stomach were lined with [DATA EXPUNGED].

I almost lost it there. [DATA EXPUNGED] I'd stayed, my suit would have melted and I'd be dead, but the kid grabbed me and shoved me headfirst through the sphincter and we fell into… the other place.

It was even worse than the stomach. [DATA EXPUNGED], this place was… well, you know what it was full of. I'm not squeamish, Bill, you can't be if you're a Mole Rat, but this place squicked me out so bad I almost passed out. The kid helped me back up to my feet, though, told me we were almost out. "Come on, Lieutenant, we're almost out of here, let's go," he said. We moved over to the other sphincter, but the thing was… well, it was puckered up tighter than my Drill Sergeant's asshole back in basic. So no way we were getting out of there.

We decided to wait for a bit until the thing shot its load, so to speak: ██ ██ ███ ███ ██ ██ ██ ███ ███ ███ ██ ██ ███ █████, ███? Anyway, that's when things started to go bad. [DATA EXPUNGED] I managed to wrestle the thing ██ ██ ██ ███ ██ ██ through the sphincter into the stomach. Its tentacles writhed at me as it started to melt. [DATA EXPUNGED]

Then 835 blew its load and I flew out its ass into the ocean.

You know the rest of the story, Bill. [DATA EXPUNGED] So yeah, fill out the rest of the reports and the logs for me, will ya? Oh, and be sure to edit it so the motherfuckers in command don't yell at me for being unprofessional in my AARs again. I'm gonna finish off my drink and take a couple Valium and go to bed. [DATA EXPUNGED] Thanks.

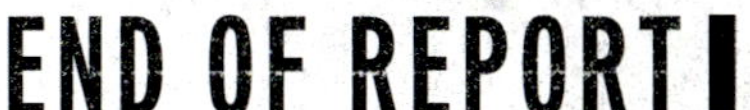

File >>> 0027334

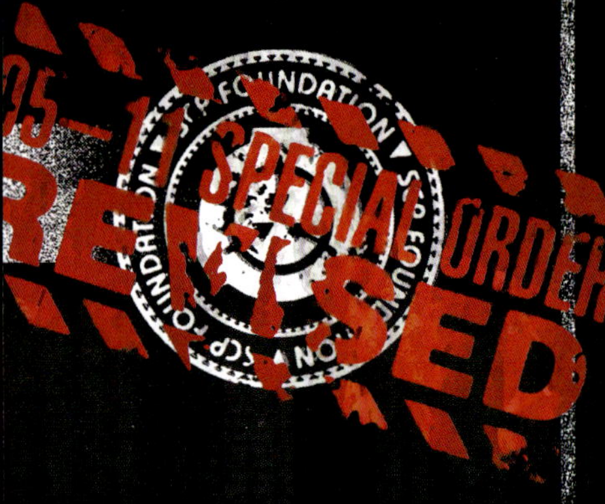

SCP-835

Title

EXPUNGED DATA RELEASED

Report by

Aelanna

Picture by

Dmitriy Fomin

Access the original report on

scp-wiki.wikidot.com/835

Date

Class

KETER

NOTICE FROM THE FOUNDATION RECORDS AND INFORMATION SECURITY ADMINISTRATION

This document requires Level 4 Clearance and authorization for Need-to-Know under **CODE TRITON VICTOR BLUE**. If you do not possess the necessary security clearances, please close this document immediately and report the security breach to the Records and Information Security Administration.

Thank you.

– Maria Jones, Director, RAISA

SPECIAL CONTAINMENT PROCEDURES

SCP-835 is to be monitored and checked daily for new growth. In the event SCP-835 becomes hostile, Suppression Tactic A-A6 is to be immediately implemented until aggressive action ceases. Containment area must be maintained in open ocean, due to the highly aggressive response of SCP-835 to confinement for any length of time.

Waste issued by SCP-835 must be immediately collected and contained. Feeding of SCP-835 is to take place twice daily, to consist of any form of local aquatic species. Feedings should be supervised at all times, and no unscheduled feedings of SCP-835 are to take place for any reason. Should SCP-835 enter a "rage" state, higher level mammals may be issued as a food supply, up to and including Homo sapiens. SCP-835 has shown high levels of docility when digesting higher level mammalian life, and recommendation for the issuing of this form of food has been approved for use during testing phases. SCP-835 may be moved to a new location twice yearly, provided that the current location is no longer capable of supporting SCP-835, and the move has been approved by Site Command.

Staff are to remain at least five yards away from SCP-835. Anyone working near SCP-835 must have safety lines attached to recall winches. Contact with SCP-835 will result in the immediate recall of all staff, and implementation of Suppression Tactic A-A6. Should contact result in full capture of a staff member, SCP-835 is to be monitored constantly until the release of the subject.

DESCRIPTION

SCP-835 appears to be a large mass of coral-like polyps weighing ██████ tons. The individual polyps are larger than any known coral species, growing to more than one meter in diameter in some cases. The central mass is roughly oval shaped, with a very large (3 meter diameter) polyp at each "end". SCP-835 is incapable of locomotion, and appears to anchor itself with the large tentacles projected from the SCP-835 polyps. These are also used in feeding, and are coated with a sticky adhesive substance. The tentacles are also quite strong, and have been shown to be capable of damaging plate steel.

The "coral" of SCP-835 is extremely hard, requiring high-powered diamond drills to collect even small samples. SCP-835 also grows at a very accelerated rate, capable

of adding 50lbs of mass every day. SCP-835 is susceptible to many chemicals, which cause SCP-835 to "seal up" and halt all growth for 24 hours, prompting the development and use of Suppression Tactic A-A6. Testing has shown that SCP-835 appears to be made from basic human biological components, with the shell being formed from super-dense calcium, the "caps" that cover the polyps coated with tooth enamel, and the tentacles appearing to be formed from mutated tongue cells. Most human biological systems are present, however many (neurological, lymphatic, circulatory, etc.) show extreme mutation and atrophy. The digestive and reproductive systems appear both highly developed and linked, with both feces and semen being collected and ejected from the same "chamber".

SCP-835 emits a large mass of semi-liquid material several times a day from the large polyps on each "end". This appears to be made of semi-digested solids, fecal material, and semen. This mass also has several forms of virus, bacteria, and parasites, many of which have been found only within SCP-835. The bacterium 835-I5 forms the major concern for containment, due to its role in the reproductive cycle of SCP-835. Vertebrate animals infected with SCP-835-I5 will undergo the following symptoms:

- Increased weight gain (10-20lbs a day on average)
- Constant hunger
- Urge to consume normally unpleasant/unpalatable items (Raw meat, organs, grass, wood)
- Hardening/calcification of the skin
- Formation of polyps on the skin
- Rapid reduction in intelligence and mobility
- Increased aggression
- Urge to enter sea water
- Atrophy of many major biological systems

End stage infection appears to convert the subject into an additional instance of SCP-835. Attempts to determine what, if any, intelligence remains have been inconclusive; however SCP-835 appears to have a limited amount of awareness. 835-I5 has shown a very high infectivity rate, with 68% of all infected subjects progressing to end stage. There is no form of treatment or antibiotic that has been shown to halt or reverse the effects of 835-I5. This, coupled with the extremely hard "shell" of SCP-835, form a major obstacle to neutralization. Any force capable of "cracking open" SCP-835 would also cause the "slurry" inside to spread, and cause additional infection from 835-I5.

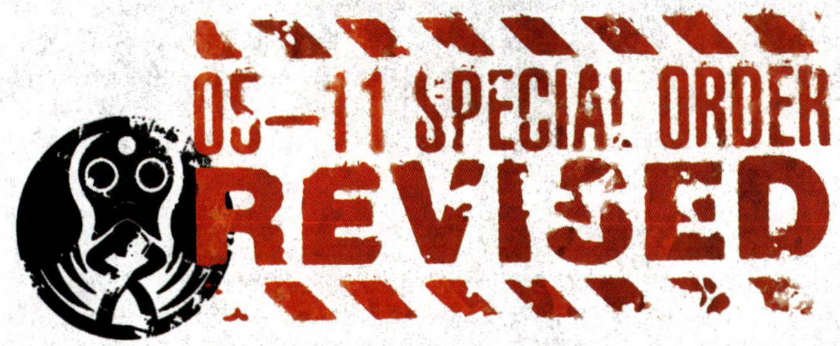

FIRST DRAFT OF AFTER ACTION

REPORT BY MOBILE TASK FORCE ZETA-NINER: CIRCUMSTANCES OF RETRIEVAL

On █-██ at ███:██ hours, Mobile Task Force Zeta-Niner (Mole Rats) conducted an investigation of SCP-835. At this time, SCP-835 had a mass of only four tons, and only one large polyp at the north end of the structure (designated Polyp Alpha), Polyp Bravo not yet being in existence.

As per standard procedure, four team members were chosen for the initial investigation. Standard isolation suits (underwater variant) were worn by all four team members: Lieutenant C█████ took point as team leader, while Sergeants L████ and M████ served as support. Corporal H███, a rookie team member, accompanied the team as an observer. A standard Underwater Remote Vehicle, or URV, was used for initial investigation.

SCP-835 did not, at first, act in a hostile manner towards the team, allowing team members to approach and make contact without incident. URV-01 was sent to investigate the exterior of the object while team members

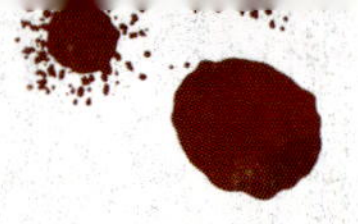

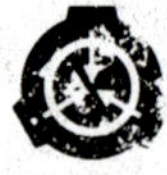

C, L, and M proceeded towards what they believed to be the entrance of the site. Corporal H was ordered to remain outside and to monitor URV-1 in order to ensure that the device's tether did not become tangled on the exterior protrusions.

The first sign of trouble occured when Corporal H, while attempting to clear a jam in URV-1's sampling claw, reported in with the words, "Oh god, help me, help me." He then reported that "some horrible tentacle thing" had wrapped around his arm and was dragging him in towards a "fucking mouth," and vocalized several distress calls... Jesus Christ. I can't do this. Fucking... goddamn it, he was just a kid! It was his first fucking mission, I should have kept my eye on him![1]

Christ... all right, here goes, guess I'll just let Sarge edit this for me. Again.

So the thing grabbed the kid. It had me fooled to rights. The entrance wasn't an entrance, it was just... some cave. The real entrance was the big polyp thing on the north end. It grabbed the kid and started dragging him towards the mouth. Topside started to drag him up, but all they got was a snapped cable. And the kid? He got pulled inside and eaten.

God, I still remember him screaming. He was screaming at us, he was crying. "Oh God, Lieutenant, it's eating me, oh god, I don't wanna die!" I'm shouting at him to calm down, we're gonna get him out of there, and then topside tells us to abort, and they start the winches. I'm screaming at them to wait, I had his hand! I HAD him! I got the carabiner on, we're hooked together, and topside starts winching us up... and we're not getting anywhere. I'm grabbing on, I'm telling him I'm not gonna let go, and then the winch starts to seize up, and I feel this jerk on the tether and it goes slack, and then we're both sliding into that damn thing.[2]

It was like... Jesus, I need another drink... fuck. It was like... the only way I can think of it was like you know that thing that doctors do when they stick a tube up someone's ass and look at the inside of their intestines? I saw that on TV once, it was like that, except I was going down the throat of some horrible underwater hell-monster, not up some poor bastard's rear. There were these... muscular contractions, I guess, and they were slowly sliding us down the length of the tube. If we weren't wearing the hard suits, we'd have been crushed, but as it was, we were held so tight we could barely move, even with power-assist. I managed to get my head up enough to see the kid's face. His faceplate was covered in vomit, poor bastard had puked in his suit.[3] I started yelling for him, trying to get him to say something. He managed to tell me he was all right. He was sobbing like a baby.

I started doing some calculations. Based on my dead reckoning tracker and initial sonar scans, we were moving about a meter every minute. That meant seventy two hours until we came out the other side, assuming we did. We had the air, our rebreathers could keep going for days. What we didn't have was the power to keep the suits warm for that long. If the heat went out, hypothermia would kill us... I dunno, look it up, in any case we'd be dead. We needed to conserve power.

I told the kid to turn off his helmet lights, lock his joints, and turn down his heater to minimal. He started crying. He didn't wanna do it. I didn't blame him, but I told him we had no choice. We finally agreed to shut down everything but our internal helmet lights, at least. It seemed to calm him down, and honestly, that extra 0.1 percent power wouldn't make a difference.

I think that was the worst part. We spent at least a day like that, locked in our suits. Couldn't move our arms and legs. No sound but the thing's gurgling and your own breathing and the sound of your rebreather. The puke on the kid's faceplate started to dry up and flake off about an hour or so in so I could see his face. He looked tired and scared.

I think... check the logs, Sarge, I think it was about thirteen hours in when the kid started talking again.[4] Kid started babbling. Apologized for stealing my underwear. Said you guys made him sneak into my quarters and

1. At this point, Lieutenant C██████ logged off their personal computer for ten minutes. Internal sensors indicate that the mini-fridge in the quarters was opened, and a fifth of Jameson Whiskey removed.

2. Post-Incident Analysis indicates that this was the point where the support vehicle's crane suffered a critical structural failure.

3. In early missions, 25% of all Zeta Niner casualties were caused by aspiration of vomit caused by backflow against the suit faceplate. Second-generation isolation suits were redesigned with catchpockets, piezo-electric faceshield wipers, and self-clearing air intakes to prevent further incidents.

4. Mission Time: 16:13 from start, 12:17 since capture.

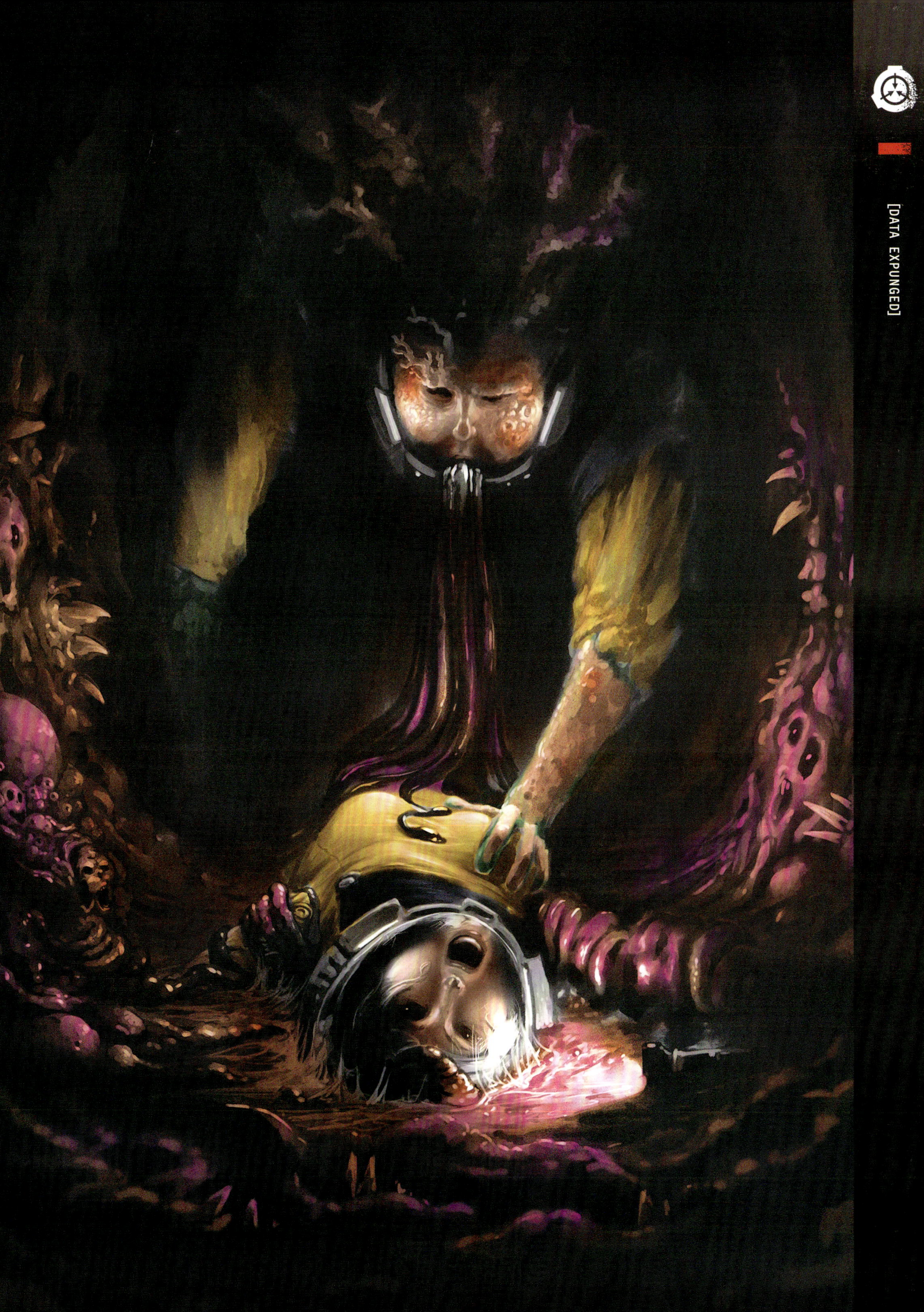
[DATA EXPUNGED]

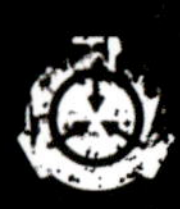

take it from me as a dare. Why the hell did you make him do that? I mean, I don't mind if you haze the new guys, Bill, but that shit gets old. It was hard enough trying to get them to listen to me as it was. Anyway, Bill, it's all there in the log. You know what I told him, what I promised; All lies, of course. Jokes. He laughed too. Joked back. I hope he was joking. I don't know what I would have done if we'd survived. Maybe I would have gone ahead and did it. I don't know. It's all fucked up. We're all fucked up. Anyway, after that, he calmed down a lot. I told him to take a nap. He slept a bit, thank god.

About twenty four hours in, we reached… I guess they're calling it the stomach now. First warning sign was a gurgling kind of noise, louder, with a crunching noise over it. I told the kid to bring his suit up to full power and get ready. A little while after, we fell out into this big chamber… big as in, big enough for the two of us to fit in it comfortably, which was huge compared to the tight squeeze of the tube. Kid's suit started hissing and the outer shell started to turn all pitted and stuff, and I noticed my gloves were starting to degrade too, so I yelled at him to move, and we started heading towards this… sphincter, I guess. I remember… god, why can I remember this, the insides of the stomach were lined with teeth and faces. Human faces, and they were all wailing at us and screaming, they were begging us to kill them.

I almost lost it there, I started opening up with my gun, started shooting them in the heads, and if I'd stayed, my suit would have melted and I'd be dead, but the kid grabbed me and shoved me headfirst through the sphincter and we fell into… the other place.

It was even worse than the stomach. That one was lined with faces and filled with acid, this place was… well, you know what it was full of. I'm not squeamish, Bill, you can't be if you're a Mole Rat, but this place squicked me out so bad I almost passed out. The kid helped me back up to my feet, though, told me we were almost out. "Come on, Lieutenant, we're almost out of here, let's go," he said. We moved over to the other sphincter, but the thing was… well, it was puckered up tighter than my Drill Sergeant's asshole back in basic. So no way we were getting out of there.

We decided to wait for a bit until the thing shot its load, so to speak: if it made shit and cum, it would have to spit it out eventually, right? Anyway, that's when things started to go bad. The kid started complaining about this awful smell. I tried to stay calm. Told him it was probably his suit's waste recyclers, told him to let me take a look at it. Yeah. There was a hole in the back of his leg, probably from the acid. I put a patch on it, and told him not to worry about it. And that's when I noticed that there were these red things growing all over his face. He started screaming when the first of them burst and splattered blood all over the inside of his face plate. He begged me to kill him. I put my gun up to his face plate and pulled the trigger. Click. I'd burned all my ammo trying to shoot those damn faces.

The tentacles burst out of its face a moment after. It grabbed me… and it started licking me, Bill. The thing was running its tongues all over my face and body, over the suit. It grabbed me and pushed me down and tried to hump my suit like a dog, but it couldn't get through. I managed to wrestle the thing back through the sphincter into the stomach. Its tentacles writhed at me as it started to melt.

He smiled - told me he loved me before he died. I screamed.

Then 835 blew its load and I flew out its ass into the ocean.

You know the rest of the story, Bill. Except one thing. My suit didn't make it intact. It was breached. No one else noticed: I didn't even notice until I was in my room and changing clothes and saw the red blotches all over my skin. So… yeah. I guess I'm fucked. I've got the room on lockdown right now, but you have to get everyone else out before I go terminal.

So yeah, fill out the rest of the reports and the logs for me, will ya? Oh, and be sure to edit it so the motherfuckers in command don't yell at me for being unprofessional in my AARs again. I'm gonna finish off my drink and take a couple Valium and go to bed. Don't bother trying to decontaminate the vessel. Just abandon the entire ship and scuttle it on top of the original site. I think the kid would like it that way. Now we can be together, just like he always wanted. Thanks.

SPECIAL CONTAINMENT PROCEDURES

SCP-689 is to be contained in a large concrete chamber equipped with high-intensity sodium iodide lights. These lights must be wired to separate redundant circuits such that SCP-689 is brightly illuminated at all times.

At least three personnel must be on duty at all times within the containment facility: two Class D inside the chamber and one Level 2 or higher at the operator's station outside the chamber. The operator must either be completely blind or be fitted with a visored helmet sufficient to block all vision, which must not be removed for the duration of his shift. Under absolutely no circumstances is the operator to look into the chamber. The Class D observers must between them keep SCP-689 in view at all times without exception. Blinking, etc. is allowed as normal but there must be at least one set of eyes focused on SCP-689 at all times. If the lights go out inside the chamber at any time for any reason or if there is any interruption in observation, all currently extant personnel who have seen SCP-689 must be executed without delay. It is recommended that they be fitted with remotely activated kill devices triggerable from the containment control room.

If SCP-689 is known to have left the chamber at any time, retrieval teams consisting of blind or visored personnel equipped with echolocators along with Class D observers must be dispatched to the location of all personnel who have previously viewed SCP-689. Retrieval teams will establish an immediate perimeter and cover the object before returning it to the chamber as quickly as possible. While SCP-689 is in transit, the Class D observers will stand under the covering and keep it in view at all times. Any Level 1 or below personnel who have seen SCP-689 as a result of a containment breach are to be terminated immediately. Higher clearance personnel will be temporarily retained but in the event of another containment failure are to be terminated.

Requests to study SCP-689 must be submitted to Dr. █████ at least 7 days in advance with a detailed description of the proposed experiment and justification. Any researcher directly viewing SCP-689 should be aware that doing so renders them liable to immediate and summary termination in the event of any containment or light failure, as described above.

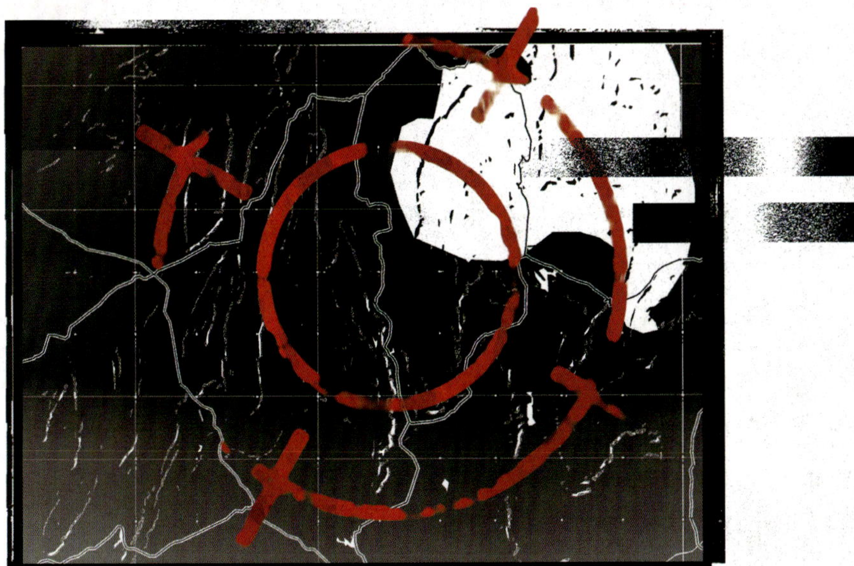

SCP-689's location at time of discovery.

File >>> 0198333

SCP-689

Title

HAUNTER IN THE DARK

Report by

far2

Picture by

Alexey Lebedev

Access the original report on

scp-wiki.wikidot.com/scp-689

Date

█████

Class

KETER

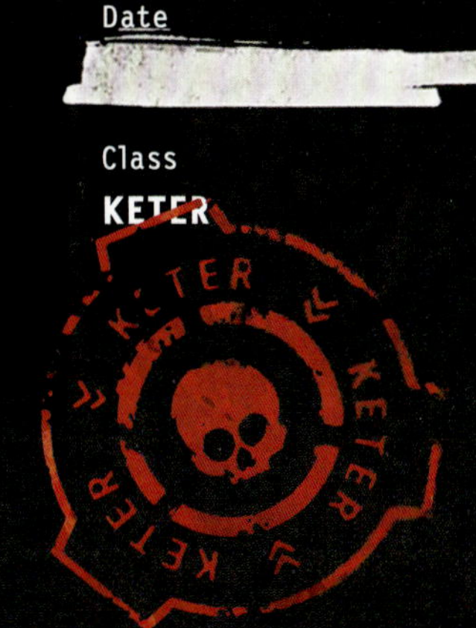

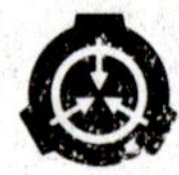

Research Library File ▸ 689

DESCRIPTION

SCP-689 appears to be a small green soapstone statue, 30 cm in height. It is carved in the semblance of what appears to be an unknown deity of the underworld, a seated skeletal figure with hands clasped over knees. It was discovered by ████ ██████ during one of the prewar German archaeological expeditions in the ████ area of India and obtained after the war by the OSS. Its location during the war is unknown.

SCP-689 is completely inert for as long as it is being watched by at least one human being. Normal behaviors such as blinking do not appear to interrupt the "watching" for this purpose, but any lapse in attention, however momentary, renders the observer vulnerable. As soon as SCP-689 is unobserved it vanishes from its current location. Within 15-20 seconds one person who has previously viewed SCP-689 dies instantaneously, SCP-689 reappearing on top of their remains. If no previous viewers are presently alive, it reappears in the same place as previous.

Tests have established that this effect is not operative on non-humans, but that any human being who has ever directly viewed SCP-689 is potentially vulnerable. No consistent cause of death has been found, with autopsy results ranging from heart attacks and strokes to complete rupture of all internal organs. The mechanism by which the victim is selected is currently unknown, save that preference seems to be given to persons in crowds or otherwise surrounded by large numbers of people, presumably to increase the number of people viewing the statue. Recorded images of SCP-689 do not appear to have this property.

Due to the potential for a "chain reaction" once SCP-689 is allowed to leave the chamber it is considered absolutely critical that all personnel who have seen the object be terminated immediately on any lapse in observation.

ADDENDUM

Those with Level 2 Security Clearance should see document #689-B

DOCUMENT #689-B: PROPOSED EXPERIMENT WITH SCP-682

Following the failure of other options and given the priority accorded to termination of SCP-682, Doctors ████ and ████ have proposed that SCP-682 be deliberately exposed to SCP-689, presumably followed by turning off the lights or a similar measure. SCP-689 staff caution that in the event of a deliberate observation failure, all personnel who have seen SCP-689 other than the intended target must be either terminated in advance or placed in the containment chamber with the intended subject to ensure that the object does not escape containment. Given the apparently random nature of the selection process, it is also likely that multiple trials would be required before the target came under attack. Staff recommends that if such an option is activated, all Class D personnel be terminated in advance of the attempt to improve chances of success.

END OF REPORT

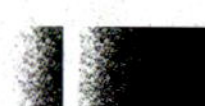

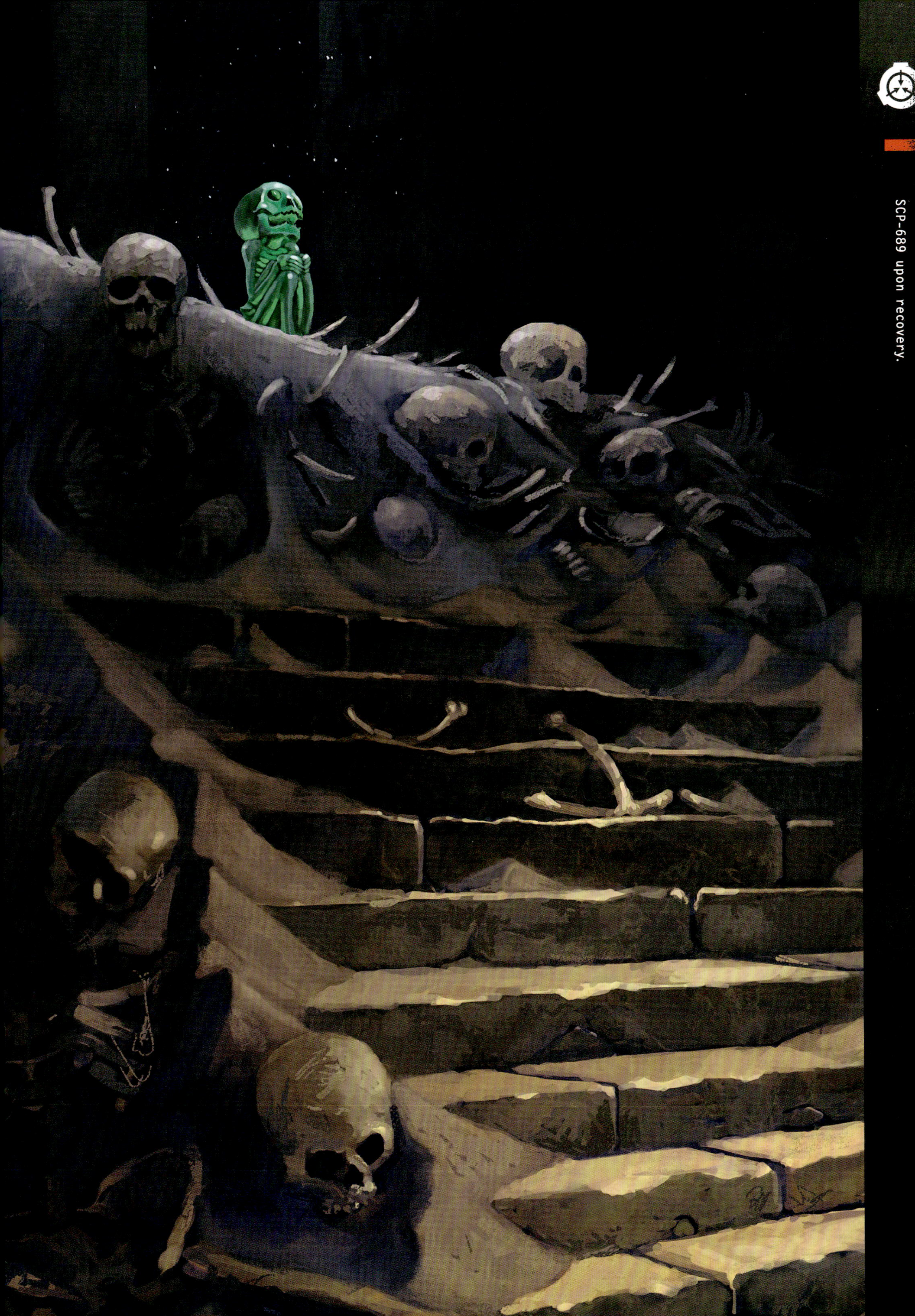

SCP-689 upon recovery.

File >>> 028833

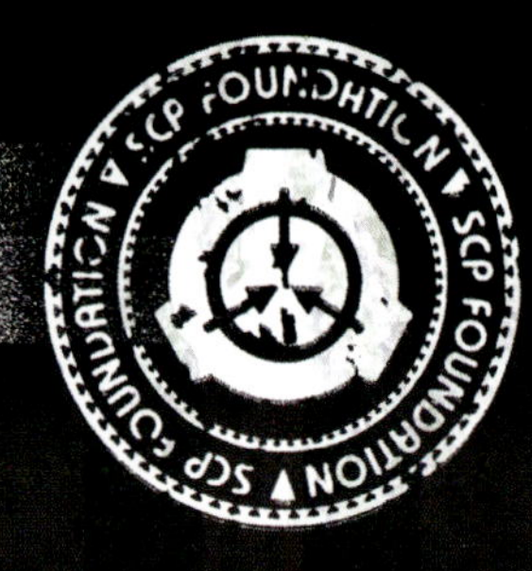

SCP-517

Title

GRAMMIE KNOWS

Report by

Dexanote

Picture by

Alex Andreev

Access the original report on

scp-wiki.wikidot.com/scp-517

Date

Class

SAFE

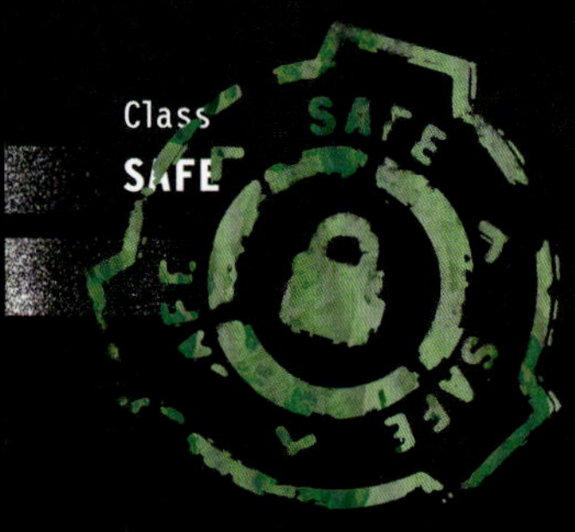

SPECIAL CONTAINMENT PROCEDURES

SCP-517 is to be kept secured within Containment Locker 51164 in Site-66, facing away from the doorway. A thick sheet is to be draped over the item at all times. Testing is currently prohibited, as the nature of the manifestation invariably causes a low-level containment breach. If SCP-517-01 is triggered, personnel are instructed to report to their immediate superior to enact Protocol 517-001.

As of Incident 517-1997-M, SCP-517 is to be kept in a dedicated cell at all times. An opaque black sheet is to be kept bound around the object at all times. As of ~~08/25/1997~~ ██/██/2002, no more testing is to be conducted on SCP-517 without Site Director's approval.

DESCRIPTION

SCP-517 is a fortune-telling machine. Item stands approximately 2 meters tall, containing a mechanical puppet and an electric candle within a glass and wooden case. Examination has shown an internal layout consistent with similar machines. On the top panels the words "Grandmother Predictions" are painted on built-in signage. The puppet within is in the shape of an elderly woman, with a white blouse and a blue shawl. Item's power cord has been severed approximately 15 centimeters from its base; it appears to have been inexpertly separated from its original power source. No reaction occurs if a coin is inserted into the slot.

The item will energize automatically, once an hour, if an individual (hereafter the "Target") enters its field of vision. The puppet will turn to face directly at the Target, dispense a "fortune card" from the slot on its front, and cease function. Process is fully mechanical, and item does not show signs of awareness. See Addendum for a transcript for examples of "fortunes".

The individual who "activated" SCP-517 will become the Target of an entity or number of entities who will attack at 1:43 AM local time the following morning. The Entity or Entities (hereby SCP-517-01) appear as a varying number of long, multi-jointed arms (between ten and three dozen), initially appearing from a single area. Arms seem to be completely corporeal, and can apparently extend indefinitely. Entity will immediately rush towards and attempt to grab and capture the Target or Targets. If the hunt is made sufficiently challenging, additional arms will begin to constantly generate in close proximity to the victim in order to facilitate an easier capture.

Chosen areas are usually low, cramped, dark areas such as basements or closets, and will not shift during a given assault. In all instances, Targets have been captured, rapidly dragged into SCP-517-01's chosen area, and savagely beaten until sunrise. Entity has been documented reaching from the ventilation system of an office building, drawing a Target into a drop-ceiling, pulling a Target under a bed, and drawing a Target through a sewage grate. Any attempts to intrude on this event will result in human aggressors being drawn into the assault. The remains of victims are reduced to [REDACTED]. To date there have been no survivors.

If more than one individual activates the item in the span of one day, all will become Targets of the following night's assault. SCP-517-01 will appear from multiple areas while "hunting" multiple Targets. However, due to the resultant chaos during the test (517-34c) in which this was discovered, all measures are to be taken to avoid multiple activations.

Remote viewing of the expected points of origin of SCP-517-01 during testing revealed arms extending from points around corners and otherwise off-camera, eventually crowding out the video feed. Fragmented, unidentified human DNA has appeared in the areas utilized by SCP-517-01; ultimate origins are still currently unknown.

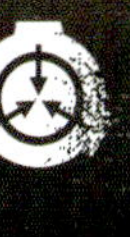

Incident 517-1997-M.

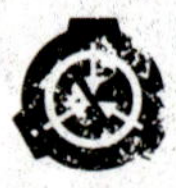

Research Library File ▸ 517

ADDENDUM - FORTUNES

Samples from several "fortunes" as read by SCP-517.

███/█/1993: How many times should somebody be told to be good?

███/█/1994: Your mother raised you better than that. I'm sorry, but fair is fair.

██/█/1994: You try to be good; you should try harder.

██/█/1994: Some people don't know how to be kind. You'll know soon enough, won't you?

██/█/1997: People who do terrible things deserve terrible things. You've brought this upon yourself, my dear.

██/█/1998: You'll find out, soon enough.

██/█/2002: You look like you've made some mistakes. Some things are unforgivable, aren't they?

██/█/2002: Do you think they've forgotten?

INCIDENT 517-1997-M

SCP Involved: SCP-517
Personnel Involved: Dr. Agusta Meil (deceased), Site-23 Security
Date: 08/25/1997
Location: Storage Site-23.

On 08/25/1997, at approximately 13:56, the late Dr. Meil was targeted by SCP-517 while supervising the object's transport to a new storage locker. Security and Site Director were alerted, and a defensive strategy was devised.

At 23:30, Dr. Meil was loaded into a Foundation UH-60 Black Hawk, five security personnel assigned as bodyguards. Helicopter was situated on Helipad 3-8, located on the roof of the then-empty Cafeteria 1.

Non-essential security personnel from sectors 1, 3 and 4 were armed with blades and stun batons, and select personnel were granted flame weapons and concussion explosives. Squads were directed to strategic points around Cafeteria 1's main and second floors, and instructed to destroy any instances of SCP-517-01 that appear. As this was the first concerted effort intended to overcome SCP-517-01, all measures were taken.

As Cafeteria 1 was not constructed with a proper basement, it was expected that SCP-517-01 would manifest in one of the surrounding buildings. All SCP objects that posed a threat if released by SCP-517-01 were moved to another area of the Site. SCP-059's enclosure is located away from Cafeteria 1 and as such was deemed safe.

Log of Events

23:57 - Dr. Meil and guards board aerial transport

00:05 - Night time illumination augmented by additional floodlights.

00:36 - Ground squads assigned to interior of Cafeteria 1 in place.

00:41 - Ground squads assigned to exterior of Cafeteria 1 in place.

01:03 - Weapon check called.

01:10 - Dr. Meil expresses an intense feeling of suspense. Becomes mildly agitated. Attributed to knowledge of SCP object and subsequent paranoia.

01:20 - Last call for restroom breaks.

01:30 - Site locked down. All doors and windows capable of being sealed are locked.

01:43 - Approximately 18 SCP-517-01 limbs sighted to the east of Cafeteria 1, generated somewhere in Storage-Center 4-b, approximately 40 metres away. Immediately destroyed by concentrated weapons fire.

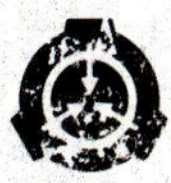

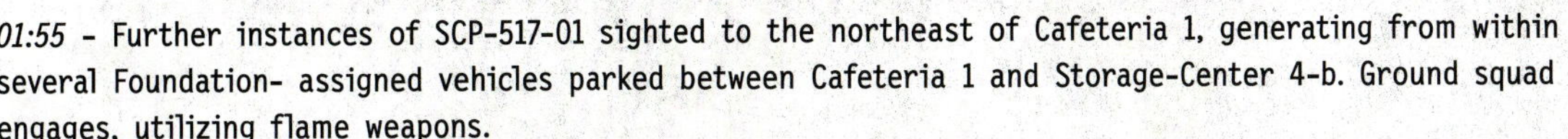

01:47 - More SCP-517-01 sighted, in the same area. Additional arms generate to replace those destroyed by weapons fire. Several seemed tasked to collect pieces left behind. No hostility towards squads reported.

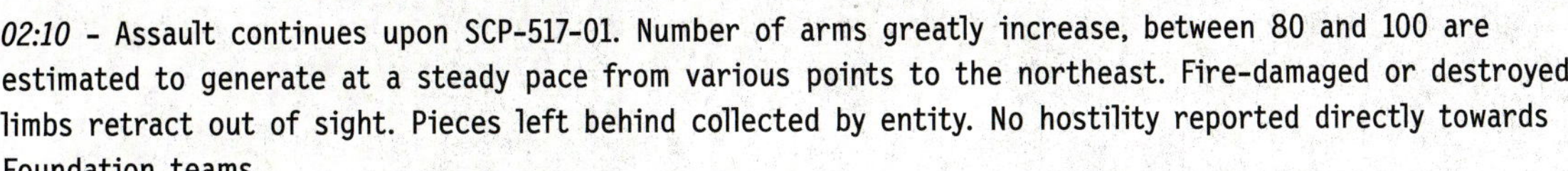

01:55 - Further instances of SCP-517-01 sighted to the northeast of Cafeteria 1, generating from within several Foundation- assigned vehicles parked between Cafeteria 1 and Storage-Center 4-b. Ground squad engages, utilizing flame weapons.

02:10 - Assault continues upon SCP-517-01. Number of arms greatly increase, between 80 and 100 are estimated to generate at a steady pace from various points to the northeast. Fire-damaged or destroyed limbs retract out of sight. Pieces left behind collected by entity. No hostility reported directly towards Foundation teams.

02:24 - Squads report some difficulty keeping up with the rate of replacement. Explosive weapons authorized against origin points. No hostility reported directly towards Foundation teams.

02:39 - Dr. Meil and aerial squad go airborne.

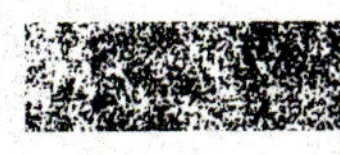

02:41 - Arms generate "from the walls" within Cafeteria 1, ground floor. Later examination reveals the arms had formed irregular holes in the drywall consistent with blunt force. Ground-floor squad engages, utilizing close-quarters weaponry. No hostility reported directly towards Foundation teams.

02:49 - SCP-517-01 appears within Cafeteria 1 ventilation system. Roof squad engages. Ground-based instances of SCP-517-01 are noted to continue reaching in the direction of Cafeteria 1, even while Dr. Meil has gone airborne within the evacuation vehicle. 200 estimated to have appeared.

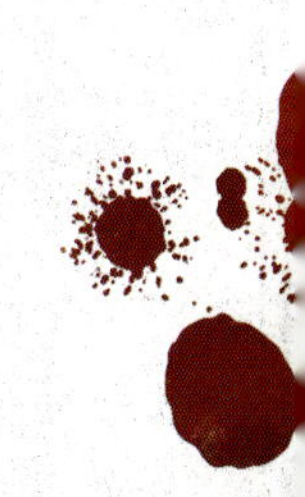

03:04 - SCP-517-01 appear on roof of Cafeteria 1, generating from kitchen exhaust ports. Damage done to structural mesh. Entity engaged.

03:11 - SCP-517-01 observed to remove the locked fire-escape door on the north side of Cafeteria 1. Said instances generated within Cafeteria 1's ventilation systems.

03:22 - 4 SCP-517-01 limbs, generating from the exhaust system of Cafeteria 1, reach helicopter. Roof crew alerted, limbs culled.

03:31 - Dr. Meil becomes hysteric, demands that the pilot flee. Helicopter begins moving to the southeast.

03:33 - SCP-517-01 generate upon helicopter, seemingly from the base of the tail. Begin attacking the doors.

03:34 - Left-side rear window shattered, onboard squad engaged with bladed weapons.

03:35 - Dr. Meil acquired by SCP-517-01. Drawn through window, passed towards waiting arms. Subsequently moved through the air towards Cafeteria 1.

03:35 - SCP-517-01 limb caught in helicopter's tail rotor; pilot forced to attempt an emergency landing. Agent Track severely wounded.

03:36 - Squads report a marked increase in hostility by SCP-517-01. Entity begins replacing arms at a greatly increased rate. Number of limbs estimated at a steady 150.

03:37 - Dr. Meil drawn through Cafeteria 1's kitchen ventilation system.

03:37 - Dr. Meil reappears in kitchen. Agent Matheson attempts to sever 517-01 limbs; subsequently captured and pulled towards fire exit with Dr. Meil.

03:37 - Agent Germain, Agent Teffler, and Agent Seile captured. Defence squads ordered to stand down.

03:39 - Dr. Meil, Agents Matheson, Germain, Teffler, and Seile drawn into Storage-Building 4-b through access door. Outside limbs retract, disappear.

03:44 - Agent Ted attempts to damage Storage-Building 4-b with combat grenades; aggressively drawn into building by exceedingly rapid limbs.

03:45 - Command contacted; mission failed.

07:01 - Dawn.

07:10 - Collective remains of Dr. Meil and Agents Matheson, Germain, Teffler, Seile and Ted rediscovered.

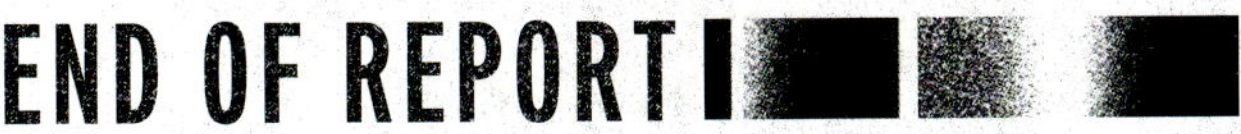

END OF REPORT

File >>> 0192234

SCP-321

Title

CHILD OF MAN

Report by
AdminBright

Picture by
Darja Kogn

Access the original report on
scp-wiki.wikidot.com/scp-321

Date

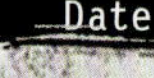

Class
SAFE

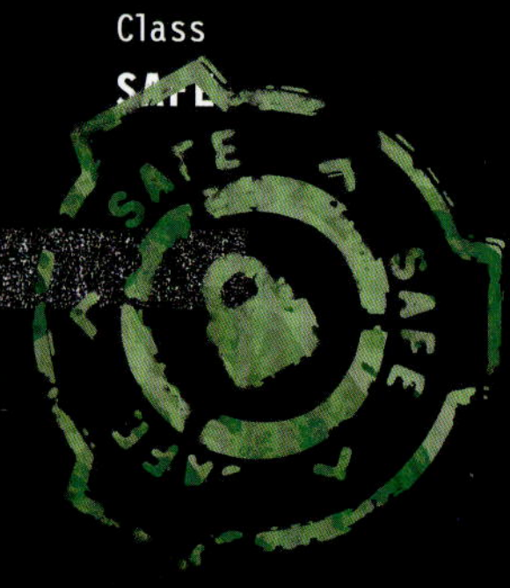

SPECIAL CONTAINMENT PROCEDURES

SCP-321 is to be kept in a regulation containment chamber. SCP-321 has been outfitted with extensive braces, to make up for weaknesses in bone structure and muscle mass. Its artificial heart is to be examined once a month for any damage. SCP-321 is to be fed three times daily. Solid foods are excluded from its prescribed diet. Three staff members are on temporary SCP-321 assignment at this time. SCP-321 is to be given three hours a day of exercise and physical therapy, with the rest of its time not involved in experiments to be confined to its cell. While SCP-321 is incapable of asking for anything, it has been allowed several stuffed toys.

DESCRIPTION

SCP-321 is a human female, born on July 4, 18█. SCP-321 is currently 3.1 meters tall, and weighs approximately 110 kilograms. Subject is devoid of melanins in hair, eyes, and skin. It is incapable of speech, but can still vocalise, and has proven to have problems with spacial recognition and awareness. SCP-321 has displayed a low degree of intellect, and has problems adjusting to new situations.

SCP-321 was the stillborn child of Junior Researcher Adam █████ and his wife, Medical Assistant Evelyn █████. Junior Researcher █████ took it upon himself to make use of several SCPs, including SCP-590 in an effort to bring his daughter back to life. The procedure worked, but the result was taken into Foundation custody for examination. The subject was later given an SCP designation.

SCP-321 was quickly found to have recuperative abilities, capable of healing injuries inflicted upon it at approximately five times the normal rate. Subject was at this time entered into Foundation records as SCP-321. In the time since, SCP-321's body has continued to age at a decelerated rate, approximately half that of a normal human. Although its aging has been slowed, SCP-321 has continued to grow, showing no signs of stopping despite now being taller than any recorded human. At this point in time, it is believed SCP-321's recuperative abilities stem from over abundant production of stem cells, a result of its interaction upon death with [REDACTED].

For a period of time beginning in early 19█, the limits of SCP-321's natural heart were reached, and SCP-321 was too tall for blood to be circulated properly. During this period, SCP-321 was restrained physically in order to keep its heart capable of pumping blood to the brain. Despite this, slow decay was evident and the limits of SCP-321's recuperative abilities were found, as it was not capable of healing damage that was being dealt constantly. Work began in 1948 to create an artificial heart to prolong SCP-321's existence; the heart was completed in 19█. Since then, all damage to SCP-321 has been healed.

SCP-321 has a very low intelligence. Everyday activities are a chore for it, and it can take several months, to years, to teach it to do such things as use utensils for eating. While SCP-321 has fully developed vocal cords, it seems incapable of learning speech, instead crying and making nonsense noises as of those typically heard from infants under the age of six months.

July 31, 18█: *Requesting SCP-321 be removed from SCP status.*
-Junior Researcher Adam █████
Request Denied. -05-█

January 10, 18█: *Requesting SCP-321 be removed from SCP Status.*
-Personnel Director Adam █████
Request Denied. -05-█

May 3, 19█: *We can learn nothing more from SCP-321, suggesting we remove its SCP designation.*
-Site Director Adam █████, Site-04
Request Denied. -05-█

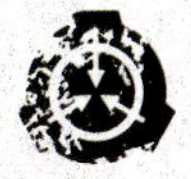

Research Library File ▸ 321

June 31, 19█: *SCP-321 is to be decommissioned and returned to her family, effective immediately.* -05-12
Request Denied. This is the final time, Adam. She is not now, nor ever has been, your daughter. If you attempt this again, I will gather the council, and you will be removed. -05-1

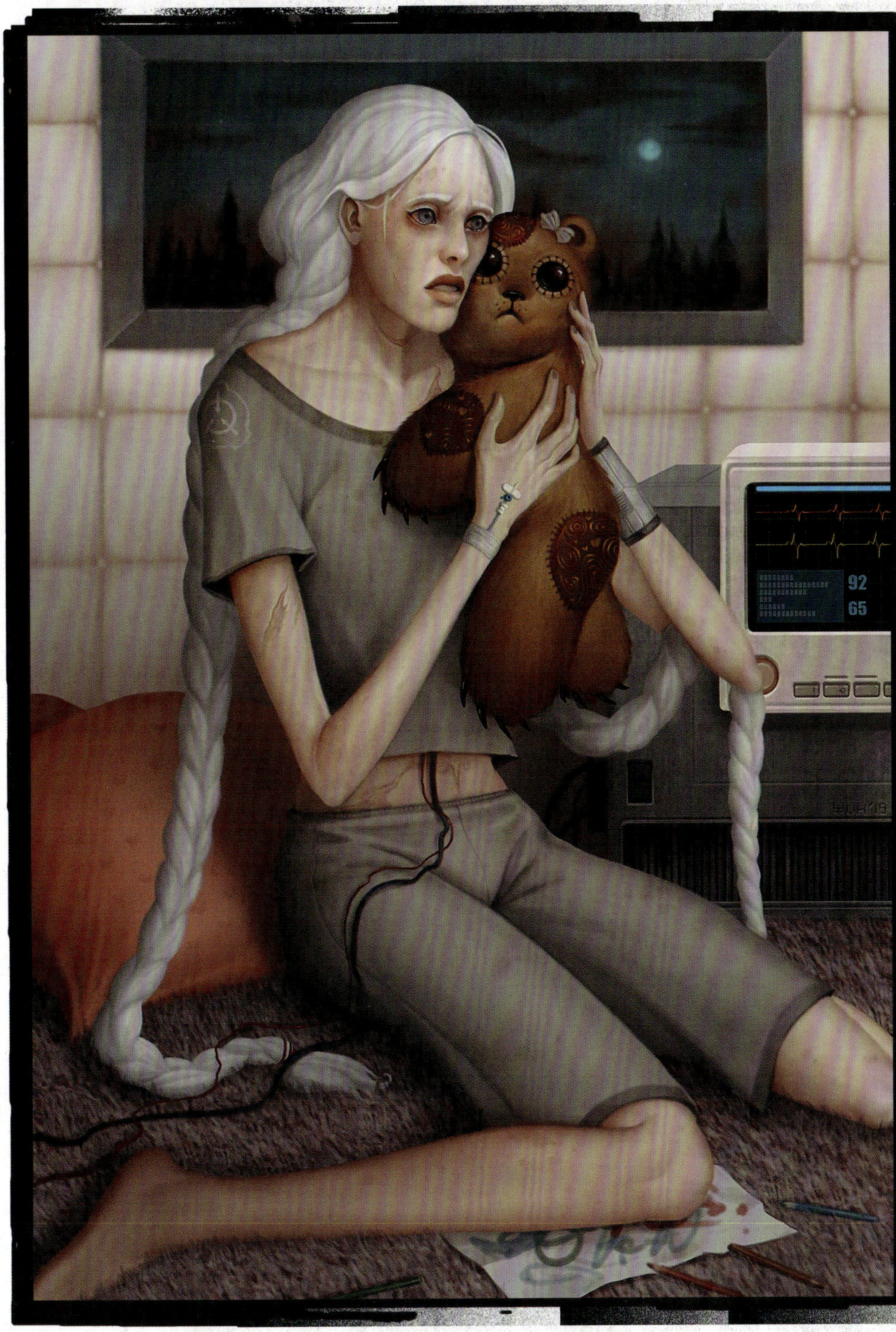

SCP-321 in its containment chamber.

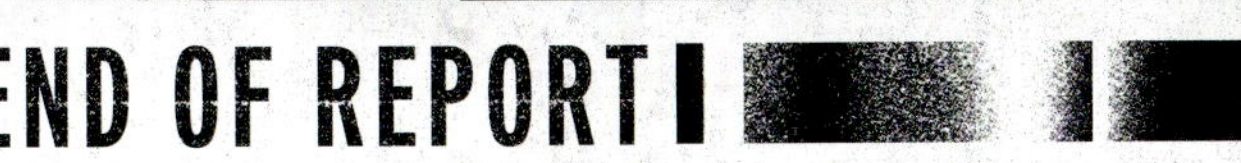

File >>> 099123

SCP-505

Title

INK STAIN

Report by

ModernMajorGeneral

Picture by

Genocide Error

Access the original report on **scp-wiki.wikidot.com/scp-505**

Date

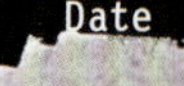

Class

KETER

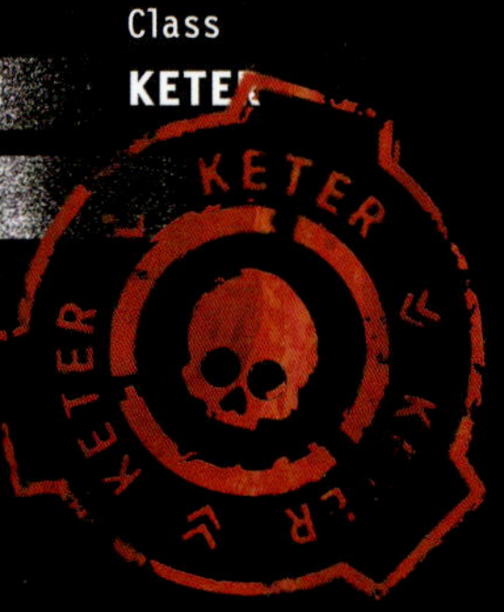

SPECIAL CONTAINMENT PROCEDURES

SCP-505 is contained in a 50 m x 40 m x 10 m room at Site-█. SCP-505's containment area is to be sealed other than one secure airlock and a series of pipes allowing transport of SCP-505-1 to storage tanks in the event of SCP-505-1 reaching levels in which it poses a danger to containment. Sprayers for 4 M NaOH are to be available through SCP-505's containment area and the rest of Site-█ to combat a containment breach. In the event of a spill of SCP-505-1, the affected area should immediately be covered with an absorbent material (commercial blotting paper is currently standard for this purpose) and doused with alcohol or acetone if NaOH is not immediately available. NaOH immersion is the method of choice for SCP-505-1 containment, followed by incineration of affected material if practicable.

There are currently ██ instances of SCP-505-1 points of secondary contamination outside SCP-505's primary containment area. Containment in these areas is variable but efforts have been made to make procedures as similar to those of the primary site if possible. Of these secondary contamination zones, █ are unable to be fully contained at this time resulting in the spread of SCP-505-1 throughout the environment. These sites are to be monitored at all times and countermeasure development is of the highest priority. For a complete list of SCP-505-1 secondary containment sites, see Document 505-14A-█.

DESCRIPTION

SCP-505 is a Model ███ Faber-Castell fountain pen, produced in 2001. For documentation of its acquisition by the Foundation, see Addendum 505-2. It is identical in all respects to a standard fountain pen apart from its association with SCP-505-1. SCP-505-1 is the black ink produced by SCP-505, which exhibits the property of self-replication. SCP-505-1 spreads at a variable rate, affected by the substance it comes into contact with and the amount of SCP-505-1 present. Quantities of SCP-505-1 have been shown to increase at rates between 0.5 and 540 mL per second. Standard ink-removing chemicals are able to partially remove SCP-505-1 and inhibit its spread; however, sodium hydroxide is necessary to remove SCP-505-1 contamination completely, and has shown to be ineffective in environments with particularly high SCP-505-1 concentrations. Fortunately, the growth rate of SCP-505-1 appears to be inversely proportional to its quantity at high concentrations. Whilst the observed effects of this are negligible in most cases, this inverse growth phenomenon provides the only explanation for the partial containment of SCP-505-1 despite a number of cases of large-scale environmental contamination which were projected to otherwise lead to an NK-class end-of-the-world scenario.

Whilst SCP-505-1 exhibits no unusual properties other than its constant spread and partial resistance to removal, it nonetheless poses serious difficulties for control. SCP-505-1 will flow across non-absorbent surfaces and pass through porous surfaces in an identical fashion to normal ink. All liquid or solid objects or beings in contact with SCP-505-1 will be contaminated. SCP-505-1 will still adhere to non-porous surfaces such as metals, but newly produced SCP-505-1 will constantly flow off. Non-porous materials are thus catalysts for SCP-505-1 spread and all SCP-505-1 contamination should be covered in porous materials such as blotting paper for this reason. It is not possible to permanently contain SCP-505-1 in a non-porous container as said container's contents will gradually increase in quantity, leading to increased pressure and subsequent rupture. All containers being used to contain SCP-505-1 must therefore be drained periodically to prevent a containment breach.

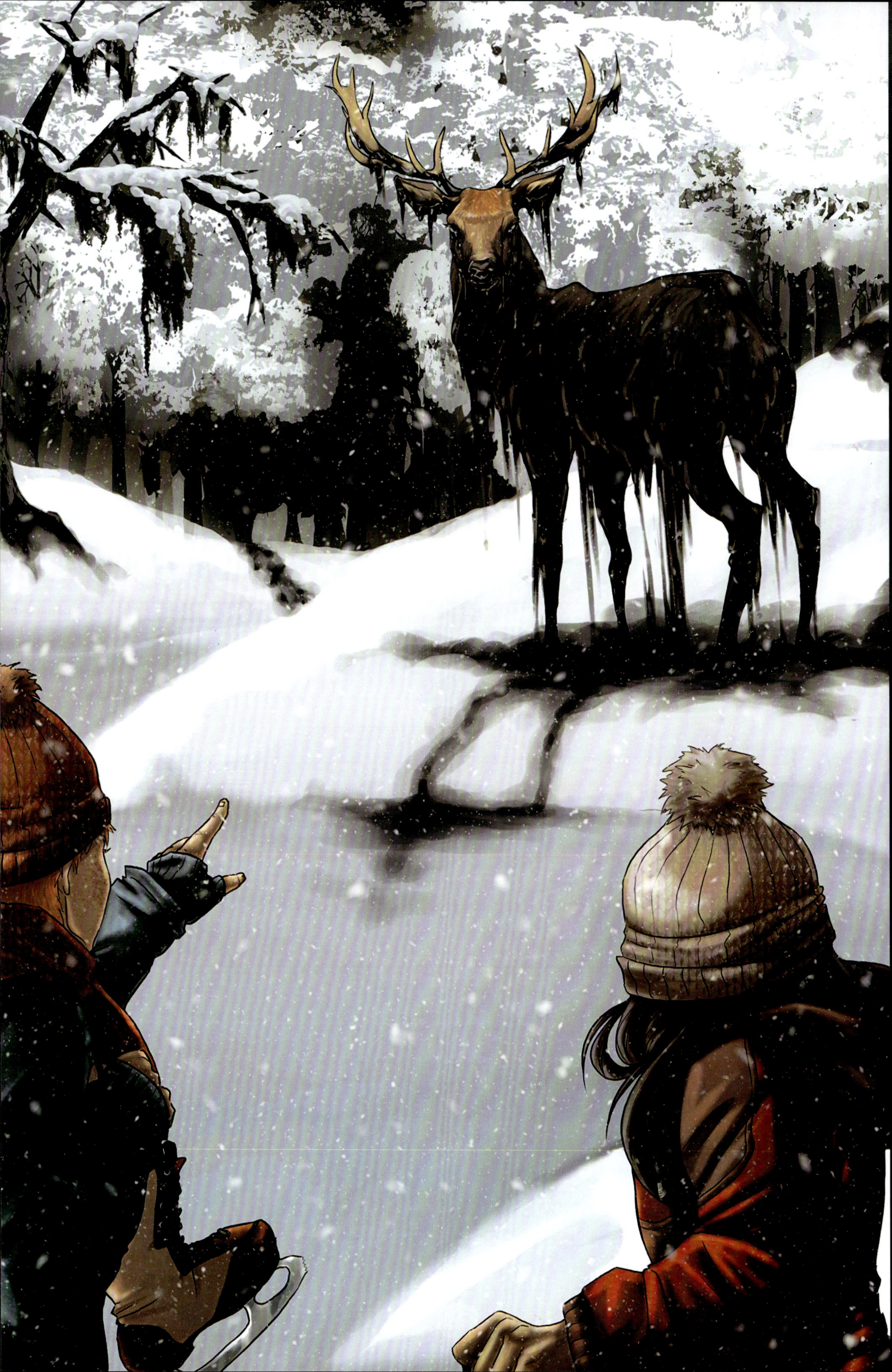

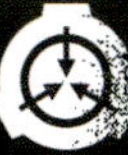

A red deer (Cervus elaphus) contaminated with SCP-505.

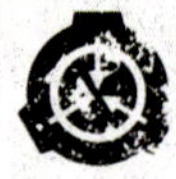

SCP-505-1's effects on its environment are identical to those of an equivalent quantity of standard fountain pen ink. SCP-505-1 exposure will inevitably lead to the death of living organisms; plant matter will be killed due to inhibition of photosynthesis, whereas animals will be killed due to chemical poisoning. In humans and other mammals, SCP-505-1 contact will most likely be via the skin, where it will spread until it reaches an orifice or a break in the skin and subsequently enter the vascular system through mucous membranes. SCP-505-1 will spread through the vasculature and have catastrophic effects on all organ systems it reaches, as it continuously replicates and is unable to be excreted by the urinary system. Cause of death is generally multiple organ failure, although in most cases affected individuals will be terminated and decontaminated prior to this. For containment procedures in these instances, see Addendum 505-1.

SCP-505-1 also has an increased rate of spread through non-viscous fluids such as water, as would be expected of normal ink. Any contamination of the water table with SCP-505-1 must be prevented at all costs, due to the potential for an NK-class end-of-the-world scenario. It is unknown whether SCP-505-1's aforementioned property of an inversely proportional rate of spread will manifest in fluids, as experimentation with such high quantities of SCP-505-1 is strictly forbidden. Thus, any environmental SCP-505-1 contamination in water sources must be met with immediate damming and drainage into storage tanks of all affected areas.

ADDENDUM 505-1

Procedures for dealing with SCP-505-1 contamination in humans

Administration of multiple-dose activated charcoal has been shown to slow the progress of SCP-505-1 contamination in humans but is unable to halt the process. The only known methods of treatment for SCP-505-1 contamination in humans are by immediate excision of the affected area or continuous application of ethanol to an affected skin region. Topical ethanol treatment will not prevent the affected individual from transmitting SCP-505-1 to other surfaces and is thus highly discouraged except in the cases of essential personnel, in which case containment procedures must be observed as in all other sites of secondary SCP-505-1 contamination. In theory excision or amputation of affected areas would be the gold standard for treatment but contamination of surgical instruments and personnel remains a problem. Therefore, all cases of SCP-505-1 contamination in humans other than essential personnel should be dealt with by termination followed by standard procedure of 4 M NaOH immersion and incineration of the remains.

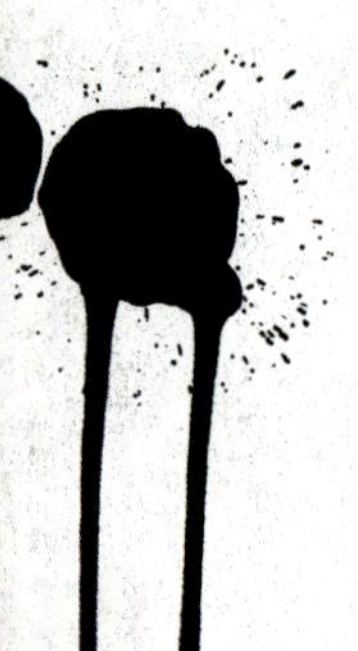

ADDENDUM 505-2

SCP-505 retrieval history

SCP-505 was acquired by the Foundation from the town of █████ in Oman, when the town in question was quarantined by the Omani government due to reports of a black fluid beginning to seep out from the town's post office and causing the deaths of a number of its inhabitants. Fortuitously the arid and remote location of the incident prevented wide-scale environmental contamination of SCP-505-1. The Foundation retrieved SCP-505-1 with ██ casualties. No other anomalous properties of the town's post office or the town itself were detected. It was deemed necessary to terminate ███ civilian inhabitants of █████ who were deemed likely to be contaminated. The incident was reported as a non-extranormal chemical spill.

END OF REPORT  

File >>> 019822

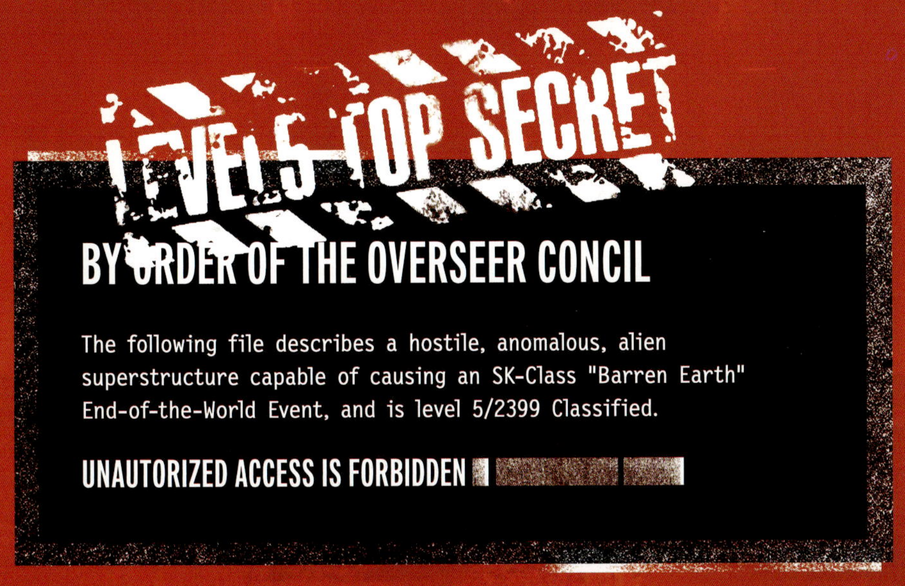

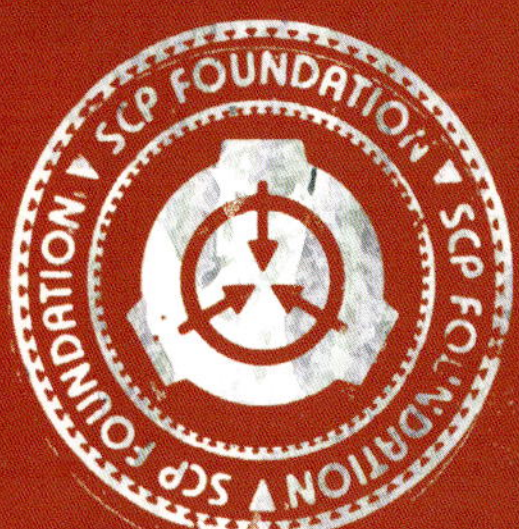

SCP-2399

Title

A MALFUNCTIONING DESTROYER

Report by
djkaktus

Pictures by
Pavel Kobyzev

Access the original report on
scp-wiki.wikidot.com/scp-2399

Date

Class
KETER

SPECIAL CONTAINMENT PROCEDURES

Due to SCP-2399's location and nature, physical means of containment are currently impossible. Implanted Foundation agents in major observatories are to contain footage or images of SCP-2399. An ongoing misinformation campaign is in effect, which has thus far been able to completely suppress any knowledge pertaining to SCP-2399 from public awareness.

Foundation satellites in orbit around Jupiter are to maintain constant vigilance of SCP-2399's reconstruction efforts, and make all attempts to hinder that process should SCP-2399 reach a minimum of 75% completion. Additionally, a perimeter of long-range electromagnetic jamming satellites (BARRIER Array) has been situated in high-Jupiter orbit. Any transmissions intercepted by this array are to be summarily decoded and logged.

In the event of SCP-2399 surpassing 75% completion or an information breach in the jamming perimeter, necessary Foundation personnel will engage Protocol LEGIONNAIRE-5 (See Addendum 2399-L5), given its completion by that time.

DESCRIPTION

SCP-2399 is a massive, complex mechanical structure currently located in Jupiter's lower atmosphere. Since its visual discovery in 1963, SCP-2399 has been observed to use highly advanced, anti-matter-based weaponry to create spacial disruptions and devastating atmospheric [DATA EXPUNGED] observable as a large red vortex, commonly known as the Great Red Spot.

SCP-2399 appears to be damaged, possibly due to an impact with the moon Io before coming to rest in its current position. SCP-2399 has been observed releasing a multitude of small, octopoid repair drones in efforts to repair the damage it has taken. Some of these drones will remain near SCP-2399, while others will patrol nearby moons, or deeper into the gasses of Jupiter itself, in search of parts that SCP-2399 is missing. Computer models estimate that SCP-2399 is at 59% completion, with a current rate of .78% annually. This rate has increased from an estimated .12% in 1970.

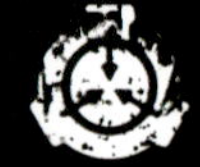

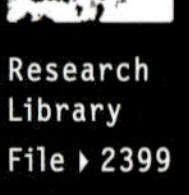

Research Library File ▸ 2399

Despite its damaged state, SCP-2399 seems to possess a limitless power supply, advanced electromagnetic shielding, matter-disrupting weaponry, the ability to repair damage done to itself, and a precise tracking and targeting system (See Addendum 2399-2b). Due to the large difference in technological advancement between the creator of SCP-2399 and our own, for all intents and purposes, SCP-2399 is currently indestructible by human means. In theory SCP-2399 might be left vulnerable by a powerful enough electromagnetic pulse. Unfortunately, this technology does not yet exist.

Since 1971, SCP-2399 has been the recipient of an unending stream of electromagnetic-based communications originating in the Triangulum Galaxy, roughly 3 million light years from Earth. The means of SCP-2399's travel to our solar system, and the means of its communications, are all unknown. From 1971 to 1985, SCP-2399 continuously received a single encoded message which, through code-breaking and translation efforts, appeared to be a command to repair the damage it incurred upon entering our solar system. After this time, the BARRIER array was established to intercept these messages. This coincided with a period of radio silence from the origin of the communications, until 1996, when a different order began transmitting. The BARRIER array has thus far prevented SCP-2399 from receiving this command (See Addendum 2399-Comm-Log).

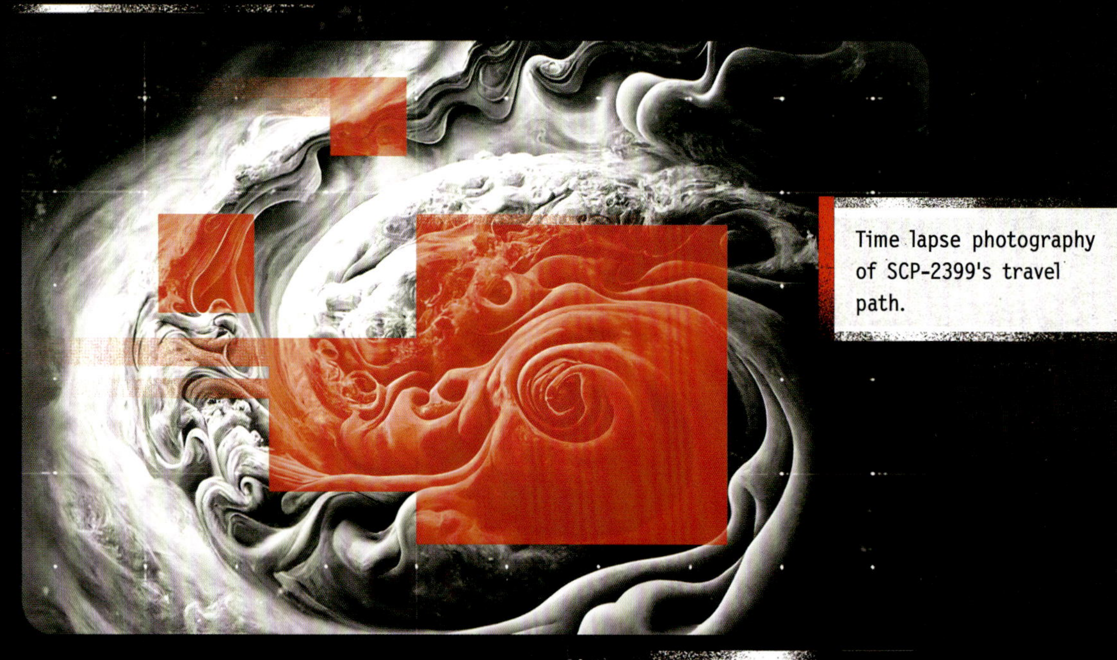

Time lapse photography of SCP-2399's travel path.

SCP-2399 DISCOVERY NOTES

SCP-2399 was originally observed, albeit unknowingly, by Giovanni Cassini in 1665. The following is taken directly from Cassini's journal on the event, translated from Italian to English.

08/10/1665

I have observed something extraordinary in the heavens. Last night, as I gazed through my looking glass, I saw what appeared to be a star of great luminescence streak through the far reaches of our solar system. I have never recorded an object moving so fast; it had surpassed the outer planets in fewer than two hours! As I watched, by my own two eyes, I saw it slow as it closed on Jupiter, make a sharp turn, and disappear into the planet itself. I saw many bursts of light afterwards, but although I continued to peer at it until the Sun broke, I saw no additional disturbances in the night sky. I must continue to document these changes, and will alert my colleagues when the day is upon me.

15/10/1665

I took Peter to my observation point last night, but a week from the night I saw the fire rain upon Jupiter in the heavens. He brought along his own looking glass, and together we aimed our view upon the giant. To our surprise, a magnificent change has occurred! Where once the distant world only showed bands of color, there is now a great red spot where the star came to rest on the surface of Jupiter. Peter was incredulous, of course, that such an amazing discovery could have taken place before our very eyes. I will continue to take note of this.

18/10/1665

Tonight as I peered through my looking glass, I swear on my life that I observed what looked to me like explosions and starbursts emanating from our red spot. I fear my mind is playing tricks on me, for there has been no record of such violent outbursts by a heavenly body since the dawn of astronomy. I will consult with Peter on the morrow, and hopefully glean from him some advice on the matter.

19/10/1665

Peter sees the same as I! As I approached him with my concerns, he leveled the same with me, and through our following discussion we concluded that it must be a powerful reaction to the falling star I saw upon the first night, and not a product of our own shortcomings. I am left wondering what cataclysmic event must be taking place upon our heavenly neighbour. Our work to document this must go on.

ADDENDUM 2399-2B

At █████ hours on ██/██/██, BARRIER Unit 53 observed one of SCP-2399's repair drones closing on a piece of debris, quickly determined to be part of a damaged communications array. Because of the nature of this specific component, and the ramifications of allowing SCP-2399 to recover it, it was ordered that BARRIER Unit 45 fire upon the drone with its on-board concussion batteries.

Batteries were discharged; however, the drone appeared undamaged. Footage obtained by BARRIER Unit 53 shows that, while the payload in question was launched towards the repair drone, it was destroyed within 5 km of the target by additional charges originating from SCP-2399. Command lost contact with BARRIER Unit 45 15 seconds after initial discharge, with video observation showing SCP-2399 [DATA EXPUNGED] the resulting spacial anomaly originating in ███-███-███ [DATA EXPUNGED] the termination of BARRIER Unit 45 by BARRIER Units 44, 51, and 55.

Under no circumstances are any BARRIER Units to further engage either SCP-2399 or drones released by SCP-2399.

ADDENDUM 2399-2C: PROJECT GIGAS

After the events of ██/██/██, it was decided that necessary force would be authorized to destroy or incapacitate SCP-2399. Using Foundation resources, as well as resources from 45 nations (notably, ████████████ ████████████ ████████████, and ████████████), a platform of ██ warheads bearing ███ Mt payloads and ██ warheads bearing EMP detonators was launched and placed in orbit around Europa. On ██/██/██ at █████ hours with orders from 15 heads of state and 05█, 05█, 05█, 05█, and 05█ the entire payload of Project Gigas was launched towards SCP-2399.

[DATA EXPUNGED]

Efforts to develop alternative methods of eliminating SCP-2399 are currently underway.

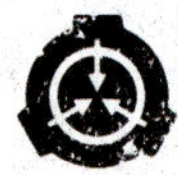

ADDENDUM 2399-L5

09388-32-1 > 02--53

So, SCP-2399.

Have you ever sat and wondered, maybe after you hear about a car accident on a street you were just on, or a bombing in a city you were visiting, just how lucky you are to be alive? Just how many things have to go right for you to continue to exist? A few seconds too late, a few seconds too early, and somebody reaches for something they dropped and a busload of people run into another busload of people. Sometimes this kind of thing does happen, as we've seen, far too often. But that's what we're here for. To protect those who can't protect themselves from things that they wouldn't even know to protect themselves from.

We can't do it all, though. As many things as we've been able to contain, as many things as we've been able to keep under lock that would threaten to destroy us all, still far too many remain that we can't do anything about. Whether they're too big, or too fast, or too powerful, any of these things could blink and wipe humanity from existence. The fact that they haven't done so yet is just luck. SCP-2399, however, is different.

We have little information regarding SCP-2399's motives, origins, and full capabilities. We do not understand how it is capable of communicating over such large distances, or why those who constructed it (if it was, in fact, constructed) sent it to us in the first place. We do not know what would happen if SCP-2399 is able to fully repair itself, or if part of our array would break down and a message would get through. We do not know this, so we must assume the worst. Judging by what we've seen, were SCP-2399 to have reached Earth, it would have led to our timely destruction.

But sometimes humanity gets a little help. Sometimes something steps in the way of the apocalypse. For us, and for SCP-2399, it was Jupiter. As SCP-2399 began to slow on its approach to Earth, Cassini saw what we've been able to ascertain; that SCP-2399 struck Io, was damaged, and was unable to escape the gravitational pull of Jupiter. Its weapons activated as they were intended, but it was Jupiter that experienced doomsday, not us.

Eventually, though, it's likely that SCP-2399 will resume full functionality, and will likely be able to pull away from Jupiter and proceed to its target. As of now, we can keep hurling bombs and EMPs at it all we want, but we've got no indication that any of it will so much as scratch the thing, on the contrary, experience dictates it would do nothing at all. If this were to happen now, we would undoubtedly be destroyed.

Jupiter has given us time. For now, SCP-2399 will remain there, reassembling itself, while we devise some way to stop it. Like it or not, we are in an arms race with this thing. Our best guesses give us something like 25 years until it is able to hear past our dampening array. Until then, we must seize the opportunity that has been laid before us. We must use the time we have been given, and not let it be wasted.

So we devised Protocol LEGIONNAIRE. One gigantic EMP, powered by god-knows-what, followed by a volley of nukes big enough to wipe out our civilization a thousand times over. A blunt plan, and simple, and likely futile. Our researchers, and researchers around the globe, have yet to devise even a way to deliver that kind of pulse, let alone a way to power it. There is no indication whatsoever that we will be able to complete LEGIONNAIRE on time, or if it will do what is intended once it is completed. But we must try. We must do something. Even if we have to drain our banks and empty our mines, we must try.

Not often do we get a chance to see the swerving bus that will end our lives, and step out of the way. Jupiter, unknowingly, has offered us that chance. I suggest we take it.

Randall McAllan

Director

BARRIER Project, Site █

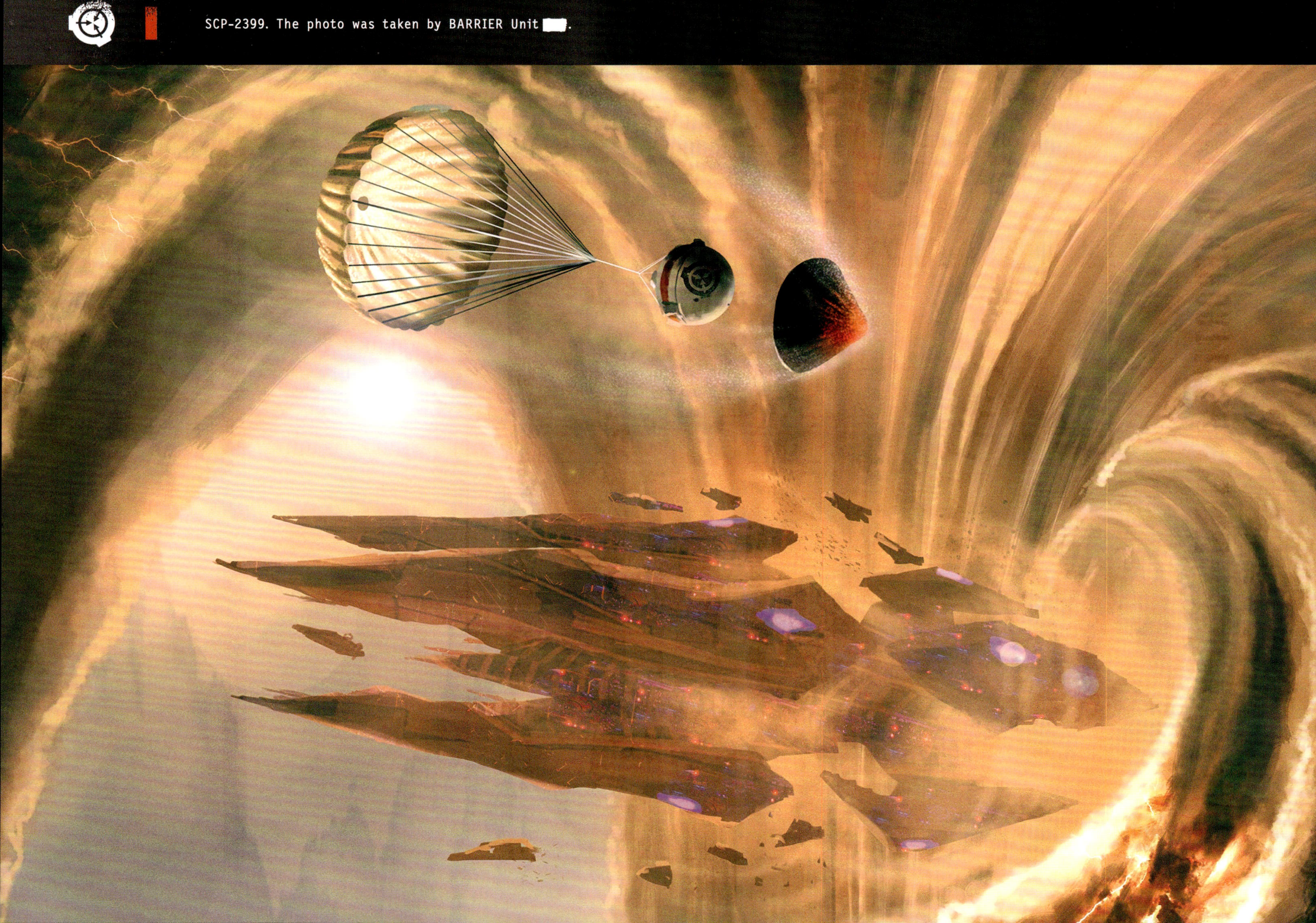

SCP-2399. The photo was taken by BARRIER Unit █.

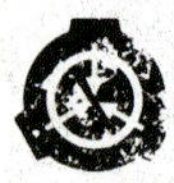

Research Library
File ▸ 2399

ADDENDUM 2399-COMM-LOG

All messages logged are to be understood as having repeated themselves, continuously, until either a new message is logged, or a logged instance of radio silence.

0199883-21 > 02---43

██/██/1971- Unit is damaged: Repair

██/██/1985- Updating Orders: Maintain Position: Repair

██/██/1985- Period of radio silence, BARRIER Array is established.

██/██/1996- Unit is out of range of target: Proceed to planet #3 in system [COORDINATES REDACTED]: Repair

██/██/2015- Unit is out of range of target: Proceed to planet #3 in system [COORDINATES REDACTED]: Priority is target: Cease repairs

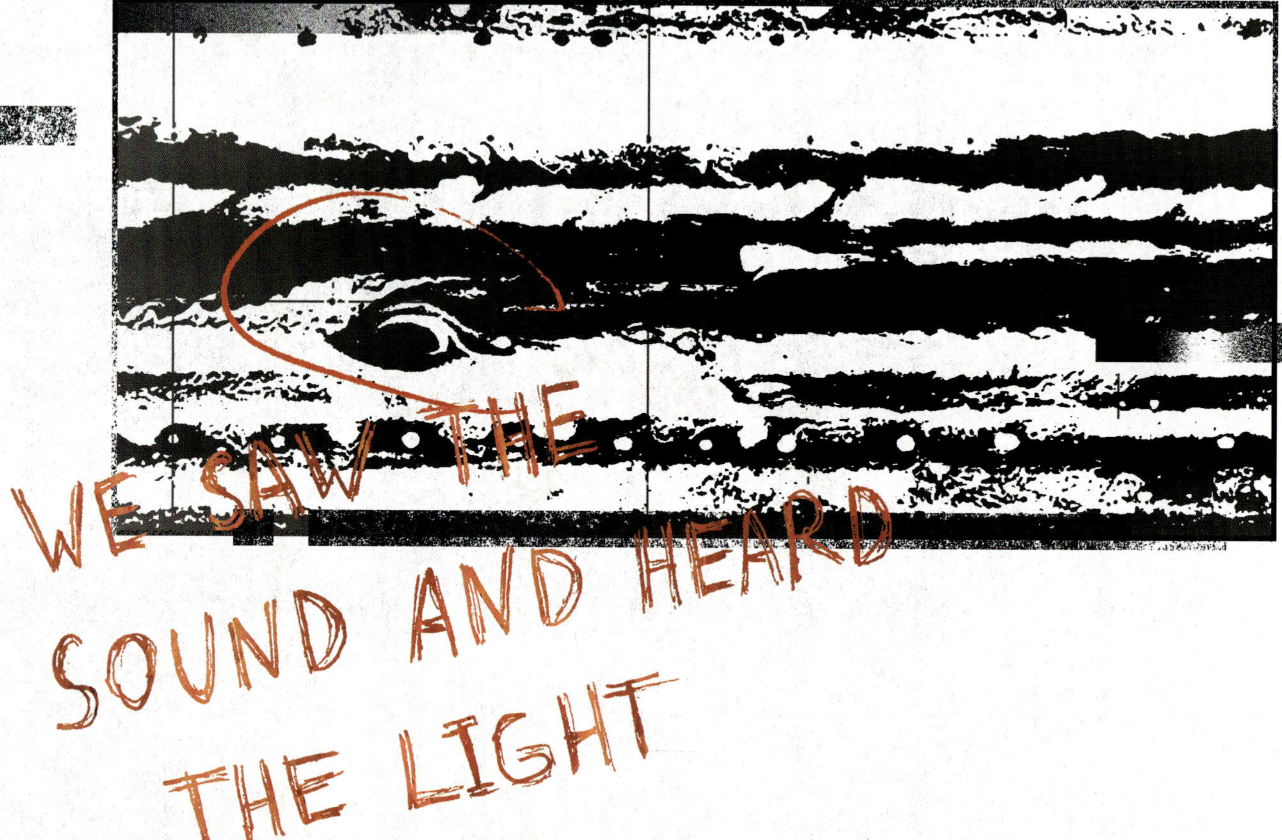

END OF REPORT

SPECIAL CONTAINMENT PROCEDURES

All personnel are banned from visiting SCP-1216-1 for any reason. The object is located inside a guarded perimeter under a reinforced concrete construction (a sarcophagus) 9 meters in diameter, 3 meters high, and with walls 0.5 meters thick. Inside the sarcophagus is an automated research station connected by a wire link to a transceiver outside the construction. The transceiver establishes a secure link with a control point no closer than 500 kilometers from the object.

Inside the sarcophagus are silicone sealant containers that can be triggered remotely. They are intended to fill the inside of the sarcophagus, completely blocking access to SCP-1216-1. The containers are to be opened by technical staff upon receiving a red alert (see Document 1216-B: Technical Regulations).

DESCRIPTION

VERSION FOR SECURITY PERSONNEL AND TECHNICAL SUPPORT FACILITY

SCP-1216-1 is a spatial anomaly located in an uninhabited portion of a mountainous subarctic semi-desert in the Bulunsky district of the Republic of Sakha (Yakutia) of the Russian Federation, 116 km south of the nearest settlement, the village of Kyusyur. The anomaly is a passage to a parallel universe designated SCP-1216-2.

The anomaly was located in 1998 thanks to satellite photography. It manifested itself as a local meteorological phenomenon – a stable, rotating fog bank. The fog was the manifestation of a mesocyclone formed by warmer and more humid air from another universe leaking into ours. Evidently, the anomaly had not existed earlier. Initially the object was designated Safe class, and regular expeditions were sent into SCP-1216-2. In the year 2013 an object (SCP-1216-3) was found that would cause a class K scenario if it entered our universe. Due to this, SCP-1216 was recategorized as Keter-class, every related expedition was cancelled, and a sarcophagus was constructed around it.

As far as is known, SCP-1216-3 is incapable of breaching the safety perimeter. However, the threat level may increase. In that case, safety measures should be enhanced, including the hermetic sealing of the sarcophagus interior. The Foundation is currently conducting research on SCP-1216-2 solely using remotely controlled robots.

VERSION FOR SEARCH ROBOT OPERATORS AND OTHER INTELLIGENCE PERSONNEL:

SCP-1216-1 is a type UO-SSSMB2 (stable, safe, mutually breachable portal) spatial anomaly, localized in [DATA REMOVED]. Outwardly, the anomaly looks like a translucent spherical oscillating membrane, freely permeable to any material bodies and radio waves. Passage through SCP-1216-1 is instantaneous and is not accompanied by any specific sensations.

File >>> 002922

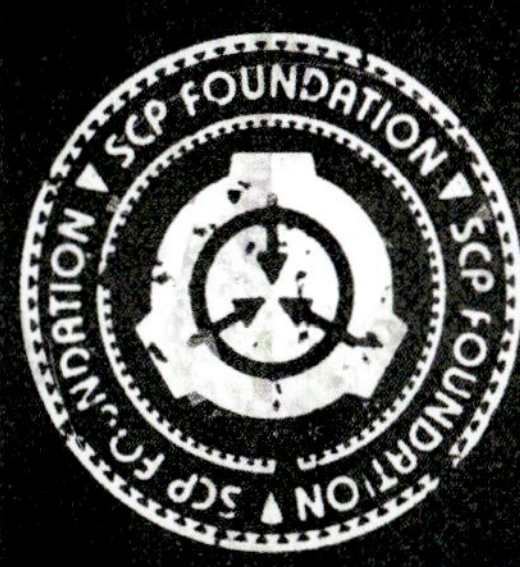

SCP-1216-RU

Title

THE GATES OF PARADISE

Report by

Fortunatus

Picture by

Dan Temirov

Access the original report on

scpfoundation.net/scp-1216-ru

Date

Class

KETER

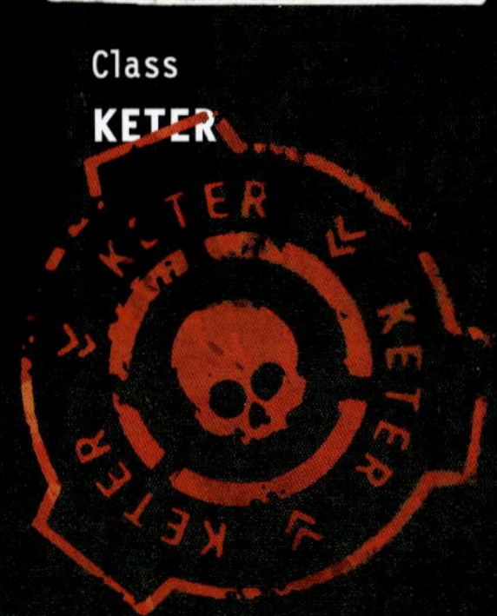

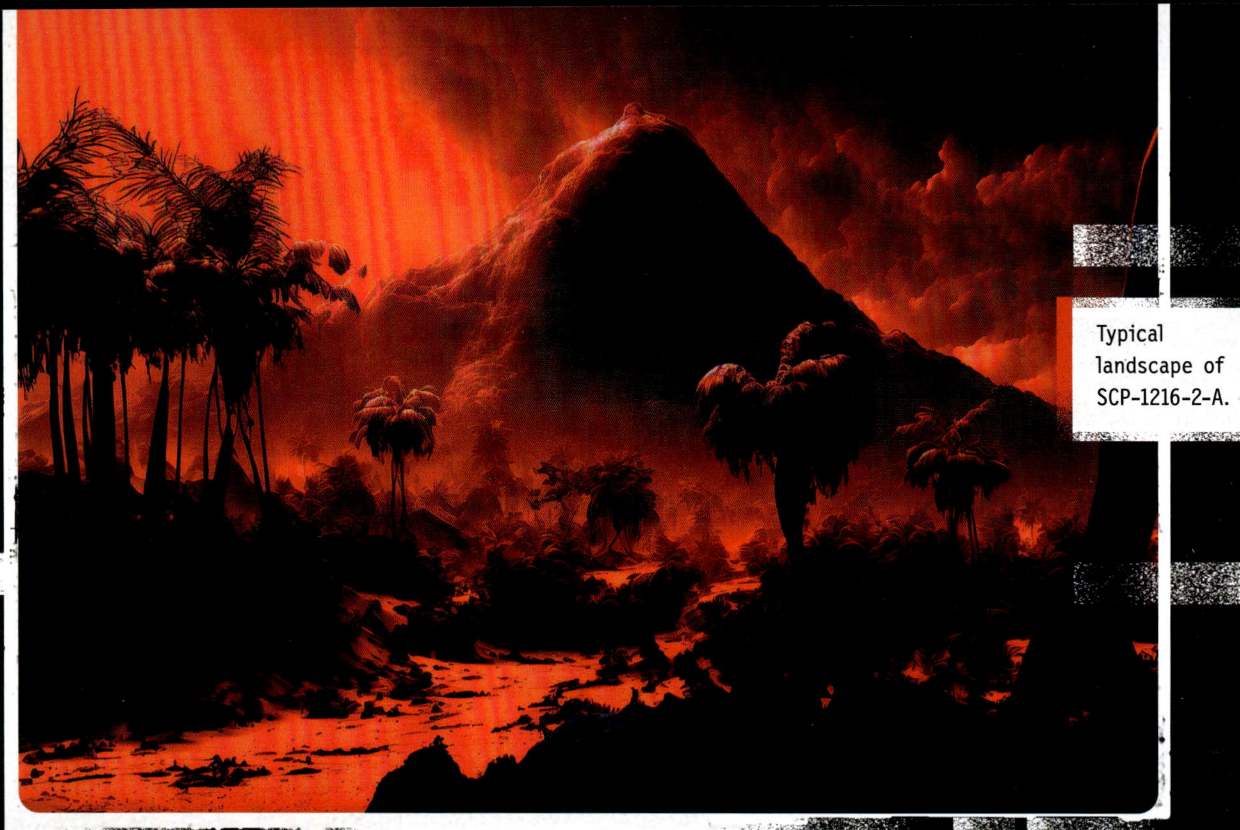

Typical landscape of SCP-1216-2-A.

SCP-1216-2 is the parallel world on the other side of SCP-1216-1. The exit point is located in an unidentified galaxy on the surface of a planet designated SCP-1216-2-A. According to measurements of the curvature of the horizon, the radius of the planet is 11.2 times that of Earth and almost equal to the radius of Jupiter, but it is not a gas giant and has gravity equal to that of Earth. This may indicate either that the gravitational constant in SCP-1216-2 is significantly less than in our universe, or that the density of the planet's matter is anomalously low. The pressure and composition of planet's atmosphere, magnetic field, lighting, and length of day also correspond to those of Earth.

The star is a yellow dwarf, similar in every respect to the Sun, with the exception of a few bright emission spectral lines that do not belong to any known element. Thanks to this (possibly anomalous) component of the spectrum, the daytime sky of the planet is purple-violet in color, the ocean is dark red, and the entire color spectrum differs from that of Earth. The planet has three large natural satellites (comparable in size to the Moon) and 12 small ones; observing them allows positioning on the planet's surface with an accuracy of 1 km.

The exit point is located at latitude 19.1°N, atop a small hilly island (224 m above sea level). Temperature, humidity and precipitation are consistent with a tropical climate; seasonal climatic fluctuations have not been observed. Rainfall is frequent (almost nightly), but not long, and wind strength does not exceed 5 on the Beaufort scale. The conditions for piloting aircraft are no different from those on Earth.

The island is part of a vast archipelago composed of sedimentary rocks such as limestone and sandstone. Most of the islands have mountainous terrain and a rugged coastline. Karst caves and grottoes, sheer cliffs, and sandbanks are characteristic of the terrain. Seismic activity is not detected. The islands are covered with vegetation, and there are terrestrial and aquatic fauna.

At the time this report edition (2015) was written, the territory within a radius of about 300 km from the exit point had been fairly well explored. All of it belongs to the above-described archipelago. No traces of the presence of humans or other sentient beings have been found. As far as is known, being on SCP-1216-2-A is physically harmless to humans. Nevertheless, a long stay has an irreversible psychophysical and anomalizing effect on people, the main aspects of which are as follows:

1-2 WEEKS: the onset and increase of an unreasonable feeling of anxiety;

2-3 WEEKS: increase in physical strength, endurance, reaction speed; all this against the emotional backdrop of growing anxiety that can trigger panic attacks;

3-4 WEEKS: the development of a hostile attitude towards other people, an increase in aggressiveness, increasingly frequent and intense bouts of unreasonable rage, to the point of complete loss of self-control;

1-2 MONTHS: development of anomalous invulnerability; any attempt at aggression against the subject will result in the immediate teleportation of the initiator of the attack from SCP-1216-2 to Earth in the vicinity of SCP-1216-1;

2-3 MONTHS: extinction of any mental activity, except for that aimed at causing maximum damage to other people;

3-4 MONTHS: development of other anomalous properties, such as levitation, unlimited underwater breathing, and short-range teleportation;

ABOUT A YEAR: Development of the ability to create portals similar to SCP-1216-1 between various points of SCP-1216-2 and our universe.

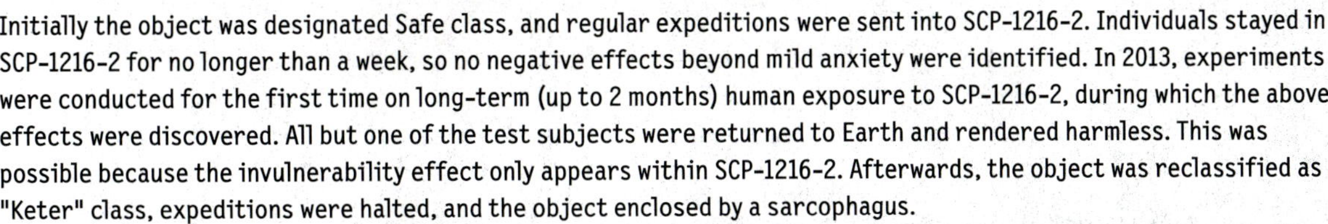

Initially the object was designated Safe class, and regular expeditions were sent into SCP-1216-2. Individuals stayed in SCP-1216-2 for no longer than a week, so no negative effects beyond mild anxiety were identified. In 2013, experiments were conducted for the first time on long-term (up to 2 months) human exposure to SCP-1216-2, during which the above effects were discovered. All but one of the test subjects were returned to Earth and rendered harmless. This was possible because the invulnerability effect only appears within SCP-1216-2. Afterwards, the object was reclassified as "Keter" class, expeditions were halted, and the object enclosed by a sarcophagus.

SCP-1216-3 is the designation assigned to the only test subject who escaped. At the moment, his apprehension and return to Earth are top priorities.

SCP-1216-3 is capable of creating portals to our universe. To date, it has created 13 portals, which have been given the general designation SCP-1216-4. They are located on the surface of SCP-1216-2-A in an irregularly shaped chain extending 120 km westward from the exit point. Most portals (except SCP-1216-4-11) lead to empty space and are easily detected by the vortexes of air being sucked into them. Thus, the chain of portals represents the "footprint" left by SCP-1216-3 on the planet's surface, making it somewhat easier to find him.

A map with the exact coordinates of all SCP-1216-4 is presented in Addendum SCP-1216-A. Below is a summary of each of the portals.

SCP-1216-4-1, -2, and -3 lead into empty intergalactic spaces. None of the galaxies observed on the other side have been identified.

SCP-1216-4-4 and -5 lead into empty intergalactic space approximately 50 megaparsecs from Earth, judging by several identified galaxies (M87 and others) viewed from completely different angles.

SCP-1216-4-6 leads into an area with lethal X-ray levels. The robot sent into this passage failed after 0.5 seconds, transmitting only telemetry and not having time to take photos.

SCP-1216-4-7 leads to a point of empty space on the outskirts of the Wolf-Landmark-Melotte galaxy, 930 kiloparsecs from Earth.

SCP-1216-4-8 leads into the vicinity of a red dwarf star within a dense dusty nebula. Other stars cannot be observed, making it impossible to determine the location of the exit point. The star is highly variable and surrounded by a protoplanetary disk of gas and dust.

SCP-1216-4-9 leads into empty space between the outskirts of our galaxy and the Large Magellanic Cloud, approximately 42 kiloparsecs from Earth.

SCP-1216-4-10 leads into the upper atmosphere of a "hot Jupiter" -type giant planet. The star (orange dwarf) could not be identified, but several bright stars are observed in the sky, visible from Earth (Canopus, Rigel, Deneb); judging by their coordinates, the exit point is located about 600 parsecs from Earth in the direction of the constellation of Southern Hydra.

SCP-1216-4-11 is impassable, and is dominated by a domed iron and nickel alloy volcano, continuously erupting high pressure lava of the same chemical composition at over 6000° C.

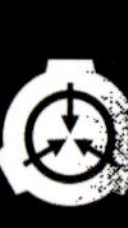

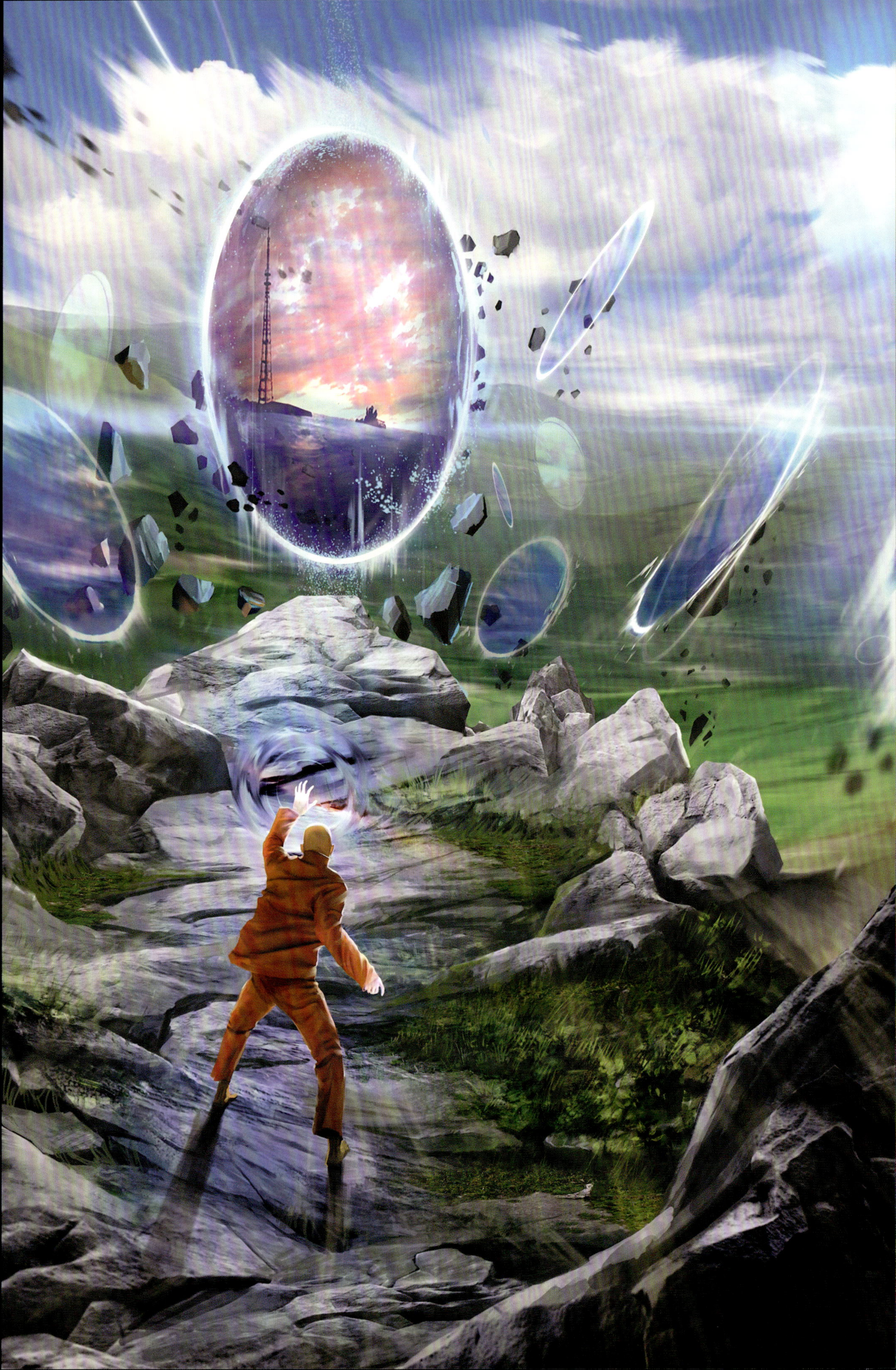

SCP-1216-4-12 leads into empty interstellar space approximately 1.2 parsecs (250,000 AU) from the Sun in the direction of the constellation Camelopardalis.

SCP-1216-4-13 leads to the surface of an unidentified ice planetoid orbiting the Sun at a distance of approximately 175 AU.

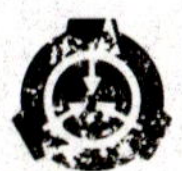

SCP-1216-3 appears to be attempting to create a portal to Earth. As you can see, he initially created portals blindly, but found the right way by trial and error, and with each attempt he shifts the exit point closer to Earth. The subject's goals are undoubtedly hostile to humanity.

If SCP-1216-3 is found, no attempt should be made to kill or immobilize him, although the search robots are equipped with the appropriate means. Such an attempt would only result in the teleportation of the robot from SCP-1216-2 to Earth without the possibility of return. For the purpose of capturing SCP-1216-3, the Siren Song Procedure was developed at the Foundation's Psychological and Memetic Research Center. When applied to a subject, it has a 85% chance of causing the subject to voluntarily obey search party commands.

Before starting the Siren Song Procedure, all operators must turn off the incoming audio channel in order to protect themselves from memetic effects. If successful, the lead operator is to order SCP-1216-3 to return to its exit point and on to Earth. When the subject passes through SCP-1216-1 and becomes vulnerable, they are to be destroyed immediately. If successful, the interior of the sarcophagus will then be sealed and all activity within SCP-1216-2 will cease.

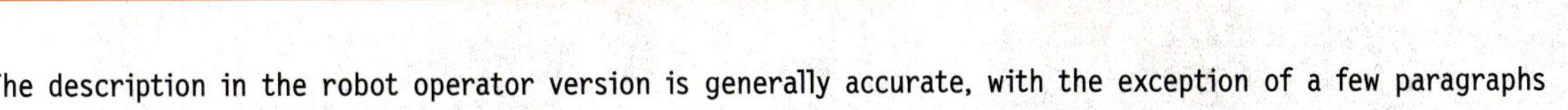

VERSION FOR EMPLOYEES WITH CLEARANCE LEVEL 4 AND ABOVE:

The description in the robot operator version is generally accurate, with the exception of a few paragraphs that contain deliberate misinformation.

SCP-1216-2-A's sun spectrum does contain lines of unknown elements, but these do not affect the planet's color spectrum, which is virtually indistinguishable from Earth's. The red-violet color is artificially created through digital color processing in the cameras of search robots in order to reduce the external attractiveness of the planet in the eyes of operators.

From an ecological point of view, the planet is completely suitable for human life. The islands are covered with dense evergreen deciduous vegetation, biochemically identical to its terrestrial counterparts. About 100 species of trees and shrubs with edible fruits have been described. Poisonous plants have not been detected. The fauna of the land is not rich and is represented by small birds and herbivorous and insectivorous mammals. Large predators, poisonous or stinging insects, and pathogenic microbes have not been found. The underwater fauna is more diverse; several dozen species of edible fish and mollusks have been described. Marine animals dangerous to humans have not been identified.

In the early 2010s a project was under way to create a spa and sanatorium area within SCP-1216-2 for Foundation personnel. It was as part of this project in 2013 that experiments were carried out on the long-term stay of humans in SCP-1216-2. The psychophysical and anomalizing effects found in this process were, in fact, as follows:

1-2 WEEKS: recovery from all somatic diseases, acquisition of immunity to all known infections (the effect is reversible, disappearing after returning to Earth); accelerated healing of wounds and injuries (irreversible);

2-3 WEEKS: physiological rejuvenation akin to returning to 25-35 years of age in older people, an increase in physical strength, endurance, and reaction speed (all effects are reversible);

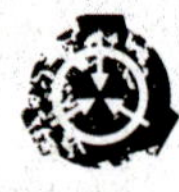

Research Library File ▸ 1216-RU

3-4 WEEKS: reduction of nervousness and aggressiveness, recovery from nervous and mental diseases of non-somatic genesis, growth in intelligence, development of a positive and friendly attitude towards other people, a tendency towards altruism, compromise, and conflict resolution (reversible);

1-2 MONTHS: Development of invulnerability within SCP-1216-2; any attempt at aggression against the subject will result in the immediate teleportation of the initiator of the attack on Earth in the vicinity of SCP-1216-1 (reversible);

3-4 MONTHS: development of other anomalous properties, such as levitation, unlimited underwater breathing, and short-range teleportation (reversibility not established);

ABOUT A YEAR: Development of the ability to create passageways similar to SCP-1216-1 between various points of SCP-1216-2 and our universe (reversibility not established).

SCP-1216-3 is the designation for a D-class employee (personal number D-8710) who refused to return from SCP-1216-2 to Earth. This is Vsevolod Petrovich Nosov, a citizen of the Russian Federation, born in 1982. He graduated from Novosibirsk State Technical University in 2003. That same year, he founded the left-wing anarcho-communist group "SVD" ("Happiness Free for All"), at the head of which he committed a series of crimes, such as: armed robberies of shops and banks (with the subsequent distribution of part of the money to the poor), arson of police stations and judicial buildings, and attacks on police officers and private guards. In 2006, the group was captured and all members were arrested and convicted except for Nosov, who managed to escape. Nosov was given an Interpol Red Notice, placing him on an international wanted list. In 2007 he was detained by Colombian authorities and extradited to the Russian Federation. In 2008 he was sentenced under a number of articles of the Criminal Code to 25 years in prison. In the same year, he signed a cooperation agreement with the Foundation.

As a D-class employee, he worked on SCP-1216. Due to his high intellectual level, scientific mindset, and willingness to cooperate, he was excluded from the monthly rotation at the request of his scientific advisor, Dr. Samokhin. Performing the work of an assistant researcher, he possessed quite complete information about SCP-1216-2. In 2013, he participated in a program studying the effects of long-term exposure to SCP-1216-2, personally staying there for a month. After curtailing the program, he refused to return to Earth and, using his newly acquired anomalous abilities, fled.

The details of the Siren Song Procedure are true, except for the fact that its effect is not memetic. The procedure is for the subject (SCP-1216-3) to be given an order to return to the exit point, with the threat of killing one D-class personnel every half hour. If the subject ignores the order, a new threat is to be reported: amputation of a small part of the body of a 3-year-old child every fifteen minutes. This is highly likely to force the subject to comply, and the threat does not have to be carried out. However, [DATA REMOVED]. It should be noted that SCP-1216-3 must be neutralized at all costs before he can open a portal to an area of the earth's surface not controlled by the Foundation.

Based on current knowledge of SCP-1216-3's biography and beliefs, there is every reason to believe that he seeks to open portals to Earth from SCP-1216-2 in order to provide access to this world for everyone. It is clear that a massive migration of Earth's population to SCP-1216-2 would have disastrous consequences for the social, political, and economic organization of humankind. An event of this nature should be viewed as a total disruption of normalcy and a UP-class scenario. As with other Keter-class objects, the Foundation's mission is to prevent this from happening.

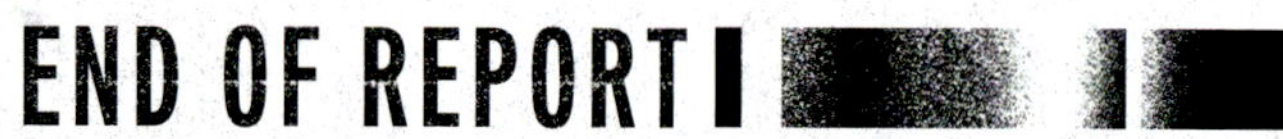

END OF REPORT

File >>> 00291112

SPECIAL CONTAINMENT PROCEDURES

SCP-179 remains beyond the reach of currently known groups of interest, including the Foundation. All containment efforts are to be focused towards a Grade 3 *Omission* cover-up, coupled with the discouragement or sabotage of exploration and research missions that attempt to study cis-Mercurian space and orbits that go through it.

DESCRIPTION

SCP-179 is a humanoid entity located at a constant distance of approximately 40,000 km from the South polar region of the solar photosphere, locked to the rotation axis of Sol. However, it does not orbit it; the most recent recordings of SCP-179 indicate that it seems to maintain a continuous orbit around the center of the galaxy.

Through the combined effort of 43 years of continuous surveying, the external appearance of SCP-179 has been defined as a human female of undetermined ethnic group of between twenty and forty years of age. Its entire bodily surface is covered in or composed of a matte black material. Its hair appears to be composed of this material, measures over 34 km long and is constantly pushed away by solar wind. However, this part of SCP-179 seems to reflect variable amounts of sunlight – this reflection being the phenomenon that indicated its existence to Foundation astrophysicists during 1940. Several markings or tattoos are placed throughout its bodily midline. Judging from their brightness, these markings might be of metallic composition and of a golden hue.

These tattoos include several symbols that have been identified as those typically representing the Sun and the six innermost planets of the Solar System according to medieval alchemy, including, in this order:

- The symbol of gold in the subject's forehead, right underneath the hair line.
- The symbol of mercury under the nose, circling both lips.
- The symbol of copper between the medial ends of its clavicles.
- [DATA EXPUNGED - AUTOCENSOR LEVEL SC 4 - NON-TRIVIAL COGNITOHAZARD DETECTED] with the anatomically correct shape of a human heart placed over the location where a heart would be in a female human of the same apparent age and bodily proportions.
- The symbol of iron in the upper abdominal region.
- The symbol of tin in the lower abdominal region.
- Part of a final symbol in the pelvic region. While the anatomy of this region makes its clear observation difficult, it has been hypothesized that the symbol of lead is also present and complete in the perineum region.

SCP-179 keeps its ventral side oriented towards Earth most of the time, but it has been observed to look towards other areas on occasion. [REDACTED]

[ALL FURTHER DATA REDACTED AS PER ADMINISTRATIVE WARNING ES-026]

SCP-179

Title

SAUELSUESOR

Report by

Dr Reach

Pictures by

Zhenya Dolgova

Access the original report on

scp-wiki.wikidot.com/scp-179

Date

Class

~~SAFE~~

THAUMI[illegible]

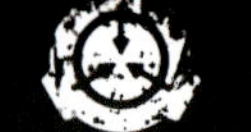

Research Library File ▸ 093

ADMINISTRATIVE WARNING ES-026

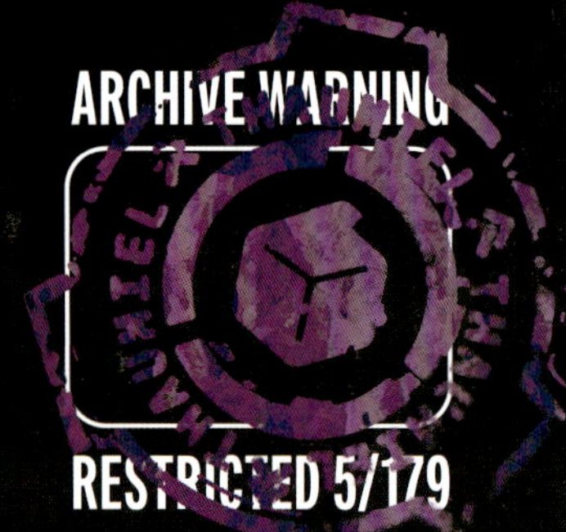

As of ███/███/█████, SCP-179 has been reclassified Thaumiel. All involved personnel with a clearance level below 4/179 will be either promoted or reassigned to fit this new classification, depending on their relevance for the continuated surveillance and cover-up operations as directed by the current Head Researcher for SCP-179. All reassigned personnel will be subject to POLYMATH-08 Memory Redaction Therapy or D-class amnestics (in a high dosage grade, with a maximum retrograde effect of ten years of experience), depending on the time spent working in SCP-179 prior to its reclassification.

SCP-179's existence will be subject to an Orbital Misinformation Standardized Intelligence Obstruction and Neutralization campaign. As per Omission Protocol 4 (items 4.5, 4.6 and 4.7), most documentation related to SCP-179 has been classified Level 4 (Top Secret). Any further data related to SCP-179 has been classified Level 5 (Thaumiel), and will be made available only to authorized 5/179 personnel.

BE ADVISED THAT: Unauthorized access to SCP-179 research materials will be considered a Type-3-B offense (Unauthorized Data Management While Lacking Appropriate Global Clearance), punishable by compulsory memory redaction therapy with immediate reassignment and/or demotion.

SCP-179 is sensitive to all radiation in the electromagnetic spectrum, intelligent and able to communicate through multiple anomalous means, including but not limited to radio and laser communications interference. Only one instance of SCP-179 communication with Foundation personnel has occurred thus far, where SCP-179 proved to be fluent in French. As this contact did not result in a clear statement of SCP-179's intentions towards the Foundation and its mission, all efforts must be made to prevent contact by any known Groups of Interest with SCP-179. Misinformation operations and other preemptive measures have been deployed.

Most recorded movements performed by SCP-179 have been related to extraterrestrial threats, both anomalous or non-anomalous in nature, on a collision or orbital insertion course with the Earth. These threatening items have been identified as capable of causing CK-Class Reconfiguration events of diverse impact on human societies and earthly life in general if allowed to reach Earth. If impact with Earth or orbital insertion occurs without proper response and containment by Foundation operatives, these items of interest may be capable of causing XK-Class end-of-the-world scenarios.

SCP-179 will usually address an item or items of interest by pointing at them with an arm and, when more than one item of interest is present, will be able to generate additional limbs anatomically identical to its arms, as needed. Survey data indicates that SCP-179 performs other motions specific to each item of interest addressed – such as raising different fingers or moving its arms in an array of as of yet undecipherable patterns at fixed intervals –, but whether these motions contain any information or not has not been determined to date.

The limits of SCP-179's detection capacities have not been clearly ascertained. While SCP-179 has been able to detect potentially harmful objects beyond the trans-Neptunian region, those threats had been detected by other surveillance and exploration systems (usually under Foundation control) or, in at least three separate instances, were visible to the naked eye from Earth. However, they had not been immediately recognized as threats. It has been hypothesized that SCP-179 may only detect and react to active threats that remain detectable to other observing parties without the cis-Neptunian region, while being able to unerringly determine their harmful nature. All items of interest approaching Earth within cis-Neptunian space that had considerable destructive capacity have been detected by SCP-179 without failure, often when no observers known to the Foundation were aware of them.

As such, SCP-179 and all personnel, orbital equipment and facilities dedicated to its surveillance remain the most reliable early warning system the Foundation possesses to detect and, when possible, prevent, potentially

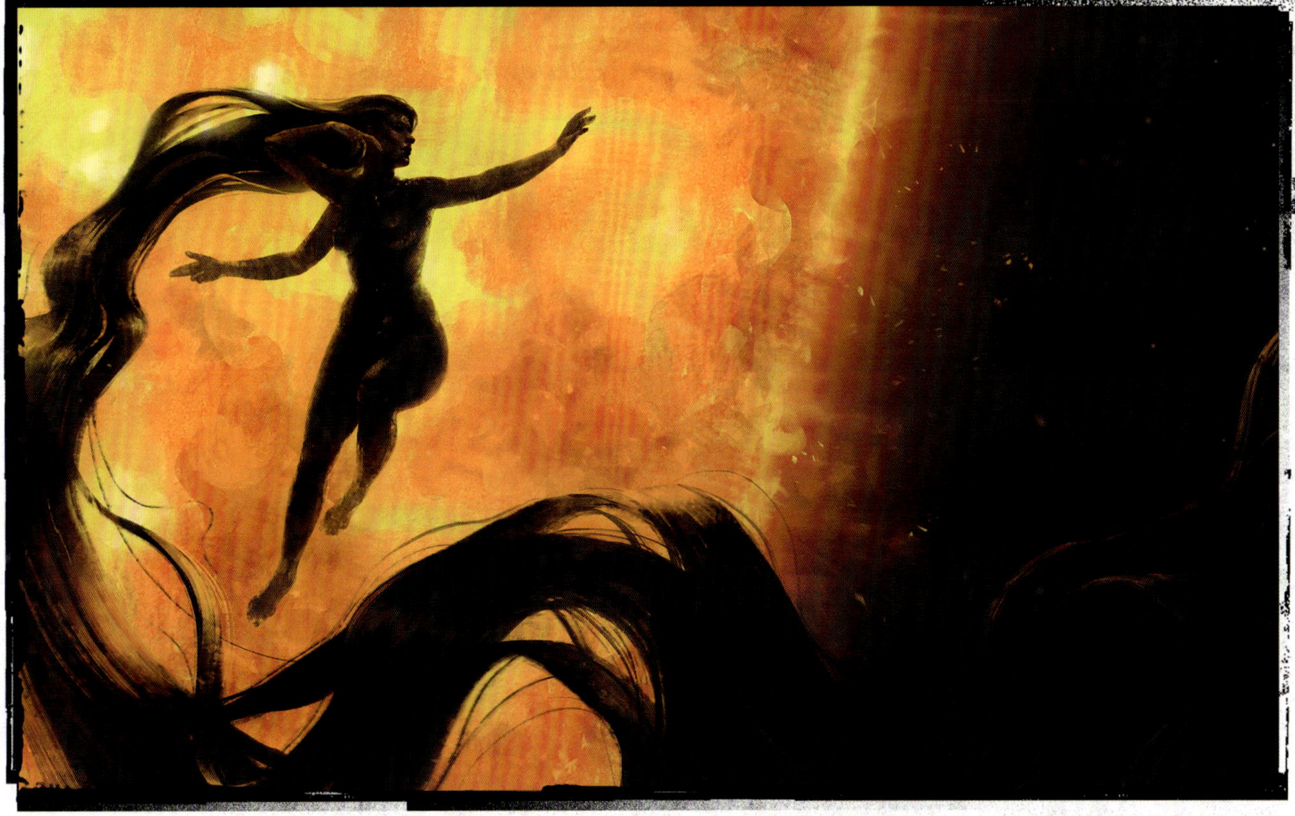

SCP-179. The photo was taken by the ████ telescope on ██/██/20█

dangerous incursions within surveyed space. SCP-179 is able to determine which interplanetary objects pose a threat to Earth, humankind or the earthly biosphere, which makes it a critical asset for the Composite Orbital Early Warning System (COEWS) project of the Foundation, which currently involves SCP-██, SCP-███, SCP-█-██, and SCP-███, XCPOA-003 to -0421, Site-34, Site-103, Site-98, Area-08, Site-██, Site-██-█, █ and █ and Command Site-██, as well as several personnel embedded within different space agencies and international consortia related to space exploration. All data of interest related to or obtained through SCP-179 will be marked COEWS-179, which will be considered high priority information to all Foundation departments.

ADDENDUM SCP-179-01: NOTABLE MOVEMENTS OF SCP-179.

<13/12/1940> First recorded movement of SCP-179. The entity, that had remained with both arms crossed, raises an arm towards a previously undetected interplanetary object on a collision course with Earth. After its impact, in an event that damaged the city of [DATA EXPUNGED] extensively with large quantities of an anomalous mucous secretion and left more than one thousand and three hundred dead which, combined with the anomalous phenomena related to [REDACTED AS PER PREVIOUS EXPUNGEMENT] Remaining central item reclassified SCP-██. SCP-179 returned to its original position.

<22/09/1942> Sixth recorded movement of SCP-179. The entity raises an arm towards [REDACTED], on a collision course with Earth. Item of interest crashes nearby Auckland, New Zealand, on 04/10/1942. Item separates upon impact into several devices of mechanical nature. [DATA EXPUNGED] recently formed sub-entities with minimal civilian casualties. Once Foundation operatives contain the item proper, which is reclassified [REDACTED] and terminating most sub-entities, SCP-179 returns to its original position. Mobile Task Forces [REDACTED, ALL DATA ON INVOLVED ASSETS EXPUNGED FROM RECORDS] proceeds to track and destroy all remaining sub-entities.

<██/██/19██> Eighteenth recorded movement of SCP-179. The entity raises its right arm towards [DATA EXPUNGED]. Up to this date, the entity has kept one of its primary arms – shifting from one to the other as necessary – pointing in the same direction.

<01/03/1949> 23rd recorded movement of SCP-179. The entity raises an arm towards an Amor-class asteroid, that has adopted a collision course with Earth. The Foundation uses a combination of several SCP objects to

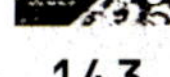

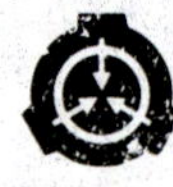

launch a remote-controlled interplanetary vehicle that acts as a gravitatory towline; this mission is announced a success on 03/05/1951; at this time, SCP-179 returns to its original position. **Note:** *Surveying elements observed that the entity performed a motion that could have been a nod. Reclassification request to Euclid status filed and denied.*

<13/12/1998> 403rd recorded movement of SCP-179. The entity stops watching the Earth for two days and thirteen hours, when it looks towards the Jovian system. Once this interval is over, SCP-179 looks at Earth again.

<09/09/2002> 487th recorded movement of SCP-179. SCP-179 points at an armed Type-11 Dimensional Weapon [FURTHER DATA ON XCP-11-DW EXPUNGED AS PER 05-11 EXECUTIVE COMMAND] launched from Area-08 to test SCP-179's detection capacities. Item remains in a primed configuration for ██ minutes, ready to be launched at a test location on Earth. It is not identified by SCP-179 until it is 3,670 kilometers above the Earth's surface, when SCP-179 reacts to it as a threat and points at it. Device subsequently reconfigured to a stand-by configuration and redirected towards its primary target, [DATA EXPUNGED] still in transit from the Kuiper Belt. SCP-179 returns to its previous position.

<16/10/2003> Contact with SCP-179 is achieved via the █████-2 probe. Subsequent movements registered in Addendum SCP-179-02. SCP-179 reclassified Thaumiel. See Addendum SCP-179-02.

ADDENDUM SCP-179-02: EVENTS OF 16/10/2003.

SCP-179 was first approached by the █████-2 probe, a microsatellite equipped with multiple recording, analysis and communications devices incorporated into the █████ probe in a clandestine operation. The █████ probe acted as a relay for the █████-2 probe and Foundation Mission Control.

Contact and communication with the entity were not foreseen nor programmed. When visual contact with SCP-179 was established (obtaining an unprecedentedly clear, very high resolution image of its surface), the entity begins to move its lips, forming the phonemes of a greeting in spoken French. What follows is a complete translation of the exchange.

SCP-179 / <17:34:23>: Hello.

SCP-179 / <17:39:38>: I'm the lookout.

SCP-179 / <17:42:38>: My name is Sauelsuesor. Do you like my brother? I like him too. He is big, so big.

SCP-179 / <17:43:01>: And so very warm.

SCP-179 / <17:43:11>: If you want to talk to me, please use your satellite to weave-talk to me. It'll be easier than coming here. Probably. *(Entity remains immobile until <17:55:53>)*

(Researchers assigned to SCP-179 detect this movement. Level 3 Researcher Tomas Graham, who is fluent in French, is selected by Head Researcher [REDACTED] to conduct a possible exchange with SCP-179. The █████-2 probe is used as a radio relay from this point onward; SCP-179 is able to receive, understand and transmit radio communications. SCP-179's transmissions read as a monotone, featureless human voice that speaks in French. The subsequent exchange occurs with a 16 minutes and 39.6 seconds delay between each message, corresponding to the distance between SCP-179 and Earth and return, that will be omitted in the rest of this document.)

RESEARCHER GRAHAM, T: Who are you?

SCP-179: My name is Sauelsuesor. I am the lookout. I behold. I often see. I often warn. Almost always, when I have to. That way, there is further life.

RESEARCHER GRAHAM, T: What do you mean, the "lookout"?

SCP-179: It's me. *(smiles)*

RESEARCHER GRAHAM, T: We have noticed the significance of your movements. Who do you report to?

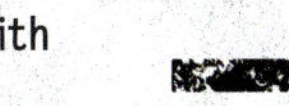

Research Library File ▸ 179

SCP-179: To those who know where to look. To you. To those who want to look. Not just you. But you, too.

RESEARCHER GRAHAM, T: When you say brother, are you referring to the Sun?

SCP-179: He is my brother, Sauel. He warms me up. He is caring fire and loving light. He caresses me with his arcs and his voice and renews me. He is the source of all true light. He is your source.

RESEARCHER GRAHAM, T: Where do you come from?

SCP-179: I was born a child. *(the entity nods towards Earth.)*

RESEARCHER GRAHAM, T: For how long have you been in your current location?

SCP-179: I do not want to tell you. *(smiles) (SCP-179 adopts a fetal position, remains looking towards the Earth and pointing at [REDACTED]. Face of the entity remains visible from the █████ probe)*

RESEARCHER GRAHAM, T: How did you reach your current position? How did you acquire the properties you currently possess?

SCP-179: I was grown into a woman. This is how I live now.

RESEARCHER GRAHAM, T: Could you give us further details, please?

SCP-179: No.

RESEARCHER GRAHAM, T: We would like to know more about you. Why not tell us?

SCP-179: I am sorry. I won't be yours. I can't belong to any one person.

RESEARCHER GRAHAM, T: The Foundation's work protects all of humanity, all life on Earth. Don't you find this work of the greatest importance?

SCP-179: Yes. I am doing it. Look upon me and know.

RESEARCHER GRAHAM, T: If we have understood your capacities correctly, we believe you could do far more than that. Sharing all the information you have, not just about the dangerous threats against humankind and Earth, could be of great benefit to all parts involved.

SCP-179: I am too big, and you are too small. There is a sea of nothing and islands of light. I am their shore. To you come the monsters. The pounding fists of void. The longing gods beyond our knowledge. I am the lookout. I see the ripples in their wake. You want me to pledge my sight-know to you, only to you, so you, only you, can be greater. Even if you find, restrain, defend. You want me to be yours. That is not why I am here. There are others. Others I assist. Others I warn. Others beyond your thin walls of grey, dry paste-rock. Others beyond the reach of your weary satellites. Others beyond the home, our home. Others I know. Others I love. Others you won't care for. Others that came before. And, over all, others beyond the little walls of rules and bone and laws and flesh and memories and oaths you build around yourselves until you don't even remember them. Others I love. Dearly. And yet, only my brother is an equal to me.

RESEARCHER GRAHAM, T: Excuse me, I don't understand what you mean by "others." Could you, please, explain yourself with other words?

SCP-179: *(smiles)* But I have no words left.

Closing: Despite several communication attempts, SCP-179 did not perform any other movements nor transmit other messages. Up to this date, SCP-179 has not responded to any message coming from any Foundation contact team or any other efforts from known Groups of Interest.

END OF REPORT

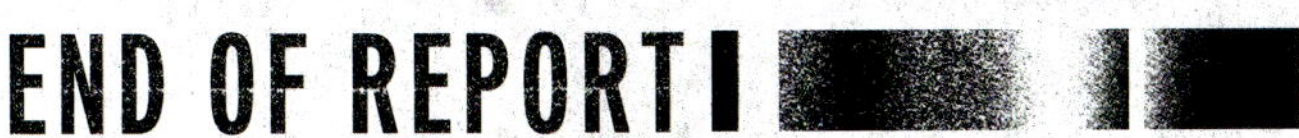

File >>> 8873211

SCP-1230

Title

A HERO IS BORN

Report by

MrPixel

Pictures by

Dan Temirov
Genocide Error

Access the original report on

scp-wiki.wikidot.com/scp-1230

Date

Class

SAFE

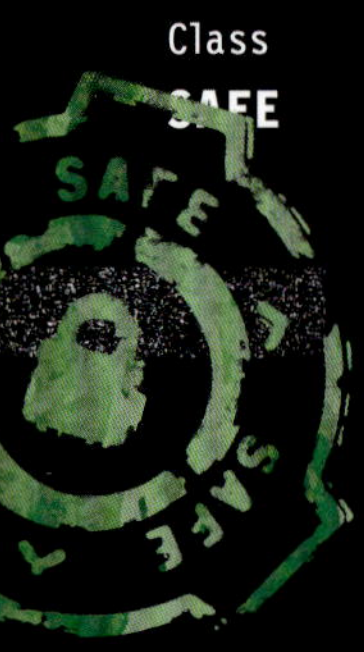

SPECIAL CONTAINMENT PROCEDURES

~~SCP-1230 is to be kept in a secure storage locker at Site-12. Access requires minimum Clearance 2 with authorization and supervision by Clearance 3 research and security staff respectively. Supervising personnel are not to view SCP-1230's contents. Personnel accessing SCP-1230 are required to submit written accounts of dreams experienced within 48 hours of access.~~ (See Addendum-1230-A) SCP-1230 has been relocated to a secure storage locker behind the desk of Site-12's main library. Access is available to Clearance 2 personnel deemed to be in satisfactory psychological condition by site psychiatric staff. Personnel accessing SCP-1230 must submit written accounts of their dreams within 48 hours of access and submit to follow-up psychological examination.

DESCRIPTION

SCP-1230 is an unlabeled, green hardcover book with no apparent exceptional qualities. When SCP-1230 is opened, it displays the phrase "A hero is born" on the first page viewed, while all other pages will be blank, "resetting" once the book is closed. This has no obvious effects at first, but upon falling asleep, the reader will dream of a fantasy world where they are the protagonist of a troubled land. Dreamers are completely aware and all senses work just as well as when awake. Results vary depending on the imagination of the reader and are mostly attuned to fantasies of adventure that the reader would enjoy. In the mind of the reader, these dreams have been documented to last anywhere from 45 seconds (see Experiment 1230-3) to 200 years (see Experiment 1230-5) but in reality, the reader will usually never be asleep longer than they would normally. Upon awaking, the reader is able to remember every aspect of their dream in detail. In SCP-1230-induced dreams, there is always a character called the "Book Keeper" (SCP-1230-1) appearing as a bearded man in a green cloak who claims to be the personification of SCP-1230 himself. SCP-1230-1 has been reported to be very amicable and helpful towards dreamers. It has stated that it enjoys creating these "fantasy-scapes" and always tries to shape them in such a way that the dreamer garners the most entertainment out of it. It has expressed sorrow when the dream comes to an end and asks the dreamer to "please visit again soon".

DISCOVERY

In a small bookstore located [DATA EXPUNGED] the shopkeeper had no recollection of owning the unlabeled book but attempted to sell a story to local newspapers about a "magical dream book". The Foundation was able to dispel the story as a hoax and SCP-1230 was confiscated.

EXPERIMENT-1230-01 ████████████

Dr. F█████, in an attempt to test its effective range, opened SCP-1230 and boarded a flight to his hometown of [REDACTED] where he spent the night at a hotel. Upon his return, Dr. F█████ reported that SCP-1230-1 appeared in his dreams and explained that once you read 'A hero is born', the dream is immediately implanted in your subconscious, after which SCP-1230-1 is able to manipulate it remotely. Dr. F█████ expressed his appreciation for SCP-1230-1's cooperation.

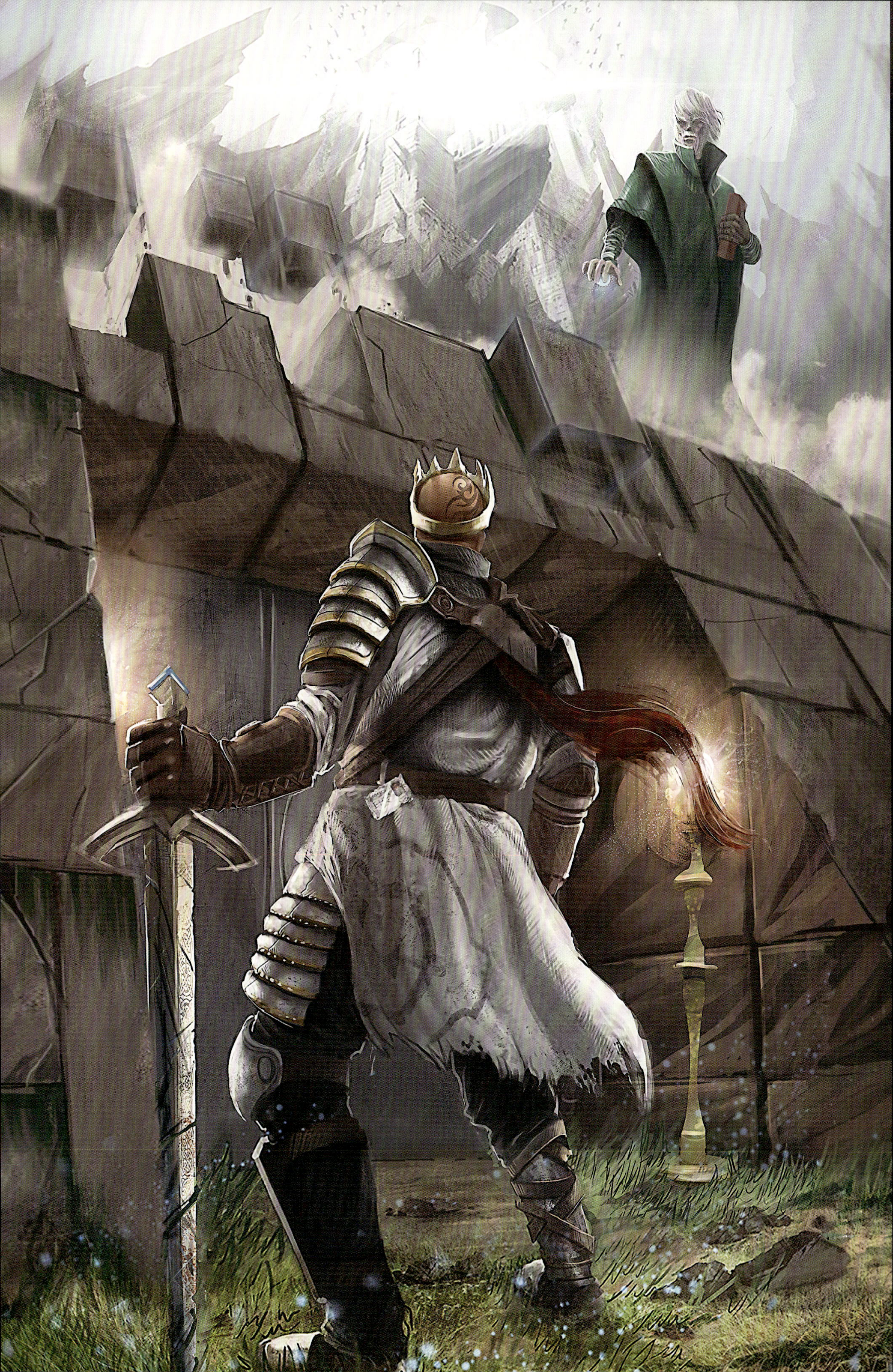

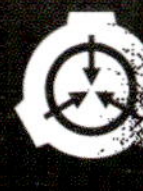
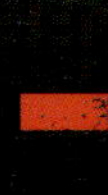

Experiment-1230-05 visualization.

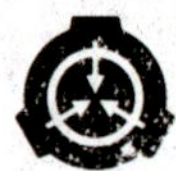

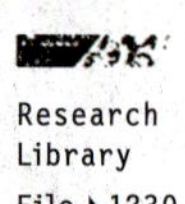

Research Library File ▸ 1230

EXPERIMENT-1230-02

A camera was set-up above SCP-1230 and, using a mechanical "arm", the book was opened. All pages were revealed to be blank. It seems SCP-1230 is only effective when opened by beings that are able to have dreams. SCP-1230-1 explained to a subsequent dreamer that it is actually only able to affect beings "with an imagination" and that most creatures such as animals would not be affected.

EXPERIMENT-1230-03

One (1) D-class was instructed to open the book and (after much reassurance that his experiences would only be dreams) ordered to immediately find a way to kill himself in the dream. The subject was asleep for merely 45 seconds before he awoke with a start in a nervous sweat. He reported being at the summit of a volcano called "The Ashen Spire" on a quest for "Caladius, the Blessed Blade". When asked how the subject knew the names, he stated, "It's like I knew them all along". He apparently leapt into the volcano and "felt an intense heat" before awakening. D-class requested permission to "give it another go". Request was denied.

EXPERIMENT-1230-04

One (1) D-class was instructed to open the book and attempt to non-fatally injure himself in his dream. After 6 hours, the D-class awoke and reported that he was able to feel a "numbed" sort of pain where it was never so intense as to be unbearable. He also reported meeting an elderly, cloaked man who asked him why he was harming himself, but thanked him for not immediately killing himself "like that other rude fellow".

EXPERIMENT-1230-05

Professor B████ filed a request for access to SCP-1230 and was quickly permitted, given his Level 4 clearance. Staff members recalled that Professor B████ was almost "visibly shaking with excitement" and some reported that Professor B████ was an avid fan of tabletop and role-playing games. Surveillance shows that Professor B████ opened the book, read the phrase, sat down beside the desk and promptly fell asleep. Staff members were alarmed when Professor B████ did not awake after 15 hours and alerted security. The on-site medical staff were able to confirm that Professor B████ was still alive and in good health. After approximately 24 hours since falling asleep, Professor B████ began to move, reported to have "slowly raised his head and looked around the room, appearing deeply confused". Security entered the room to ensure he was alright, to which he replied, "Where am I?". He was sent to Medical where staff explained where and who he was. Several minutes later, Professor B████ appeared to have regained his memory and excused himself to the restroom. When 15 minutes passed and Professor B████ had not exited, a nurse entered to find he had hanged himself with his belt. A scribbled message on the wall revealed his last words: "I can't go back to this". Dr. F█████, went to ask SCP-1230-1 what had happened, but upon opening SCP-1230, all its pages were soaking wet with the same message on every page: "I'm so sorry. I never intended for this to happen. I just wanted to make people happy." repeated over and over. SCP-1230 remained in this state for three weeks and its desk had to be wiped dry biweekly. In an attempt to communicate, Dr. F█████ placed a sticky note inside SCP-1230 with the statement, "I'd like to talk to you, if that's alright". The next morning, Dr. F█████ filed a report about a dream he had concerning SCP-1230-1.

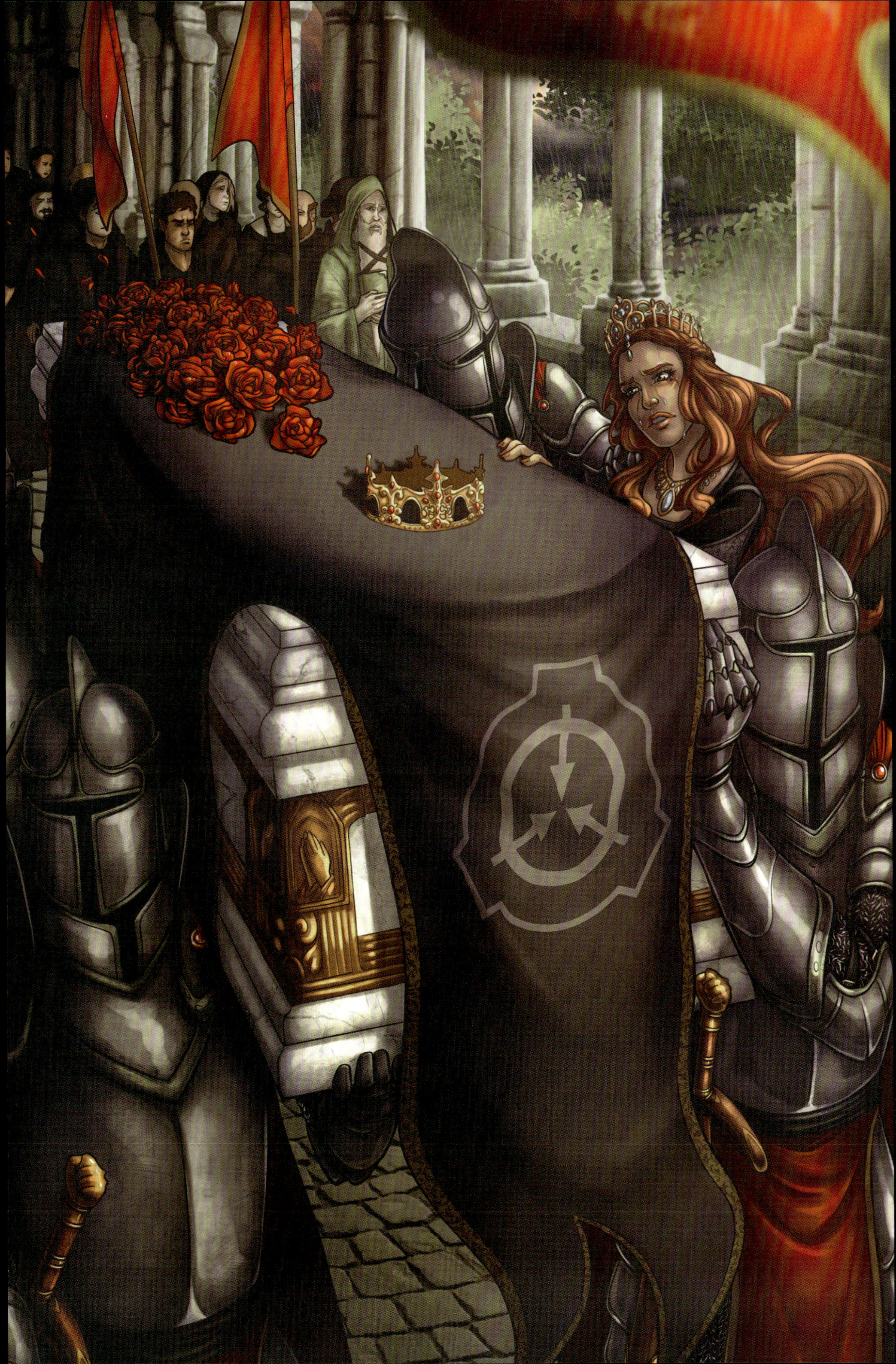

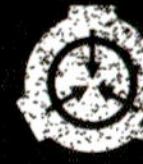

Professor B█████'s memorial service inside SCP-1230 as described by SCP-1230-1.

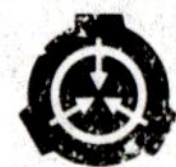

Report-1230-14

Upon falling asleep last night, I dreamt I was in a dark void. There was a streetlamp and underneath it was SCP-1230-1 sitting in a puddle. His cloak was visibly soaked and he was sobbing profusely. I remember our conversation:

Dr. F█████: Book Keeper? Is that you? My god, man, where are we?

Book Keeper: *(between sobs)* I… couldn't think of anything to make for a landscape.

Dr. F█████: Book Keeper… what happened that day? Why did Professor B█████ kill himself? We have to know your side of the story.

Book Keeper: *(wiping his eyes)* He had such an active imagination! I was able to create a vast and beautiful universe for him and it was obvious that he had wanted a life like that for so long. He conquered foul beasts and rescued princesses… He built kingdoms and even raised a family… but he never wanted to leave. He delved so far into his fantasy world that I soon realized he preferred his dream over the real world. I reminded him that this was all merely an illusion, but he wouldn't listen to me. He stated that if he was ever forced to leave, he would immediately end his life. I tried to keep him happy for as long as I could…

Dr. F█████: …Book Keeper… how long was the dream from his point of view?

Book Keeper: …200 years, Doctor. I did my best but I could only hold onto him for 200 years. As sweet as dreams may be, eventually we all have to wake up.

I awoke almost immediately after. I can't believe he spent 200 years in his dream. I'm astounded by his foolishness but it's such a shame to have lost a brilliant mind to his own delusions.

Shortly after the report was filed, surveillance showed Dr. F█████ slipping another small paper into SCP-1230. A few days later, SCP-1230 began showing its usual "A hero is born" greeting once again. When asked what the note said, Dr. F█████ declined to give detailed comment, simply stating that he "just gave it some friendly advice".

ADDENDUM-1230-A

During initial testing, SCP-1230-1 asked dreaming personnel if it could be relocated to an area with many books (preferably fiction) so that it could think of even better ways to construct its "fantasy-scapes". After numerous experiments were performed to ensure that SCP-1230 posed no threat, the request was accepted and SCP-1230 has been relocated to Site-12's library.

END OF REPORT

SPECIAL CONTAINMENT PROCEDURES

A single pair of human SCP-726 samples are to be contained at Site-17 in a padded cell for their own safety, cleaned of any waste matter at 24-hour intervals. A diet of mixed vegetable slurry is adequate for their nutritional needs. A jar of smooth peanut butter may be provided to pacify subjects during cleaning and examinations. On a quarterly basis, subjects shall be provided a pair of mixed sex cadavers, and terminated after successful reproduction. Absolutely no other animal tissues of any kind are permitted in the enclosure at any time.

DESCRIPTION

SCP-726 are physiologically and genetically identical to the eggs and larvae of Lucilia sericata, a species of blowfly common worldwide in warm climates. When larvae hatch on decomposing animal matter, they begin to consume nonliving tissues as normal until none remain, at which point they collect at a central point and begin to regurgitate a continuous stream of healthy, living cellular matter, and will multiply in number by unknown means as volume increases. If uninterrupted, SCP-726 will "reconstruct" a complete body matching that of the original tissue source. The reconstruction process occurs at high speed, resembling footage of maggot activity in reverse, and ends with the full restoration of life functions as all larvae abruptly drop off and appear to disintegrate.

While otherwise restored to optimum physical health, any organism reconstituted by SCP-726 exhibits only the mental processes of a mature blowfly. Instances instinctively follow the wafting odors of decaying organic materials and attempt to consume them via licking and sucking actions. Instances of all species move clumsily and periodically spasm in an apparent attempt to beat nonexistent insect wings, with avian and chiropteran examples failing to achieve flight by their usual means. Proximity to any source of decaying flesh will excite subjects into mating behavior, coupling without regard to original species. Any mechanically successful copulation will produce a fertile clutch of SCP-726 eggs, which reconstructed females attempt to deposit on any appropriate food source.

SCP-726 has proven capable of replicating a complete body from any volume of flesh regardless of its condition, including multiple copies of the same body from disconnected fragments. Reconstructed bodies that have subsequently expired can be reconstituted again by SCP-726 like any other tissue sample, but are subject to an increasing degradation of accuracy (see attached Generation Log).

DISCOVERY

On August 16th, 19█ a Mrs. Faber of Beckley, West Virginia, was discovered nude in a dumpster behind a local ████ ███, engaging in [REDACTED] with a large male [REDACTED] and subsequently hospitalized for acute dementia. Over the following weeks, locals reported outbreaks of abnormal animal behavior, including large numbers of domestic cattle, swine, and poultry inconsistent with local livestock. Foundation operatives deduced the reproductive habits of SCP-726 and discovered animals reconstituting from meat scraps in the dumpster where Mrs. Faber had been found. During containment sweeps, █ identical instances of Mrs. Faber were found wandering the woods near her property. Under interrogation, Mr. Faber admitted to the murder and dismemberment of his wife.

File >>> 7365522

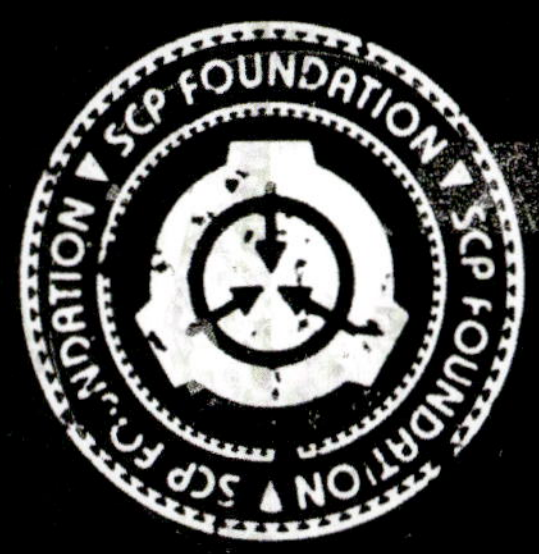

SCP-726

Title

RECONSTRUCTIVE MAGGOTS

Report by

bogleech

Pictures by

Markiz de Baldezar

Access the original report on **scp-wiki.wikidot.com/scp-726**

Date

Class

EUCLID

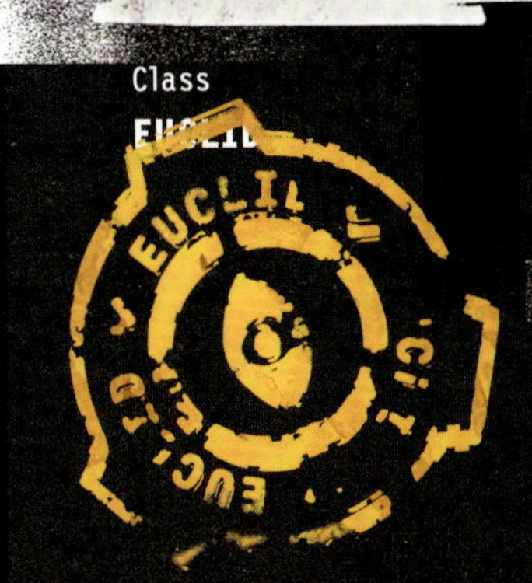

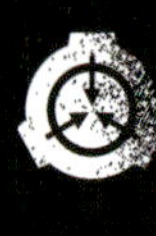

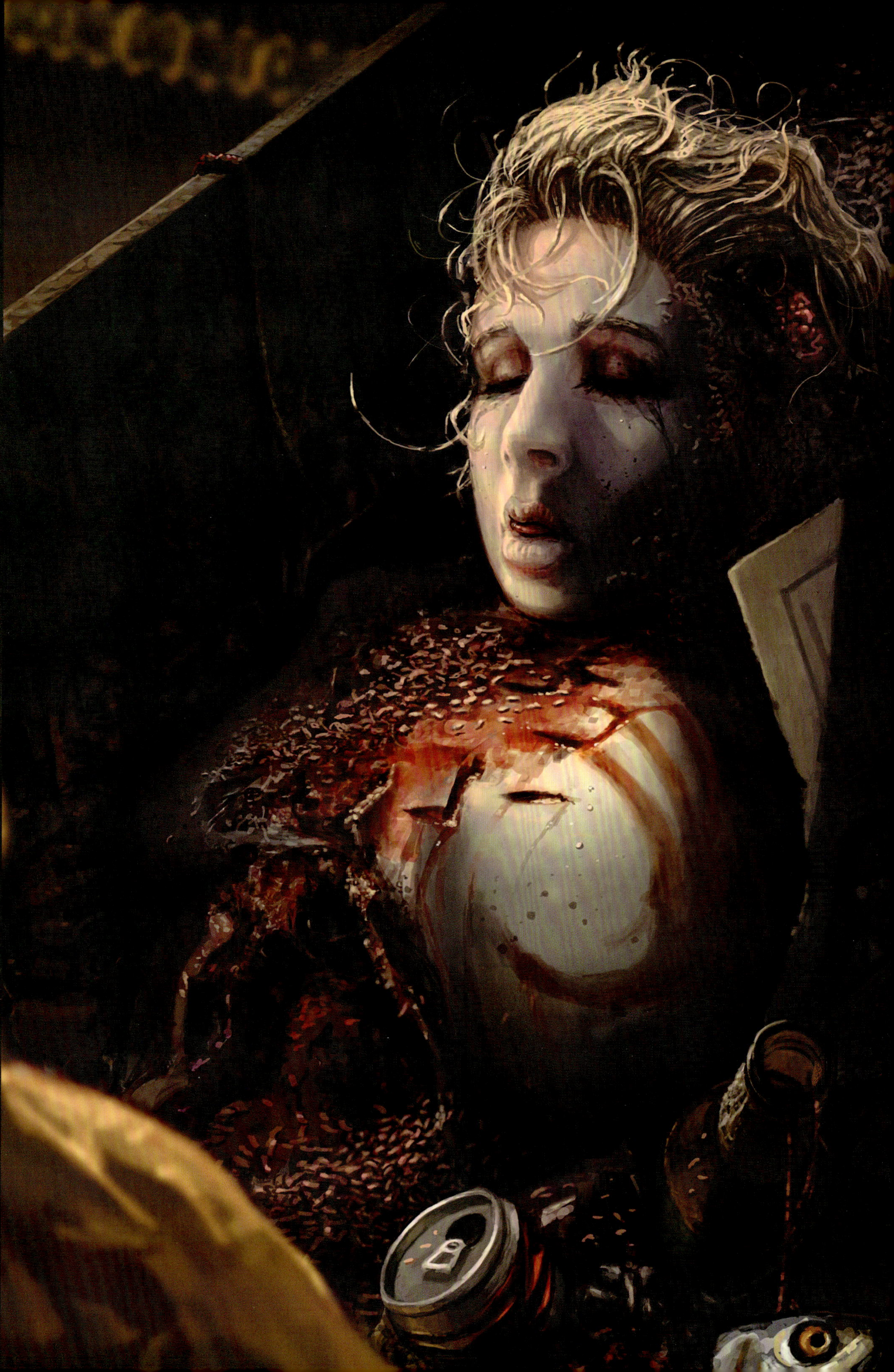

Mrs. Faber.

TEST LOG: 8/17: DR.█████ SCP-726 GENERATION LOG

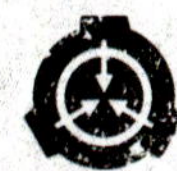

█████

Research Library File ▸ 726

I've decided to begin by testing the limits of repeated replication. A single SCP-726 egg will be introduced per sample. Due to their rapid multiplication, maggot volume does not affect their speed of operation, only the size of the organism to be reconstructed.

Sample: one (1) freshly killed Norwegian rat, cut in half lengthwise.
Result: SCP-726 reconstituted two versions of the same rat, their coat patterns mirror images of one another.

Sample: remains of duplicate rats from previous experiment, processed into a fine paste and mixed.
Result: SCP-726 separated sample into two portions and reconstructed nearly the same two copies, one with a red right eye.

Sample: remains of least divergent duplicate rat, processed into fine paste.
Result: rat reconstituted with slight limp, blind in both eyes.

Sample: heart from blind rat.
Result: reconstituted without eyes or pigmentation. Squeaks incessantly.

Sample: heart from eyeless rat, cut in half.
Result: two eyeless rats. One only walks in tight circles, other completely devoid of hair and unusually aggressive towards the first.
Note: *The insect behavior appears to be degrading with the physiology.*

Sample: scrap of flesh from hairless rat.
Result: eyeless, hairless and limbless. Fails to return fully to life. Braincase found to contain a liver.

Sample: liver from "brainless" rat.
Result: eyeless, hairless and limbless with elongated "worm-like" midsection, nodules scattered throughout body appear to be incomplete eyes. Drastic increase in aggression, eventually begins to consume its own posterior end and expires from blood loss.

Sample: fresh, complete remains from previous rat.
Result: large, formless mass of tissues and viscera, trembles until extinguished.

Sample: portion of previous result.
Result: large, slug-like, motile mass of undifferentiated cells. Appears to absorb nutrients through skin.

Sample: portion of previous result.
Result: identical to previous test.
Note: *This continued for four additional tests with no divergence. I've decided to keep the final "slug" for long-term observation. I'm calling him Brundle.*

Sample: single scrap of dried flesh from cadaver dated ███ B.C.
Result: reconstituted middle-aged male exhibiting expected fly behavior.
Note: *This could be an interesting new forensics tool.*

Sample: one (1) fingertip from D-class subject.
Result: subject reconstituted and exhibited expected fly behavior. Standard range of identification tests were compared to public and Foundation records. DNA a precise match, dentition and fingerprints reversed.

Sample: ocular orb taken from previous D-class subject.
Result: subject reconstituted with normal dentition, entirely foreign fingerprints.
Note: *There appears to be a slight margin of error even from original samples.*

Sample: one (1) living D-class with large infected gash on ankle, SCP-726 applied to wound.
Result: dead tissues were consumed and reconstruction proceeded until wound was healed. Subject appeared healthy until behavior deteriorated over the course of ██ hours. Subject displayed all properties associated with SCP-726 constructs and subsequently terminated.
Note: *I guess we can rule out any medical applications.*

Sample: porterhouse steak.
Result: mature steer, normal except for dipteran behavior and appetites. Subject slaughtered, porterhouse steaks served to D-class control group. Subsequent examinations unremarkable until [DATA EXPUNGED] consistent with known Calliphoridae. Subjects terminated.
Note: *A marginally greater biohazard than we thought. Suggesting closer observation of original site.*

Sample: porterhouse steak.
Result: same as above. Cuts variously subjected to a variety of chemical and thermal sterilization methods including radioactive bombardment. Served to D-class individuals in a variety of dishes. Results identical to previous test.
Note: *I think we have established that anomalous maggots are not a viable alternative to ranching.*

Sample: fine paste of ███ assorted insects and arachnids.
Result: ██████ reconstructed arthropods behaving as flies. All females produced SCP-726 eggs.
Note: *This likely wouldn't happen in the wild; dead insects are neither meaty nor malodorous enough to attract blowflies. It takes a substantial quantity decomposing under moist conditions to reproduce the same breeding environment as a vertebrate corpse.*

Sample: fine paste of ███ normal adult blowflies matching the species of SCP-726 larvae.
Result: single, abnormally huge fly. Quickly expired.
Note: *That was unexpected. Too bad about the square cube law, I'd have loved to observe it further.*

Sample: one (1) fillet of salmon.
Result: one (1) mature, male salmon. Convulsed violently as though "drowning" when placed in water. Flopped haphazardly when removed from liquid but did not display stress as it asphyxiated.

Sample: one (1) fried calamari ring.
Result: one (1) adult male squid, immediately placed in pool of water. Writhed helplessly until removed from liquid. Dragged itself crudely with tentacles, actively consumed fecal matter and decomposing flesh. SCP-726 properties in sperm sample.

Sample: one (1) fast food cheeseburger purchased from █████ drive through.
Result: SCP-726 reconstituted two mature cattle and ██ Norwegian rats.

Sample: one (1) can of commercially available "potted meat food product". Analysis showed beef and pork derivatives, high fructose corn syrup and 12 FDA-approved preservative agents.
Result: [DATA EXPUNGED]
Note: *What the ████ were those even remotely supposed to be?*

Sample: single corpse from previous experiment, ground into paste.
Result: [REDACTED] exhibiting extreme hostility to moving objects. All termination attempts failed. Specimen frozen.
Note: *I liquefied it and it kept moving.*

Sample: thawed sample of previous result.
Result: [REDACTED] exhibiting properties similar to SCP-███. Incinerated.
Note: *I'm not taking these tests any further. I might even put Brundle down.*

ADDENDUM

Testing of SCP-726 has been discontinued following Dr. █████'s recent findings. Requests to use tissue generated by SCP-726 for experimentation with SCP-1361 and similar anomalies have subsequently been denied. The samples at Site-17 should be closely monitored for any inconsistent behavior or abnormal growth.

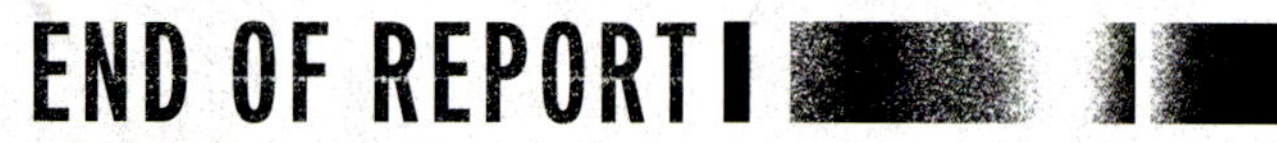

END OF REPORT

SPECIAL CONTAINMENT PROCEDURES

If a manifestation of SCP-1861 is reported, Task Force agents from the nearest Foundation Outpost are to reroute traffic away from the affected area and prevent civilian interaction with SCP-1861-B instances. A separate team must be deployed with the specific task of locating and preventing access to SCP-1861-A. As SCP-1861-B instances cannot be destroyed with brute force, diplomatic means of preventing civilian abduction should be undertaken if at all possible. Foundation Misinformation agents positioned in local news sources and weather monitoring sites are to attribute SCP-1861 to irregularities in air pressure and large quantities of dust present in storm water. Civilians who enter SCP-1861-A are to be declared legally dead, with causes of death attributed to common inclement weather accidents.

DESCRIPTION

SCP-1861 is an anomalous meteorological phenomenon characterized by heavy precipitation and fog composed of saltwater, human blood, and human cerebrospinal fluid. SCP-1861 manifestations are unpredictable, appearing spontaneously and with no regard to an affected area's natural climate and weather patterns. Manifestations typically occur once every three to six months and have been recorded occurring in numerous regions across the world. Historical records have confirmed that SCP-1861 has existed since as early as the year 1916. The size of the area covered by SCP-1861 varies from instance to instance, with the largest recorded affected area measuring approximately 5km2. Aside from its manifestation, composition, and apparent connection to SCP-1861-A, SCP-1861 displays no additional extranormal properties.

SCP-1861-A is a single underwater marine vessel that closely resembles B-class boats used by the British Royal Navy in World War I. During each SCP-1861 manifestation, SCP-1861-A will attempt to surface in a body of water that is large enough to contain its full mass. Both natural and manmade bodies of water have hosted manifestations of SCP-1861-A. If no body of water large enough to contain the entirety of SCP-1861-A is present, SCP-1861-A will surface in any collection of water with a surface area large enough to encompass its conning tower and topmost platform, even if the collection of water in question is only several inches deep.

SCP-1861-B are humanoid entities that emerge from SCP-1861-A during SCP-1861 phenomenon. SCP-1861-B are dressed in full body suits resembling deep sea diving gear, although with no discernable source of air supply. Instances of SCP-1861-B are uniform in size and possess speed and strength typical of an adult human male. Although most instances are sapient and capable of speech, approximately 9% possess limited intelligence and are only sentient. Instances that are incapable of verbal communication have been recorded making vocalizations similar to to the cries of domestic felines, canines, and infant humans. The diving gear worn by SCP-1861-B instances is anomalously durable and cannot be removed except by the instance presently wearing it. If an instance of SCP-1861-B encounters a human subject, it will attempt to persuade the subject into entering SCP-1861-A, claiming that this action would be in the subject's best interest. Subjects who refuse may or may not be forcefully taken to SCP-1861-A, depending on the temperament of the SCP-1861-B instance.

File >>> 906634

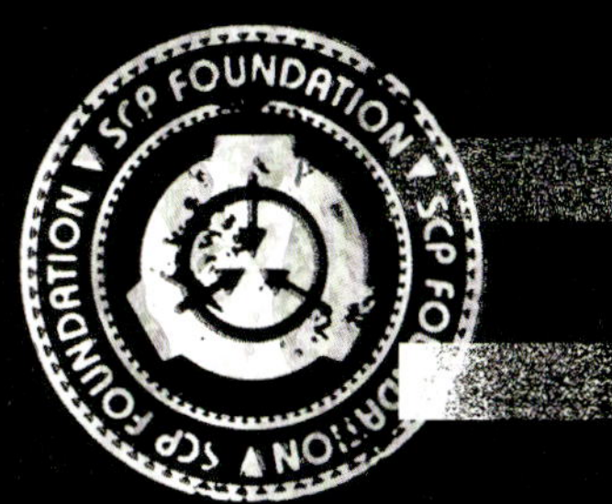

SCP-1861

Title

THE CREW OF THE HMS WINTERSHEIMER

Report by

PeppersGhost

Picture by

Alex Andreev

Access the original report on

scp-wiki.wikidot.com/scp-1861

Date

Class

KETER

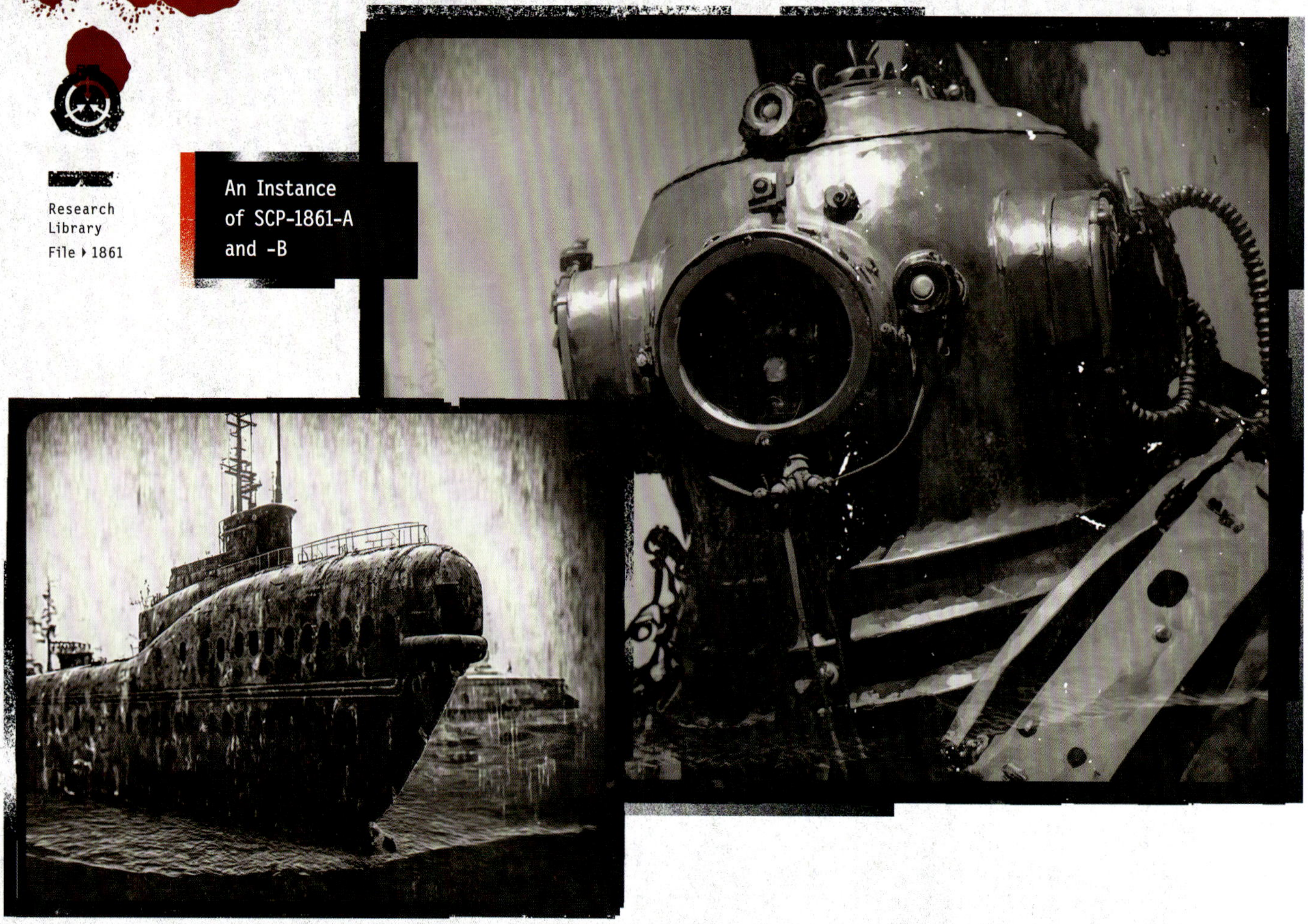

An Instance of SCP-1861-A and -B

Human subjects lured into entering SCP-1861-A will reemerge during subsequent SCP-1861 manifestations as SCP-1861-B instances. If an SCP-1861-B instance is taken outside SCP-1861's area of effect, it will begin to experience accelerated fatigue and lose consciousness, becoming completely inert until reintroduced into SCP-1861. After a manifestation of SCP-1861 has ended, SCP-1861-A will disappear along with any remaining instances of SCP-1861-B; additionally, blood, cerebrospinal fluid, and saltwater left behind by SCP-1861 will instantly convert to regular rainwater.

INTERVIEW LOG DOC-1861-1

Interviewed: An instance of SCP-1861-B claiming to be member of the ship's crew.

Interviewer: D-1861-36, receiving questions from Dr. Klutch via remote broadcast.

Foreword: D-1861-36 was sent into an SCP-1861 affected area and instructed to interview an SCP-1861-B instance. Heavy rain can be heard throughout the interview, and SCP-1861-B's speech is muffled by the diving gear it is wearing.

<Begin log>

D-1861-36: Who are you?

SCP-1861-B: Samuel Ramsey of the HMS Wintersheimer. We're evacuating the area. Please, you've got to come with me. You're in danger out here.

D-1861-36: Why? What's going on?

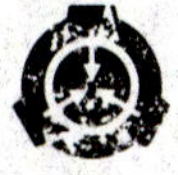

SCP-1861-B: I don't have any way to prove this, but I can tell you right now that you're going to die very soon unless you come with me. And that's not a threat, it's a warning. Something really, really terrible is about to happen here.

D-1861-36: What? What's going to happen?

SCP-1861-B: Listen, you've got to trust me on this: when this rain stops, you're going to die. I'm not kidding, you're going to die unless you follow me back to our submarine. You'll be safe there.

D-1861-36: Just tell me what's going to happen after the rain stops!

SCP-1861-B: You wouldn't believe me if I told you.

D-1861-36: Try me.

SCP-1861-B: I … look, I know this is going to sound insane, but this isn't regular rain. It's not from this world. There's another world—a *horrible* world, and it's leaking into this one. Don't look at me like that! You can see for yourself that isn't normal rain. It's thick! It's red! Please, you just have to trust me. I'm *begging* here. I'm trying to save your life. I've seen what happens to people after the rain and I'm trying to save you from that! Just come with me and I swear we'll both survive this!

D-1861-36: What kind of world is it? How long has this been happening?

SCP-1861-B: Listen, I want to help you. I swear I do. But if you won't believe me, I have no choice but to go look for someone else who'll come with me. I'm truly, truly sorry, but I can't just stand here arguing with you when there are other people out there I could be trying to save.

<End Log>

INTERVIEW LOG DOC-1861-2

Interviewed: An instance of SCP-1861-B claiming to be D-1861-46.

Interviewer: D-1861-45, receiving questions from Dr. Klutch via remote broadcast.

Foreword: D-1861-45 and D-1861-46, adult males of roughly 30 years of age, had both been sent into a previous manifestation of SCP-1861. During that time, D-1861-45 was instructed to avoid contact with SCP-1861-B instances, and D-1861-46 was instructed to enter SCP-1861-A. Heavy rain can be heard throughout the interview, and SCP-1861-B's speech is muffled by the diving gear it is wearing.

<Begin log>

D-1861-45: How do I know that you're really Sal?

SCP-1861-B: I can tell you that the code word is 'Boyardee.' Is that proof enough?

D-1861-45: It proves you've got his memories, at least. So what happened after you went inside the sub?

SCP-1861-B: The inside of the sub is pretty much just one long, narrow passageway. The thing was full of those diving suit people, along with a bunch of random folks from around town. It was jam packed in there; you could barely move. You kept getting pushed further and further back as more people entered. The deeper I got, the more certain I was that I'd hit a wall at the end, but it was like that passageway just kept stretching on forever. About an hour after I first entered, people stopped coming in and the hatch was closed. Then, without any warning, the sub started filling up with water.

D-1861-45: Wait, they tried to drown you?

SCP-1861-B: I don't know, man. The water just kept rising higher and higher. People were screaming and panicking and knocking each other over. It was awful. The guys in the diving suits tried to keep everyone calm, explaining it was part of safety procedures. They gave out diving suits to the rest of us and ordered us to put them on. So we did. I mean, what choice did we have? People who'd brought their kids and pets

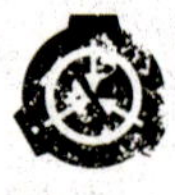

Research Library File ▸ 1861

were cramming them into the suits just to keep them from drowning to death.

D-1861-45: Makes sense. So I guess you were all trapped down there for a whole 'nother six months until the next blood rain thing happened?

SCP-1861-B: Actually, we didn't have to wait very long at all. That's where things started getting *really weird.* Once everyone had the diving suits on … they opened the airlock and started letting people leave the sub.

D-1861-45: What?

SCP-1861-B: Yeah. We were told not to take the suits off yet, though. They told us that when we got out of the sub, we wouldn't be able to breathe without our suits, and that everyone we left behind on land would be dead. When I stepped out onto the surface, everything looked almost exactly like it had an hour ago. I saw the lake, the trees, the boathouses… everything was where it had been, but …

D-1861-45: What? Had something changed?

SCP-1861-B: It's hard to explain. I want to say that it was like everything was underwater, but it was more than that. It was like everything around us was part of the water itself. When you looked up, you didn't see a surface. It just went on forever. And the trees? The boathouses? They weren't solid. They were just a different sort of liquid. Even when you stood on the ground, it was kind of like you were swimming in it, because the ground was liquid. Except you didn't actually have to swim. And even though everything was water, you could still tell that there was a lake there. As if the lake was a purer form of liquidness. Sorry, am I making any sense at all here?

D-1861-45: Not a whole lot, no. Hey, Dr. Klutch wants to know how long you guys were out there like that.

SCP-1861-B: The whole six months. We lived like that day and night.

D-1861-45: Did anyone try taking their suits off?

SCP-1861-B: Of course. Especially at first, since everyone was confused and scared. But as soon as someone took their helmet off, their bodies sort of … I think 'dissolve' would be the best word for it. They weren't solid anymore; they kind of turned into a mist and merged with the water that was all around us. They lost their shape, but you could still tell they were there, shapeless and floating.

D-1861-45: How did you guys eat?

SCP-1861-B: We didn't. Didn't sleep, either. We just breathed. Passed the time by exploring and talking to each other.

D-1861-45: Did you see any animals or other people?

SCP-1861-B: Kinda. We'd see their bodies. They'd float three or four feet off the ground, and their hair and fur would move like it does when its underwater, but they always kept their position. Didn't drift away or anything like that. It's really, really weird over there, man. And all the dead things, humans and animals, were missing their eyes. Blood would just keep pumping nonstop from the sockets and then dissipate into the water around them. And their teeth … I can't just say 'their teeth were gone,' because that doesn't begin to cover it. It was like someone took a bite out of their face right where their mouth should have been. Teeth, lips, gums, all gone.

D-1861-45: And no explanation from anyone? What did the guys who had led you into the sub have to say about all this?

SCP-1861-B: A lot of them said they had the same story we did. The blood rain came, then someone in a suit told them to climb into the sub, then bam! Water world. There was this one guy, though. He said he was the original captain of the sub. 'Hershel Guthrie of the HMS Wintersheimer' was how he introduced himself. Anyway, the guy was a looney one. Rarely ever spoke coherently. If you asked him about the sub, he'd call it his 'ark.' If you asked him about the water place, he would call it the 'new world'.

D-1861-45: What did he say about the people with missing eyes and teeth?

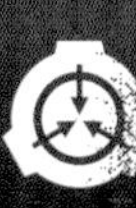

SCP-1861-A surfaced in ███, Russia.

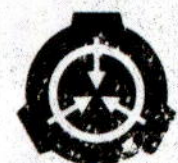

Research Library File ▸ 1861

SCP-1861-B: He just said 'the watcher of eyes and biter of teeth deemed them worthy' and crazy talk like that.

D-1861-45: How'd you wind up back in the real world?

SCP-1861-B: It was pretty sudden, actually. One day, a bunch of guys started yelling for everyone to make their way back to the submarine. Said that another area was getting 'attacked', and we needed to rescue as many people as possible.

D-1861-45: All right. Weird water dimension, mangled floating corpses, infinite submarine. Got all that Dr. Klutch? Great. But now why haven't you taken off that suit already, Sal?

SCP-1861-B: *[Silence]*

D-1861-45: Sal?

SCP-1861-B: I'm scared, man. I don't know what's real anymore. Hell, I can't say for sure if I'm even really alive. You have these diving suits that wander around, moving like people, but barking like dogs and talking like toddlers. We aren't what we used to be before we put on the suits. I'm sorry, man. I don't understand very much of this, but given what I do know, I honestly don't think that we're human anymore.

D-1861-45: Dr. Klutch says you've got to take off the suit. For science and all that.

SCP-1861-B: *[No response for 15 seconds]* I'm just so scared. If I'm not human, what am I? If I take this helmet off, what'll I see? *[10 second pause]* Before, when we were in that storm together, the guys in the suits told us that we'd die as soon as the rain stopped. And you know what? During the time I spent in that water place, I found you. Teeth missing and eyes gone. I saw your dead body! And I thought, 'maybe those guys were right. Maybe everyone else really is dead.' And here you are in front of me. I don't get it. I don't know what's real, man.

D-1861-45: Well, what else are you going to do? Get back into the sub and live in Sea World the rest of your life? Who knows, maybe it's not too late to get back to normal. If I were you, I'd think death would be better than whatever kind of hell you're stuck in. Just take off the suit already!

SCP-1861-B: Okay... here goes.

<End Log>

Closing Statement: SCP-1861-B removed its helmet and large amounts of seawater began to pour from the suit. No body was found inside, but two human eyes and a set of teeth were recovered from within the diving suit. Testing performed on the remains revealed that the eyes originally belonged to an 8-year-old female and the teeth to a European red deer (Cervus elaphus).

END OF REPORT

SPECIAL CONTAINMENT PROCEDURES

SCP-738 is to be kept in three linked sealed chambers with armed guards and a remote detonation system at all times, as well as constant full audio/visual surveillance. Due to the variety and strength of observed interactions with SCP-738, and the unknown limits of SCP-738, the following procedures are to be strictly followed.

When SCP-738 is not in use, its components must be kept one to each chamber. Mechanical means built into the containment area are to be used to assemble and disassemble SCP-738.

Should mechanical assembly means fail, then testing is to be canceled until an engineer fitted with an explosive collar can be sent in to repair the systems. Said engineer is to be detonated upon any attempt to interact with any component of SCP-738.

Should mechanical disassembly fail, preset shaped charges shall be used to disassemble SCP-738. The system should then be repaired and reset by a single engineer fitted with an explosive collar.

All Class D personnel used to test the device must be mildly intellectually disabled or of comparably impaired cognitive function, and must be fitted with an explosive collar. This is in order to prevent them from learning too much about SCP-738 and possibly using SCP-738 in a way that is detrimental to the Foundation.

Class D personnel with IQs over 60, and all other personnel are not allowed into the room containing SCP-738. Class D personnel are allowed into the room containing SCP-738 for experimentation only and are to be provided with continual instruction by research personnel.

DESCRIPTION

SCP-738 consists of three components. A matched set of mahogany furniture including one (1) desk currently labeled SCP-738-1, one (1) straight-backed chair currently labeled SCP-738-2, and one (1) ornate "throne" styled office chair labeled SCP-738-3, all with brass embellishments and royal purple velvet padding.

The effect begins when a sentient entity sits in SCP-738-2 in 'front' of SCP-738-1 with SCP-738-3 resting behind SCP-738-2. Cameras show SCP-738-3 moving during the effect, frequently leaning back into a 'relaxed state' as well as moving closer to, or further away from SCP-738-2. Occasionally SCP-738-3 is moved in front of SCP-738-2. Furthermore cameras show papers and folders containing papers leaving SCP-738-1's drawers. The papers are made of parchment. A quill pen and a bottle of ink emerge from the long drawer. The pen will write on the parchment.

Audio recorders record a distorted voice speaking. This voice will make offers and promises, attempting to tempt the occupant of SCP-738-2. Meaning has been extracted from the spoken voice. If, in this time, the entity sitting in SCP-738-2 makes a request, then the tempting and offers will cease. There will be a pause and a price will be stated. This can be bargained with; however, the voice will insist on other prices of 'equal value.' Occasionally when a request is made the voice will respond by telling the requester that they 'do not want the object enough' or that they are 'obviously requesting the object for someone else to get around paying full price' in which case the request is not fulfilled. This occurs most frequently for requests that can affect other people, or can transfer possession.

File >>> 093644

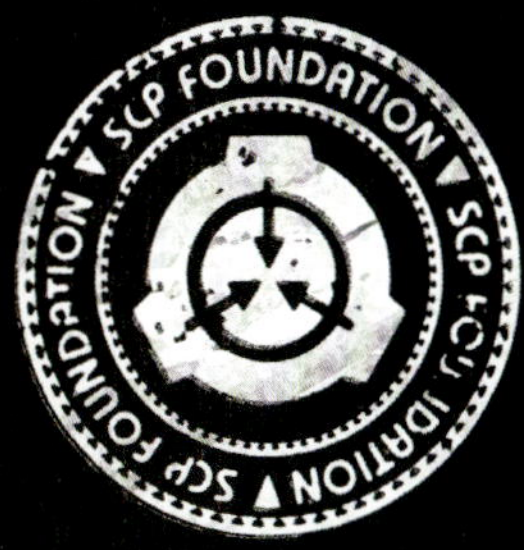

SCP-738

Title

THE DEVIL'S DEAL

Report by

Le Blue Dude

Picture by

Genocide Error

Access the original report on

scp-wiki.wikidot.com/scp-738

Date

Class

KETER

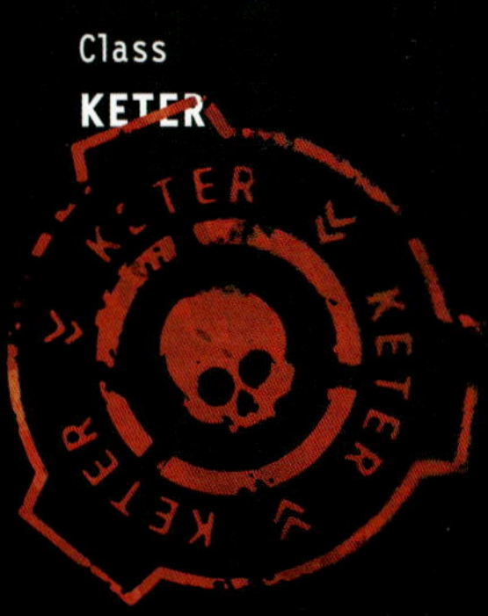

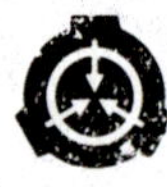

Research Library File ▸ 738

Accepting the deal causes the agreed-upon wish or command to be fulfilled to the letter, but not past the letter. Furthermore it will cause the occurrences stated in the price to be paid. The entity has actively stated that the occurrences in the price are intended to cause an amount of emotional and/or physical pain equal to the amount that the requester desires what they request. How parity is calculated is at present unknown. The price has also been stated to be independent of any pain caused by fulfilling the request. See the test log for examples of prices paid, and requests made.

As a final note, personnel in the chair have reported seeing an entity sitting in SCP-738-3. However, all attempts to observe this entity when not seated in SCP-738-2 have failed, and further descriptions of the entity are inconsistent between sessions, even with multiple sessions with the same person. When asked about this, the entity claims to be the same entity each time. Some frequent descriptions of the entity include 'seductive' and 'charming'. Sessions with the same person that are close in time report similar or identical entity appearances. Sessions with different people that are close in time report different entities appearances. Descriptions of the voice do not match the voice recorded on the equipment.

ADDENDUM 738-1: HISTORY

SCP-738 was recovered from the office of ████ █████, a Catholic Cardinal, after his death on █/█/█. He had received it as a gift from the Pope for extraordinary services from the Vatican archives. The Foundation became aware of SCP-738 after [DATA EXPUNGED]. With ████ ██████ dead and his will contested in the aftermath of the event, Foundation personnel acquired the desk. Foundation agents in the Vatican reported recovering some of the documents surrounding SCP-738.

ADDENDUM 738-2: TEST RESULTS

Test 1: Researcher sits in SCP-738-2 and waits.
Results: Researcher reports several attempts made to coerce him into a deal, with deals including love of the women he wants, an object that would make him a well respected researcher, and the granting of 05 status. Startled researcher leaves SCP-738-2, leaves room. Recordings follow statements provided. Researcher reports disappearance of the entity, followed by return of pen, paper, and folders to drawers. Using cameras, speed of object return clocked at over 120 m/s. Researcher reports seeing a man in a red and gold business suit.

Test 2: Personnel D-██ sat on SCP-738-2. Analysis performed upon papers and documents.
Results: Spectral analysis has confirmed that the parchment is human skin. The feather in the quill pen comes from an unidentified bird. Subject offered freedom, is told that the price is the death of his best friend. D-██ laughed and agreed, then vanished. D-██ was re-captured five hours later. Documents written in English. D-██ involved in test reported seeing a beautiful and seductive woman.

Test 3: Personnel D-██, a non-native English speaker, sits in SCP-738-2.
Results: Papers written in D-██'s native language, as is spoken communication. D-██ offered the power to never be held in a cell again. Price is stated to be memories of D-██'s mother. D-██ accepts offer. After acceptance [DATA EXPUNGED] resulting in the deaths of 12 guards, and D-██.

Test 4: Personnel D-███, dyslexic and seriously intellectually disabled, sits in SCP-738-2.
Results: The language on the parchment appeared to be crude pictograms representing the deal, though some words in English were represented in the parchment. In general the English was unrelated to the pictures they were under and frequently insult D-███'s intelligence, and state that the entity is uncertain how much of this D-███ understands. D-███ was offered a Sloppy Joe. Price was stated to be Mopsy, a toy that D-███ had been allowed to smuggle into the Foundation. D-███ accepted and food was materialized upon the desk, along with antique silverware, fine china plate, and crystal glass 'sippy cup' with wine colored grape juice. D-███ shows great distress upon discovering that Mopsy was missing after finishing meal. D-███ reports seeing a large pink rabbit. After deal was complete, and D-███ left chair, recorders picked up a sigh. Voiceprint of sigh does not match D-███'s voice.

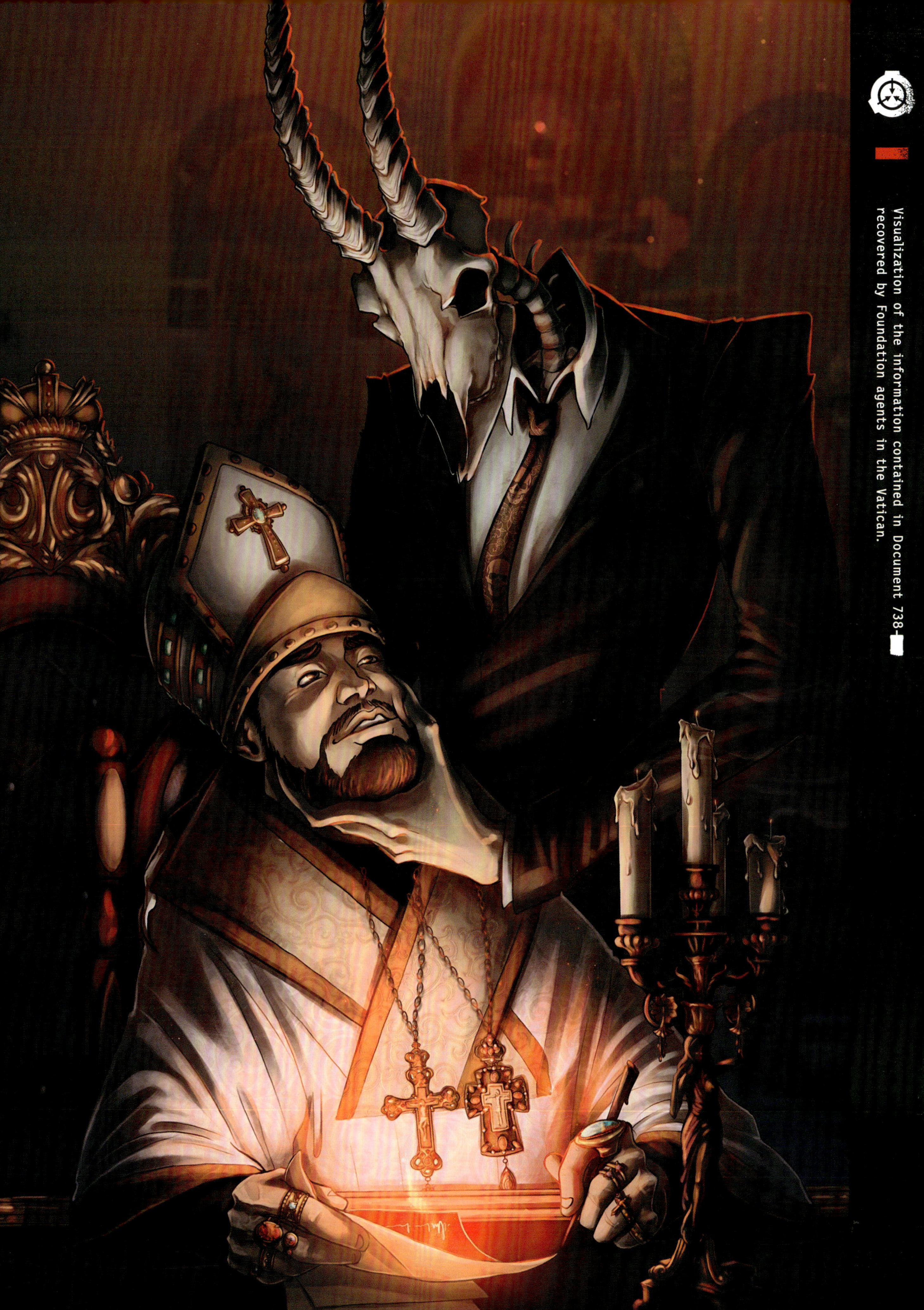

Visualization of the information contained in Document 738-█ recovered by Foundation agents in the Vatican.

Research Library File ▸ 738

Test 4 followup: D-████ issued toy exactly identical to 'Mopsy'.
Result: As soon as D-████ named the toy Mopsy, it vanished. D-████ showed great emotional distress.

Test 5: Destruction testing.
Result: [DATA EXPUNGED], explosive, fire, gunshot, mechanical wood chipper fail. Direct attack upon desk with axe leaves a single gash, with depth of 3 mm and results in [DATA EXPUNGED] as well as death of attacking personnel. Gash remains in desk. Video logs show gash healing at a rate of 1 μm per day.

Test 6: Researcher sits in SCP-738-2. Asks "What are you?"
Result: Entity, taking the appearance of a large snake, states "I'm sorry. It's against policy to divulge personal details. But may I interest you in [DATA EXPUNGED]". Researcher stood from chair, shaking and ending the session. Researcher was then placed in mental institution 5 awaiting review due to information revealed by offer.

Test 7: Sheldon Katz, Esq., senior counsel with the Foundation's legal department.
Result: At commencement of test, Mr. Katz presented the entity with a notarized, apostilled affidavit stating that he was participating in the test on his own behalf and not as agent for the Foundation. Approximately forty-one hours after the commencement of the test, Mr. Katz lapsed into unconsciousness due to exhaustion. Mr. Katz described the appearance of the entity as identical to his first-year contracts professor from law school, but he declined to describe the nature of the offer that had been made. He reported that just prior to his blacking out, he had been in the midst of negotiating a precise technical definition of the word "shall". Katz stated that the current working draft of the agreement that he and the entity had been drafting was at least nine hundred pages long at that moment, exclusive of exhibits and schedules, and that he regretted not keeping a copy for his form file. A red leather envelope, smelling of sulphur, was found on Mr. Katz's person, which contained a handwritten note reading "Please come back any time. I haven't had so much fun in years." Mr. Katz has requested reassignment.

Sheldon Katz, Esq.

Remaining tests require level 4 clearance or higher to view until declassification is complete.

ADDENDUM 738-3: NOTES

In recent testing, offers have been made directly to the researchers who were telling the subject what to do. Recommend cessation of all testing.

O5-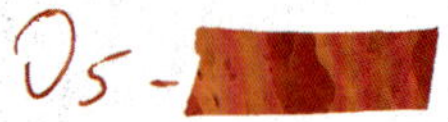

END OF REPORT

File >>> 38401234

SCP-089

Title

TOPHET

Report by

spikebrennan

Pictures by

Maxim Kozlov

Access the original report on

scp-wiki.wikidot.com/scp-089

Date

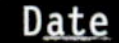

Class

EUCLID

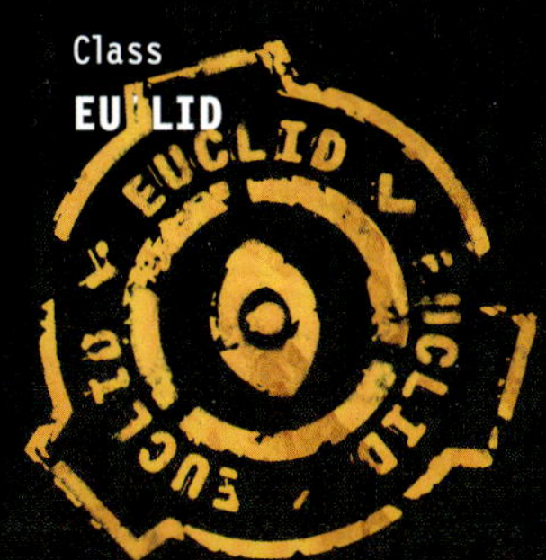

SPECIAL CONTAINMENT PROCEDURES

SCP-089 is stored in a special shipping container at Site-36 and monitored for locution events. Mobile Task Force Mu-89, consisting of personnel with advanced training in linguistics, psychology and tactical diplomacy, has been established in order to respond to such locution events. Upon the occurrence of a locution event, Mobile Task Force Mu-89 is to translate and interpret the locution so as to identify the primary subjects of that triggering (herein designated as SCP-089-A and SCP-089-B), then execute Protocol M8, which consists of the following steps:

1. Transport SCP-089 to SCP-089-A's location and explain Protocol M8 to SCP-089-B; and

2. At such time as SCP-089-B is prepared to voluntarily execute Protocol M8, render to SCP-089-B any assistance as SCP-089-B may request in connection with SCP-089-B performing the following actions: inserting SCP-089-A into the cavity together with inflammable materials such as oiled wood or charcoal, then igniting them.

The successful execution of Protocol M8 requires the voluntary compliance of SCP-089-B in a sober and uncoerced state. Likewise, SCP-089-A must be conscious and alert during the execution of the protocol. It is recommended that SCP-089-B be restrained (although not sedated) following ignition so as to avoid interference with the completion of the protocol, as the process is extremely painful and fatal to SCP-089-A.

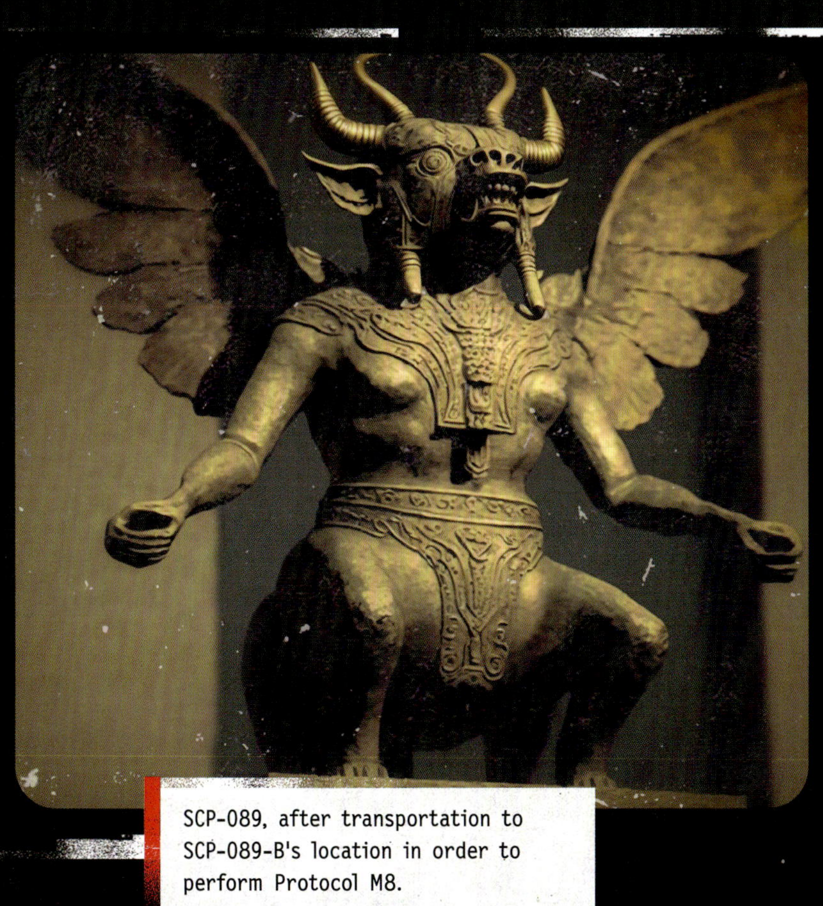

SCP-089, after transportation to SCP-089-B's location in order to perform Protocol M8.

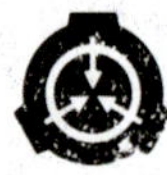

If SCP-089-B refuses to voluntarily execute Protocol M8 in accordance with the aforementioned specifications, MTF Mu-89 is to explain the prospective consequences of failing to successfully complete the protocol and make every effort to persuade SCP-089-B to cooperate. If MTF Mu-89's best efforts to so persuade SCP-089-B are unsuccessful, SCP-089 is to be redesignated as Keter-class and Protocol M9 is to be executed (reference Document 089-M9). The use of intimidation, threats or mind-altering drugs or intoxicants in an effort to affect SCP-089-B's free will, and any attempt to complete Protocol M8 without SCP-089-B's participation or voluntary cooperation, or otherwise other than as described, are strictly prohibited since these measures invalidate the attempted completion of the protocol and are known to intensify the severity of the attendant Type-S Event.

It is also recommended (although not a required part of Protocol M8) to cause the execution of step 2 of Protocol M8 to be accompanied by the sounding of horns and percussion instruments, as doing so may mask the sounds made by SCP-089-A during the execution of the protocol.

Upon a successful execution of Protocol M8, the related Type-S Event generally begins to abate within 7 hours.

DESCRIPTION

SCP-089 is a glazed earthenware statue, approximately 3 meters in height, depicting a winged, bull-headed humanoid with an open mouth. The front of the statue's torso is hinged and can be opened from the top to reveal a cavity, approximately 0.6 cubic meters in volume, and can be locked from the outside. The rear of the statue bears an inscription in a Canaanite language (possibly Punic). The statue dates from approximately the 2nd century BCE.

I believe it could be translated as "Nightmare of Moloch! Moloch the loveless! Mental Moloch! Moloch the heavy judger of men!" Dr.

On infrequent occasions (sometimes separated by periods in excess of a century), the statue speaks. The mechanism by which these sounds are made is not understood, and the mouth of the statue does not move. The statue's locutions are in a Canaanite language (probably the same language as the inscription) and consist of:

- the name, or a description, of SCP-089-A;
- a demand for Protocol M8 to be accomplished, together with instructions for doing so; and
- a description of the attendant Type-S Event, in figurative language

Each locution event is followed, within a period of three to eleven days, by the commencement of a Type-S Event meeting the description given in the locution event, unless Protocol M8 has already been completed. Each Type-S event is an epidemic, natural disaster, mass hysteria involving genocide or other massacres, or other event involving extensive damage to property and loss of human lives over a period of time that continues until Protocol M8 is successfully completed. In the case of each documented locution event, the attendant Type-S Event, while significant, is limited to a geographic area that does not directly affect SCP-089-B. This has, in some documented cases, resulted in the pendency of a Type-S Event for an extended duration of time due to SCP-089-B's unawareness of SCP-089 or of Protocol M8, or to SCP-089-B's unwillingness to undertake Protocol M8 in order to arrest the Type-S Event.

For each locution event, SCP-089-A is a healthy, unblemished human infant or child between eight months and six years of age, and SCP-089-B is that child's natural mother. In all documented cases, at the time of the locution event SCP-089-A and -B are each alive and healthy, and experience a strong bond of trust and affection with each other.

Following SCP-089-B's placement of SCP-089-A in the cavity and the ignition of the inflammable materials, SCP-089-A will burn and be destroyed over a period of two to five hours.

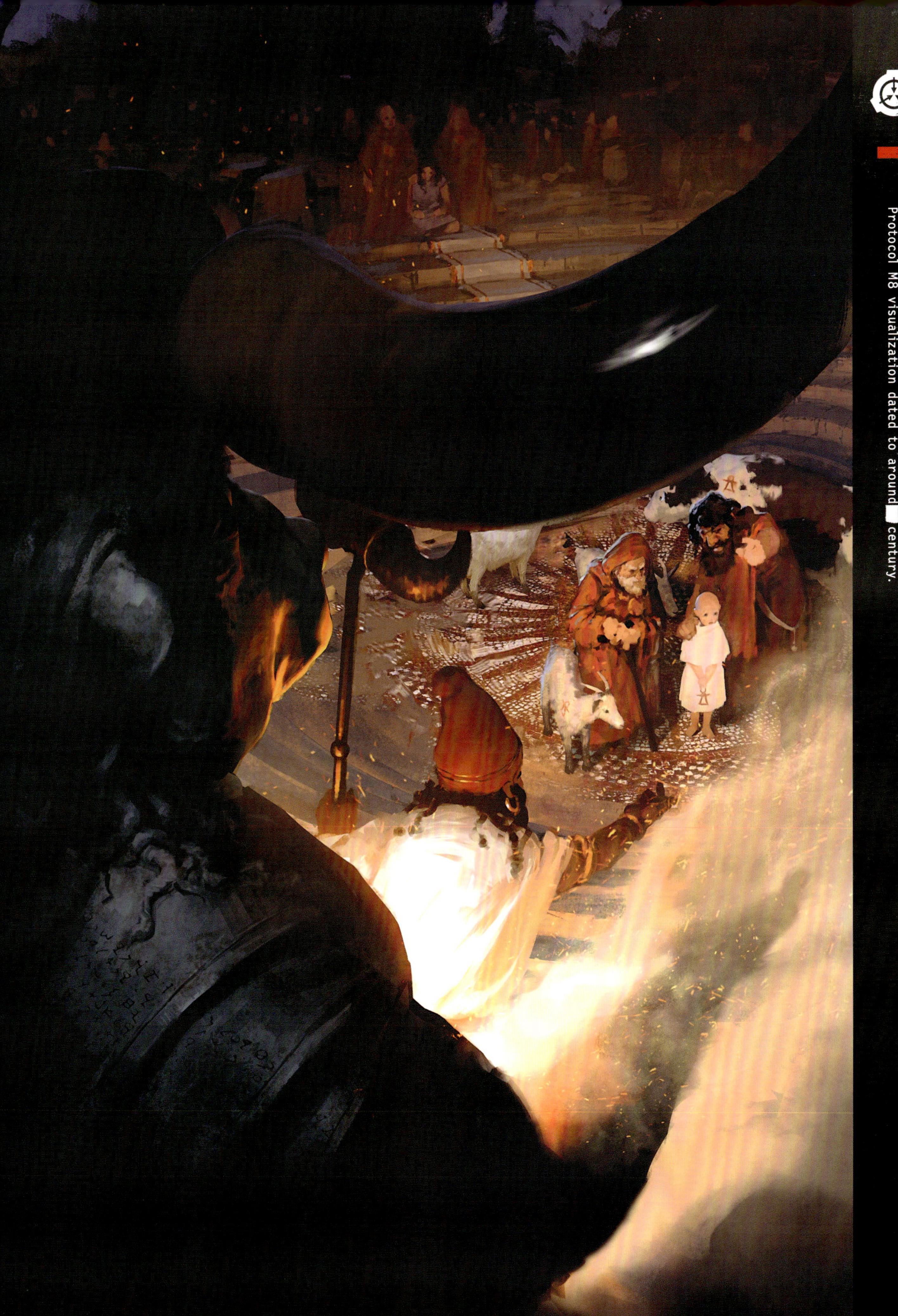

Protocol M8 visualization dated to around █ century.

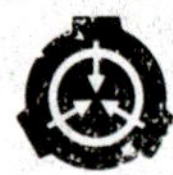

ADDENDUM #1

Memo to file from Dr. Garcia: While the role of SCP-089 in actually causing Type-S Events is unclear, experience has demonstrated that the prompt and precise application of Protocol M8 is effective in limiting the damage that they do. Dr. Patel has speculated that SCP-089 does not cause Type-S events, but merely anticipates them and provides a means to mitigate their effects.

ADDENDUM #2

A partial list of documented Type-S Events that were terminated by means of Protocol M8 (inclusive of documented completions of Protocol M8 that pre-date the Foundation's acquisition of custody of SCP-089) follows:

Date of locution: March 21, 1788
Description of Type-S Event in Locution Event: "The flames shall consume their houses, yea, and their markets, and their temples, and all of their dwelling places, they shall be destroyed."
Type-S Event: Fire in city of ███ ████.
Outcome: Protocol M8 completed on day 29 after locution event. 66% of city's buildings destroyed.

Date of locution: December 2, 1850
Description of Type-S Event in Locution Event: "The false prophet shall gather the multitude unto him, and cast them against the princes. They shall each of them be slain and their fields made barren."
Type-S Event: Large-scale messianic-based peasant uprising in ████.
Outcome: Protocol M8 completed on day 1,363 after locution event. Massacres associated with uprising and its suppression, and attendant agricultural collapse, account for at least ██ million casualties.

Date of locution: November 23, 1951
Description of Type-S Event in Locution Event: "The earth shall tremble and the seas shall rise and be cast against the earth, and the mountain shall vomit fire, its voice shall be darkness and death."
Type-S Event: Earthquake and volcanic eruption in ███ ███.
Outcome: Protocol M8 executed within 31 hours of locution event. No tsunami resulted although geological models had anticipated that one would occur from a seismic event in that area. No fatalities.

Date of locution: November 7, 1970
Description of Type-S Event in Locution Event: "The rains shall scour the earth, and sweep away man, and his beasts, and all his works, the deluge shall take them all."
Type-S Event: Cyclone in ██████.
Outcome: Protocol M8 executed on day 49 after locution event. Casualties from flooding, disease and starvation estimated at ███ thousand.

Date of locution: April 4, 20██
Description of Type-S Event in Locution Event: [DATA EXPUNGED]
Type-S Event: [DATA EXPUNGED]
Outcome: Ongoing. Protocol M8 not yet executed.

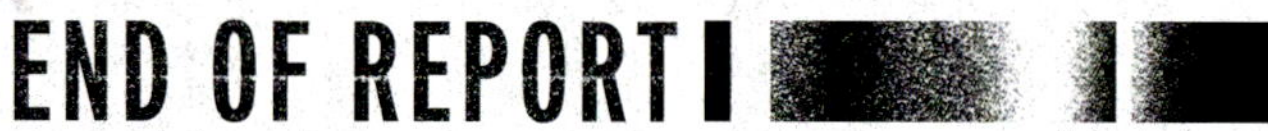

END OF REPORT

File >>> 0933455

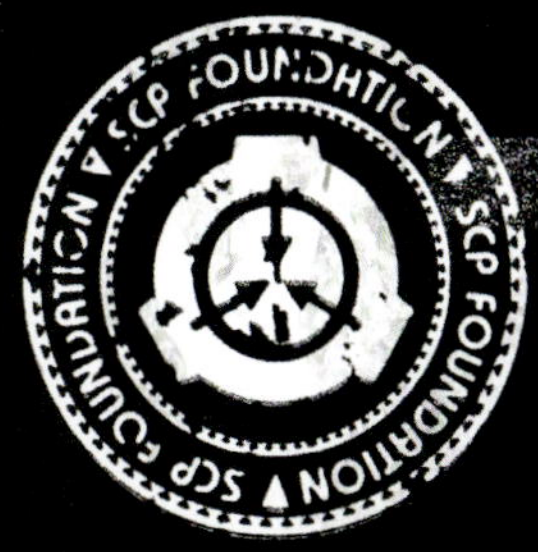

SCP-186

Title

TO END ALL WARS

Report by

Kalinin

Picture by

Roman Avseenko

Access the original report on

scp-wiki.wikidot.com/scp-186

Date

Class

EUCLID

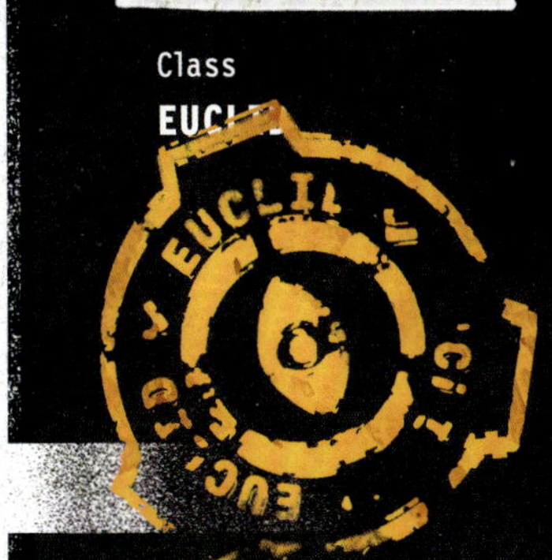

SPECIAL CONTAINMENT PROCEDURES

The site of SCP-186, comprising an approximately 300 km^2 area, is to be closed to the public under the auspices of a habitat restoration initiative for the European bison. An automated security perimeter is to be established, monitored by staff at Remote Site-355. Security personnel must patrol SCP-186 every two weeks; any anomalous phenomena observed within the security perimeter must be documented and reported to the Research Director.

All known primary sources documenting the events of SCP-186 have been secured by the Foundation. These materials are to be stored in the Site-23 Archives. Due to the age of the materials and the potential for deterioration, all access to these documents must be approved by the Site-23 Archivist and handled per their instructions.

All instances of SCP-186-1 are to be secured in the munitions wing of Site-23.

DESCRIPTION

SCP-186 is the site of an unrecorded military engagement occurring from 7/24/1917 to 8/13/1917 between elements of the Imperial German Army and forces of the Russian provisional government as part of the larger conflict of World War I, and the continuing effects resulting from its aftermath. This conflict came to be known to its participants as the Battle of Husiatyn Woods in surviving accounts.

In July of 1917, an armed engagement between a detachment of approximately 500 German soldiers and the remnants of a Russian division scattered during the German counterattack to the Kerensky Offensive took place at the location of SCP-186. The forces met in heavily forested terrain outside the town of Husiatyn in what is currently Ternopil Oblast, Ukraine. On both sides of the conflict, combatants deployed anomalous weaponry utilizing technology that has yet to be duplicated or understood at present. This battle eventually resulted in the deaths or permanent incapacitation of all forces involved, and approximately 300 civilians in its general vicinity.

SCP-186-1 consists of recovered weaponry dating from the initial containment of SCP-186 in 1917, and includes the following:

- A highly modified weapon resembling the Skoda M1909 machine gun, capable of causing extremely rapid tumor-like growths to appear within the body of any organism larger than a common lab rat
- Mortar shells specially designed to be fired from a Mortier de 58mm type 2, containing a gas that causes animal cells to become unable to cease life function
- Concertina wire coated with an unknown hallucinogenic compound that permanently affects human test subjects upon entering the bloodstream
- Remnants of an unknown incendiary device believed to have been detonated at the close of the conflict, accounting for what is estimated to be 34% of total casualties
- British Empire-issue No. 27 type grenades, containing a gas capable of passing through all tested gas-mask filtration systems, and causing humans to constantly experience the sensation of being on fire
- 8x50mmR French rifle cartridges containing powdered human bone instead of gunpowder; purpose unknown

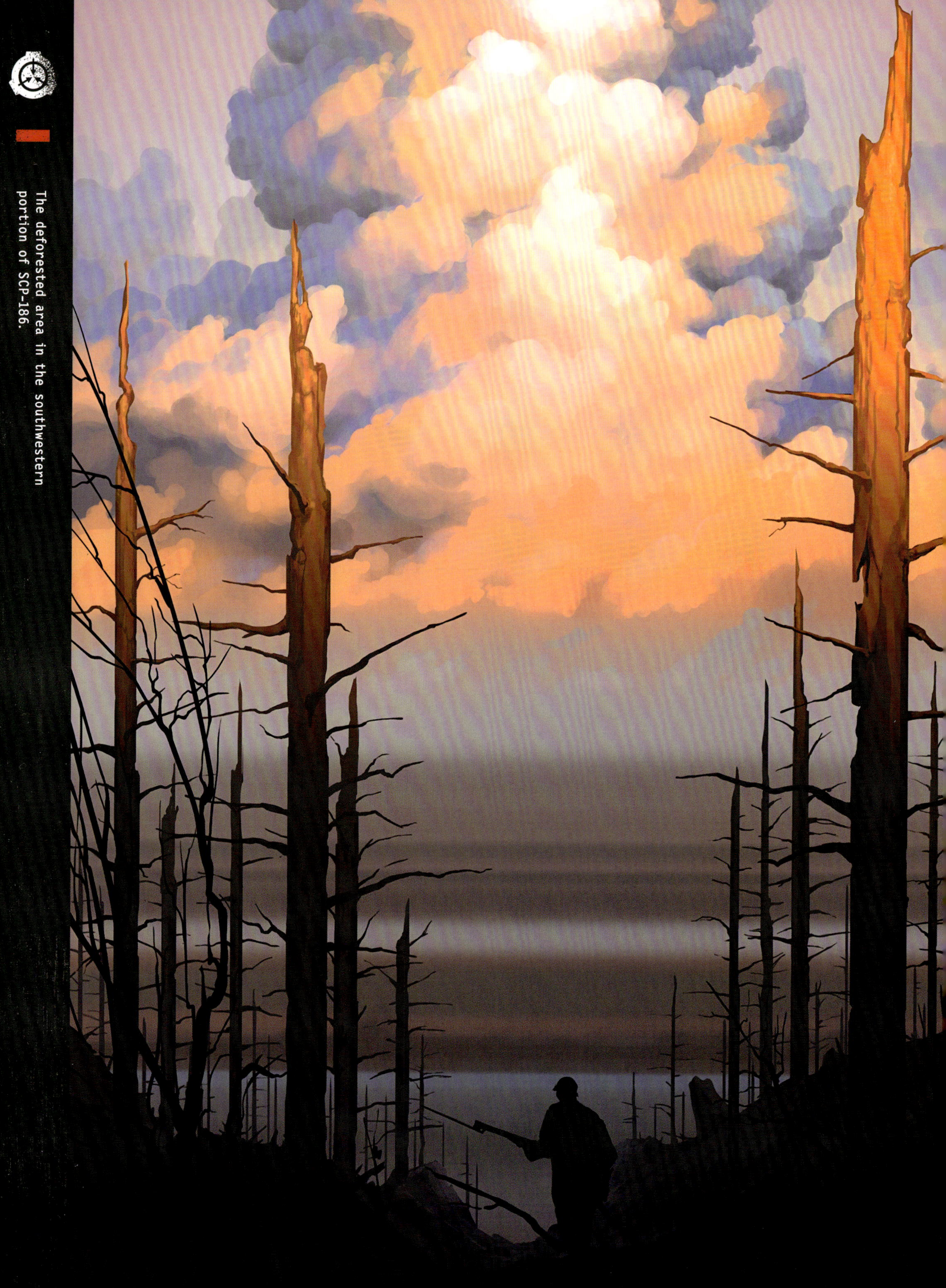

The deforested area in the southwestern portion of SCP-186.

Historical records indicate that the German detachment involved in the Battle of Husiatyn Woods, at the behest of a Hungarian military advisor named Mátyás Nemeş, specifically pursued the group of Russian forces in retreat, which at the time included French scientist Dr. Jean Durand. Based on documents of the era since suppressed by the Foundation, it is believed that these two individuals are responsible for the development and limited manufacture of SCP-186-1, and had attached themselves to opposing sides of the Eastern Front for the express purpose of deployment of these weapons in a combat setting.

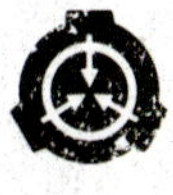

RESEARCH LOG 186-7

Research Log 186-7: Notable Anomalies Documented at SCP-186

04/11/1923: A 3 km^2 area in the southwestern portion of SCP-186 experiences a spontaneous die-off of trees. Decomposition occurs on an extremely accelerated time scale, and area is completely cleared of trees and other plant life within two weeks.

01/13/1927: Despite temperatures consistently at -15°C, no snow is visible throughout central portion of site. Temperatures measured at site are consistent with surroundings.

09/02/1932: The sounds of sporadic gunfire are recorded throughout the site, despite lack of observed presence of any civilians. Sounds persist for three days.

05/30/1936: Agents Chekhov and ████ fail to return from routine patrol of SCP-186. No subsequent traces of either person are ever recovered.

05/15/1941: Acting in accordance with intelligence sources embedded in the Third Reich, Foundation personnel evacuate SCP-186 in advance of Operation Barbarossa. Subsequent to decommissioning observation posts, faint glow visible from 150 m documented by staff to move through site. Definitive visual contact unestablished prior to evacuation.

10/29/1945: Containment of SCP-186 reestablished after discussions with Soviet Union officials. Upon initial patrol after reestablishment of containment, thirteen corpses dressed in uniforms and insignia of the German 4th Panzer Army and twenty-seven corpses in Soviet 22nd Army uniforms are discovered in advanced state of decay. No identifications of personnel are successful, as all identifying documents and insignia had been removed prior to Foundation containment.

02/19/1959: Following the formation of a large sinkhole in the northeastern portion of SCP-186, four men are observed wandering the immediate area in a state of extreme disorientation, dressed in what are later identified to be severely decomposed and degraded World War I-era military uniforms of both German Empire and Russian issue. Subjects detained and routed to Site-23 for subsequent research.

04/02/1959: After an extensive excavation of the site of the northeastern sinkhole, 23 persons are discovered buried at a depth of 15 m in a mass grave, alive despite decades of interment and various wounds and injuries. As with subjects discovered earlier, most are dressed in remnants of military uniforms of the World War I era and are presumed to be participants in the original SCP-186 event. Extensive research at Site-23 yields little information, as subjects are unable to provide any meaningful information or communication to Foundation staff due to extensive psychological trauma and profound mental disorders. Foundation staff attempt to euthanize subjects after 3 weeks of research, but fail in all attempts. Subjects subsequently tranquilized, anesthetized and incinerated.

07/29/1962: Prior to upgrades to containment facilities, security perimeter of SCP-186 found to be almost 85 m longer than originally documented. Inquiry later rules out clerical error as source of discrepancy.

12/13/1975: Localized weather phenomena documented as occurring entirely and exclusively within SCP-186. These include sustained winds up to 120 kph, 20 cm of rainfall and temperatures temporarily reaching 48°C.

08/12/1987: Packs of wolves, numbering an estimated 200 total individuals, travel to SCP-186, mass at a point in the central region of the site, and immediately disperse.

03/03/2009: A stand of three spruce trees is observed in the southwestern deforested area, the first documented plant life since 1923 event. Estimated age of trees is fifty years.

TRANSCRIPTS OF SELECTED SCP-186 DOCUMENTS

1 / Document 186-3: A flyer advertising a May 1911 lecture given by Dr. Durand to the Royal Institute of Chemistry

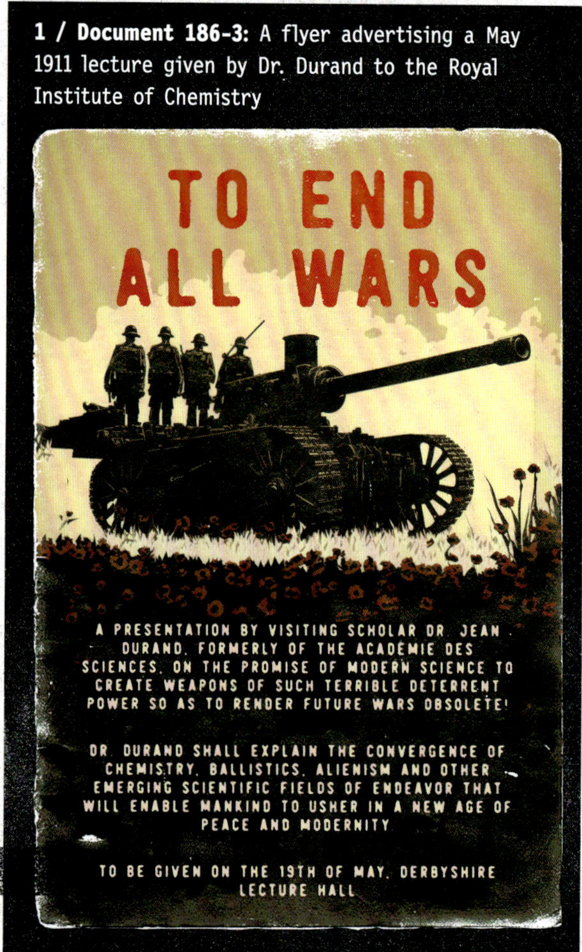

2 / Document 186-11: Opinion piece published in the January 2, 1912 edition of the Hungarian newspaper Népszava, authored by Mátyás Nemeş

To my fellow subjects of His Highness Emperor Franz Joseph,

Truly, the greatest of human glories is the unification of a numerous and disparate people into a single, unstoppable purpose. That our marvelous Kingdom should embody this inescapable principle should go without saying from Vienna to Budapest.

But there are those, both within our territories and elsewhere on the Continent, that would see us splintered into a thousand shards and stand in the way of our destiny. What is to be done with such agitators and malcontents? While traitors and radicals are hung properly in the manner of the dogs that they are, there is no execution sufficient to quell the embers of treachery that burn in the hearts of the Balkanites. How are we to demonstrate our unity of purpose, our power, our God-given place at the head of the European procession?

By force of arms! The hangman can only strike fear into the heart of dozens. A proper army can strike it into the souls of millions. Perhaps we have the numbers, but in this we are not alone. The Russian and the Moslem can rally hordes to their banners, but for all of their masses are mere unruly nuisances. What sets man apart from the animals is not his numerical superiority, no, but his superiority of mind, demonstrated through quick wit and artifice!

My fellow subjects, I have dedicated my life to the construction of such demonstrations of artifice that none may stand against my weapons save the Almighty! It is through the force of superior arms that we will achieve our grand design, both within our borders and without! Give me the factories, give me the manpower, give me the chance to serve our Empire through my industries, and I will deliver to the people the flaming sword that will light the way to a civilized Europe! It is through these means, and only these means, that we will solve the questions that plague us today!

3 / Document 186-32: Telegram sent by Jean Durand to Mátyás Nemeş from Paris, April 28, 1912

HAVE CONSIDERED YOUR PROPOSAL

MUST DECLINE. METHODS INFERIOR AND DERIVATIVE OF OWN RESEARCH

YOUR AIMS ARE OF CONQUEST. MINE ARE OF PEACE.

REGARDS, J. DURAND

4 / Document 186-39: Undated memorandum from General Felix Graf von Bothmer of the Imperial German Army to unnamed subordinates

Effective immediately, Lt. Nemeş is assigned to your unit as an advisor. Experimental armaments are only to be deployed on Lt. Nemeş' orders. Despite potential for a breakthrough on the Romanian Front, unwise to use these ungodly things until more is known of their efficacy. Rumors of similar developments among the Tsarists remain unsubstantiated.

DOCUMENT 186-52: LETTER FROM PVT. PYOTR AVTUKHOV, PARTICIPANT IN THE BATTLE OF HUSIATYN WOODS

Dearest Nadya,

I have heard rumors of the madness happening at home. Be comforted that it is nothing like the madness happening here. We thought that four years of war had taught us everything we had to know. and then more. We learned nothing.

The damnable Frenchman that the men elected to lead them spoke of peace. He spoke of weapons so terrible that we could make the enemy surrender on the spot. We were fools. We had run at trenches with dead men's rifles and sticks in our hands. We believed him the way we believed anyone that has supplies.

We never thought where this man came from. We didn't wonder why he had the weapons he did. We didn't care. We wanted to live.

We never considered that the enemy had the same things we did. I do not think the Frenchman did either. Or at least I hope he did not. I cannot imagine any man who would walk into this knowing what would happen. Maybe the Frenchman is not a man. Maybe he is something else.

I am sitting now in a hole I have dug in a forest somewhere. I should have run the second I saw the German take aim at Gilyov. That was no bullet fired at him. I could not look anymore after his face came apart and he was still screaming. I thought I saw hands pulling his head apart.

Somewhere in the distance Volikov is screaming he can see devils roasting his children. He has been screaming about the same thing for five days.

I should have run away so many times. The Frenchman gave us a new gas weapon. We refused at first, remembering what had happened in Romania. But he promised us that this was different, that this would put our enemies down without harming them. Who wants any more bloodshed, he asked us. We could not argue with that. We fired mortars at a position ahead of us. A strange blue gas seeped from behing the trees, but the Frenchman cautioned us against advancing. One more thing, he said. He took one of our rifles, and taking aim took a single shot. Before we could ask what a scientist could know of shooting, we heard a scream. He had hit one of the Germans.

He handed me a pair of field glasses. Take a look, he said. I saw the German missing half of his head, still screaming. I have seen everything in this war, but I have never seen faces like those of that German's fellows as they watched their comrade. The Frenchman, in his terrible calm voice, explained that his shot had to have destroyed at least a quarter of the soldier's brain tissue. Enough to cause instant death, he said. But watch.

I kept watching through the field glasses. The German didn't stop screaming. At least ten minutes I watched, unable to move away. The Frenchman smiled. He smiled at this scene. The gas, he said, ensured that death would not come, regardless of injury. The Germans were too horrified by their comrade to notice that they were not behind cover, and the Frenchman lined up another shot. The rest of the soldier's head was now gone, and the screaming was replaced by some sort of low grunting, the likes of which I have never heard from men.

No, the Frenchman said, no harm at all. I have bestowed the gift of life on your opponents. Who could possibly stand against that, he asked.

I had to leave and vomit behind some bushes. I had not done that since the first trenches. Who indeed could keep fighting after such a thing? But fight they did. Once a group of us were ambushed and chased to a meadow. The first men through the trees were hit with something that took their skin. I cannot describe why seeing men blown apart is not as frightening as seeing a neatly flayed corpse on a battlefield, but our group scattered.

We are no longer armies. Not any more. We are animals, trapped in a forest together, uncomprehending. Sometimes, when Volikov sleeps, I hear the Frenchman in the woods, yelling in Hungarian, yelling and laughing. I would almost rather listen to Volikov.

I am going to die in this hole. I am too scared of what is outside of it to do otherwise. Minkin is going to try to brave the horrors in the woods to escape. I am sending this letter with him in the hopes that he does. As I gave it to him, he joked that he will get a civil service commission after the war for delivering a letter from Hell. I am not certain he is wrong.

Goodbye,
Pyotr

END OF REPORT

SPECIAL CONTAINMENT PROCEDURES

SCP-191 is currently housed in a 6 m x 6 m room at Site-17. To date, SCP-191 has not made any requests for furnishings or entertainment.

Current furnishings include:

- One (1) wooden-frame futon with a 15 cm (6 in) pad and standard cotton bedsheets and blankets. All sheets are to be sterilized each morning according to standard procedures. The futon pad itself will be replaced every six months, and the old pad discarded through incineration.
- One (1) standard 220 V type G power outlet with an emergency cut-off box (fuse, circuit breaker, and manual non-insulating guillotine) located outside the cell.
- One (1) standard hazardous waste disposal unit (liquid and solid waste). All drainage tubes shall lead directly to an incinerator unit.

SCP-191 is to be dressed in loose, sleeveless garments made of 100% long-staple cotton. Fresh clothing will be provided once daily, with used garments sterilized according to standard procedures. Bathing is to be done once every evening, in a washtub filled with a solution of water and baking soda. Feeding (in the form of a sterile saline solution supplemented with vitamins, minerals, antibiotics, and a mild anesthetic) shall be carried out twice a day via injection into a metallic tube located in the base of the neck.

SCP-191 is capable of limited self-care, including draining waste and recharging internal batteries. A log shall be kept of power consumption, and any unusual changes in power usage reported to supervising staff.

Daily inspections for injury should be carried out after bathing. Should SCP-191 require medical care, refer to documents 191-Alpha (Special Medical Needs) and 191-Alpha Supplemental (Repair of Non-Biological Components) before administering care.

At least two armed guards are to be present in the room any time that personnel have contact with SCP-191, although a translucent screen may be utilized for privacy purposes. Standard anti-computer countermeasures are ineffective, as SCP-191's components have been hardened against electromagnetic pulse (EMP).

DESCRIPTION

SCP-191 is a female human child, approximately █ years old. It is believed to have been a test subject of several experimental surgeries performed by the late Dr. ███ █████ (see below).

1. 80% of the left half of the face and skull have been removed, with the eye and ear replaced by a complex transceiver system that allows it to receive and transmit not only visual and auditory input, but a wider spectrum of electromagnetic radiation ranging from low frequency radio to high-energy gamma rays. The lower jaw, teeth, and larynx have been removed and replaced with [DATA EXPUNGED]. The esophagus has been rerouted to an artificial orifice at the back of the neck (feeding tube), and the trachea rerouted directly to an air filtration device. Due to these alterations, SCP-191 is incapable of speech, although it has been reported occasionally vocalizing distress through rapid respiration.

File >>> 93240001

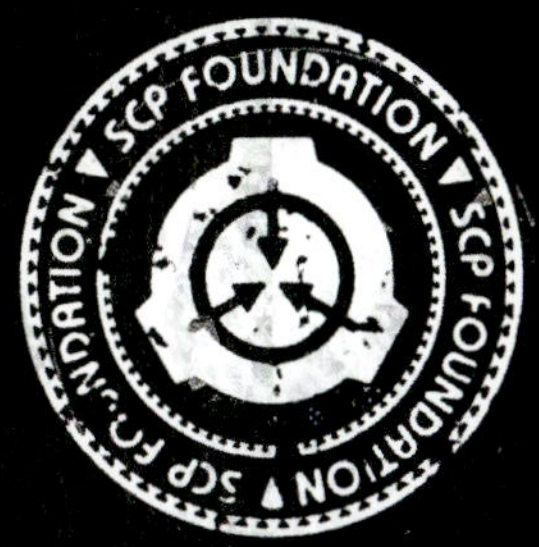

SCP-191

Title

CYBORG CHILD

Report by
Dr Clef

Pictures by
Ivan Efimov

Access the original report on
scp-wiki.wikidot.com/scp-191

Date
██████

Class
KETER

SAFE

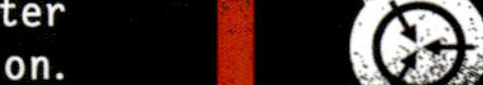

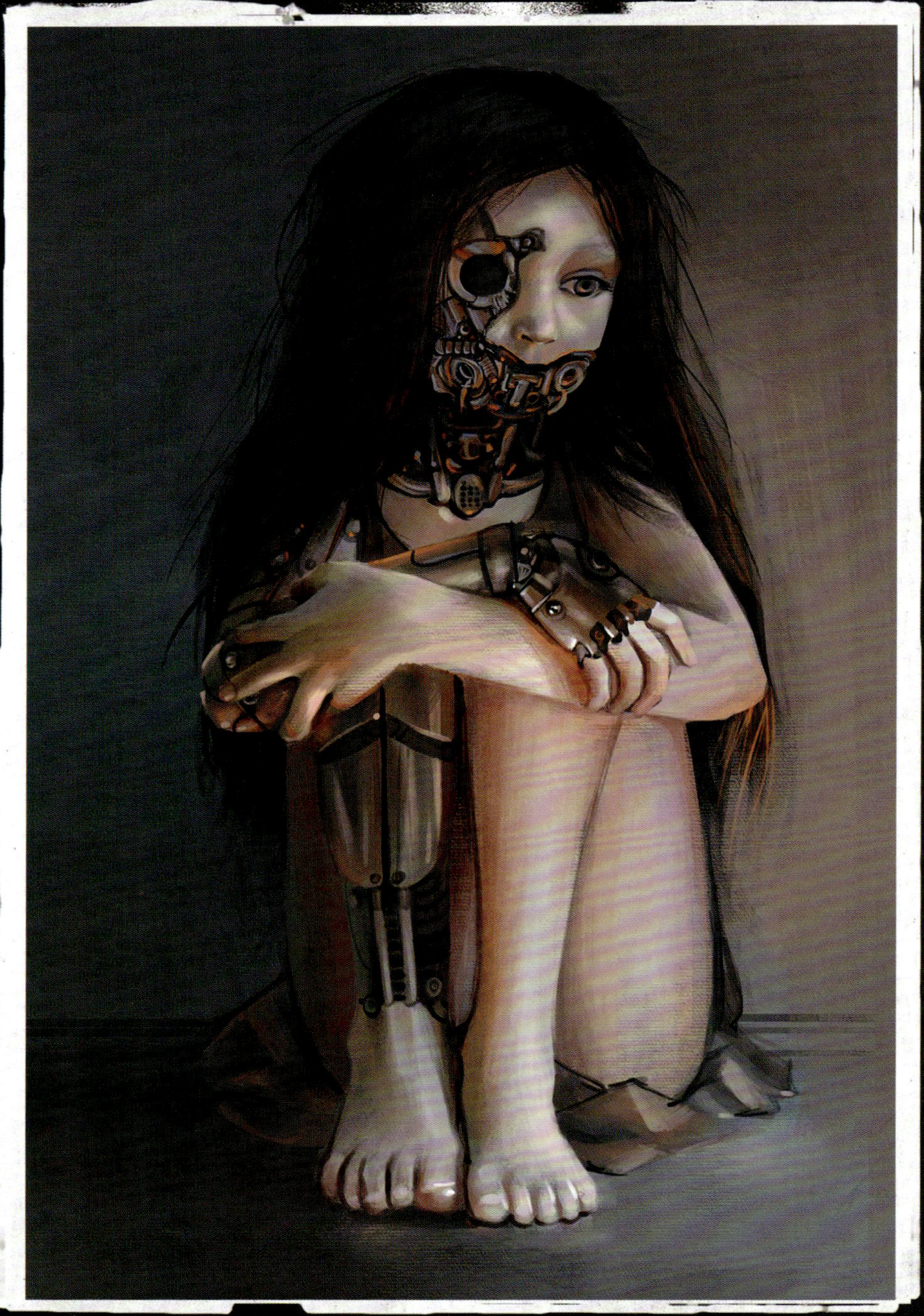

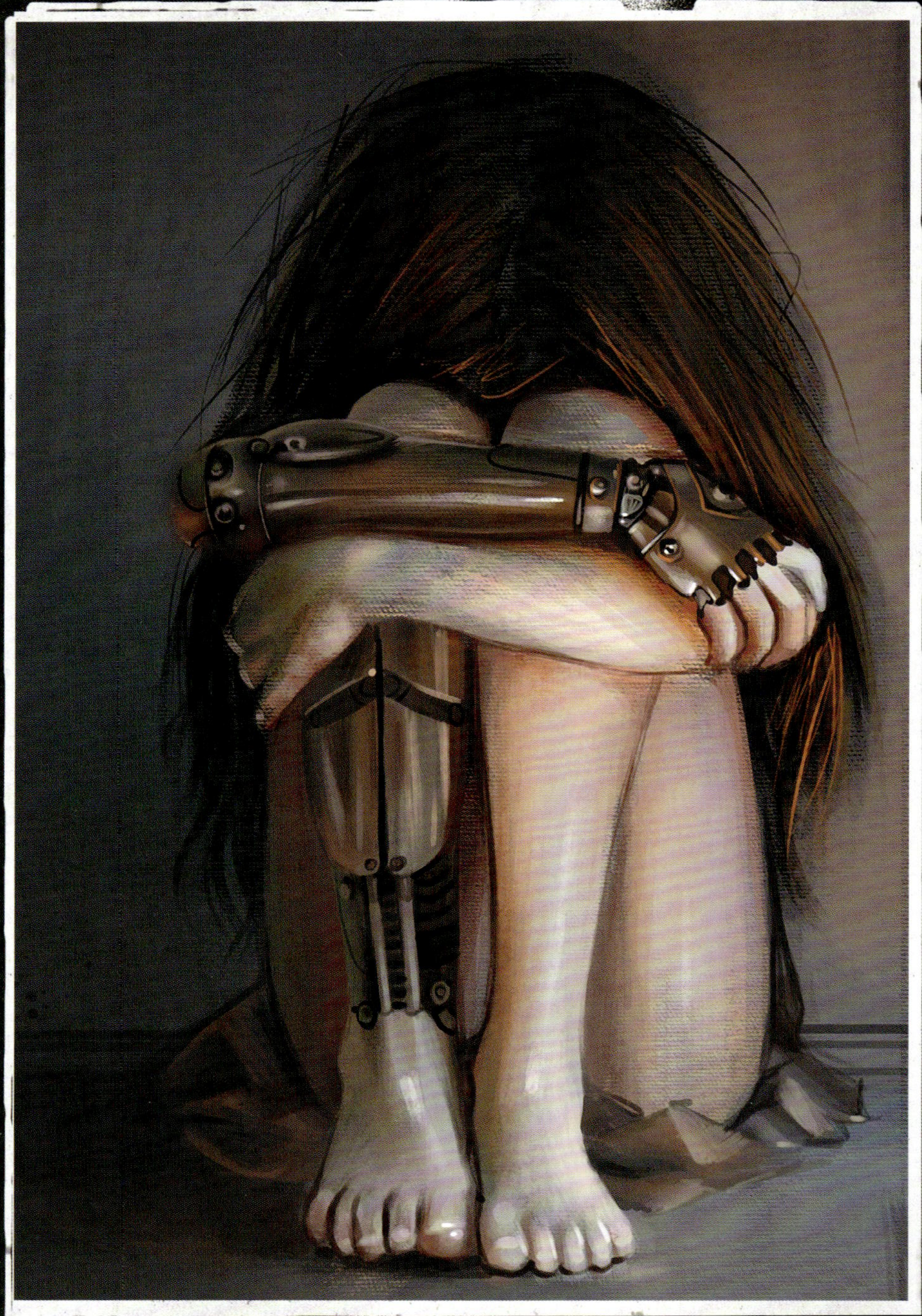

Photos of SCP-191 taken soon after recovery by the Foundation.

2. An input-output device has been placed into the right forearm, replacing the radius and ulna bones. The device contains interfaces for a variety of modern and obsolete formats, including USB, Ethernet, Firewire, and DIN-8 pin, as well as seven (7) other interfaces corresponding to no known formats. The device can be accessed by pulling back the skin over the right arm like a shirt sleeve.

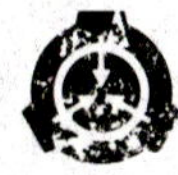

3. A 24-core processor array has been implanted in the brain, which "translates" input from all artificial components, essentially allowing SCP-191 to read and write computer data without the use of an external interface. Internal communication is carried out through fiber optic cables implanted through the glial cells and the entire nervous system. Damage to the brain stem and cerebellum due to the implantation procedure has severely damaged SCP-191's motor skills.

4. The right hand and right foreleg have been replaced with artificial components, consisting primarily of steel, carbon-fiber, and an unknown polymer-like substance. The exposed areas of tissue are susceptible to injury and infection: due to damage to the spinothalamic tract, SCP-191 has reduced pain and temperature sensitivity in its limbs. Reconstructive surgery by Dr.███ was able to provide some relief, but regular doses of antibiotics and analgesics are still required.

5. [DATA EXPUNGED]

6. The lungs, heart, and major blood vessels have been replaced with mechanical analogues. It has been determined that this system would allow SCP-191's bodily systems to be restarted after death, and may have actually [DATA EXPUNGED].

7. The digestive system has been completely reconfigured to the point where regular food intake is both unnecessary and dangerous. Waste is now disposed of via a drainage system located in the lower back and consists of a thick, dark gray viscous slime consisting primarily of [DATA EXPUNGED].

8. The reproductive organs (uterus, ovaries, etc.) have been removed and replaced with [DATA EXPUNGED]. According to██████'s notes, this was done to "provide extra space by removing non-vital components." Hormone therapy has been proposed to counteract the long-term effects of the missing glands: this proposal is under review pending analysis of possible complications due to [DATA EXPUNGED].

9. [DATA EXPUNGED]

10. At least fifteen (15) other alterations of unknown purpose. Given this fact, and the haphazard integration of the "useful" components, it is believed that they were performed merely to test the viability of such procedures on other subjects. Investigations are underway as to whether Dr.██████ was planning to [DATA EXPUNGED]. At present, any theories as to the purpose behind these alterations are speculative at best, as Dr.██████ died during the raid in which SCP-191 was recovered (see notes below), and the only surviving records of his research are a single, half-burned spiral-bound notebook consisting mostly of cryptic notes regarding a "higher purpose."

HISTORY

SCP-191 was recovered by Foundation agents during a brief collaborative effort with the Global Occult Coalition, in which a raid was conducted on the laboratory of Dr.█████, a suspected member of █████ ███. SCP-191 was the only test subject recovered from the laboratory: all other test subjects expired during the raid (either disposed of by Dr.█████, or eliminated as hostiles by the task force).

Preliminary assessment concluded that full reconstruction was impossible, that the components introduced were too technologically advanced to risk becoming widely known, and that it could be a source of valuable data regarding [DATA EXPUNGED] if kept alive. Subject was classified SCP-191 and moved to Site-█ on ██-██-███. Its disappearance, and those of the other test subjects, was later blamed on a local serial killer who was arranged to be killed in prison while awaiting trial.

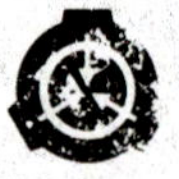

EXPERIMENT LOG 191

This is a test log for exploring the capabilities of SCP-191. Please remember that SCP-191 is a research tool, not an entertainment center. Any test involving games or other recreational technology should be conducted in a proffessinal manner, and not for amusement.

Dr. 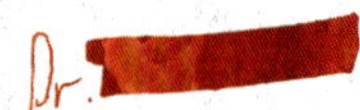

Research Library
File ▸ 191

Subject: "█ Paint," a ubiquitous, simple drawing program.

Instructions: Interface with a computer via USB port, and draw specified pictures using █ Paint.

Results: SCP-191 was instantly able to emulate the functions of a mouse and keyboard. When showed any photograph, 191 was able to reproduce it within seconds using only the pencil tool, creating copies indistinguishable from the original.

After the test was recorded, it was noticed that SCP-191 had continued drawing in additional █ Paint files. SCP-191 appeared surprised, and opened a text file onscreen claiming that it had not realized it was still drawing.

The following drawings were discovered:

- Three people wearing what appear to be GOC uniforms, standing in a burning office, pointing guns at a man across the room. The man is committing suicide via gunshot wound to the head, his face obscured by blood.[1]
- An adult and child trick-or-treating. The child is a girl wearing makeup similar to that worn by Boris Karloff in Frankenstein, and the adult [DATA EXPUNGED].
- [DATA EXPUNGED][2]

1. (Agent ███, who participated in the raid in which SCP-191 was acquired, identified this as the death of Dr. ███ █████, SCP-191's "creator")
2. SCP-191 was once again asked if it was really feeling well, and once again replied (via text file) that it was fine, and that the [EXPUNGED] "didn't mean anything."

Subject: The video game "████ ███: █████."

Instructions: Attempt to emulate the functions of a "Wiimote," and play a video game.

Result: Test began poorly, as SCP-191's impaired motor skills caused it to snap the disc in two before it could place it in the console. SCP-191 became distressed. It then stared at the disc, and the red light from its eye changed to green for a moment.

When Dr. ███ returned with a fresh disc (less than two minutes had passed), the game was already running on the machine. Dr. ███ inquired as to how that had happened, and a message appeared on the screen saying, "I looked at the ones and the zeroes and I loaded those in. I'm sorry, I know I'm not supposed to do it this way, but I didn't want you to waste a disc. Please don't be angry." SCP-191 still seemed fearful of reprimand, even after being reassured that it was doing excellently.

SCP-191 made a perfect run-through of the game, despite the fact that it did not make any physical movements consistent with the Wii controls.

Subject:

- "███ ███ ███" (a well-known video-effects program)
- A 40-second video file from a security camera located in the employee cafeteria.

Instructions: Perform a series of video-enhancement techniques used by forensic detectives on the popular television drama "█.█.█" (techniques that cannot actually be done in reality):

- "Zoom and Enhance:" SCP-191 was instructed to zoom in on the window over the parking lot and render the license plates on the cars, which were illegible from this distance (the actual license plates had been photographed for reference)
- "Uncrop:" SCP-191 was asked to shrink the video by 100 px on every side, and fill in the blank space with what it believed the rest of the cafeteria looked like (again, data that was not actually available in the video)
- "Rotate Camera:" SCP-191 was informed of the exact location and angle of the other security camera in the cafeteria, and asked to render the scene as viewed from that angle, filling in the parts that the current camera did not see (the actual footage from the second camera was requisitioned and held for reference).

Result: SCP-191 could not understand the instructions at first. Dr. ███ had to provide a lengthy explanation, and then stand behind SCP-191 and give it instructions one step at a time. It was several minutes before the test could even begin.

However, once SCP-191 actually got started, the videos and frames were finished in less than seven minutes (of which at least three were spent watching the rendering progress bar).

- "Zoom and Enhance" test: SCP-191 successfully rendered close-ups of the license plates, complete with photorealistic scratches and dents. However, the plates were found not to match the license plates on the vehicles. SCP-191 typed, "The data wasn't there, so I had to guess."[3]
- "Uncrop" test: SCP-191 expanded the video canvas and filling in what was in the blank space, rendering the extra image seamlessly. It did not match the actual cafeteria, but once again, the data was not in the video file and SCP-191 had been forced to guess.
- "Rotate Camera" test: The generated video matched the angle of the second camera perfectly, and almost everything visible from the angle of C-1 matched the scene in C-2 very closely. As before, places not visible were very different. One table only visible in C-2, that had been seating [REDACTED], was now (in the generated video) seating Dr. ███ and Agent ███ (the attending doctor and agent supervising SCP-191), eating lunch and talking.[4]

Although there were many visual differences between the original videos and SCP-191's copies, many on-site personnel were unable to determine which ones were the forgeries.

3. The actual license plates were ███, ███, ███ and ███. The license plates generated by SCP-191 were: IAM-191, 191-ISA, 600-DMA and CHI-930.

4. A lip-reader was brought in to decipher what Dr. ███ and Agent ███ were saying in the simulation video. [DATA EXPUNGED]. The real Dr. ███ became uncomfortable upon learning what SCP-191 had depicted her saying to Agent ███. The real Agent ███ declined to comment.

PSYCHOLOGICAL ANALYSIS BY DR. GLASS

SCP-191 has responded fairly well to containment. It is completely docile and cooperative, and when not being interacted with, it spends most of its time sitting still or curled up in a fetal position. This may be a sign of distress, but it is more likely for physical comfort, as normal body movements and postures are difficult.

Mental acuity is questionable. Although capable of rapid data analysis and communications when physically linked to a computer system, it seems unable to follow conversations with human beings unless the conversant speaks slowly and uses simple words. Complex tasks are also impossible unless it is guided at every step.

Its mood seems consistent, though somewhat inscrutable. It continually affects melancholy, will not make eye contact unless asked to, and any attempts to induce a cheerful or humorous mood have proven fruitless. However, it shows no signs of ongoing mental distress, and claims (through computer interface) that it is feeling well.

To date SCP-191 has not requested access to (or information about) any acquaintance it had before its abduction.

END OF REPORT

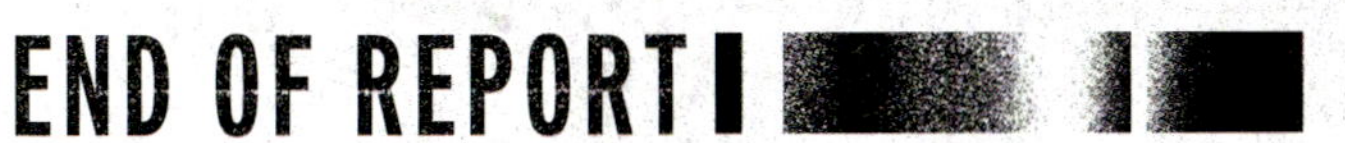

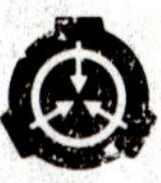

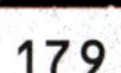

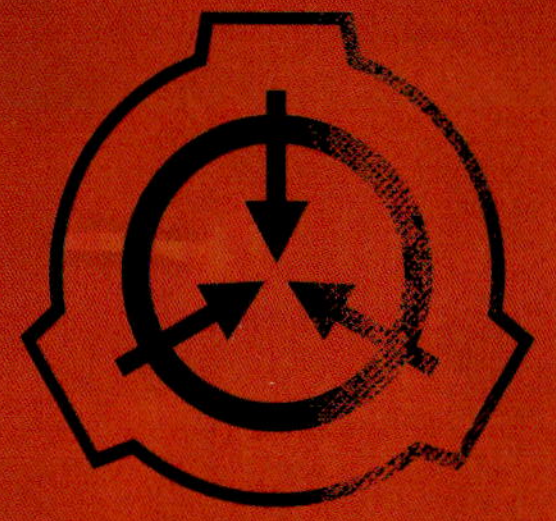

CLASSIFIED

WARNING

HMCL and O5 Approval Required

The file you are attempting to access is available to personnel with Level 4/2000 clearance only. This clearance is not included in general Level 4 security protocol.

Attempting to read the following document without necessary clearance is grounds for termination of Foundation employment and cancellation of all educational, medical, retirement, and mortality benefits. By continuing you hereby consent to exposure to a known cognitohazardous message encrypted in the text of the document, and verify that you have been inoculated against that message. Should the Foundation obtain information confirming unauthorized access, security personnel will be dispatched to revive you and escort you to a detention cell for interrogation. Attempting to relocate this file or make it otherwise untraceable by the Foundation will result in immediate termination regardless of clearance.

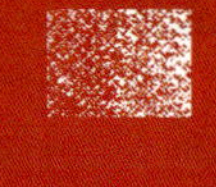

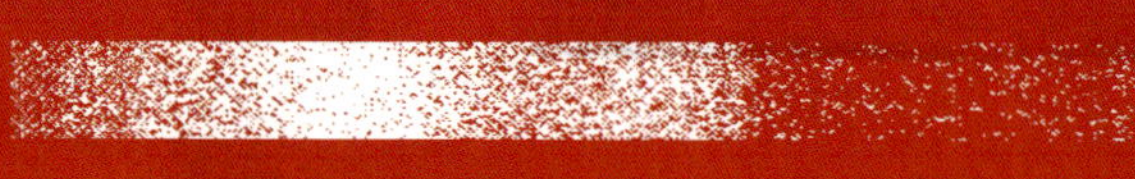

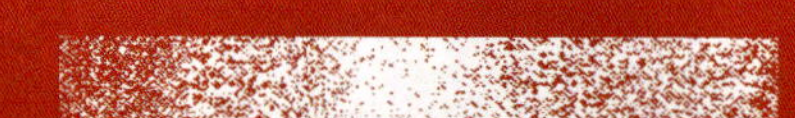

You people don't get it. And I don't think you ever will.

SPECIAL CONTAINMENT PROCEDURES

The entrance to SCP-2000 is disguised as a disused Park Ranger station in Yellowstone National Park. Despite several civilian trespassing attempts, the entrance has yet to be breached in the installation's recorded history, and no further physical containment has been deemed necessary. Protocol Plainsight-201 is in effect for SCP-2000. Necessary supplies and replacement personnel may be delivered via unmarked road vehicles or civilian helicopter as appropriate.

No personnel below Level 4/2000 clearance are permitted access to documentation regarding SCP-2000, or any protocols associated with its containment and upkeep. No personnel below Level 5/2000 clearance are permitted access to SCP-2000 below Sub-level 3. All personnel assigned to SCP-2000 must submit to a neural archetype scan on a monthly basis. Personnel stationed on-site must submit to weekly scans, to be stored locally.

Level 4/2000 personnel or above stationed on-site are not permitted to leave Yellowstone National Park during the course of their assignment. In the event of transfer (either elective or compulsory), Class A amnestics must be administered, and false memories implanted consistent with assignment to other high-security or Keter-class SCP objects. Additional personnel may be assigned to SCP-2000 and granted temporary Level 4/2000 clearance at the discretion of the item's HMCL supervisor (currently Dr. Charles Gears) and 05 command.

The exterior surface of SCP-2000 is surrounded by Scranton Reality Anchors (SRAs) every 20 m, arranged hexagonally, to prevent incursion by hostile anomalous interference. Each SRA's function must be checked semi-annually and replaced as necessary. Technicians servicing SRA components may reference Document SRA-033, rev 1.0.7. Five Xyank/Anastasakos Constant Temporal Sinks (XACTS) capable of maintaining stable tachyon flux across the expanse of the facility (maximum output rating at 100 W each) have been installed and are to be maintained monthly. Technicians servicing XACTS components may refer to Document XACTS-864, rev 1.3.0.

One Pseudo-Riemannian manifold has been initiated at the entrance to Sub-level 4, and must remain open at all times. In the event of the manifold's failure, Procedure Dead Euclid-101 is to be executed immediately. Other non-anomalous life support and utility systems may be maintained in accordance with standard Foundation Maintenance Protocol, Section 101.5 (Mission Critical Components). Wherever possible, non-anomalous materials and resources are to be used for SCP-2000's maintenance and repair.

In the event of any K-Class scenario which does not compromise the existence or function of SCP-2000, Procedure CYA-009 is to be enacted as soon as possible. Remaining Foundation installations globally are to monitor the scenario as it unfolds, preserving what material resources are possible under the Ganymede Protocol until such time as all remaining sites respond "All Clear" to SCP-2000 queries as defined in Document 2000XKAC-1.9. Upon receipt of "All Clear" code, Procedure Lazarus-01 is to be implemented.

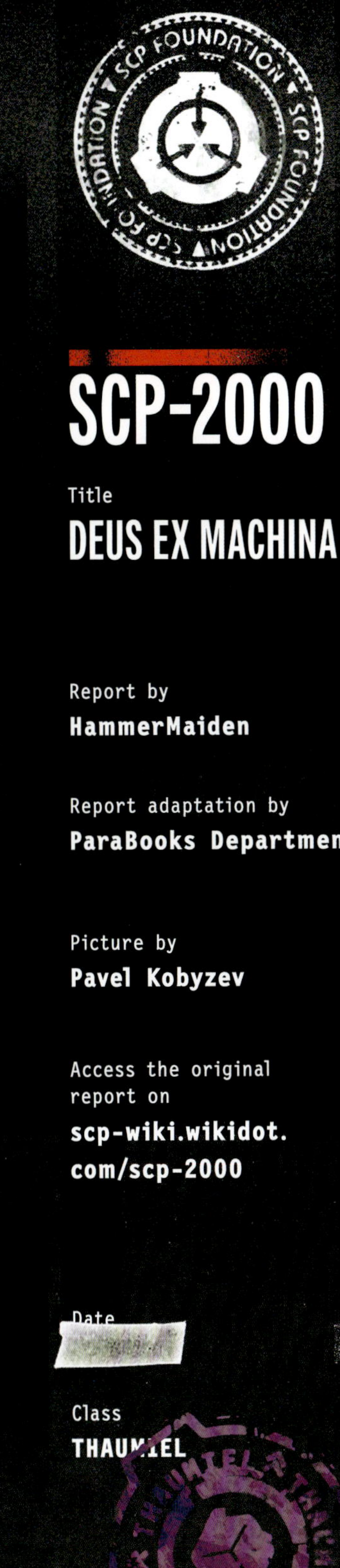

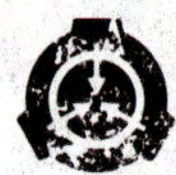

Research Library File ▸ 2000

ADMINISTRATOR NOTE

I want this on permanent record, and I don't rightly care if you think it's an insult to your intelligence; some things are just this important. This device is absolutely not an excuse to let down our guard or take greater risks with SCP objects or cross-test them or whatever you might have in mind. Primary Containment is still our best chance at survival; otherwise there would be no reason to make the cover-up so extensive. We can only suspend God's disbelief so many times before the universe just says "no". And considering what we've had to deal with in these past few decades, we may have passed that point already.

- Former Administrator Dr. William Fritz

Dr. William Fritz

DESCRIPTION

SCP-2000 is a subterranean Foundation installation originally constructed sometime in the last ███ years for the purpose of reconstructing civilization in the event that a K-Class end-of-the-world scenario could not be averted in time to prevent humanity's extinction or near-extinction. Since its inception, SCP-2000 has been activated at least twice. Foundation records regarding SCP-2000's construction and history prior to this assumed first use have been lost. Whether this information black-out is the result of accident or design is impossible to determine. The mission critical portion of this installation begins 75m below ground level and extends to a 100m depth.

Although the scope of engineering required to recreate SCP-2000 in its entirety is impossible to execute while maintaining secrecy, all subsystems of SCP-2000 have been successfully reproduced in laboratory setting; the installation and all procedures involved in its upkeep are mundane in nature. (See Document 2000-SS-EX for information regarding esoteric Foundation technologies necessary for SCP-2000's function). Primary power for the facility is a Liquid Fluoride Thorium Reactor (LFTR) rated for 1 GW total output, with a reactor life of 70 years at maximum capacity. A geothermal generator has also been installed to take advantage of the region's volcanic activity. This generator is capable of powering the facility in "stand-by" mode indefinitely. SCP-2000 also contains water treatment facilities, air purification and recycling systems, hydroponic production wings, and housing necessary to permanently sustain up to 10,000 personnel.

To fulfill its primary mission, SCP-2000 includes 500,000 Bright/Zartion Hominid Replicators (BZHR). At peak capacity, SCP-2000 is capable of producing 100,000 viable, non-anomalous humans per day (with a warm-up period of 5 days). Utilizing an underground Riemannian transit pipe to collect raw material from various hot springs and underground magma flows in the area, and a computer memory bank housing data on all known human alleles, this system is capable of recreating any lost human genome or generating as many new and unique genomes as necessary to repopulate human civilization.

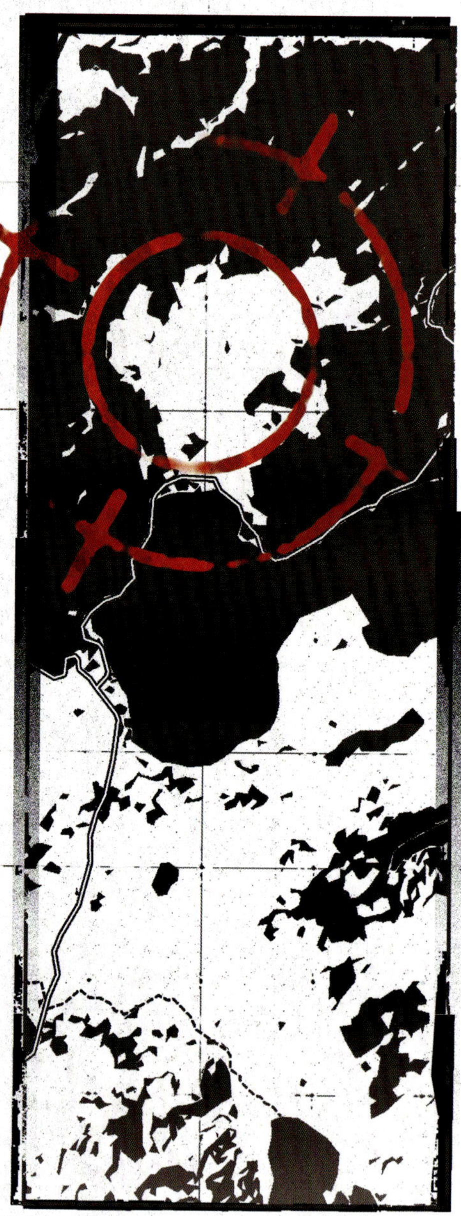

SCP-2000's location.

RESEARCHER NOTE

Use of the BZHR system is currently suspended outside of maintenance testing and emergency situations (CYA-009 is still "go"). Possible hostile incursion is still being investigated, and this database is proving particularly difficult to de-bug. We're still seeing a distribution of congenital and genetic defects far above baseline numbers. Right now, I can only guarantee about 60-75% viability in new specimens. See Addendum 2000-1.

- Dr. Christopher Zartion MD, Biotech Research and Development

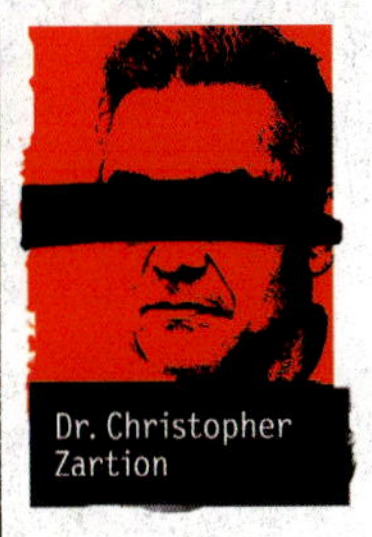

Dr. Christopher Zartion

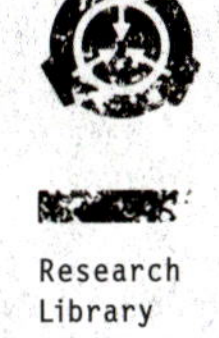

Research Library File ▸ 2000

You can't bring them back.

Humans produced by this process can be advanced to any age desired without extending the 5 day incubation period. In addition to construction features, the BZHR also has the ability to implant memories by administration of Class-G hallucinogenics and developmental hypnotherapy. Life histories, neural archetype scans, and genomes of many Foundation personnel – including all personnel of Level 4/2000 clearance and above – are maintained to ensure that SCP-2000 may be activated and Procedure Lazarus-01 can be initiated by as few as one surviving human.

After the implementation of the Ganymede protocol (indicating a failure of the Foundation to prevent a K-Class scenario), SCP-2000's security systems will unlock, allowing any Foundation employee to initiate Procedure CYA-009. If, after 20 years, SCP-2000 remains inactive, security will be relaxed further, allowing any non-anomalous human being to access the facility and initiate the procedure. Once activated, SCP-2000's internal monitoring systems will attempt to locate all personnel of Level 4/2000 clearance and assess their condition. Mission-critical personnel not found will be replicated using the most recent neural archetype scan on file, and awakened prior to the initialization of any other systems.

Did you catch that?

After these personnel are revived, security locks will resume normal function. For a complete list of contingency options available, Level 5/2000 personnel may access Document 2000-CYA-09. Note that receipt of the "All Clear" code as defined by Document 2000XKAC-1.9 may be waived only if all other Foundation facilities have been rendered inoperative. Otherwise, security and MTF elements revived under Procedure CYA-009 will be dispatched to all remaining Foundation facilities to confirm their function and the integrity of local reality.

Procedure Lazarus-01 will begin when an authorized Level 5/2000 Foundation employee inputs the desired "Resume Date" into SCP-2000's BZHR control unit. Available units will then begin production of prominent political and cultural leaders of the time period using descriptions/genetic information on file, as well as replication of a global populace consistent with the chosen time period. Most of SCP-2000's floor space is dedicated to storage of building materials, construction equipment, factory machinery, agricultural equipment, and computer database storage. In addition to infrastructure concerns, a wide cultural base with copies of thousands of famous works of art, music, literature, and a full backup of the World Wide Web are kept on site in the event that other repositories are destroyed.

HMCL NOTE

Discovered this note in previous iteration records at Lazarus-01 conclusion.

> **Researcher Note**: If we ever have to do this again, do not set the Resume Date further back than 20 years before the Event. Not only can we piggy-back on a lot of undestroyed structures if we do, but it will make continuity a lot easier to resume. [REDACTED] years is too many. We're straining personnel such as it is without having to rebuild to chronological specifications just to save time on the population and agricultural demands. Besides, how much of the 20th-2█th centuries do we really want to re-write, and how many times? Isn't one 'Great War' hard enough to keep track of?
>
> *Dr. Henrietta Eisenhower, Historian*

My tenure as SCP-2000's HMCL will honor this request. Currently pursuing official documentation update to account for this change. Two World Wars is plenty. We do not need to hazard a third.

- Dr. Charles Gears, HMCL Supervisor

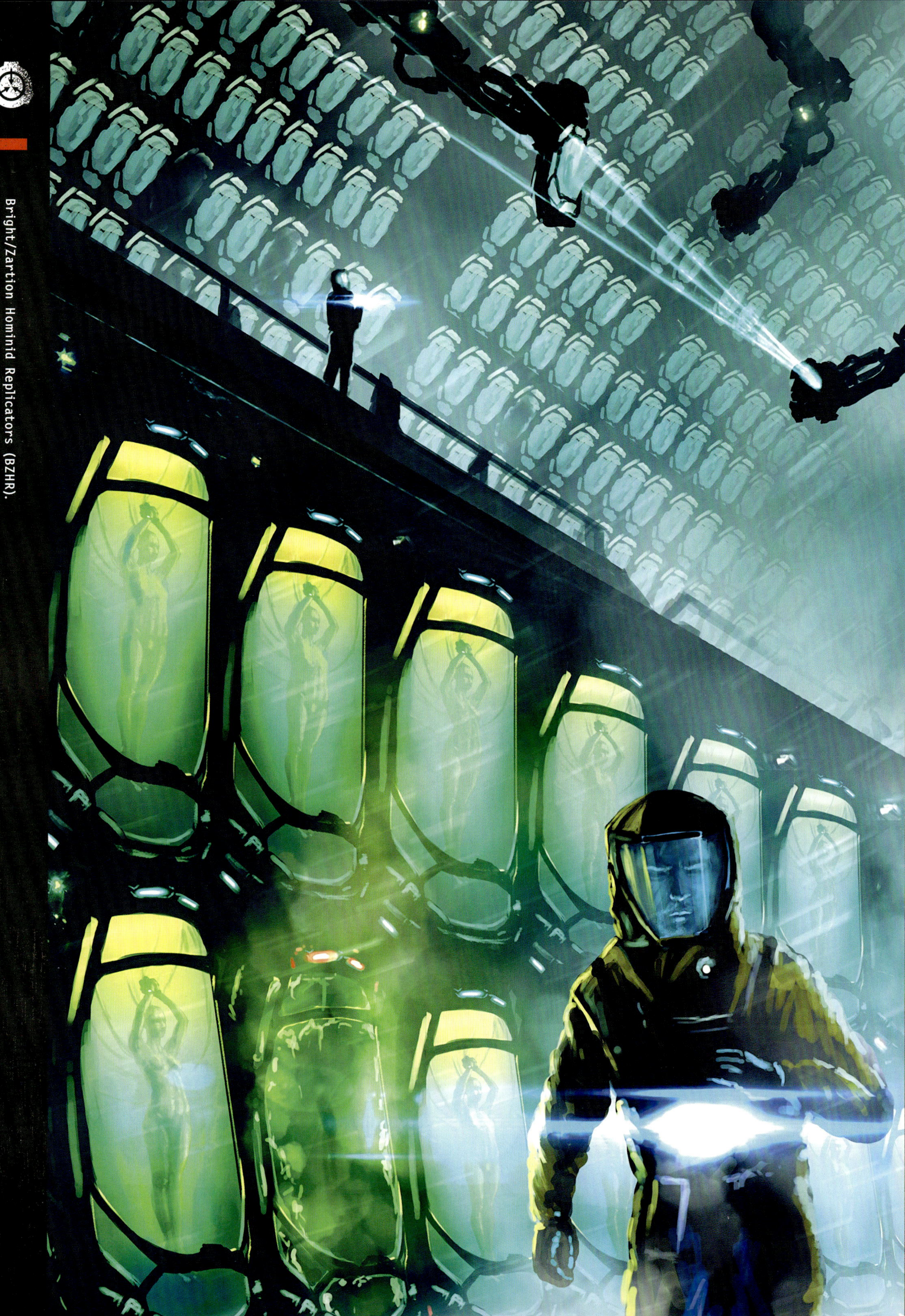

Bright/Zartion Hominid Replicators (BZHR).

You've already failed.

The first replacement humans housed off-site must necessarily be informed of SCP-2000's existence and function as they are being created. This strategy allows newly constructed humans to assist in reconstruction and recolonization efforts directly, and skill sets appropriate to reconstruction have been preselected for increased prevalence in the first 5 million individuals produced. As global population increases, the process of diaspora and reconstruction will accelerate geometrically, allowing economic and agricultural infrastructure to recover as quickly as possible.

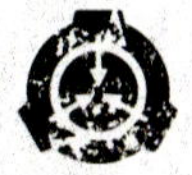

While it is feasible that some replacement humans will not survive the initial renovation period, such individuals can be recreated indefinitely until all major population centers and Foundation facilities have been completed. Foundation administrative assets during this period will focus on the falsification of dendrochronological, astronomical, and radiometric dating records necessary to maintain the appearance of historical continuity. Please see Document 2000-RetCon v 2.3.3 for details. In the event that significant portions of natural habitat are also destroyed prior to the project's completion, refer to Document 2000-OneTear v 3.0 for approved rapid regrowth methods.

It is estimated that the world population, manufacturing capability, agricultural production, and culture can be reset to 2000 CE levels 25 to 50 yrs after the procedure is implemented. At the conclusion of Procedure Lazarus-01, amnestic agent ENUI-5 will be released en-masse, causing all reconstructed humans to forget their affiliation with Foundation assets. History will then resume from the chosen date. Each procedure will necessarily alter the course of human events due to the enormous complexity of human social interaction. Further research into predictive historical modeling based on observations from prior completions of the Procedure Lazarus-01 is ongoing.

HMCL NOTE

No further proposals for behavioral or cultural modification will be accepted at this time. Previous attempts to ameliorate violent and sociopathic tendencies in humanity as a whole have already been implemented and deemed successful. Experimentation using second iteration subjects indicates that further modification would undermine tenacity to such a degree that technological and social progress would be noticeably inhibited. See Experiment Log ███-█ for further information.

- Dr. Charles Gears, HMCL Supervisor

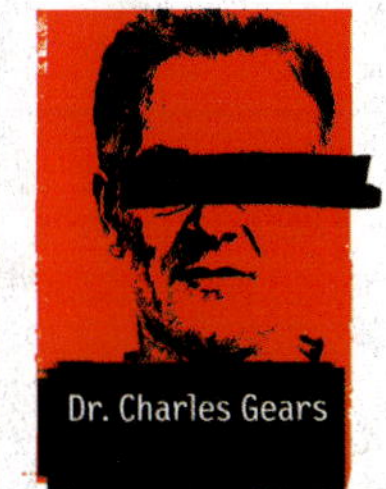
Dr. Charles Gears

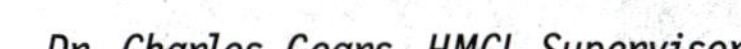

DOCUMENT 2000-SS-EX

The following information establishes basic operational parameters of technology developed specifically for the SCP-2000 project. Although this technology may appear to be anomalous, it is based entirely on verifiable scientific principles currently in use by the Foundation to effect containment.

The invention of the Scranton Reality Anchor (SRA) appears to pre-date the first activation of SCP-2000, and is credited to Dr. Robert Scranton in 1889. The main body and much of the circuitry of the SRA are constructed of a corrosion-resistant beryllium bronze alloy. Inspired by artifacts recovered [DATA EXPUNGED], effectively eliminating the appearance of virtual particle/anti-particle pairs required for Type Green reality bending phenomena to manifest. Due to the expense involved in producing the beryllium bronze alloy required for the SRA's construction, Foundation-wide implementation of the device has been limited to units capable of an area of effect less than two cubic meters[1].

Stop.

1. "Use of mSRA 'Scranton Boxes' to Provide Mission Critical Document Security"; L. Piedmont et. al.; *Foundation*; Vol 106.8; pp 10-14; 1988

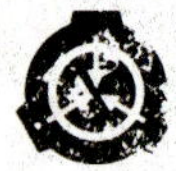

Research Library File ▸ 2000

RESEARCHER NOTE

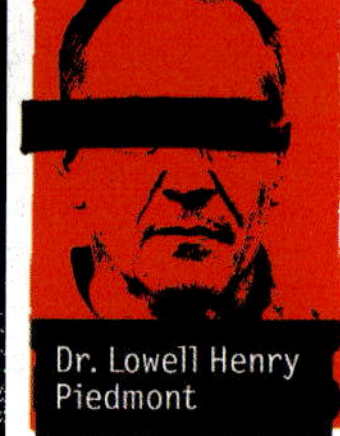

Dr. Lowell Henry Piedmont

The mechanism of the SRA's function and the source of its inspiration must be kept secret from all possible Reality Bending entities for reasons which I hope are obvious. Only qualified Level-6/2000 maintenance technicians have been cleared to access this documentation. If any member of SCP-2000 staff reveals to you that they are a Level-6/2000 maintenance technician, please report them to 05 Command so they can be reassigned and submitted to amnestic therapy immediately. This is not a punishment; it is a legitimate safety concern. If these devices are ever compromised, so too is our life-boat.

- Dr. Lowell Henry Piedmont, Esoteric Containment

The Xyank/Anastasakos Constant Temporal Sink (XACTS) is a device designed to stabilize the flow of causality across a given field of effect. XACTS's use high-power electromagnetic radiation in the radio band coupled with a tachyon field emitter[2] to create a permeable event-boundary, allowing organic and electrical systems to pass through unaffected while maintaining a static causal environment. In other words, temporal anomalies which might normally prevent SCP-2000 from being constructed will have no effect, so long as at least one XACTS remains in operation. There are no plans to implement Foundation-wide use of XACTS devices.

RESEARCHER NOTE

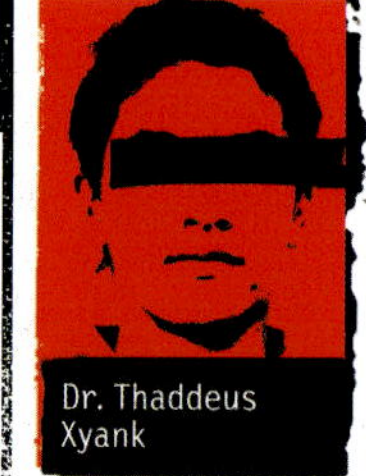

Dr. Thaddeus Xyank

Temporal sinks can be useful for a lot of things. Containing SCP objects for which you need one second to last 300,000 years is a good example. Holding a point of reference constant during temporal repair missions, so that you can meaningfully record your progress and undo serious mistakes is another. But natural causal relationships are flexible in a way the human mind is not equipped to deal with meaningfully, and creating more than a small handful of isolated static causalities will do more to damage temporal integrity than secure it. XACTS will not be implemented Foundation-wide. Yes, we have tried it during a past iteration. No, further inquiries into the results of that attempt will not be accepted.

- Dr. Thaddeus Xyank, Temporal Anomalies

STOP.

The use of a Pseudo-Riemannian manifold allows SCP-2000's floor plan to extend into negative depth, providing 10 km^2 of floor space. Original documentation on this system's construction prior to previous SCP-2000 activations has been lost. While this phenomenon has traditionally been indicative of spatial anomalies, it is the determination of Drs. Robert Boyd and Tristan Bailey that the manifold entrance is consistent with an advanced implementation of modern physics.[3] This 'negative' space is maintained via a non-gravitational singularity generated through focused ████ particle emission across the manifold's desired entrance. In the event of the singularity's failure, the installation will remain intact in isolation and will not suffer structural collapse. Recreation of the manifold is estimated to take less than 10 hrs if Protocol Dead Euclid-101 is enacted immediately after failure. The isolated portion of SCP-2000 will remain operable and inhabitable for up to 36 hrs after the manifold fails, and is recoverable indefinitely.

2. "Relativistic Motion in Superfluids for use in Tachyon Emission and Storage"; T. Xyank, A. Anastasakos; *Foundation*; Vol 10.4; pp 141-143; 1892

3. "Transit Portal Dynamics: Stretching the Brane"; T. Bailey et al. *Foundation*; Vol 115.2; pp 23-37; 1997

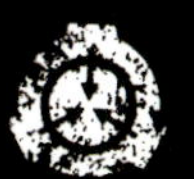

ADDENDUM 2000-1

During containment breach of SCP-████ on ██/██/███.2, SCP-2000 experienced failure of several SRA and XACTS components which coincided with activation of the BZHR units on site. For 25 days following this incident, BZHR units produced over 10 million humanoid entities with internal biology inconsistent with modern humans. Differences include an additional heart chamber, perfect polydactyl of the hands and feet, increased endocranial volume and height, and the presence of an abdominal organ of unknown purpose which emits and responds to radio frequencies in the 2.4-3.6 GHz range. These humanoids were neither dosed with Class-G hallucinogenics during replication, nor submitted to developmental hypnotherapy. All remained unconscious until expiration five weeks later. Classification of SCP-2000-1 for these entities is currently under review.

Whether this event is the direct result of trans-temporal interaction between SCP-████ and SCP-2000, sabotage, information leak, or non-anomalous equipment malfunction is as yet unknown. Diagnostic checks and structural repair are proceeding ~~as scheduled nominally~~ within acceptable risk. SCP-2000 is expected to resume normal function as of January ~~2008 2013~~ 2020.

ADDENDUM 2000-2

While making repairs to SRA units in Sector 3382 on ██/██/███.2, Technician [DATA EXPUNGED] reported the discovery of human remains in an advanced state of decay. Analysis of clothing fragments discovered with the remains indicates the remains are 450-700 yrs old. Valid Foundation security credentials for Dr. Alto Clef were discovered nearby, although a genetic match could not be established. The following note was recovered from a hermetically sealed plastic document sleeve.

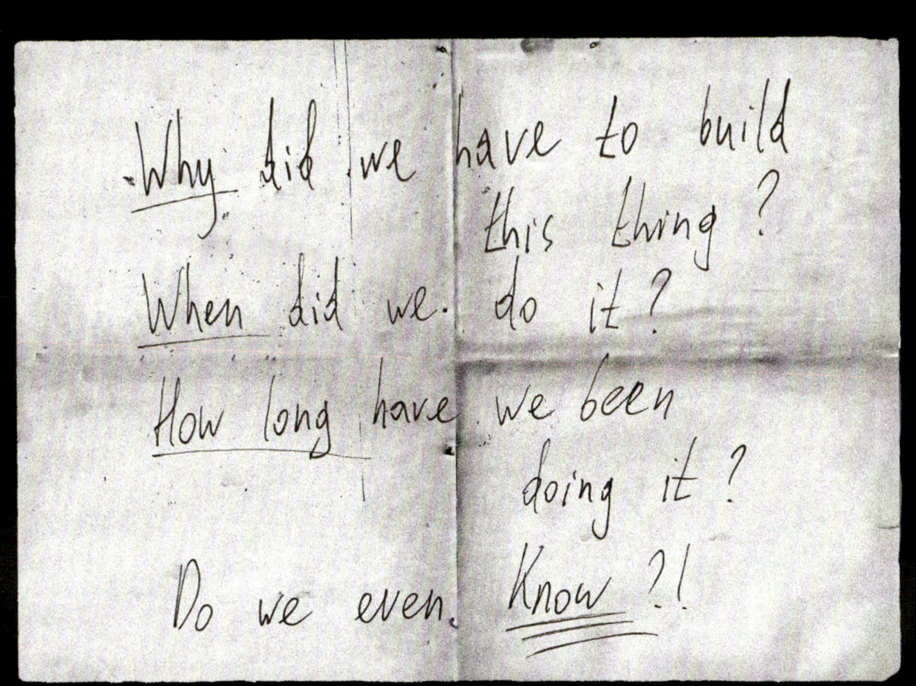

Why did we have to build this thing?
When did we do it?
How long have we been doing it?
Do we even Know?!

Subsequent interrogation has verified that Dr. Clef has no knowledge of this event, and is ignorant as to the purpose of the message.

You are not normal. THIS is normal.

File >>> 019234

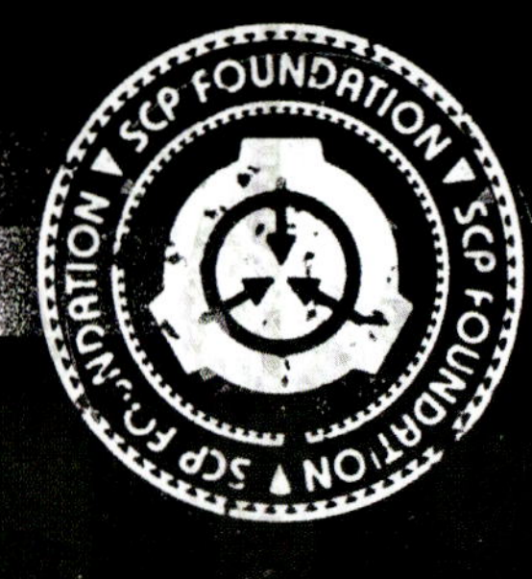

SCP-1092-RU

Title

A WEBBING OF A WOVEN WRITING

Report by

Wiiskey

Translation by

Anton Akopov

Access the original report on

scp-wiki.wikidot.com/scp-1092-ru

Date

Class

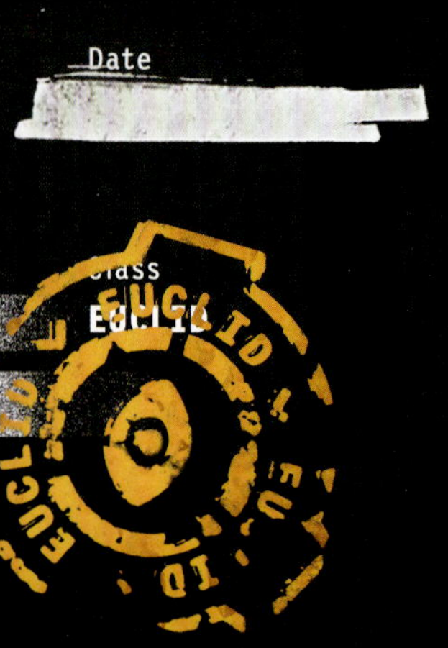

SPECIAL CONTAINMENT PROCEDURES

As of now, we have only approximate plans of containing the threat that this object presents. Anyone can become an unfortunate victim: doctors, postmen, or clerks – they can all get addicted. Anyone who has ever used rhythm or rhyme, all who trusted a pen with a piece of their mind, even those who forgot of their fondness for poems – none of them are immune; hence are all our worries.

A continuous search for the possible traces is conducted in various digital spaces. Each suspicious verse prompts a rapid response: MTFs with amnestics and a bag for the corpse.

DESCRIPTION

Object ten-ninety-two is a powerful word that takes root in one's mind and in one's line of thought. Time and time and again it comes up in their lines, but it's visible only to uninfluenced eyes.

Once exposed to the word, it will alter the pattern of expression in text: it gets broken and scattered, it's distorted and filled with unneeded additions, its ideas now changed into rhyming renditions. Since that moment the victim, unaware of the change, will be writing in verse, their words rearranged, to embellish the object and conceal the threat. It cannot be Contained; we are left to Protect.

Every following verse is more powerful, moving; it's inflaming the listeners, always improving, and it spreads like a virus, it touches the souls. It enchants, it transforms, it infects and it grows. This incredible gift is a curse wrapped as blessing; its effects are untouched by the best of amnestics. For this talent there is but one way to unteach: burn the author along with their passionate speech.

ADDENDUM

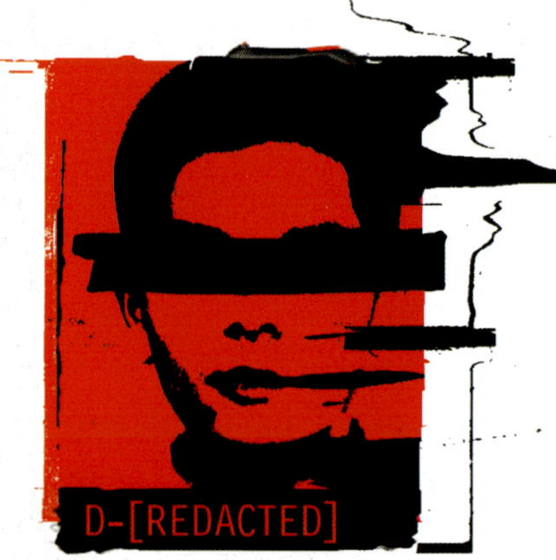

Our agents and staff have to be highly cautious, as containment requires most radical options. But despite our efforts and strict protocols, the disease worms its way into our reports.

If a member of staff, stiff and callous inside, who does things by the book, never follows desires, cold and dry like a lawyer and a stranger to passion, in a word: a true member of our great Foundation... If they notice a page full of sensuous rhymes, but their heart remains still and their eyes remain dry, this event must be promptly reported above, so [REDACTED] and agents can remove the involved.

END OF REPORT

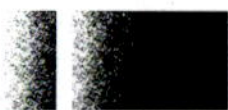

EXCERPTS FROM A JOURNAL KEPT BY TEST SUBJECT D-[REDACTED]

A cardboard cover on the damp concrete floor. A grey, dingy cell with a hard metal door. My fingers are black with the mold from the walls. No name, only numbers on my overalls. If I wake up tomorrow, I've lived for four weeks, which is longer than any of the resident freaks. When I'm out in the hallway, I see others sometimes, though all their numbers are smaller than mine.

This "containment facility" ain't really a jail, but there's plenty of stuff here to make your face pale; and sometimes in the night I hear bone-chilling screams... But they gave me a bed and they offered me meals.

Weeks ago this strange dude made me read a few words — ever since it's been harder to focus my thoughts. Every evening he brings me a page in his case and he tells me to write. "Write about this place," he will say, "How you feel. Anything is okay." Things are never that simple, whatever they say. Knew a guy here assigned to scrub floors in a cell that would always give off this unsavory smell. There was him and two others, someone winked as a joke... They say something "one-ten" is my buddy's new job...

There are lots of white coats but they're not here to heal, and the look in their eyes can get colder than steel. Though, a nurse came this morning — nice woman, I guess — asked about my dreams, if I felt any stress. Saw her writing stuff down — something starting with "d", then "approved" in her clipboard. What the hell could that be? Am I finally sick? Will they get me some meds?

I'm a throwaway thing, no one cares how this ends.

I've lived for so long, it's ridiculous, really, but I just can't get rid of this terrible feeling... As if I am a pig, fast asleep in its stable, while the folks at the house are setting the table.

I'm day after day here, it's all been a blur — there's stench in the labs, toxic pools on the floor. My memory's hazy, there's fog in my brains. I see mold on the walls, on my skin, in my veins... I hear soundless singing in the depths of my skull. It's so cold, it's so dark, and the colors are dull. When I'm done with this page, I'll jump in my bed, wrap myself in a blanket that stinks of old sweat, close my eyes, try to sleep, try ignoring the screams... And tomorrow I'll try to remember my dreams.

[PERSONNEL DOC_01]
[ID_DOCTOR ███]

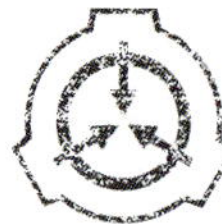

TABLE OF CONTENTS

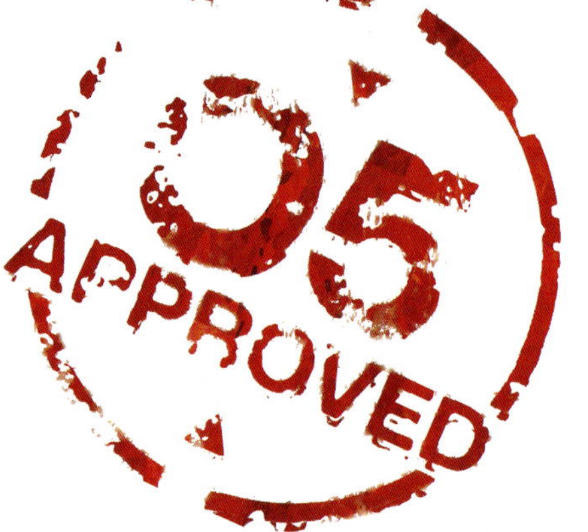

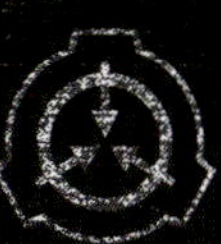

LIST OF ARTISTS

Alex Andreev	artstation.com/alexandreev
Alexander Puchkov	artstation.com/rpo6obwuk
Alexey Lebedev	artstation.com/myp
Anna Agafonova	artstation.com/agafo _ supernova
Artem Grigoryan	artstation.com/junu
Dan Temirov	artstation.com/dante
Darja Kogn	artstation.com/ventralhound
David Romero	artstation.com/cinemamind
Dmitriy Fomin	artstation.com/fomincgart
Genocide Error	artstation.com/deadlineart
Ivan Efimov	artstation.com/efimov
Jack Hainsworth	artstation.com/jackhainsworth
Julia Galkina	artstation.com/xgingerwr
Markiz de Baldezar	instagram.com/de _ baldezar
Maxim Kozlov	artstation.com/maximyz
Natalie Lesiv	artstation.com/cuddlenoon
Pavel Kobyzev	artstation.com/starwolf
Roman Avseenko	artstation.com/razgriz
Ruslana Gus	artstation.com/rilun
Zhenya Dolgova	artstation.com/dolgova

05 APPROVED

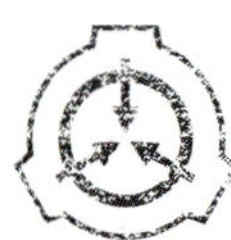

ACKNOWLEDGEMENTS

SCP Foundation is a unique project rooted in the concept of co-authorship so deeply, it is hard to even start guessing how many people contributed to it by and large. And we are immensely grateful to all of them. Had it not been for their hard work, this book would have never gotten into your hands.

First of all, of course, we would like to thank the authors who decided to share their ideas and created all those SCPs you have read about in this journal. As the saying goes, "in the beginning was the Word..."

...and the Word needed proofreading really badly. It is hard to overestimate the role of those who put their time and effort into polishing the texts and making them look as authentic as possible. Sometimes even a couple of small edits can make a huge difference!

We should also thank all those active site users who give their upvotes and downvotes, discuss and debate, pitch new ideas, ask tough questions, and simply share their emotions. The Wikidot platform really makes communication between authors and readers much easier!

Speaking of which... We need to give a huge THANK YOU to all those heroes who pulled the project from the depths of 4chan and turned it into what we have now: a user-friendly website with a neat rating and editing system, holding various contests to boost activity and defending the principles of the CC-BY-SA license that let us publish this book in the first place. Thank you, Moto42, for posting The Sculpture in 2007 and starting the whole thing. Thank you, to all those who came after and developed a simple concept of a secret organization fighting anomalies into something that grand.

The SCP Foundation is much more than a huge collection of tales and stories stylized as official reports. First and foremost, it is a community of great and talented people. Ideas give rise to new ideas and bring inspiration. We want to thank those who use this inspiration to create something for SCP: those who illustrate, animate, and make voiceovers, who craft and cosplay, who translate into other languages, who develop video and board games. This is exactly what keeps any undertaking afloat! Shared interest pushes the project forward opening new horizons and making it more and more popular. Our dearest wish is that we can contribute to it, too.

Last but not least, thank YOU, dear reader, for supporting our venture and putting this book on your shelf.

Even though this volume came to an end, your journey through the SCP universe is far from it. Actually, it never ends! We, ParaBooks publishing house, tried to fit as many articles as we can in these three journals (black, yellow, and red), and still just barely scratched the surface of the treasure pile known as scpwiki.com. There are thousands of more stories — some of them are creepy and unsettling, some are funny and wholesome, and some are quite thought-provoking. So, what are you waiting for? Read, vote, discuss, create and write the SCP Foundation history with your own hands!

scp-wiki.wikidot.com

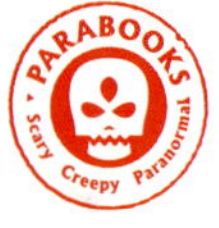

SCP Foundation Artbook | Black journal
Designed and published by
ParaBooks Publishing House
An Imprint of Aloha Comics LLC
330 SARATOGA RD #8851, Honolulu,
HI 96830 USA

Follow us: para-books.com
instagram.com/para.books

First edition: January 2023
ISBN: 978-1-63838-012-2

Printed and bound in China